On the Dragon

On the Dragon's Breath

... a tale of Merlin

Jenny Hall

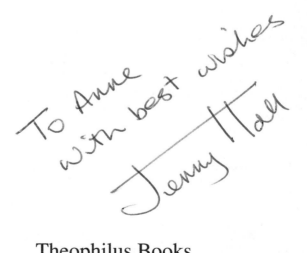

To Anne
with best wishes
Jenny Hall

Theophilus Books

Published by
Theophilus Books
62 Greenleaf Road
London E17 6QN
England

A catalogue record for this book
is available from the British Library

ISBN 0 9545423 0 4

The famous, short one-liners that appear in this novel are
extracted from the works of that famous bard, William
Shakespeare, to whom I am, of course, extremely grateful.

Front cover design by Cecil Smith, EVERGREEN*Graphics*
Illustration by Tony Masero

Printed and bound in Great Britain by
Antony Rowe Limited, Chippenham

To the memory of
Leslie Bunkall
(1953-2001)

Acknowledgments

I am very much indebted to Claudia Holness and Alex Hall for all their hard work and patience in reading and re-reading my work and correcting more errors than I care to admit. I also very much appreciate Jim Hutchinson's knowledge and help with the mysteries of the computer. I wish I could thank my late friend, Leslie Bunkall - even during his last illness, regardless of how he was feeling, he gave me so much encouragement. I am also very grateful to Ian Barnes, friend and farmer in New Zealand, for his help in explaining the workings and parts of farm equipment. And for my old dog, Sandy – I believe that much of her character and sense of fun is bound up in my hero's hound, Cabal.

On the Dragon's Breath – a tale of Merlin

Telling them about those mysterious days by way of his very first encounter with anything supernatural, Jack introduced his two young grandsons to the time he had travelled back – on the dragon's breath – to a time of magic, sorcery, the faerie, giants, dragons, a mad witch and, most importantly, Merlin. It had all started with the discovery of the Arthur Stone and - but this was much more bizarre - the photograph!

During the school summer holidays, mother would take my brother James and me to Tintagel Island for a treat, once the haymaking was finished. My dad would pile all of us into the trap, mother already having harnessed the pony, and wish us well on our way. From the beatific look on his face, I think he was only too happy to get some peace! Mother drove the trap, the pony would jump to the kiss of the whip and off we'd go. Funny some of the things you remember, but one of them is watching mother as she raised the whip to the pony's flanks - she had really strong muscles in her arms - like a man I often thought. I reckon it was all the hard work she did in the home and around the farmstead - pummelling the dough to make bread and turning the handle on the churn to make cheese needed a lot of energy and strength; yes, she was a very strong woman. The best piece of advice I ever got from my dad - and I have to admit that it was sensible advice given to me after a good hiding from my mum - was "Don't upset your mother, son". Those muscles of hers were not wasted on my backside! I learned my lesson fast that day.

When we got to Tintagel, we would spend part of the morning combing the small beach. It was a hard job getting down onto that beach, as the cliffs were very steep and quite crumbly. However, there were always lots of shells, bright stones and other things washed up onto the shore. If we were lucky and the tide was well out we would explore the largest cave under the island as well. There were a few smaller caves but the huge one went all the way through to the other side, though the tide was always in at that end - well every time we went there at any rate and my mother told me that the wizard Merlin was supposed to have lived in that one.

As far as I can remember, in all the years we visited the island, we only ever swam once, but that was a day on which the water was very calm and warm. Mother, ever protective, always kept an eye on us, as the tide could come in quite rapidly and, when it did, it was very rough and covered the whole of the bay, sending great torrents of spray up and over the rocks; it would be extremely dangerous to be cut off.

Just about mid-day all three of us would go across the causeway, climb to the top and eat mum's wonderful lunch, after which we'd explore Tintagel Island itself. At the top of the steep slope on the island were the remains of an ancient castle, which appeared to be situated almost directly over "Merlin's cave". I can remember trying to think of what it must have been like before it became a ruin, with Merlin making his way up a secret stairway to the castle (mind, I didn't find the remains of any stairway); I could imagine kings and knights to-ing and fro-ing, saving maidens in distress and fighting off dragons and invaders - there must have been raiders from the sea - and I would gaze out and almost see the sails of enemy ships coming my way with their frightening figureheads - always with horns and teeth - adorning their prows.

Exploring the island pushed my imagination into overdrive and I was sure I could see back through time many hundreds of years; I secretly hoped to find a skeleton encased in armour and was always on the look out, but was continually disappointed, as I never did. My mother told me I had a macabre and over-imaginative mind that would get me

2

into trouble one of these days. And, as I was to find out sooner rather than later, it did! She was very down to earth and couldn't understand my fantasies but, upon reflection, I suppose that working so hard in a farming community didn't give her much time to daydream and had, therefore, made her the way she was. I, though, still dreamed on. The very last time my mother took James and I to the island was when I was eight years old and James was 13; after that he was considered too old to be going on trips "with his mum" and the annual outing dropped out of the calendar. Some things are very sad in their passing, aren't they? Still, the last time that we all went together proved to be a turning point in my life.

Looking back, I see it as a time that had been set down somewhere back in eternity, waiting for me to reach it - yes, set in stone, and in more ways than one! I believe that each one of us has that time in their life where if they don't grab hold of what is set before them, on a plate so to speak, well, they will never have that opportunity again. So, as I said, I believe I had been called to that place at that specific time for a specific purpose. I felt it was as though the impossible had happened – a bit like two parallel lines meeting, just briefly - and I had somehow crossed over. As I have already told you, I didn't find that skeleton on my explorations but I came across something that would change my life forever.

I literally stumbled over a very large stone and, being annoyed with it for obstructing me, but more annoyed with myself for tripping over it, I turned to give it a kick for its trouble. However, when I did so, it dislodged some dirt and I noticed that engraved upon it, among other marks, was some writing, like the beginning of the word "Arthur", and, as we had been learning about myths and legends at school, my interest was aroused. All I could see when I first found it were the first three letters "Art". I rubbed a lot of the dirt away and was a bit disappointed to find that it did not say

3

"Arthur" at all but something like, I believe, "Artogno". It was some time later, when I was reading some history books I'd borrowed from the library, that I found other words similar to "Artogno" and the books told that their source could be of either Roman or even of Celtic origin. What excited me most was the comment in one particular history book that it could have come from Arthur's time; well, in any event, perhaps I should say during the time when the Romans ran the country.

Anyway, to get back to our trip, mum had a very cheap box camera that took black and white photos and I managed to get her to take a couple of shots of the stone. They weren't printed until a good few months later and then she gave me the two photos of the stone for my scrapbook. Each print was just slightly bigger than a special occasion postage stamp - about four centimetres by four centimetres - treasure indeed!

From that time on I started to get really interested in the things of King Arthur and of what the stone could possibly mean - I couldn't get it out of my head. I was convinced that at some time it had definitely been King Arthur that had carved his name into that stone. Was he injured at that time? Had he been chased by invaders and been pierced through by an arrow or a sword? Had he, like St George, fought a dragon? Did he have to swim ashore after being thrown overboard from a ship, or had he and others escaped when their ship went down? I wove the fantasies through my mind, getting into trouble at home and at school but, oh, I didn't care about that, I just wished I knew! After finding the stone and then seeing the photographs, I ate, drank, dreamed and daydreamed "Arthur". I devoured every book I could lay my hands on in the library and how disappointed I was when there were no books at all in it about him. Every penny I could, I saved until I had enough to buy anything to do with Arthur, at which time I would travel into the larger market town, if I could cajole anyone into taking me, and once there would trawl the very few bookshops or get lost in the library. I was, at first, heartbroken when people told me that I was wasting my time and that Arthur was merely a legend but I consoled myself with the knowledge that they didn't really know that for sure, as they were not around fifteen hundred years ago, so couldn't swear to it. Well, they couldn't, could they? And *I* had seen his name carved in stone. I did not get upset too much when they ridiculed me; in fact I believe that at that time I felt quite superior to them all. In a way that I couldn't explain at the time, I knew that I had been privileged to see this for a special reason.

That stone had been the catalyst with regard to my destiny! Why? I had no idea; but I would have to be patient and wait. One day all would be revealed.'

Jack stood up and stretched and both boys complained that he wasn't going to stop the story there, was he? It was barely 8 o'clock and their mother wouldn't be home until about nine.

Laughing at their dismay, Jack held up his hands in surrender, commenting, 'No, I'm just going to put the kettle on for a cup of tea and put some logs on the fire. It's getting cold now that the nights are drawing in, especially with that wind finding every nook and cranny in this house to get past and chill us to the bone.

Besides, if I don't have something to drink soon, my voice will completely give out and that wouldn't do, would it?'

Both boys agreed and jumped up to help their grandfather.

Before long, the tongues of flame started, cautiously at first, to sample the new logs that had been carefully placed on the grate, licking around their edges before deciding they were delicious enough to be consumed. Then, while the fire crackled and crunched through the logs, the tea was poured and a good chunk of fruitcake cut for each of them before Jack sat back in the old rocker to continue his tale.

5

TWO

A whole year passed and it got to the time of year when mum would have taken my brother and me on our outing to the beach at Tintagel, if those trips had continued. The funny thing this year was that on the day we should have gone there was a shocking storm; as I said before, it had always been fair weather on our days out up till now so this was really quite strange, not to say eerie. Fortunately the weathermen had said some few days earlier that this storm was on its way. The weathermen are almost like gods to the farmers. Farming relies totally on the weather doing what it is supposed to do at the time it is supposed to do it. So all farmers listen religiously to the weather and shipping forecasts. By this time, most of the harvest had been gathered in and so virtually everyone in the village got stuck into helping with the rest of it. The harvest was all in only the day before, when the wind picked up to such a degree that if we ventured out we had to hold on to anything that was bolted down to stop ourselves from being blown away! This storm was ferocious; overnight many trees were uprooted and lots of houses lost their roofs. We were very lucky in that we only lost a couple of apple trees. The man on the wireless …'. Jack stopped when he saw the boys sniggering at him. 'Oh well, it was called a wireless in those days – even though it was full of wires! Hmm, I wonder how it got that name. Anyway, the man on the *radio* said that people should stay indoors, unless it was absolutely essential to go out, until the storm had passed. By the second day, with no let-up to the weather, I was bored out of my socks. My brother, being older, was allowed to go out with his friends but I had to stay indoors; my dad was in his smithy and mum - well mum was always busy. So I had to amuse myself. I'd played patience with an old deck of cards until I thought I must surely rub all the spots off them.

Putting them into my drawer, my eye was caught by my old scrapbook, which was almost buried under a load of school exercise books and other paraphernalia. I took it out and started to look at all the things I'd glued into it over the last, how many – four, or was it five years? Well, since I had started school at any rate. Never mind, I was completely engrossed as I stared at pictures I'd cut out of newspapers and comics, a Christmas card I had spent ages making for my mum but had retrieved after the holidays to add to my collection of memorabilia; bits and pieces I could just about remember and some that I couldn't. Even though I was still engrossed with Arthur, I had completely forgotten about the photos of the "Arthur" stone and so, when I turned the page upon which they were glued, I literally jumped out of my skin, not least because as I did so a huge flash of lightening lit up the room, followed swiftly by a gigantic clap of thunder. I dropped my album and bits fell out of it, scattering across the floor. Steadying myself, I collected all the bits and pieces and put them in a pile on the bed. It would take me ages to sort it all out and put everything back into the right place but right now I needed to look again at those photos.

Curling myself up on the bed I stared at the first one, which was just taken up with the stone itself. There was a tuft of grass making a shadow on it but it was clear that the word etched upon it was as near to the name of Arthur as any ancient word could be. I turned and looked at the other photo. My mum had been standing back a bit to take this one and there was quite a bit of space, mainly grass and sky, all around the stone. As I stared at this second photograph I thought I could just vaguely see someone standing beside the stone and staring into the camera. "*No*", I thought, "*that's just my imagination*", but I wasn't completely convincing myself even though my mind echoed my mother saying it would get me into trouble one day. I thought back to the time, and, yes, it was exactly one year ago that weekend,

7

when I had dug around the ruins and had come across the stone. Closing my eyes I tried to recall what had happened and who had been around. My brother had gone further along the headland to explore and was not at that moment in sight. In fact, we didn't see him for well over an hour; I remember mum had got quite concerned about him because there were sheer drops into the sea all around the island.´ However, getting back to the photograph - my mother and I were standing side by side and, obviously, as she was taking the photograph and I was next to her, neither of us would be in it. No, there was no one else around, so perhaps the photo had got a bit dirty. I was chewing my lip as I pulled out my handkerchief and rubbed at the photo. No, it had not been dirty: the outline of *what?* was still there. Jumping up from my bed, I returned to the drawer and rummaged around for my magnifying glass. Bringing it back over to the bed, I turned on the lamp and, closing one eye, held the glass over the picture, moving it up and down between the picture and my eye to get a clearer view.

I got a real creepy feeling and the hair started to rise at the back of my neck - I could literally feel my heart beating in my ears. There *was* an outline of someone – yes it was definitely someone, not something – staring at me out of the photograph. I dropped the photographs into the album and snapped it shut with a bang. I was pretty shaken up at what I had just seen, I can tell you. I asked mum later on if she could remember our last outing to Tintagel and the roundabout way I got her to tell me if she could recall whether there was anyone else nearby when we took the photos of the stone I had found. She said that we were quite alone. I asked if she still had the other photos and could I borrow them. She gave me the packet of photographs and negatives and so, later on, in my room again, I got out the magnifying glass and, holding the negatives up to the bedside lamp, checked to see what was on the ones with the stones. If

I thought the photographs were small - well, you should have seen the negatives – they were tiny! Anyway, using the magnifying glass I searched through the negatives. Nothing! There was no outline of anyone or anything on it. But there was most definitely something on my photograph. I was more than a bit scared, I can tell you.

I didn't open my album for almost a week, although I was tempted to - it played on my mind, particularly when I went into my bedroom. Every time I went into the room I found my eyes swivelling round to stare at the chest of drawers and if I opened the drawer to get out either my school books or a pencil or something, my eyes would be drawn to it lying there, almost willing me to pick it up and open it. Once I thought the book looked almost like a finger beckoning me to come closer. I would slam the drawer shut and get out of the room as fast as I could or, if it was bedtime, dive into my bed, switch off the light and pull the covers up over my head. I even got told off by my dad for slamming around too much and he usually left the telling off to my mum, so I knew it was serious.

After a week, however, the temptation was too much. I took out the scrapbook and put it on the bed. I sat looking at it for at least ten minutes, arguing with myself inside my head for and against opening it, before I actually did. As soon as I got to the page with that photo on it I could feel myself squinting my eyes to look at it. As I searched, I knew that there was definitely someone there – a ghost maybe – and I needed to work out who, why it was there and, more particularly, what on earth was happening to me? Was I going mad?

I got out a few books from my bedside cupboard. I only had the half a dozen that I'd purchased over the last year – all about King Arthur – and one that was on loan to me from the library. I started going through those pages that had pictures on them to see if they could give me any clues. I suppose I

9

had got to my third book before any light started to dawn. I was suddenly drawn to a page upon which a bard or sorcerer was painted. He had a long flowing beard, although the outline of the man in the photograph did not appear to have a beard at all, but what *was* similar was the long garment he wore and the staff he held.

The book told me that the man's name was Myrddin, that he was a Druid, prophet, bard and magician; that he advised Arthur, who was a king who would bring peace and prosperity to the land but that when Arthur was dying, Myrddin prophesied that the king would be taken across the sea to a safe place - an enchanted isle - to be healed, returning when Britain was once again in dire peril and in need of a High King. The book also went on to say that when the king returned, he, Myrddin, would return with him to be at his right hand, to serve him and protect him as he had done all his life.

I put the book down and picked up the photograph. The wraith-like outline seemed more substantial and I noticed that, where before the man had been leaning on the staff, now he held it aloft. My mouth dropped open! I knuckled my eyes to see if I could clear them to make sure I was not imagining things, but, no, he still held the staff aloft and, not only that, he appeared, with his other hand, to be beckoning to me.

I can remember that I was so unsettled by this that I decided to show mum the photograph and ask her what she saw. She took it off me and gave it a perfunctory glance. However, I got quite agitated and, when she saw how concerned I was and after feeling my head to see if I might have a fever, she took the photograph back; she stared at it for a good few moments and then told me what she saw.

I held my breath. She saw the stone we had found with the writing on it, the grass, some sky and that was it. I waited for her to mention the figure or at least a shadow and, when she didn't, I looked over her shoulder at the photograph – the outline had disappeared! I really thought I must have been going out of my mind.

What on earth could it all mean? I really didn't know. I can remember saying, inside my head, *"If there is anyone there, please let me know what is happening"*. However, at that time, I got no response. But I had a gut feeling that things were not going to be the same again.

Funny thing is, though, that many years later, when I went to Tintagel, I never ever found that stone, though I looked for it high and low.'

'Right, lads, time for bed! No!' he held up his hand, 'I'm tired, even if you are not and my voice is just about to give out.'

The two lads, grumbling a little, finally made their way up to bed. It was quite late and very soon they settled down and all was quiet.

'Do you ever miss those days, Cab?' Jack spoke softly.

'Ah, there is never a day goes by …,' the hound replied.

Kate returned to the cottage soon after the boys had gone to sleep and almost directly went up to bed.

Jack and Cabal took a turn around the smallholding, checking all was secure – a job they had always done – just to make sure!

Returning to the cottage, Jack pulled off his work gloves and, tossing them into the corner of the huge fireplace, leaned against the mantle shelf as he poked at the settling embers with the toe of his boot, trying to bring the fire back to life. He watched as a shower of sparks danced up the chimney like demented sprites. Adding a few slivers of wood to the smoking ash to get it going and then putting on some of the smaller logs, a huge pile of which was always kept stacked at the side of the fireplace, he moved his chair closer to the fire and settled himself into it for a few minutes while he pulled

11

off the boots he had forgotten to remove. He prodded the fire again, this time with the poker while the wolfhound crept up to him to be closer to the warmth of the fire and, of course, keep his guard over him. Crossing his ankles and resting them on the brass fender which surrounded the fireplace Jack sighed as he looked down fondly at the old dog and then, after scratching the flat area on top of the hound's head, ran his fingers through the rough hair at the back of his neck commenting, 'We're both getting on a bit Cab', and the old dog nodded.

Shaking his head and bringing his thoughts back to the present, Jack stretched, hearing more than a few of his bones crack as he did so, and repeated, 'Yes, certainly showing the signs of wear and tear, Cab!'

'But not too much if we were called to go back again, though, eh?'

'No, Cab, not too much. *Never too old for that.'*

Jack sighed as he thought of when they'd travelled back to the times of Merlin; but, after ten years of adventures they had ceased, quite abruptly, and it had taken over thirty-five years before there had been even a glimpse of a sign that they might be called to go back again. Well, that had happened just recently - some three years after his family had arrived on his doorstep and asked him to take them in. So, thinking about it, it could easily be another twenty-five before it happened again! 'Then, I reckon we would be much too old,' he laughed. He looked again at the old dog - a miracle in himself at his great age! Cabal just wagged his tail and they then settled down comfortably, both remembering, in their own ways, the exciting, and sometimes frightening times they had spent together.

THREE

'You remember me telling you that Merlin was a very good looking man?' The boys nodded as Jack continued with his story the next evening. 'Well, I believe he was a quite vain in that regard. Not that he ever said anything, but, when he was in the presence of the fairer sex, he would somehow seem to stand even taller and even though he was wearing a long robe it looked like he might be flexing his muscles. It was the only thing I ever noticed that was a weakness in him. Mind you, the only female he ever really loved was a young woman called Nimue, who was also someone fairly knowledgeable in the Old Way. Suffice it to say that Nimue was a crafty female. She was lovely to look at but she had a cunning heart - that is, if she had a heart at all and knew just how to twist Merlin round her little finger to get what she wanted.

She started off as an apprentice to a sorceress called Morgan le Fey, another practitioner of the Old Way; Morgan was also a cunning and evil woman, but when she couldn't get any further with her she tried to apprentice herself to Merlin.

I'll tell you about how I first met Merlin, all those years ago and what he told me about the Old Way, and I'll tell you another time how crafty Nimue affected him and the terrible consequences that followed. She was almost his downfall, yes, but, as I said, I'll tell you all about her another day. Right now, though, I'll get back to our story, are you ready?'

The boys nodded.

'Do you want anything before I start?'

They shook their heads. 'No, granddad.' Daniel sat, round eyed, on the edge of his seat while Ben lay down on the ragweave rug in front of the fire, chin resting on his hands, both ready to be transported back over the years to a time of legend and romance. Cabby 'harrumphed' in the corner.

Jack began.

'I was about nine years old when I first met Merlin. My grandparents had had to move to the west country during the first World War, taking my father and Uncle John with them, as the government needed more farriers out here.'

'What's a farrier?' asked Ben.

'Mostly a blacksmith, a man who works in metals - mainly shoeing horses - but who also treats a horse's ailments - a bit like a vet. They needed lots of them in my granddad's time, in the First World War. Not so much in World War II, although because of his great understanding in his field, my father was often required to help the authorities in the blending and use of metals. When he had the time, he used to show me how to make horseshoes. I never actually made one, though - well, not one that would have fitted any horses I knew - they would have had to have been either as small as a chicken or as large as a barn to fit the ones my dad let me make! - but it came in handy knowing how and I did learn how to heat and shape metal. Yes, because my dad showed me a lot about the different metals and how to work them, it came in handy, as you will hear. More than that, though, he showed me how to deal with all sorts of animals, getting to know their problems and their characteristics. He had such a way with them that they seemed automatically to trust him. I, too, felt that trust - it seemed to rub off onto me until I found that I was able to have an empathy with them as well. But, to continue ...

We'd moved further inland then, some few miles north of Cadbury. One day, a man from the Government came to visit my father and gave him lots of instructions. I was in the smithy but I watched them as they strode up and down outside. They argued a bit because I think that as my mother had gone to help her sister-in-law, who was having a baby, my dad did not want to leave his smithy as first, he'd have to let it cool and it took a great deal getting it going again but,

14

mainly because he'd have to take me with him on this job and he didn't want to. The man said he had no choice - it was for King and Country. Years later my dad told me that it was something to do with the communists. My dad had learned a lot about hard metals and so he was often called upon by the government to do something or other to help them.

Anyway, the next morning the two of us set off, just before it got light, for a place a bit further north-west of where we lived.

Dad had hitched the old horse to the cart, which he had loaded up the night before. I was still half asleep when we left and spent most of the journey fast asleep in the back of the cart. I suppose we got there late morning.

When we arrived, my father, wanting to get the job done and return home as soon as he could, had all but forgotten my existence. However, I decided it was time to explore.

As I started nosing around, he must have remembered me because he leaned back and told me to keep close to the house. I mumbled some sort of agreement but decided that as there was no other building for miles around I was hardly likely to get lost.

The man who had let us in was a huge mountain of a man, with a large, round, reddish face, purple nose and scruffy, unshaved chin. In fact, it looked as though someone had been pulling his beard out in clumps. When he opened his mouth I could see that his teeth were brown and a few were missing; also, almost every time he did open his mouth, he spat. I could feel myself grimacing. He wore trousers that were kept up by thick braces – he had no waist to support a belt - and a collarless shirt that strained over the largest stomach I had ever seen.

We had gone into a very unkempt kitchen where a couple of cats eyed us with some curiosity, as did the man's sons - I believe they were his sons - who were eating doorstep-sized bacon sandwiches with the grease running down their chins.

The man led my father off through the back of the house and their voices gradually faded away. After being stared at by the two boys until I became aware of my face going hot, I decided it best to follow my father outside and felt great relief once I was away from them.

I followed the sound of voices into the huge barn and settled myself into the corner just inside the door. Like any nine year old, after a while I got totally bored. I asked if we were going to be there long and my father said that it could possibly take most of the day. So I wandered outside.

I started to explore. Again, dad told me not to go too far but to keep the house in sight. "Stay close, Jack. Don't get lost", he shouted out at me. I agreed, but at my age the mind doesn't really remember to hold on to warnings, especially when there was too much that was new and an obvious adventure to be had. I had my penny whistle and my clockwork mouse in my pocket, along with a piece of string, some smooth stones, two pennies (the old, big ones) and a few bits of other kinds of kids' stuff.

I realised it would be a long day so, to stifle boredom, decided to see how many steps it would take to walk right round the outside of this farmstead. Well, farmstead was the best I could call it. It was a mixture of barns, lock-ups, a house, animal pens, a silo and other various storage buildings, but it wasn't like a real farm. True, there were a few pigs and chickens but, on the whole, it did not appear to make sense. But I was young and so it didn't really bother me.

I started counting my steps around the outskirts and I suppose I had got as far away from my father as I could get, when I turned the corner and literally bumped into one of the man's sons. With hindsight, I don't think it was by accident on their part.

'Who d'ya think you're pushing, eh?' he sneered at me as he shoved me to the ground. I thought how lucky I was that it had not been raining, as I would have got pretty muddy and

16

my dad would've gone mad. Silly, the things you think of, isn't it? If I knew just then what those two boys had in mind for me, I would have realised that getting dirty was the least of my worries.

'I'm sorry, I didn't mean to knock into you and I wasn't pushing anyone,' I said as I struggled up from the ground. I shouldn't have bothered; he pushed me back down again and put his foot on my chest. He didn't press, so it wasn't hurting me but I certainly couldn't get up and started to feel a little scared.

The older boy - well, I call them boys but I suppose the one with his foot on me was about 11 and the other one 12 years' old or so, so they were both a lot bigger than me - told his brother, 'Teach him a lesson, Alf'. I wasn't looking forward to the type of lesson he might teach me, as by the look on their faces it wouldn't be very educational - not in an academic sense at any rate. I started to squirm as I tried to push his foot away.

Luck, so I believed, was on my side as at that moment a man came out from behind the silo and looked over at us. Alf, looking a bit sheepish, removed his foot and I scrambled to my feet. As I started to walk away - I couldn't run, that would make me look pathetic - Alf whispered, loud enough for me to hear, that he would still teach me that lesson. I had not gone very far when I felt a sharp impact, followed by a burning sensation on my face. Putting my hand up to it, I removed it to find hot, sticky blood on my fingers. Turning, I was alarmed to see the two boys not far behind me. Their faces showed they were determined to keep up their mischief and that I was the object of their plans. They grinned even wider when they saw that their missile had found its mark. I, on the other hand, could think of nothing to smile about and had a sudden dread of the tears, ever ready to run down my face, making me look very foolish; and not just that, I believed I might even wet my pants, being as scared as I was.

17

Nevertheless, all brave intentions forgotten, I started to run and seeing some trees at the far side of the field, I made for them, hoping to hide myself among them. I wondered why they had picked on me. What had I done to them? It wasn't fair. I recalled one of my mother's favourite sayings, of which she seemed to have a never-ending supply: 'Who said life was fair, dear?' Yes, the tears were starting to flow; at least its only tears, I thought! I found a handkerchief in my pocket and dabbed at my face. The blood had eased a bit but there was still quite a lot of it. After trying to staunch it, I felt along the cut and found that it went from my cheekbone to the outside of my eye. Hence the scar that I carry to this day,' Jack said as he felt along the now not so visible line on his face. 'It was not very deep but I wondered if it would leave a scar.

Looking all around me for signs of the two boys and listening as hard as I could I sat down on the massive roots of some old tree and leaned back against the trunk, catching my breath and closing my eyes for a second or two. I felt a bit dizzy but wasn't sure if it was from fear, shortage of breath or loss of blood.

Whump! A clod of earth landed just above my head and broke up, falling over me and down into my shirt. I jumped up, eyes wide with fear, tears flowing and bladder threatening to do the same. The older of the two boys, whose name I had yet to discover, burst out laughing as he watched me scramble up the hill and into the trees. With a whoop, they were after me like a pack of wolves. I ran as though my lungs would burst, gradually moving through the trees, away, I thought miserably, from the safety of my father. I wondered what on earth they would do if they caught up with me.

Trying not to think of that - it was too awful to contemplate - I took one quick look over my shoulder, without slowing my pace, after I had plotted my next move. They were gaining. 'Good grief,' I thought, 'They're going to murder me'. It must have spurred me on to greater speed as I felt that I had wings, the rate at which I was running.

The younger boy, heavier, but in a very unhealthy way and obviously prone to eating large amounts of pastries and fried food, was surprisingly quick on his feet. I had run as fast as I could, hoping that his excess weight would tire him but I heard his breath as I darted among the trees. Was he getting nearer or was he just breathing louder? I suppose that being bigger than me they were very much faster and the younger boy's breath now seemed to be warming my neck. He dived suddenly and grabbed at my elbow as I ran. 'This is it,' I thought with dismay. 'I'm dead.' Wham! As he grabbed me I fell and my head went straight into a tree when I tripped over a root. I saw bright lights and flashes. Then, as I tried to straighten and run on, he landed on top of me with a wallop that knocked all the breath from my body. Lifting me from the ground by my shirt collar, my feet dangling in the air, he laughed as he raised me high off the ground. He pushed me up against the tree and over his head I could see the older boy closing in with a dreadful grin on his face. Again, I nearly wet myself. I was petrified! The tree, which had a lot of sharp bits where new branches, probably years ago, had snapped off and become broken stilettos, scratched along my back. I could feel a bump starting to grow at the side of my head over my ear, where I had collided with the tree. The boy was still breathing heavily and his face was so close to mine that the pungency of his breath almost knocked me out again.

All these particles of information came to me in a split second and, as I sorted them into the different compartments in my brain, the whorls and swirls of light and stars gradually eased their bright spinning before my eyes.

Gradually my vision cleared and I became very aware of my plight. 'Well done, Alf. Put him down and we'll have some fun.' The older boy was now towering over me. I stood stock-still but my eyes were darting here and there, looking for a way out. From where I was standing and I don't know how I was still doing that, my knees wobbling as they were, there *was* no way out! I looked from one boy's eyes to the other but there was no kindness there, even though the older boy had a face that could easily pass for an angel. I realised that even if I were to shout or scream, no-one would hear me; everyone was too far away by now and the trees would hold on to my words and bounce them back at me. I started to cry. Try as I might not to, the tears started to roll down my face. That set them off howling with laughter, which gave me just enough time to try and escape, so I thought, but, as I swirled around, Alf stuck out his leg and I was again floored, the breath once more being knocked out of my body. They were both on top of me then. Alf pulled me up by my hair and thumped me against the tree - more daggers in my back from the rough bark, more scratches down my shoulders. How will they be able to get away with it? Surely they must be frightened of the consequences of beating me up? They must know that they will get the blame for it! But these thoughts brought me no comfort right then.

'Let's toss a coin to see who thumps him first,' suggested the older boy, digging in his pocket for the object that would decide who my first torturer was to be.

'Oh, come on, Bryn, I caught him. Let me go first!'

'Oh, please,' I begged.

'Oh, please,' they both mimicked. 'Oh, please, oh, please, oh please,' they chorused, and then they started laughing again.

Alf won the toss. Grinning, he stood in front of me, hands on hips and head to one side. 'What shall I do, Bryn?' he asked. 'Shall I pull his hair out?' Bryn nodded. 'Shall I punch his daylights out or maybe knock his teeth out or shall I just knock him out?' He obviously liked the "out" word. As he made all of these suggestions, he spluttered spittle -

some down his chin but most over me. His breath was foul, but that was the least of my worries.

Wham! Without any more warning he punched me hard in the stomach, which made me double up and then almost immediately straighten as he hit me on the already swelling bruise over my right eye. More stars and whorls spun in my head. As the mists cleared I felt a warm trickle running down over my cheek and along the lid of my eye, as he opened up again the initial cut made earlier with the stone. I was horrified to see yet more blood dripping onto my shirt. I really didn't think they would do anything to me. I thought it was all a game just to scare me. And scared I was, yes, but all along I thought it was just a tormenting game to them. I looked from one to the other - well out of the one eye that was still open as the other was almost blinded by the blood that had got into it, but I saw no compassion there. Bryn looked a bit shocked because I think that he, initially at any rate, was just tormenting. However, Alf was licking his lips and was obviously enjoying what he was doing.

Before I had time to bring all these thoughts together there was another punch, which came crashing down on my nose. I felt a crunch, which at first did not hurt but as soon as the blood was allowed to start flowing again, the pain hit. Then the most peculiar thing happened! I could feel myself falling into unconsciousness but as I floated into it I either dreamed or envisioned my salvation.

The two boys were standing in front of me, hands on hips and laughing; they were doing this in slow motion and their echoing laughter ricocheted around and through the trees in a drawn out, sluggish ebb and flow of sound, as though seconds were stretched into minutes. I believe my eyes were closed but it was as though I could see from a height, looking down at the scene. I could see that I had slid down the tree and was lying on the floor with blood pouring from my outer eyebrow and my nose; the boys were standing back a bit, looking at me

21

and laughing - probably wondering what horror to inflict on me next, when something made me turn, in my out-of-body state, toward movement to my right. I sensed, rather than saw, a huge animal - wolf? dog? - I couldn't be sure but I stared with unblinking eyes – both of which in my present, disembodied state, were wide open - as it moved, very swiftly – weird, seeing that everything else was moving in slow motion - upon those two tormentors of mine. It was very indistinct in outline – a bit like clear, rippling jelly - and I could see right through it. In fact, if it stood still I wondered whether I would have known it was there at all; it only appeared to show itself when it moved.

They did not see it at all, at first – that is, if they ever did see it - but they didn't stand a chance. I believe that even now they probably look back on that time and reckon the "heebie-jeebies" had got them. Problem here, though, is that as they both experienced it, they'd have to agree that it was a bit more than just the heebie-jeebies! Getting back to what happened, there was a rushing of wind and a deep moaning - or was it a throaty growling? Anyway, they turned around slowly and in unison.

The animal, if that is was it was, leapt from what seemed about twenty feet away and landed powerfully on top of both of them. They fell - the wind being knocked out of their lungs as they toppled backwards and were pinned to the ground. Their eyes were standing out of their sockets, fear being writ large upon their faces. I noticed that the awful Alf was lying in what appeared to be an ever-increasing puddle, just around the top part of his legs. I could hear myself laugh - an extremely hollow sounding noise - that also appeared to echo around the forest. The two boys obviously heard my eerie laughter and I could see the ginger hair standing up on Bryn's head. I thought in the recesses of my mind that because of the state I was in, I should not have been laughing - but I felt no pain, well not just then at any rate.

22

I looked back down to see the dog, yes I believed by then that it was a dog - a very large dog - with its two front paws on the chests of both boys. They were trying to get up but every time they lifted their heads the dog snapped at them - its teeth were fearsome as it worried each face. They cowered back, squealing like stuck pigs, not knowing what was happening. I don't believe they could see much of what had attacked them but I do believe they felt its hot breath, if nothing else.

After what seemed an age the dog, quite casually, stepped off the boys and they, like coiled springs, were off and running back through the forest and down the hill, tripping and falling but recovering and bolting off again, one rubbing his face and the other holding onto his torn ear, as though all the hounds of hell were after them. 'Was it a hound from hell?' I thought. 'No, not possible, it had saved me from further harm, and had possibly saved my life!'

As I looked back down on the scene I noticed that the dog had turned and was alternately looking at me up high and then down at my inert body on the ground. He moved again, this time slowly, and started, very tenderly, to lick my wounds. It was soothing and he was gentle and soon I felt myself being drawn down and down, like a pin to a magnet, into my real self until, eventually, I awoke. I came round slowly and then my heart skipped a beat as I recalled my cruel experience. I sat bolt upright before almost swooning again as a chronic pain shot through my wounded head. Taking some cautious breaths, I looked around first to see if those awful boys were there but they were not and all was very quiet. I had been holding my breath and slowly let it out. Then I searched for the dog. 'Hello! Dog! Are you there?' I whispered quite hoarsely as, first, my throat was very dry, possibly due to the blood from my nose that had trickled into it; secondly, it sounded a bit daft to be calling after a dog if it hadn't really been there in the first place. Was I delirious? Perhaps in my weakened state I had been hallucinating and the boys had left me there once their fun was over or – and this I doubted – they had gone to fetch help.

The forest was very quiet. I sat for a while to get my strength back and try to consider my next move. Eventually, not wanting to take the chance of bumping into those awful boys again, I determined I would travel up the hill until I could see the farm. I had been able to see the top of the hill from the farm and therefore believed I could see the farm from the hill. Nevertheless, I would wait there until my father came out to look for me and then I would go down only when I knew I would be safe. Yes, he would have to look for me, so I decided that only when I saw him would I wave my handkerchief from the top of the hill and wait until he came and got me. I would probably get a telling off, but it was better than a beating up.

At the thought of my trials I lifted my hand to my face and felt my wounds. My eyebrow was still sticky with blood but it seemed to have stopped bleeding; my nose was very sore and there was still a trickle of blood coming out of one nostril. My eye had swollen up and I couldn't see out of it. My shirt was ruined - not that I ever took much notice of my clothes until I was getting a telling off from my mum – they were always getting torn or dirty - but I had never before seen any of my clothes covered in so much blood. I carried on walking through the trees until I came out at the other side. The forest covered the side of a hill and when I came out of the trees I was almost at the top. If I climbed the short distance to the top of the hill I should be able to see my father when he came out and then I could blow my whistle, which I carried about with me all the time, and wave my handkerchief. Yes, he would come and rescue me from those bullies.

I knew that I was quite weak but I made it to the top of the hill. As I neared the top it started to get dark. It wasn't nighttime; I could always tell the time by my stomach and even though I had suffered an awful ordeal, my stomach was telling me I had not yet had my lunch! But the sky got more overcast and it felt muggy and warm - perhaps because of all my exertion. I was puffed and sat down for a while but I could still just about make out the house from where I was sitting.

Feeling the consequences of my frightful experience, I rubbed my injured eye, only to feel pain shoot through my head once again. I decided to lie down on the grass for a short rest and to wait for my father's departure. I must have fallen asleep.

When I did open my eyes it was really dark and I was a bit scared, I can tell you. I looked down to where the house should be but all I could see was mist. I wanted to cry but I was even too scared to do that. I can remember that I opened my eyes - well the good one anyway - as far as I could, hoping that by doing so I would be able to see much clearer. I imagine my good eye must have looked like an organ stop, sticking out of my face the way it did! I pinched myself to wake myself up, just in case I was dreaming - I wasn't! Panic started to rise up from within me, the result being that my head felt like it was being crushed in a vice. Tears, always near the surface with me at that age, again threatened but I thought I had better not cry - what good would it do up there? First, my good eye would swell up and it was hard enough to see anyway and, secondly, there was no one to hear me cry - you have to have an audience for it to be effective!

Then I almost jumped out of my skin as I was confronted by a very small man. I was nine years old and therefore not very big, but he only came up to my shoulder. He started to speak to me but I couldn't understand the language he was using. He then turned away but stopped when he realised that I did not follow, so had to come back to me. When I think of him now, I wonder how I did not laugh, as he looked very

25

comical, but then, again, I *was* close to tears. Even now, when I close my eyes, I can still recall him - as I said, he was very small, dressed all in green and with a high, pointed hat, which I expect was to make him look taller. His face was pointed, too, and he had a huge, thin nose, white hair and drooping moustache, but no teeth. In fact, when he looked displeased - and he looked that way then, with his feet apart and his hands on his hips - his mouth pursed up in disapproval and then seemed to disappear into his face. He turned, expecting me to follow but I just sat there. After a few more steps, and realising I had not moved, he came back, jabbered at me a bit more and, when I made no response, grabbed hold of my hand and made me follow him. To this day, I don't know why I didn't resist. I suppose it could be that as he was so small, I felt safe. In any event, I knew I couldn't get down the hill without someone's help.

We travelled around the hillside for about five minutes until we came up to this big rock that was jutting out of it. The little man scrabbled about on the ground, picked up a small rock with which he tapped three times on the large rock and stood back, waiting. To my great surprise - and I must admit that this was one of those days when the surprises were the norm and normality didn't seem to exist any more - it rumbled backwards, opening into a steep tunnel which had been cut into the hill. He pulled me through and then tapped the rock again; once more I heard it rumble back into place. In front of us was a stairway that spiralled downward from where we were standing. We started our descent and, although there was no torch either in the little man's hand or on the walls, the tunnel itself radiated an eerie illumination, which gave sufficient light for us to see. It was then that I started to shake, probably due to all the things that had happened to me that day, not to mention my weakened state. I think I must have passed out because the next thing I remember is opening my eyes and looking into the piercing

26

black eyes of Merlin, although I did not know, at that time, that that was who it was.

Mind you, you don't really need reminders, as, once you have met him, he isn't someone you could easily, if ever, forget. Tall - well over six feet and striking, with eyes so black and deep you could almost fall into them and drown – mesmerizing – many a misguided idiot has been fooled by those eyes! No beard – now that's quite funny! Everyone who thinks of him always pictures him with a long white beard. I don't know where that one came from! He never had a beard! Well, not when he was his real self at any rate – but I shall tell you about some of the different characters he changed into later. Hmm, now come to think of it, the only hair I ever saw on him were his eyelashes - so long that almost every woman who had the pleasure of gazing at him, and there were quite a few, you know, would primp and preen themselves to try and catch his eye - *and* those sharply tilted eyebrows, almost satanic in shape they were - but he was not satanic - oh no - far from it! He clothed himself from neck to foot in a dark blue robe which, amazingly enough, did not inhibit his walk. Even when I grew older I had almost to run to keep up with him. His hair (as I said - if he had any) was covered in a tight fitting skullcap, also midnight blue, which was decorated in silver swirls, whorls and hieroglyphs and which also sported a silver badge embossed at the front with the head of a hawk (or, should I say, a merlin as he corrected me on more than one occasion – lifting one of those eyebrows as he did so).

I had, over the time I spent with him, learned to look at his eyes whenever he made a rebuke of some kind or another: if his eyes twinkled I knew he was kidding but, and this rarely happened, if they did not well, I was really in trouble!

He had a staff, etched with similar hieroglyphs to his cap, which was black, possibly made of wood but very strong, the top of which also sported the hawk - er, merlin's, head. And the birds, on both his headgear and staff, had glittering rubies for eyes.

Still, getting back to the story, he started jabbering away at me, just like the little man had done. When he could see that I did not understand he got out a very small notebook, jabbered a bit more, looked at me again, flipped a few pages until, eventually, he said, 'Can you understand me now?' I nodded vigorously and was rewarded with a beaming smile, and a shooting pain from my injuries - I had to remember to take care at the moment. I believe I've told you that Merlin very rarely smiled. It took a lot to make him do so but when he did, well the whole place lit up. He was a wonderful man, yes! How I miss him.' Jack drifted off into some distant world until Daniel pulled at his sleeve. Jack shook his head to clear it and carried on with the story.

The little man came hurrying up to Merlin with a dish of something that was eventually given to me. I didn't know what it was but was told to eat and drink. It tasted wonderful. I hadn't realised how hungry or thirsty I was. Do you know, boys, that Merlin was one of the only people I'd ever met who knew exactly what to do or say and exactly what was needed at any given time. He gave the little man some more instructions and some short time later he was ministering to my wounds.

'I'm afraid you will have a scar just below your eyebrow as the cut is quite deep and it has been left too long before being seen to,' he said to me with a grave look on his face. 'And your nose has been cracked, so it will more than likely be slightly bent, but I have seen worse and it should heal sufficiently.'

'Great!' I thought quite happily. My Uncle John, who had been in the war, had a few scars and he was very interesting. He always had a lot of people around him and he laughed a lot. I hoped I would look like him and be as happy as he was.

28

Merlin took me further inside this cave, or whatever it was, and told me that he had sent for me and was very glad that I was there. I said that I did not know I had been sent for or even how I had come to be there and that I reckoned my dad would be frantic as to where I had got to but he just shushed me and said that it was all under control and not to worry.

I followed him around the cave, looking at all the weird things he had in there. At one end there were shelves, which had been cut into the rock face, full of different sized pots and glass jars with symbols on them. At that time I did not know what those symbols meant. There must have been about fifty containers, many of them covered in cobwebs - not to mention spiders! I shivered! On the floor beside the shelves were bundles of what I believed were herbs. On the wall at the back of the cave, half hidden behind a leather screen, were hundreds of scrolls kept in pigeonholes. At the end of the scrolls was a cage big enough to hold a large dog, but it was empty. And there were about twenty cats roaming about, all black. Other rooms or cells were situated off tunnels, which led away from the main chamber of the cave, mostly behind the racks of scrolls and these held huge glass jars, as big as Ali Baba baskets, which contained his "special" concoctions. I shall tell you about them later.

'Come here, lad,' he said, beckoning me over to the far wall just past the table he had been working on, 'I want to show you something.' I went over and looked into a huge glass suspended down the wall from the ceiling. At first glance it was like a distorted mirror but it did not reflect us in it, instead it would show to us, he said, whatever it wanted to, and sometimes whatever we wanted it to. Just like a moving picture show, I thought.

'The reason you are here, and I have to admit that it is not the only reason, is because you have the gift of the Old Way. You have also been chosen because you are intelligent and

29

physically strong. No, child, don't preen yourself! I don't want someone who's vain; I should have to send you back and find someone else. Perish the thought! It took me long enough to find you, let alone look for someone else,' he sighed. 'It took me ages to find out how to display myself in that picture you had. I kept fading and coming back and, sadly, so did you. I eventually saw that you had seen me and so I felt quite satisfied that my plan was coming together. So, as I said, don't preen yourself. It has taken over a thousand years and many a restless night to come up with you! Maybe I could have got worse; maybe I could have got better! Hm, we shall have to wait and see.'

I felt abashed.

He continued. 'Now, now – it's not that bad so cheer up. You don't really belong to the time in which you are now living, you know - you are what they call a "throwback" - you belong to the time of Arthur. You must be aware of that!' He raised an eyebrow as he turned toward me. 'There are many things you have to do. As you have the gift, I need you to help Arthur in ways that not many others can - or will', he amended. 'Yes,' he went on, 'there are many who can but will not. He has lots of enemies that would see him fail, some who want to see him die and *they* spend many a long time plotting! I have seen them when I have been in my high tower.' He seemed to stare off into space for quite some time and then, recalling where he was, shook his head as his eyes turned again to me, saying, 'then again, there are those who have a knowledge of the Old Way but are evil, so their knowledge and use of it is limited, and, of course, there are others that are good. Pendulum swings! Let me inform you of the Old Way.

'Looking back to the beginning of time, the Old Way was given to man for good. At that time it was the *only* way. It was an authority given to man covering all of creation. Now, just think, lad - to have authority over creation one must be

30

able to communicate with it. How else do you think he could have authority if he couldn't make it understand what it was supposed to be doing? Man must therefore have been able to communicate with *all* creation! Trees, animals, birds, fish, sun, moon, stars, wind, rain! You name it! Now, take Noah, for instance! How did he get all those animals to come into his Ark, if they did not understand him when he was calling to them? He could have been calling them till he was blue in the face and they would have carried on ignoring him the same as they ignore us today! Well, most animals at any rate. No, at the beginning of time all things were good and worked together and understood each other; each had its place, its job, its life! Complete balance, my boy, not like in my day – or yours come to think of it. How sad that that all had to change.

'Looking on from those now lost times, I have to warn you that there are some who have a knowledge of the Old Way that go back to a place *before* the beginning of time – before a time when all had its rightful and peaceful place - a place where chaos reigned and evil stalked about, feeding on and becoming fat from wickedness; a place they should never have even tried to enter; a place that leads to madness!' His voice rose to a crescendo as he told me the last bit and then seemed to echo around the cave as it bounced back and forth off the walls. I ducked as the echo took on an almost tangible form - I thought I was going to be hit. Time seemed to hold its breath as it weighed the consequences of Merlin's statement and then, after the quietness that followed, I thought I heard a distant rumble of - thunder? He stood, staring into space for a long time, his face showing all the emotions between fear and sadness, sanity and madness until, coming back to the present, he shook himself, turned to me and continuing said, 'Not many are left who would use the gift for good and the Glass has told me that a boy from the future who has this gift will use it to protect and promote

31

Arthur. That boy is you!' – he pointed at me as he made this declaration. *You* know he will be king and *I* know I can trust you not to change the course of history.'

'How do you know I have this gift of the, um, Old Way?' I can remember asking him.

'Ah, so you can talk,' he laughed. 'Only those experienced in the Old Way can discern others with the same gift. *That* is how I know.' He sighed as he again stared off into the distance, but then, shaking his head yet again, he continued. 'I have the privilege - but sometimes I think it is a burden - to know many things that are closed to others. For instance, I know that one day the True Way will be the only way, but, until that time, the Old Way will still reign. The Old Way, in the hands of the good is used for good; in the hands of the bad is used for evil. Too untrustworthy either way! As I said, the days are coming - and Arthur is drawn to that way - when the True Way will rule.' He sat staring ahead as though everything around him had disappeared – his eyes were a million miles away. I coughed. He slowly came back to the present and then continued.

'At that time there will be those who will try to resurrect that time earlier than the Old Way, but their attempts will be short lived, without strength – futile! Their endeavours are for their own gratification, not for the good of all. They go too far, looking to use the time when chaos reigned.' He sighed, again seeming to stare down the avenues of time. Jumping up, he shook off the melancholy of the moment. 'Until that time, those of us of the Old Way who have man's best interests at heart will try to overcome the evil around us. There is not much left of the good side now, except for a few of us who have this knowledge.

'One example is being able to communicate with nature: slow down rivers, call up a storm or calm it down, bring the sunshine to help raise a harvest or burn up a town! Another is being able to communicate with all creation, like the animals, as I said, in Noah's day; however, not all animals are receptive to this in these days, but there are still a few. A horse, for example, or even a string of horses, can communicate with us, and vice versa. Mind you, when a string of horses starts to talk, it gets a bit noisy and confusing, so a one-to-one conversation is by far the best. These animals don't talk, as you would suppose by word of mouth, but in the mind. In the mind, dear boy, in the mind,' he said, tapping his brow. 'Let me see now, another prime example is the wolf, although they are very contrary and might possibly consume you instead of converse with you, but, more, say, the dog. Now he is a wonderful example. And the prime example is between man and man. I know when you came in it seemed like we wouldn't be able to communicate at all, didn't it?' I nodded. *Speak, don't just nod.*'

'Yes, I didn't think we would. I couldn't understand you at all,' I added.

'Ha! Excellent! You answered me, and I only made that last request with my mind! Did you know that?'

I didn't know whether to be pleased or scared or, in reality, understand what he meant. I did not know he had spoken to me only with his mind. However, when I thought about it later, it seemed quite natural. At the moment, though, things were moving a bit too fast and I started to get that panicky feeling rising up in me again.

'I think I had better get back to my father, now. He'll be worrying about me,' I said, but Merlin took no notice. I felt like I might cry and could feel my lips starting to turn down and a lump starting to rise up in my throat. I could feel the drag on the cut beside my eye and lifted my hand to feel if it was still bleeding, but it had near enough stopped. Merlin had done a good job there; maybe I wouldn't get a scar. I swallowed a couple of times to try and stop myself from crying. Thinking about it, I was ever ready to let the waterworks start! I had to get this crying business under

33

control. Well, I mean, I was going to be a man one day, wasn't I? Well, wasn't I? Well, I hope I was!

Merlin had his back to me at this point, as he was staring into the Glass. However, he said, over his shoulder, 'don't worry about your father. Time will, or at least should – if the spell works - stand still in the future until you get back. No, don't start thinking they will all be standing about like they've been struck by lightening or like inanimate statues until you return - it doesn't work like that - and never fear, you will get back because although you belong to this time, you exist also in that time. If I don't let you go back, there will eventually be hundreds of people looking for you, stomping about all over my hill and causing all manner of turbulence. Yes, even down the ages, it will still reverberate and cause the most awful of disturbances and disruptions for the here and now. But first, and getting back to the more important things, I need you to do something for me.'

He then turned to look at me and, as I looked into those clear eyes, it dawned on me that he would always tell me the truth. I would find out over a long period of time that Merlin had no need to lie. He was strong, not only in his body but in every aspect of his character and, therefore, lying did not come into the equation. I would strive all my life to be like him and would often think what life would be like if we were all strong enough to always do the right thing and tell the truth - whatever the consequences. Even now, at the ripe old age of 55, I long to be like him and can sometimes hear a faintly echoed "tut, tut" if I even *think* of telling a lie.

'For now, rest, we'll start your training tomorrow. By the way, do you have a name?'

'Jack,' I replied.

'A very strange name indeed! I shall call you Percy – short for Percival - a very noble name.' He looked at me pulling a face and continued, completely ignoring any protest I might make. 'It is a more usual sounding name - in this day and age, in any event, and you look very regal - like a Percy,' he commented as he looked at me with a quizzical lift of his eyebrow. He then turned away, chuckling.

I started to argue with him. I liked my name and didn't want it changed. He raised one eyebrow as he looked back at me. 'It's no use you arguing with me, young Percy, you can't be taken seriously with a name that does not exist – well not yet, anyway! And they changed my name, didn't they? So if I had to put up with it, well, so will you!' And that was that. He changed my name.'

FOUR

The next evening, Jack sorted out with the boys just where he had got to in the story. Banking up the fire with enough logs to keep them uninterrupted for some time, he continued.

'I awoke some time later that night. My heart did a somersault under my ribs – you know, the sort of feeling you sometimes get when you think you are falling out of the bed. Daft really, as I was already lying on the floor. It took a short while to re-orientate myself but, after looking around the cave, I came back to the present when I saw Merlin busily mixing some powders on the table near the shelves, humming – at least it sounded like humming - as he worked. He had his back to me so I felt that I could watch without him being aware of it. However, he made me jump as, after a while, he spoke, 'If you are now fully awake young man, you might as well come over here and help me.' I got up and moved over to him, not knowing how I could possibly help but curious to what he was doing.

'Do you know,' he said, 'that most of the time spells are merely common sense? It's just that people believe that things will happen if you give them a potion or a bit of mumbo jumbo. Well, I have to admit that there's also a little bit of scheming involved as well! One of the reasons I have brought you back from your time is so you can tell me what is happening there, then I can use that knowledge in my magic. The best way to make people think you are a prophet is to tell them something you *know* is going to happen. However, I think I have brought you back a bit too soon, you being as young as you are, as you won't really have stored up much information in nine summers.' He stood looking quizzically at me for a while, stroking his chin, while he considered his next move. Nodding his agreement with something he had decided upon in his own head, he stated, 'What I think I will do is train you up a bit while you're here, send you back home and then bring you back again when you are a bit older. That way you will be able to give me the answers to questions I shall send you back to find out. Brilliant!' I did think him a little bit vain but then, as I thought it, Merlin pursed his lips and shook his head and I realised I would have to keep such thoughts to myself – he could understand everything I was thinking! As I thought this, I looked up at him again and saw him smile.

'Yes, exactly! But, and you have to remember this more seriously, so can some others who are not so nice!'

He started speaking naturally and as I stood listening to him, wide eyed – now that my eye was much better - and watching him, he began describing what he was doing with all that diverse equipment on the table as he measured, cut, boiled, sliced, crushed and packed various herbs and potions. Standing on tiptoe, I could just about see over the top of the table. Laughing again, he picked me up and, after clearing a space, sat me on the end of the bench. 'I will show you what all these herbs are, where to collect them, what they are used for, how much to use to hypnotise, or stun, or how much to use to, er, get rid of the enemy completely! Don't squirm, it probably won't happen. I will also show you what to mix to turn a young maiden's heart to butter in your hands.' He sighed, looked at me and then, probably realising how young I was, cleared his throat, commenting, 'Well, most maidens at any rate.'

He turned away, humming a quite tuneless tune, as he finished stirring an incredibly smelly mixture. Mind you, almost all of the potions I have seen him mix had obnoxious smells and one day, when I asked him why, he told me, 'Come, come, Percy, its obvious! Bland substances produce mild results but powerful substances – well, that's another story! You have to know your adversary, my boy. If he, or more than likely she, is more powerful than you, you are done for. You will probably only get one shot at it and if you mess that one up – gone, finished, dead more than likely. There is no quarter given in this game, my lad, none at all! It'll be you - or him – or her!' he declared with a snap of his fingers.

I think my eyes must have shown how frightened and confused I was getting by what he was telling me. So, while he was on the subject and, I suppose, to get all the frightening things over with in one fell swoop, he continued, 'We have to kill the giant.'

'Giant!' I squeaked, then coughed to try and cover the squeak, cleared my throat and said it again, hopefully in not so shrill a voice. If anything, it was higher!

'Yes, the Glaston giant! He lives above us on this hill but at the moment he sleeps and when he sleeps he cannot be seen – he's completely invisible and, not only that, he has no substance whatsoever; you could walk right through him without waking him and you wouldn't even know he was there. It's the most unusual thing! He can sleep for one night or one year and sometimes even longer. This time he has not been seen for many a moon but he will awake, yes, he'll wake up again when he's hungry. Oh, man, will he be hungry this time! The last time he slept before this was for one and a half years. He eventually woke up and when he did he ate all the cattle, hogs and chickens as far as the eye can see. Some bards made up quite frightening songs about it.' He lowered his voice to a whisper, 'and they said that at least two children disappeared and were never seen again!' He saw the fright on my face and, clearing his throat, continued, 'Well, now, that was in the song sung by a fairly unknown bard whom I believe was just trying to make a name for himself, so I don't know how true it is.' He looked over at me and as he could see I was getting quite agitated, amended his discourse by adding that he did not think this particular tale could be true as there was no outcry about lost children at the time.

38

'Generally speaking, though, what bards sing about is true, if embellished a bit. They travel all over Britain, following kings or mighty warriors, to make up a great song, story or poem about them so as to become famous themselves and enjoy the easy life. Most great men are very vain and thoroughly enjoy good songs or yarns about themselves, so they will keep a competent bard in the lap of luxury. You'll find great bards in nearly every castle but, as I said, only if they are good enough and to know if they are good enough, well, their stories have to hold up to very close scrutiny - without actually offending their lords, of course.

'I knew of a bard who, instead of being circumspect, actually made the lord of the manor look quite a fool - he disappeared, although his harp was found half submerged in a boggy field some few miles away with a glove clutching one of the strings! No one dug any deeper to see if there was a hand inside it or if anything – or anyone – was further down!

'Conversely,' he went on, 'a lord is only respected if he has a bard at his beck and call, otherwise folk will think that he is too insignificant, boring or – worse – not brave, and there is no song or poem that has been put together to show how great and mighty he is. So, as you can see, if there was nothing to be said about him, that would make him a very poor specimen indeed.' Squaring his shoulders and pulling himself up to his fullest stature, and obviously well into his story, Merlin continued, 'I was once thought to be one of the greatest bards ever, as well as the finest and truest British prophet who ever lived.' Then he shrugged one shoulder as if to dismiss the thought, stating, 'But being a bard is a bit of a cutthroat life; I wouldn't recommend it'. He turned back to his table and continued making his potions.

The hair was still standing up on the back of my neck; it was not a good thing to think of whether it was true or not that a giant may have eaten some children. More to the point, I don't know how he thought I could help to kill one! I knew

I was a good shot with a sling but I was no David against Goliath. I didn't know if I could kill anyone to save my life, let alone a giant. I earnestly hoped it wouldn't come to that.

However, Merlin did go on to say that I should put the thought of the giant out of my head, as at the moment I was much too young. 'I really thought I was bringing a man back when I got hold of that prediction; never mind, you will be a man one day!' He went on to say that it was going to be some time before he would be in a position to do anything at all other than get me trained up - so, the giant could wait.

I spent many a long day with Merlin in his cave. He had to reassure me on more than one occasion that I would eventually go back to my own time and that a minute there could well be like a year here, so I carried on, quite happily, assisting him in his mixtures and spells and, even if I say it myself, enjoyed it and became quite proficient.

Then one day, quite out of the blue - 'Ready or not,' Merlin wiped his hands on a rag and turned to me, 'let's go! I think it's about time you started your physical education. I am going to take you to someone who will show you not only how to defend yourself but, more importantly, how to attack. He will also show you how to dress yourself properly, well his wife will at any rate, and how to behave in public. Sir Ector is one of the very few gentlemen I have ever met who has also managed to raise his family and men in truth and wisdom. By that, I don't mean the sort of wisdom that appears to be in fashion at the moment - you know, the type of veneer that covers up deception, shallowness and greed, which shows itself up for what it is when it goes out of date. No, Sir Ector is a true man and his wisdom goes very deep.'

He was saying all of this, as he looked me over; at my short trousers, my shirt and my socks, one of which always seemed to be down around my ankle. He commented, again, as he had done many times before, 'Strange clothes, very strange, hmm. And your hair!' He looked at my short back and sides. 'Were you ill before you came to me or perhaps had head lice and have had to have all your hair shaved off?' I shook my head, blushing, as I recalled the ribbing that the kids at school got if they were found with nits – we all dreaded the woman we called "Nitty Nora, the flea explorer", and I was embarrassed to think that he thought I may have had head lice. 'Mind you,' he continued, 'I really do like your boots, very clever, very clever indeed!'

Changing the subject, he said, 'Once trained in the basics, I'll bring you back here to continue your training in the more subtle arts of the unexplained and the refined aspects of the Old Way. Then we will be ready for anything!'

I had often looked at the huge Glass that hung from the ceiling at the far side of the cave. We now moved over to it and Merlin, standing behind me and holding onto my shoulders, told me to look into it and tell him what I saw. I couldn't see anything at all. It looked at one and the same time shiny and cloudy, a bit like mother-of-pearl or a thick sheet of cracked ice. 'No, Percy,' Merlin sighed, 'don't just look at it - look *into* it! Concentrate! Look into its depths!' He didn't raise his voice but all the same I was aware that I didn't have a choice. What Merlin said, I did. In fact, apart from a very few people (and those were usually very bad or exceptionally stupid people) everyone did what Merlin said. It wasn't that I feared him; well, perhaps as I got to know him better I did fear disappointing him. He interrupted my reverie. 'Find a point to concentrate on, deep in the glass … focus.'

We stood there for quite some time, and I have to admit that Merlin was very patient, until, suddenly, 'I saw something!' I pointed, getting quite excited. 'Yes, look,' I pointed, 'I saw it move!' I kept on staring at the glass. Very slowly it got lighter and clearer. Soon it was just like looking at a moving picture show at the local cinema, only it was in colour. Yes, boys, in my day, most films were only in black and white! I took in the whole picture and could see a large wooden shed, which Merlin later told me was a barn, set in front of a huge forest; in front of the barn were two boys, one a lot older than the other, the younger one looked slightly older than me. In fact he was eleven years old – two years my senior.

They were playing a sword fighting game with wooden practise swords and the older boy was finding it extremely hard to see due to the fact that his eyes were streaming tears of hilarity - he was laughing not so much because the younger one kept getting "killed" but because he showed how upset and annoyed he was that he kept getting "killed".

Merlin put his hands on both my shoulders and turned me to face him. Looking very serious and hoping to get across the point that what was about to happen was very important indeed, he said 'I am taking you to this family. I shall tell them that you are the son of someone very special. The father of these two young men, and I shall tell you more of that another time, is used to taking these requests of mine and he will raise you like one of his own for as long as it takes, until I come to get you.

'Now,' he turned me back to the glass, 'it is important you remember the next few things.' He took hold of my forearm in a grip that was not painful but one that I would not easily be able to wriggle out of. 'When we get there, you are not to say anything about where you have really come from. All you need say is that you come from a very far away place. That is sufficient for everyone's needs and is not a lie.' Merlin hated lies and liars with equal passion. 'I shall tell them that you are to be taught the ways of a knight. Ha, don't grin! It will be very hard work! The most vital thing you have to remember, though, is not to let anyone, and I mean *anyone*, know anything of their history, especially that Sir Ector is not really Arthur's father. They know nothing of King Uther being Arthur's real father. If you let anything slip

42

out, the whole course of history could change and it might be the devil to pay if that happens. Do you understand?' He glared at me. I nodded. After staring fiercely at me for a further long moment, he suddenly relaxed his fierce demeanour and smiled, 'Good. Now, look into the Glass again.'

Merlin handed me a small pouch with some fine dust in it. 'Keep this on you at all times. Don't use it unless you have to.' He drew his lips together as he clenched his jaws and frowned. 'It really takes a long time to collect this stuff. It comes from dragons' droppings, you know!' My mouth fell open as he went on to enlarge upon the subject. He saw the look on my face and decided to elaborate: 'By dragons' droppings, I don't mean little parcels like the stuff you get from birds or rabbits or even cows or horses come to think of it. No, dragons only go about once a year and then only when they have been awake for some length of time and have therefore eaten sufficient, because they can sleep for years at a stretch you know. No, there is quite a mound of the stuff when they do go! *And* there is an art to collecting it as well. It has to be allowed to dry out completely; if it is only even slightly damp it will rot the shovel (or whatever other implement is used in collecting it) and, not only that, it will be completely useless as there will be no magic left in it whatsoever. What has to happen is that before it turns to dust and blows away completely, it changes, only at night you know, into a surging greenish-purple phosphorescence, and that only for that one night. It is only then that it can be collected and still retain its magical properties. By the next morning it will have turned to dust and will just disappear - puff.' As he made this exclamation, he blew on his hand and clicked his fingers into the air.

'Sometimes, on a really sunny day, you can see these motes of dust floating in the sunbeams - I expect you have. But although you can tell, well almost, that they are particles of dragon's droppings, they are by then useless and quite harmless.

'However, getting back to the subject of collecting it. Sometimes you will notice that I'll go missing for days or even months on end. Well, it's probably because I have found a mound, so to speak, and I have to sit night-by-night watching it until it is on the turn and ready. I then collect it in special glass jars and hide it away in one of my caves. Of course, I have to use my own magic on it as well, otherwise when it is used, especially if it's to transport someone, they could end up anywhere. No good if you ended up at the bottom of the sea, eh!' He fell about laughing at his supposition. When he finally got himself under control he cleared his throat and made an important assertion, 'Yes, it's special stuff and can only be processed by a master magician like myself.'

Returning his attention to the present, he went on to say, 'So, as I said, be very sparing with it. Come to think of it, I haven't found any for at least two summers now, but then the weather has been so damp that it wouldn't be any good anyway. Yes, well,' he turned to me as he passed the cord over my head and patted the pouch which now hung round my neck, 'if you are in a tight jam you must take a pinch of the dust and throw it over your head. I have said my special magic over it and under that particular spell you will be immediately transported back to this cave. Do you understand?' I nodded. 'And don't let anyone know you've got it. I didn't mean to start telling you about any of my special magic just yet, but I think, in these circumstances, you needed to know about the "dust".'

'I can't believe what you've told me. I didn't think dragons really existed; in fact I find it really had to believe that they do!'

'My boy, I do not waste words and if there were no such things as dragons I wouldn't waste my breath mentioning

44

them. You have obviously heard about them and I have been talking about them so, believe me, they exist. Hopefully, when you do see one it will be a friendly one. If not – well, its been great meeting you!'

I shivered!

Merlin then produced, from a pouch, which was tied to his waist and secreted in the folds of his robe, another pinch of fine dust. He threw it high above our heads and, catching the light from the wall sconces, it glittered down, over and around us. He said a very few words that I did not understand (some of his mumbo jumbo, I suppose – was that for my benefit or did he really need to say it? Who knows?) and then, suddenly, we were standing at the edge of the forest and looking for real at the two boys fighting.

'Quickly, now, hide the dust pouch; I think they have seen us coming.'

I tugged at the string and tucked the pouch he had given me into my shirtfront.

He went on chattering about dragons for a while, but I was only listening with half an ear as we stood on the edge of the clearing and I looked goggle-eyed at the two boys as they wielded their wooden swords.

The younger of the two saw us first and rushed over yelling and whooping. Even though he was short of breath from his exertions, he almost knocked Merlin over as he bounded over to him. Taking in as much of him as I could in the short time before he reached us, I saw a boy who was obviously about 11 or 12 years old, but already looked very much like the young man he was to become. He had long, brownish-red hair tied back in a ponytail. In fact, he had tied it back so as to enable him to see to fight. Apparently, so he told me later, the men were not really allowed to tie it back until they became fighting men, as it was then a sign that they had actually earned the right to call themselves warriors. His clothes were dark linen cloth made up of tight trousers over which he wore an almost knee-length linen jerkin tied at the waist with a thick leather belt. He wore soft leather sandals.

'Merlin, where have you come from? Why have you been gone so long? We'd heard you were locked up somewhere and that your powers had gone and you couldn't get away!' Stepping back, he laughed as he took up a swordsman's stance and pointed his wooden sword at Merlin's chest and then, throwing the sword down, threw his arms around him in an embrace.

'Now, now, young Arthur, you are getting a bit big to cuddle an old man!'

'Old man, indeed! You will never be that!' said his older brother as he strode over and clasped both of Merlin's hands, shaking them vigorously. 'Come, have some refreshment and see Father.' He led Merlin into the barn, where their father was discussing one of the horses with the smith.

I was dumbstruck! Was this Arthur? *The* King Arthur to be? I just couldn't get my head round it. I followed them all across the compound and into the small barn. I was still trying to get my head together as I took in the new smells and the sights and sounds. As Merlin and the older boy moved out of the way I saw another man - huge - dressed in similar clothing to the others but sporting a large ragged fleece around his shoulders.

Merlin and I looked at the man - Sir Ector – with his untamed yellow hair making him look so wild; Merlin told me later that over the years he had hardly altered in looks or demeanour. 'Father, Merlin is here'.

Ector turned and, showing large, good teeth in an enormous grin, greeted the magician with a bear hug. 'Why so long away, sir?' Then, holding Merlin at arms' length, he looked him over. 'You seem whole; there are no scars.' Turning toward Arthur, he commented, 'As you can see, Merlin, the boy does well and grows strong and wise. But, where have you been and what have you been up to? Nay,

46

later … for now come and refresh yourself. We have hams and a fresh game pie and a good, strong mead, which I tested yesterday and found to be full ready for consumption or, perhaps, some beer if you would prefer something lighter. Come, and when you are refreshed you can tell us your news.' His voice was as big and loud as one would expect from such a big man and interspersed with his welcome toward Merlin and me he was shouting orders to the servants, some of whom could be seen running to do his bidding, to prepare the feast.

While the men talked, Arthur took me outside, introduced himself and showed me around. I was still reeling with the knowledge that the Arthur I had read about over the last year or so was now walking about, arm in arm with me and talking to me.

When I got older and more suspicious, and possibly a bit wiser, I would look back and wish that life could have remained like it was then. Most children seem to have such an in-built friendliness and acceptance of other children and are happy to be with them and play in their games. Mind, I did think about the two bullies – there are always exceptions! Also, it's different when one grows up! But, then, everything is different when one grows up - what suspicious cynics we become! However, this was a wonderful time before I even knew there was such a word as "cynicism".

Beside the barn was a larger house, mainly made of wood but some lower parts were made of stone; this was where the whole family lived. There were various other smaller buildings dotted around and I noticed people working in the fields. 'Come, let's go hunt in the woods; there's plenty of daylight left before supper. I'll take my bow and we'll shoot some hare. Perhaps, then, old Molly will make us a hare pie for tomorrow! We'll take the dogs and they will chase out the game for us. Here, take this bow.' He thrust a bow and a quiver of arrows into my hands and I must have looked completely bewildered because he then asked if I knew how to use it.

'No. I have never used a bow and arrow but I can use a sling or a catapult,' I declared, trying to redeem myself.

'Good, but I will show you later how to make a bow for yourself - and how to use it. If Merlin wants you to be trained as a knight, you will probably not need to use a bow and arrow as you will have training with the sword and spear and, possibly, the mace or axe, but I like to use the bow. Meantime, let's go hunting. By the by, what's your name?'

'Ja, er, Percival, but please call me Percy.' I stammered, almost saying my real name.

Arthur had two dogs. They were both wolfhounds; one he called Griff and the other was called Cabal. Griff went loping off into the forest and we didn't see him again until he had apparently had his fill of hare or something. Cabal kept pace with us, ears alert and nose twitching. A couple of times I noticed he was looking at me and I felt sure I knew what he was thinking. '*No*,' I thought, '*that's daft!*' I put those thoughts out of my head and tried to concentrate on what Arthur was doing.

Arthur showed me how to track game. He wet his finger with his tongue and held it in the air. 'I'm finding out which way the wind is blowing. We need to be down wind or they will smell us. Right!' he said when he was satisfied we were in the right place, 'Follow me very quietly and don't tread on any dry twigs. Cabby,' he called softly to his dog, 'go root them out.' The dog, big as he was, moved off like a lightning shadow.

We spent most of the afternoon in the woods and caught more than six large hare. Arthur tied them onto a branch he cut from a tree and propped them against it while he showed me how to find the correct wood to make a bow and different wood to make the arrows. We would need to get back to the barn to find the twine for the bow and see if we could beg or borrow some real metal arrowheads instead of using wooden ones and also find some feathers. I had never enjoyed myself so much in my life. As we travelled back towards the house I was suddenly warned to watch where I put my foot. '*Keep still.*' I froze. I looked and there, almost three feet in my path, was an adder. There was a patch of sunshine through the trees, which was touching the moss where the adder was sunning itself. I had heard of snakes before but had never seen one. Fortunately for all of us, just then a cloud covered the sun and the snake moved back into the warmer undergrowth.

'Thanks for the warning,' I said.

'Warning? What warning? I said nothing!' Arthur replied.

Cabal trotted ahead of us, nose up, sniffing, beard pointing, tail swaying.

'We arrived back at the enclosure in time for supper. After leaving the catch of hare with Old Molly, with the promise that a fresh hare pie would be on the table on the morrow, we let ourselves into the main hall. I had a few nettle stings on my legs and Ector's "good lady wife", as she was mostly referred to, took me off to see to the stings and to "dress me properly". She gave me a pouch in which I could put all my belongings. Spreading them out on the dresser, I made a quick inventory of: penny whistle, two old copper pennies, clockwork mouse, catapult, piece of string, a not too clean handkerchief and two smooth stones. I put them in the pouch, which I tucked into my belt. When I returned I found that everyone was waiting for me so that proper introductions could be made. I felt very self-conscious as in the past I had been mostly ignored by my elders; also I stood there in what I considered to be a dress, which was made of a light brown herringbone woollen material tied in the middle by a belt; it came down to my knees. I also wore loose-fitting leggings which were a darker brown and, of course, my boots. Apart from my very short haircut, I looked just like everyone else which still didn't make me feel better – I still felt like I was in a dress.

Sir Ector was going to be responsible for my training in knightly pursuits. He introduced me to his oldest son, Sir Kay; Arthur, his youngest (so everyone thought), whom I had already met, his good lady wife, Elise, whom I was to call "Mistress". He then introduced me to his daughter, Rhianne. Wow, I was smitten! I had never considered girls as anything but sissy up to now but when I looked at her I can remember, in a very embarrassed way, trying to stand even taller and puff out my chest and, at the same time try to forget that I was almost wearing a dress! Even at the tender age of nine I had never seen anyone as beautiful as her. She took after her father in that she was fair of hair but she had deep violet coloured eyes, something very rare in those days as most people were, especially in the south, fairly dark of hair and eye and to the north and west more red of hair and lighter or even blue eyed. The pale, winter sky blue of her dress only accentuated the deep violet of her eyes. She gave a very shy smile and I blushed as deep as a berry, experiencing a new and weird sensation in my stomach. Happily, though, I don't think anyone saw, although I did notice that Cabal wagged his tail as he lay there in front of the fire looking at me with his head on his forepaws. '*Strange!*' I thought.

Supper was a very happy affair. They were a very close family and there was lots of laughter and light-hearted jesting. I really wanted to go home to my father and hoped that my mother had returned from my aunts. '*But, if I couldn't go home just yet*', I thought, '*I think I would rather like it here*'. As darkness fell, Merlin took me outside. 'You will stay with this family until I return. No, don't interrupt,' he held up his hand, 'just listen to me. They will say you are a relative from the south and that you are to be companion to Arthur while his brother goes to serve at the court of the king. Be courteous at all times. I do not want to return to find that you have shamed me! But no,' he looked me over, his voice becoming quite gentle, 'I do not think you could do that. I will return, hopefully when the giant awakes if not before. You will not be ready to confront him yet as you are too young; I shall need you to return to the other side of the mist before we make further plans. Look up at the stars,' he said, changing the subject.

We both stared up into a clear night sky, sprinkled with stars and a sickle moon - the sky seemed clearer than I could ever remember seeing it before. *Perhaps the world and the universe had got dirtier in the Twentieth Century,'* I thought.

'Perhaps you are right!' Merlin responded. I had forgotten we could mind speak. 'Ector knows as much about the stars as I, and he will teach you how to travel using them as guides. You have much to learn. Learn well, my young friend.'

At that Merlin turned into the hall to make his goodbyes and then, with the whole family bidding him "fare ye well", simply walked away.

He strode so fast, that he seemed almost to glide off into the forest. However, before he completely disappeared he turned to look at me and I felt, rather than heard, him say for me to trust Cabal - he would look after me.

I now felt very scared. Merlin had seemed the only contact with my real family, in that year 1949, or was it 449? How was I going to get home? Merlin had told me that I *would* get home because he didn't want anyone stomping about all over his hill, causing havoc. But, where had he gone? Would I be able to get home without his help? Was I stuck here forever?

I was still staring at the spot where I had last seen him, when I felt a cold, wet nose thrust into my hand. I almost jumped out of my skin and looked down to see Cabal looking up at me. Well, there wasn't much of a distance to look down to, as he was a very large dog and his head almost came up to my shoulder.

'*Don't worry,*' he said. I jumped again, this time because I believed the dog had spoken to me. I actually heard a voice. He read my mind, '*I did speak to you! No, not like people speak to each other, which would be impossible. I don't have the vocal ability or even the vocal equipment to speak like man, I can only bark or growl, or, when it's stormy, I am ashamed to say, sometimes howl. No, I speak directly into your mind, but to you it seems audible. Funny that! However, no one else can hear – well, not that many at any event. Please close your mouth, you look like the King's Fool on a bad day!*'

I realised I was staring at him with huge eyes and gaping mouth. 'I cannot believe this!' I said, aloud.

'*Shhh. Hush! Did Merlin tell you about the Old Way?*' I nodded. '*Well, this is one aspect of it. Not many people are awake to it but as soon as I saw you, I knew you were. None of them here have the gift except, maybe, Rhianne.*' I could feel myself blush. '*Hmm, you will have to control that red face of yours, Percy; it's a real giveaway! Oh yes, I can see colours, unlike most dogs who can only see in black and white and various shades of grey in between. However, so far as the Old Way is concerned, in Rhianne's case, her mind has not yet matured to understand it, it's so jumbled; I think she will need a lot of training, but you, well - you're a natural!*'

As he spoke I was only slightly reassured. He said I was a "natural" but I didn't feel natural at all and what had happened, and was continuing to happen, was so unnatural – it was creepy.

I let my mind go back to the first time Merlin had spoken into my mind. That was OK, as men are naturally able to converse with one another but this, well, this is another thing. I know that humans can train dogs to obey simple commands but I have never seen a dog command a man or, as in this case, talk to one. I just didn't think that animals had the brainpower. This was something else to add to the bizarre things I had experienced over the last day or so.

'*Not so strange, Percival,*' Cabal had followed my thinking and now, without taking umbrage, interrupted my thoughts. '*But, you will need to be able to shut off your mind at times. There are a few who have knowledge of the Old Way that would harm not only you but also those most dear to you. They, fortunately, cannot use it very effectively because they are evil and are therefore unable to use it as well as they would wish – it is corrupted, you see. It does cause them a problem but they are still able to try and confuse those of us who can use it effectively. If you are to be used to help Arthur and Merlin, you will need to be able to close off your mind to the wrong sort. I'll teach you how to do that, if you don't know already. Anyhow, back to the present! When you are with Sir Kay and Arthur, training you in these modern days to be a great knight, I shall be yours and Arthur's faithful hound; I have to tell you, though, that with me he has to come first and, like you, my job is to protect him. Arthur, however, won't be able to communicate the way we do, as he does not have knowledge of the Old Way.*

'*Merlin told me that you are also to be Arthur's friend and protector and it's because you know the Old Way you have been chosen for this role.*

'*We have met before, you know!*' I stared at him! I knew I had never met him before. '*Oh yes, we have met. Do you remember when those two bullies attacked you in the woods?*'

I stared at him with eyes bulging. 'You! But how?' was all I could find to say.

'*Now, Percy, you must remember to speak to me with your mind, otherwise everyone will think you demented! But, as for me helping you with the bullies, it's another of the gifts of the Old Way. I have this gift, so does Merlin, but not many others do. Getting back to our positions in the here and now,*

53

you are my friend so, when Arthur meets with his religious instructor, I shall take you off and train you up in my way. Perhaps we could stalk some small game in the woods and share some fresh meat?'

I looked in horror at Cabal at the thought of eating any freshly killed meat let alone some that was recently deceased. He did have the grace to look a bit ashamed, *'Well, perhaps not. Just the chase then, eh?'*

FIVE

It was a hard job to get the boys to understand when it was time to stop telling a story for that day. They would listen until he had no voice left at all, if he let them. It was almost a standing joke now, when he said that that was enough for today. He would look down at Ben and Daniel, their huge eyes showing that they were hanging on his every word. *'Wait for it'*, he would think, *'Here it comes'*.

'Oh, no, not now! Not when it's getting so exciting! What happened next? Is it really true? Does Merlin really exist? Could we go to the island one day and visit the cave or wherever that cave is? There's no school tomorrow, so we could stay up later, or even go to the ruins at Tintagel. Perhaps we might find the stone.' The boys were tripping over each sentence as they tried hard to convince their grandfather that now was not the time to stop telling the story.

'Whoa, whoa, stop now.' Jack sounded stern but his eyes were always laughing. 'It's way past your bedtime and you have to help me in the yard tomorrow. No help, no stories!'

'Oh alright,' Ben moaned, 'but you will tell us what happened after that, won't you? Tomorrow? Promise?'

'Cross my heart.'

Most nights, as the boys got ready for bed, they could be heard discussing the authenticity of Jack's stories. It would finally go quiet.

Tonight, Kate had gone for a walk with her friend Sally and wouldn't be back for another half-hour or so. Cab pushed the door open with his nose and trotted into the room. He rolled over on to his back and, twisting from side to side, gave his back a vigorous scratching on the old hardwood floorboards. 'Come over here, old friend and I'll give your back a good stiff brushing.' Cab got up and after giving himself a shake, which started from his nose and carried on through his entire body to the end of his tail, stood in anticipation of the stiff brushing. You could actually see the pleasure in the set of his head while this was going on; he looked almost regal, with his long face and pointed beard. 'How are you? Did you have good hunting in the woods today?'

'Tolerable. They've set new traps for the rabbits. I can see where the trappers have been, as they all appear to have the most enormous feet that flatten the ground all around the traps. You would think the rabbits would notice that and thus not get caught, but they don't. It's OK finding one dead in the traps, saves me the trouble of hunting, but then, mostly, they are cold and sometimes rather stiff. The pleasure of the hunt is the main thing. There's nothing like stalking a rabbit before the kill! As you know, they are very fast but incredibly stupid. I know there are those who would say that that is wicked, but nature is nature and has to be accepted. When I look at humans I have to review my thinking - nature is natural, but man is unnatural - wicked. It has ever been so, eh? Do you remember the time we were incarcerated in the Giant's Tower?'

Jack stared into the fire, remembering, and it was as if the coals themselves turned into the shapes of that long time past. Even the flames brought back memories of the sconces on the dungeon walls and the spluttering flames within them. Yes, he remembered, and even now a shiver ran down his spine at the narrow escape he had had there.

He had stopped brushing so Cab pushed his elbow up with a cold wet nose, to remind him of the job he was supposed to be doing! Jack carried on with the brushing, commenting, *'I don't think the boys are old enough to hear that one yet'.*

'No, I don't think the boys are ready to hear the story of the Giant, or the Tower of Glaston yet and, to be fair to them, you should always start at the beginning so that when you get

to something like what happened after you and Merlin came out of the cave at Tintagel, it will make all the more sense to them. Otherwise you are going to have to keep stopping and explaining bits to them. Then, of course, you'll forget where you got up to and we'll all get in a muddle!'

'Yes, you are right, my old friend. I'll continue with the first time I met Arthur.'

As Jack lay back in his rocker his mind drifted back along the avenues of the past, thinking of his family and of recent events. His daughter's face swam into his imagination, with her dark, slightly wavy hair framing an extremely pretty face. That dark hair she got from him, although her skin was fair, almost translucent like her mother's, and she had her mother's features, including her blue eyes; in fact, except for the dark hair, he would say that they were the image of one another. Jack's thoughts then drifted back to his wife. How he missed her. It was so painful to think about her. Determinedly bringing his thoughts back to the present he considered Ben who looked just like Kate, except his skin tanned easily and his eyes were brown; he was going to be tall and already had his grandfather's muscles. Danny! Well, he favoured his late father with his piercing blue eyes and he also had Jack's wife's colouring, both having fair, curly hair. He, too, looked as though he would grow quite tall but he was slim, like Kate.

The three of them were very close and took care of one another – unusual that, in the 1990s – but looking at their lives over the past few years, suffering as they had at the hands of their stepfather, if they couldn't rely on each other, there was no-one else they could turn to! No-one else, indeed! *'Well there is now,'* he had determined, when they had first arrived. As he was still thinking about his family when he drifted off to sleep, his dreams were, of course, about them.

Those first few days after their arrival Jack had given Kate his bed and made room for the boys in the other upstairs room, after clearing all the rubbish out. He had slept in his rocking chair and recalled how he had awoken very early the next morning with a start and with a rather aching back. However, in the twinkling of an eye, the happenings of the previous evening came flooding back. He stretched, almost like a cat, or, to be more precise, like a wolfhound, something Cabal had taught him many moons back. He felt some of his bones crack, and more than a few muscles complain! *'Perhaps sleeping in the rocker was not such a good idea! I'd better get myself back into shape, Cab, you never know when you might need to be fit for something or other!'* He had then noticed that Daniel was fast asleep, lying beside the hound. Cab looked quizzically up at his friend and allowed one small wag of his tail.

'My, it's cold when that fire goes out! Still, it won't take long to light.' He went outside and stripped off his old shirt and, after splashing some cold water over his face from the faucet that fed the horse trough, he very soon had a pile of freshly chopped firewood. By the time his daughter had come downstairs, the fire was laughing merrily in the hearth and the kettle was singing on the hob. As she stepped into the kitchen, Jack's heart almost stopped. Yes, she looked so like her mother. His mouth fell open.

Misinterpreting his look, she felt awkward and stammered, 'Have I done something wrong? I didn't have any clothes to wear and found this old t-shirt and trousers of yours in the cupboard. They fit me almost perfectly! I hope you don't mind.' As Jack did not answer her at once, she turned as if to run upstairs. Almost on a sob, she whispered, 'I'm sorry - I'll put them back.'

'No, no. Hush, now, Kate. It was just a shock, that's all. I thought I'd seen a ghost. The way the light got you, you looked so like your mother! No, you are welcome to anything you can find. Perhaps we'll all take a walk to the village later today. Mary, the dairyman's wife, has children a bit older and might have some cast-offs for the boys, that is until we can get into town to buy them some new ones.' He told them all to break their fast while he hurried upstairs to dress.

Kate couldn't help noticing that although her father was a lot older than she could ever remember before she had left to marry her second husband, Morgan, he was still a very big man; he was at least six feet tall, with muscles on his arms that any bruiser would be proud of. He had a full head of hair, dark brown and wavy but going rather grey at the sides. His eyes, light brown with golden glints in them, were, however, his best feature; they would flash when he was angry and sparkle when he laughed and the very slight scar that ran from his cheekbone to his outer eye gave him a merry look. She let her breath out on a long sigh. For the first time in a very long time she felt safe. The feeling brought tears to her eyes. Again, for the first time in a very long time she felt free to let those tears fall. The boys, who had by then come downstairs, looked up at their mother, not understanding why she should cry now. She tried to smile but it was a bit of a lopsided one. However, as they hadn't seen her smile for such a long time now, they felt they could relax.

Cab, curled up by the hearth with his head on his forepaws, took it all in.

Kate again felt a surge of relief to know that her father had not moved house but in the back of her mind worried whether that would make it all the more easy for Morgan to find them. She tried to put that thought out of her head. Looking around the kitchen, though, she wondered why her father didn't move with the times. Although he'd had running water installed and a bath – thank goodness – his lifestyle was still very simple. Wood served for the fire, which fed the boiler, and gas cylinders served the utensils for cooking and lighting; diesel, of course, was used for the farm equipment. She supposed being a good way from the edge of town and living alone – until now that is - he still liked to keep himself to himself. And, there was no phone! Now, that could be a good thing but at the same time she considered that it could be a bad thing.

Morgan did not appear to be interested in coming to find them. Not just then, anyway!

Over the next few months Kate relaxed and got some colour back in her cheeks. A woman's touch in the home was most welcome to Jack and, as the months passed and then the years, she put in a cottage garden, grew vegetables and helped raise hens. In fact she did so well she could sell much of what she produced. Also, over the last couple of years she had become very well known in the village for her handiwork with the needle and was called on to make curtains and drapes for quite a few of the village families.

The boys grew and, as with all boys, could eat as though they were in competition. They would help their grandfather around the cottage, repairing, cutting wood and, best of all, going out with him to catch rabbits and fish. Daniel enjoyed this most as he tried to keep up with Cab, who, being an expert stalker and hunter, would flush out the rabbits and Danny and Ben would try to catch them – they never did. On very fine mid-summer days they would pack up a basket and go out for the whole day, starting at first light, hitching up the wagon and travelling as far as the coast.

On such fine days, quite often after lunch in the meadow or on the beach, or maybe in the evening or on a winter night round the fire, Jack would tell them stories, and such stories they were – about Merlin and Arthur, castles, dragons and witches, and the like. He always had that faraway look in his eyes, as though what he was saying was actually true. But of course it was! Well it was – wasn't it?

Like all children of their age, they believed every word and then re-enacted the story in the yard, using some old willow wands as swords. There would, of course, be arguments as to who played Arthur and who played Merlin. They had spent an entire day, once, making a wizard's outfit – the cloak, the headpiece, the staff, a beard - until Jack put them right on that one! They would play in the copse, hiding and jumping out on one another and pretending they had just materialised, or they would climb the hill above the fields and claim it their castle and battlegrounds.

Yes, it seemed like yesterday, instead of three or so years' ago, since they had first arrived – these thoughts swam in and out of Jack's mind as he drifted in and out of sleep.

SIX

Jack woke early, as usual. He reckoned it should have been a bit lighter than it was and, for a moment, as he lay there half-asleep, half-awake, thought, perhaps, that he must have been disturbed by something.

Since starting to tell his growing grandsons about Merlin, he had become acutely aware of a change. He was not quite sure what the change was – in the atmosphere, his mood, a longing for the old days, a heightening of otherworldly perception – whatever it was, there was a definite change. He was aware that Cab felt it too! However, on this morning, it was no more, so it seemed, than a stormy start to the day. He opened the curtains and saw low, black clouds - menacing, ominous - making their way slowly toward him from the far side of the valley, from the direction of the village. *'Well, our day in the yard looks as though it will be cut short. I had better get a stockpile of wood ready, before it's too wet to chop, or to burn! Come on, Cab, let's get started.'* They went out into the yard as one or two drops of rain started to fall. However, it kept off while Cab bounded off through the trees and Jack chopped a pile of wood for the fire. The boys had not materialised yet and the house remained in darkness. There was a slight glow from the south as lightning twitched, preparing to launch itself, which was almost immediately confirmed by a slow, barely audible rumble, *'not too dissimilar to the sound of the giant's belly when he's hungry, which is almost all the time as he is never satisfied'*, thought Jack. *'Hmm, there I go again!'* Before Jack had the chance to start thinking more about the giant, Cab came bounding back out of the woods looking very pleased with himself and proceeded to lick his paws, washing off the residue of whatever had been breakfast from his mouth and whiskers. He looked up at Jack *'I know, I know, but it is so much better than that tinned stuff you once tried to force onto me!'* Jack gave a wry smile as he shouldered the bundle of wood and took it into the house.

Kate looked up as he walked in. She smiled, and he thought how lovely his daughter looked. She had changed so much from the bedraggled, pale creature that had first come to him some few years ago. She smiled now. Yes, that was the change. She never used to smile. She always looked frightened. However, the years had gone by and there was no sign of Morgan, so she had started to unwind and now looked radiant.

'Hello, dad. Tea's made and the breakfast is nearly ready. It feels really muggy. Did I hear thunder?' She was slicing the bread and had started to spread some butter on it as the boys tumbled down the stairs. 'Careful, you two.'

Jack went over to the fireplace, stacking the logs on the pile and positioning some wood on the fire. As he did so, it sent sparks shooting and cracking up the chimney like hundreds of miniature flaming arrows. *'Why does everything I do at the moment remind me so much of the old days?'* he queried.

'Do you think we are being called to go back? Arthur still might have need of us, you know,' Cab questioned.

Jack looked over at the old dog. Cab even looked as though he raised one shaggy eyebrow – a trick he had been taught by King Arthur himself! *'I can't see how that would help, old friend. Looking back, the king has been dead - or should I say "sleeping" - these fifteen hundred years and the prophesy, as you well know, is that he won't return until Britain is in dire peril and that, when he does come, Merlin, as always, will be at his side!'*

'King Arthur', said Daniel. Both Jack and Cab jumped, startled, 'is he going to be in the story you're telling us, granddad, or will you be leaving him and going on on your own?'

'Er, maybe, er yes, he might be, er, yes of course he will be,' Jack spluttered, having been caught off guard. He straightened up from stacking the wood at the side of the fireplace and continued, 'Help your mother. I have to secure the fence before the storm hits. Cabby, heel.' Noticing that a few more, bigger drops of rain had started to fall, Jack grabbed his Mackintosh from the peg near the door and went out to the yard. As he reached the far end he leaned against the gatepost and looked out over the meadow. He was visibly shaken by Daniel's exclamation about King Arthur. *Well, what do you think of that, Cab? Do you think he can mind-speak?*

I think he most probably has the gift but at the moment I believe he thinks that these "thoughts" just pop into his head. What do you think we should do?

I think we should be more careful for a start. I don't think he is old enough and I certainly don't want to take the chance of losing him. I nearly did that a few years ago, through my pride - almost losing all the family I have. I don't want to take the chance of losing any of them permanently.

Cabal understood exactly what Jack meant by "permanently".

Jack looked up as thunder, like the sound of stallions on a charge, rumbled across the sky. He finished securing the loose planks in the fence and then turned toward the house. *Let's go in. I don't think we will be going far today and remember to keep a hold on your thoughts.*

Me? Hrrmph! It's been such a long time since we have had the need to put up a guard, it will be hard to remember it every time, but I, at least, will try, Cab said indignantly as he stalked off toward the house with his head held high but his tail unfortunately, due to the thunder, tucked between his legs.

Jack smiled to himself.

Kate slipped her raincoat over her shoulders as she headed towards the door. 'I shall be at Mrs. Ambrose's for most of today. It's the only job I have on so I should be back about four o'clock. If not, would you please start tea. I'll bring some fresh bread when I come in. And you boys - behave for your grandfather!' With that she disappeared. Ben raised his eyebrows and looked angelically at Daniel as if to say that no-one trusted them; but they were basically well-behaved - well, like most other healthy 10 and 11 year olds at any rate! Mrs. Ambrose was fairly new to the village and had taken over old Mr. Fellowes' house. It had been empty since the old chap had died a couple of years ago and Mrs. Ambrose had asked Kate, on recommendation of course, to make the drapes and covers for her, something Kate was only too pleased to do to make some extra money.

'What are we going to do today, granddad?' Ben was tying the lace on one of his shoes and looked up at his grandfather stacking the rest of the wood at the side of the hearth. Daniel had called Cabby over to him and was scratching the dog behind his ears and over the rough coat on the back of his neck.

The hound couldn't help but show the pleasure on his face, stretching his neck forward as he soaked up the satisfaction of getting an itch scratched where he had trouble reaching.

Jack laughed at the hound's expression and told Daniel that he would have a job for life if he kept spoiling the dog.

'Ben, I think we will have to work in the barn this morning. It looks like being a bad day for tidying the yard. You and Daniel can help me move the plant and equipment over to one side and I suppose Cabby will catch some mice, or whatever. There are bound to be lots of them when we start shifting everything. So you had better dress suitably. I'll get some thick work gloves for you both. Mind you, don't touch anything unless I say. That barn hasn't been cleared out for years and some of the stuff in there is rusted and quite dangerous. Goodness knows what's in the back; I haven't been right back there since your mother was a little 'un!' He went upstairs to get their gear.

They spent the next few hours helping in the barn. Cabby caught (and most probably ate) more mice than he had seen in a month in the woods. He had the good sense to go off and hide before he ate them. Jack recalled him once telling how he had been used to catch wolves - a great sport and one that he and Griff had prided themselves in. There were quite a few of them around at one time, especially when the country was running with wild boar; but that when they had become scarce in Britain they had been reduced to chasing and catching hare or, when there was nothing else, the odd mouse. There were still quite a few hare in the forest but mostly, unfortunately, there was only the odd rush of mice - however, as he said, he had acquired quite a taste for them. Jack had, by that stage, asked him, none too politely, to shut up.

By lunchtime they were all ready to eat as they had worked up an enormous appetite. That is, all of them except Cabby!

'I think we will take the afternoon off boys,' said their grandfather. 'You have worked so hard and we have got so much done this morning, that I think we all deserve a good rest. We'll get scrubbed up and have our lunch. Then we'll decide what to do this afternoon, after that.'

The storm had been threatening all morning but it was only as they were eating their lunch that the first real streaks of lightning brightened up the otherwise very dark sky. The thunder sounded like battering rams against castle walls. It always made the hair stand up on the back of Jack's neck. It had the same effect on Cabby who hoped that the storm would not last too long as it made him howl. It took all his self-control not to start howling as soon as he saw the first streak of lightning. Today was no exception and as he looked across the room he tightened that control when Jack scowled at him. The funny thing was, though, Cabby thought, it didn't

66

seem to have any effect on the boys. *'I wonder if that is because they haven't been in the thick of battle.'*

'Granddad', said Daniel, 'you've told us about meeting Merlin. Was he really the man you saw in the photo? Are you going to tell us what happened after you met Arthur? Did you and he take part in any battles together?'

Again, Jack was unnerved by the fact that Daniel seemed so aware of his and Cabby's thoughts. Once more, he buried them behind a guard and hoped that Daniel was not aware of what he was doing. 'First of all, let's prepare the tea, as your mother asked. Then we'll see.'

'Oh, can't we do that later?' asked Ben.

'No. If I have things on my mind that I need to do when I am telling a story, I cannot get into it properly and then I miss bits out. Let's get all the jobs done first and then we'll settle down to Merlin.' Jack then gave a wry smile and thought to himself, 'If one could ever "settle down" where Merlin was concerned!'

'You're like a beacon on a hill', said Kate as she came home, being whooshed in through the door with a flurry of leaves and having to really push the door hard to close it. 'So still this morning and now so windy; this storm is quite frightening. I've never known one last as long and I have had to come home early because the power lines are down on the hill and all the electricity has gone off in the village. Mrs. Ambrose was quite put out that I couldn't hang the rest of her downstairs curtains. I said I would come home and sew the last of the swags and tails and hopefully be able to press and hang all of them for her tomorrow. I suppose it's when these things happen that it makes sense to have a cylinder of gas standing by, but in your case not just standing by but being used all the time, eh dad!' They laughed.

The storm moved on taking the last of the daylight and the wind with it, leaving a calm that was more ominous than a relief. The children did not seem to have any fear of the brooding atmosphere and quickly helped their mother with the dishes and the clearing away after lunch. They were relieved that, because their mother was home early, they wouldn't now have to prepare things for tea. There was then no getting away from it, as the boys sat down in expectation of the story unfolding and anticipation of excitement.

The next day arrived and it took a short while for me to re-orientate myself. I was lying on a wooden pallet, which was covered with an animal's fur. I had somehow managed to get myself completely tangled in it as I tossed around during the night. The dawn was just starting to lighten the room and, as it crept up over the windowsill, I studied Arthur's belongings. He, meanwhile, was still fast asleep on the pallet next to mine while Cabal was lying across the entranceway, alert as ever. As I lay there, looking around the room, I was amazed at the things that made up Arthur's goods and chattels. The walls were covered in weaponry - a mixture of spears were propped up in one corner, a shield leaned against them upon which was drawn a red flame; there were two bows, one without twine, and many arrows, some with wooden heads and some made with metal, all at different stages of construction. I sat up and looked at the clothes I had been given to wear the day before. They were rough, felt like linen and were mostly kept together with thick laces. I put them on and tied the pouch around my neck with a longer piece of cord. I had been allowed to keep my boots, upon which everyone had commented. They seemed to like the lace holes the best, as they had not seen rivets like them before. They thought it was an excellent idea for keeping the leather from fraying and would start to make and use them like that themselves. I started to wonder then just who inventors might really be! Were they people from the future returning to the past to show them how to do things or make things, thus making the people in the past the ones who appeared to have been the

68

inventors in the first place instead of the people from the future who had gone back to show them? But then, if that were so, who originally showed whom in the first place? Pondering this seemingly unfathomable puzzle, I slipped my feet into my boots and tied them up.

I was suddenly knocked sideways when Arthur threw a leather jerkin at me. He laughed, and I had to join in when he saw me jump. 'Put this on. There's a keen wind, by the sound of it, and you will need it to keep you warm. When we have had some exercise in the yard, that will be time enough to discard it.' We went down to break our fast.

The days went by, autumn starting to turn into winter, with Arthur and I becoming firm friends. I became pretty proficient with the bow and arrow and my muscles were starting to bulge with all the other exercises, especially with the short sword – well, we were only allowed the wooden practise sword. He told me about his family here in Devon and about the Angles and Saxons who travelled over the sea to attack Britain along the east and south coasts; he also told me about the Picts who travelled down from the north and attacked without warning. It was they who produced the most fear in everyone as they would cover their faces and arms in blue woad and thus looked very fierce. The stories about them were horrendous. Arthur had, so far, never seen any but had heard the tales. There were also Scots who attacked from the west. So, looking at all of these enemies, Britain appeared to be completely surrounded. No wonder it was essential to learn the art of warfare.

Arthur continued with his story, saying that they had apparently not been attacked for many a year now, but everyone knew the enemy, whichever one it was - if not all of them, would be back. Arthur also told me that he and his brother, both dark of feature but otherwise very dissimilar, had a different mother and that Sir Ector had married again some time after the death of his first wife.

Sir Ector's second wife was from a noble Welsh family and they spent their time between the two countries, usually taking ship from the north coast of Devon to the south coast of Wales. 'So, therefore,' Arthur told me, 'Kay is my half-brother and Rhianne is my half-sister.' He said she was a good child with a sweet temper. I was always happy to listen to him talk about her. We only really saw her at mealtimes, as her tuition was very different from ours; sometimes the whole family got together during the evening and she would be there. I would peek at her whenever I thought no one was looking. However, every time I did, I would think of Cabal and look over at him in his usual place by the fire. He always gave a slight wag of his tail as he looked at me out of one eye - just as though he was winking at me! Again, I would blush and then mentally kick myself for doing so.

Looking back, I believe that even as I got older, I would still change colour at the thought, more at my embarrassment of being found out than of my feelings for Rhianne.

We spent our mornings learning to fight, mainly with sword, spear, bow and arrow or in unarmed combat. I was able to show Arthur some moves that I had learned from my brother when he had practised boxing with me, most of which were new to him. We got it wrong lots of times but because there was no real urgency to learn to fight there and then, we would often fall about laughing.

I can remember one memorable day. We had been practising on our own with the wooden training swords and Arthur was pretending to be king, while I was his squire. We wove a story as we lunged and feinted and I managed to save him from the Black Knight. My reward was to kneel in front of him while he took the wooden sword and made me a knight. I had shivers going up and down my spine as he said, "Arise, Sir Percival". *'If only he knew!'* I thought, and then wondered if that counted and I really was a knight! But, then again, I wasn't really Percival, was I? I was merely Jack!

On fine days, we took it in turns to go into the forest and stalk each other. Sometimes, when a neighbouring lord visited, there would be ten or more of us at a time taking it in turns to stalk just one. That was great fun as there was a lot of rivalry between the sons of neighbouring lords as to who might be best at any game that was in fashion at the present time.

So far as stalking - or hunting as we called it - was concerned, I had a very unfair advantage in that Cabal would shadow me and let me know when anyone was getting too close. I would then change tack and go off in another direction, basking in the compliments I received at the end of the hunt. On the odd occasion, though, I would allow myself to get caught; I did not want to appear to be so clever that it produced resentment. Cabal, on the other hand, couldn't understand this reasoning at all. Winning was what it was all about in his book. He lost patience with me when he could see I had put myself in the way of detection. *'I mean,'* he once said, *'would you allow yourself to get caught by a hungry bear - just to stop it becoming resentful! You'd never get another chance would you?'* I guess he had a point!

We learned to make some of our own weapons, as we might never know when we would need to do so, especially if the Saxons attacked again. When joined in battle arrows ran out, javelins broke; anything could happen. I liked helping to make the arrowheads, it reminded me of home as my father, you will recall, worked in metal.

After a meal, around lunchtime – by which time, from our exertions, we were ravenous - we would sit at our books, or should I say scrolls as it was in those days. Arthur struggled a bit with his letters and numbers. It wasn't that it was hard for him to learn, it was more that he couldn't be bothered to spend all that time sitting and carrying out his tutor's instructions; there were much more exciting things that interested him than learning to read and write. He was a couple of years older than me but I had learned fast at school and could read and write very well at age seven, so at nine I was quite proficient. I could add up tolerably well too, so where, during our spare time, Arthur gave me much help in becoming a warrior, I showed him what I knew of the three Rs. Fortunately, from each other, we both learned fast.

Arthur was a very religious man. Most late afternoons or early evenings he would spend either in prayer or, if one of the monks who lived in the abbey came over, as they sometimes did, he would listen, almost like a starving man I thought, as they talked to him about God. He couldn't get enough teaching on the things pertaining to Christ. I had always gone to the church in our village because everyone did so and if you stopped going you missed out on the local social life. But, so far, church was just something that I went to on Sundays. I didn't have this passion that seemed to overtake Arthur at times, though looking at his face during instruction or in prayer, I sometimes wished that I did.

When he spent his time thus, I would go off into the woods with Cabal. We would stalk prey and I tried not to notice when Cabal came bounding through the undergrowth toward me, still with the blood of whatever he had eaten all around his mouth and happily licking his face with his incredibly long tongue. He had a great sense of fun and often, when he had got me to stalk him and I thought I had the upper hand, he would come charging at me from behind, knocking me flying and we would end up having a rough and tumble in the grass, him pretending to growl and attack me and I ending up laughing helplessly as he slobbered all over my face. He also showed me the best places to hide, away from the wind.

'If they get a whiff of you, they will be off and you will never catch them. That's one way of looking at it, isn't it? But, if they *are stalking you, you'll need to be either in a place they cannot reach you, or you'll need to be in a place they cannot smell you!'* I had not looked at it this way but I

knew, from my old story books and from the odd distant howl, that there were still wolves about and that I could not, especially at my tender age, possibly get away from one if it surprised me. Yes, I needed to learn as much as I could from this hound.

Autumn passed into winter and I became fairly well skilled in armed as well as unarmed combat. I had a good eye and could therefore nearly always hit the target with an arrow. I had a few bruises on my arms where the practise sword had managed to hit me when I was working out with one of the trained men but as time wore on, and I as I got fed up with being bruised, I improved. I sometimes wondered if my family, back in the 1940s, were worrying about me but as there was nothing I could do about it, I soon put it to the back of my mind. I didn't see anything of Merlin over this time. He seemed to have completely disappeared from the face of the earth.

Early in December, Sir Ector announced that the time had come for him to take Sir Kay on an important trip. He was to attend a meeting of the War Council and Sir Kay was to take his turn at waiting upon the king. I am not sure, even now, which king it was because there were very many kings in Britain at that time; also, if there were many kings, there were many more lords and knights. One of my dad's favourite sayings, when we were all talking at once at home and, I suppose, giving our orders, was that 'there are "too many chiefs and not enough Indians" in this house!' Looking at all the people coming and going at Sir Ector's, it seemed it was just as true back in Arthur's time.

Sir Ector told us that they would be away for some few months. Taking Arthur to one side, he said that he was to keep guard over his house, family and servants. In those days I was almost like Arthur's shadow and even now I often wonder how two boys, both of whom were twelve years old or younger, could do this. But, at the time, we puffed out our chests and said he could rely on us to do so. Then again, looking back at Arthur's twelve summers, many boys of that age were considered to be men.

For the first week, we carried on as normal. During my time there, one of the monks came down quite regularly from the abbey and spent some time with Arthur. I sat in a few times but, after a morning spent training and an afternoon pouring over our books, usually fell asleep, so, just in case I did happen to snore, I thought that in the future I wouldn't intrude.

At the beginning of the second week, some time after a new novice monk who had been schooling Arthur had left, Mistress Elise came out to the barn. She had looked all over the house and thought that Rhianne might be with us.

'We have not seen her out of the house this day, Mother' said Arthur. 'In fact, the last time I saw her was just after the monk took his leave of me.' He turned a quizzical eye to me and I shook my head. 'Shall we search for her? I'll get Cabal to help us. He has a sharp nose for smells.'

At that we all left the barn, calling for Cabal and a few of the servants to help us find Rhianne.

Cabal flew round the yard until he got the scent and then, making sure we were with him, bounded off down the hill coming to a sudden halt at the edge of the roadway - with the forest on the right and the road forking left that led to the abbey.

'*I can discern the smell of the child up to here but then it stops. The monk was here, too, and he continues not up to the abbey, but down into the woods. He smells of fear! Perhaps we should follow the monk?*'

'Arthur, I don't suppose she would have gone off into the woods on her own, would she?'

'I don't see why she should. She's always been afraid of the trees and of being lost on her own, since that Cornish bard came to stay for a few days. He sang this song of children

74

being turned insane by the evil faerie king or burned up and eaten by the white dragon. No, I don't think she would have gone into the woods! She would have been too afraid.'

'We have to go in there Percy. It's the only place she could be. The trail stops here. But the smell of at least two horses and another man starts here so I think he had them tied ready and they have gone into the forest. You must get Arthur and some of the men to follow you.' Cabal was rushing around with his nose to the ground, hunting feverishly for other traces of Rhianne.

'There! Over there, look!' shouted Arthur. 'There is a piece of her dress on that tree.' We all rushed over. Yes, it was hers. There was no mistaking the pale blue silk of her dress. My heart fell into my boots. What had happened here, then? It was nearly dark and it had started to snow again. We went as far as we could but soon lost the scent of even the monk as the snow covered all traces - both of sight and of smell. Although the snow made everything visible by its brightness, it soon became clear that we had lost all sign of where Rhianne and the monk could have gone. Before we *too* were lost, Arthur held up his hand to halt our expedition, saying that even though everything in him screamed to find his sister, we should return tomorrow, when it was light, and start again. Despondently, we turned around and started back through the forest towards the house. It was close to midnight as we entered the yard.

'Is she back, Mistress?' we scarce dared hope, as we pushed in through the door.

She had jumped up as we entered the room. Her face went pale as she shook her head. Tears started in her eyes and she almost fell swooning into the chair.

I had hoped we were wrong and that she had been at home all the time.

'I'm sorry, Mother.' We found a piece of cloth that must be part of her dress and we started to follow the scent, but, because of the snow, we lost the trail. We will get the men together and start again at first light. Please try not to fear, Mother.' Arthur went up and put his arms around her. His face was very grim as he looked at me and it was as much as I could do not to cry myself.

It was a very bad night for us all. We tried to sleep so as to be alert the next day, but all of us tossed and turned in our beds until it was a relief to get up the next morning. Lady Elise, getting up at first light, had sent a servant out into the hamlet and had asked for volunteers to go with Arthur to find Rhianne. Sir Ector was highly respected and well thought of in the neighbourhood and there were quite a few men who were happy to go. Elise chose eight of them who were not only strong but who had served their lord during some of his campaigns.

'I've got to go with you as well,' shouted a frighteningly large and wild looking man as he pushed his way through to the front of the knot of men.

'Now you know you can't see properly,' argued Elise.

'I might be short-sighted, but I've never found anyone who would want to fight me yet, Mistress,' he responded. 'It's enough when I charge at them shaking my spear and they all run away.'

'Yes, but so do your comrades, Shake Spear,' said Wite, and the others nodded in agreement. 'If I were you, I'd stick to copying out the master's lists and Merlin's songs. You've a fair hand. Yes, Sir Ector has often boasted on it, and on his choice of scribe! Perhaps you should stay here. You've chased many of us instead of the enemy and it's only by good fortune that you haven't killed one of us before now!'

'A friendly eye could never see such faults,' complained Shake Spear. 'But, seeing it,' he continued, 'I should require that you condemn the fault, and not the actor of it!' He was on the point of tears at the unfairness of their jibes, but with chin lifted in defiance of their arguments, stood his ground.

Then, 'I have written some pretty verses myself for Mistress Rhianne to sing as well as for Merlin, I must admit, and I can hear her now, in my head, as she sings some of my songs.' He looked into the distance as he thought of her. 'But,' he continued, 'I cannot just stay here thinking the worst! If I don't go to try and rescue her I shall go mad. I promise I will only shake my spear and not attack anyone. You know that would make them all run away. I'm such a giant that they will only have to look at me and they will flee. I promise I won't attack anyone. You have to let me come along. My endeavours have ever come too short of my desires,' he acknowledged, almost sobbing in his eagerness to be included, 'but I give my word that I will behave'.

'Yes, you must come,' said Arthur as he returned to the group, 'and there's an end to it.'

Shake Spear was vociferous in his gratitude, so much so that Arthur threatened to change his mind if he did not shut up.

'Go down to see Nell, the innkeeper, and ask if her son is around. We might need him to take us across the river.'

Brosc said he'd heard that Nell's son was working at the port at the moment, and that, in any event, they wouldn't find any substantial rivers in the forest; not any that he knew of, in the direction they were headed.

'He would have been good to have had around, though; he has such a knowledge of the heavens to be able to guide us rightly,' Arthur stated.

Nevertheless, splashing cold water on our faces and, getting provisions of cheese and bread together, a few apples from the winter store and skins of water, we saddled some ponies and set off with the men in the direction of where we had turned back the day before. However, before getting halfway there, Arthur held up his hand for us to stop, 'I think we should go to the abbey and speak to the monks; maybe we will find Brother Marcus there or even Rhianne! If she had

77

been lost, she may have sought sanctuary there. Perhaps we will meet them bringing her home?' Turning the reins on his pony's head away from the forest, he hurried along the path that led up to the abbey. When we arrived, we were ushered into a cold, stone-built room and were instructed to wait for Brother Aebbe, who was at his prayers. We were there for quite some time! When one is in a hurry and the matter is urgent, even a few minutes seem too long, but he was over half an hour - which seemed an inordinately long time to pray! He eventually appeared and asked us how he could help us. We told him of our concern for Rhianne and asked if we could possibly speak to their novice, Brother Marcus.

If the first part of this story was frightening, the second sent shivers down my spine. 'We have no Brother Marcus here! We have had no novices either, for at least two years. It is such an out of the way place that not many of them want to come here.'

'Oh, but Brother Marcus said he had come to teach me due to the fact that Brother Geraint was ill!' Arthur was almost beside himself with worry.

'Brother Geraint was ill,' remarked the priest, scratching his bald pate. 'He ate something we purchased from a travelling tinker and it laid him low for a week. He is now well on the road to recovery, thank God, and was about to come and resume your lessons. However, I know nothing of a Brother Marcus,' he reflected, frowning a little.

We described Brother Marcus and the monks agreed that we had described the tinker. Something bad was obviously afoot and they said they would add our troubles to their prayers. They provided us with some extra provisions and, as we wanted to start out straight away before the trail went completely cold, we continued immediately on our way with their blessing.

Even so, we left the abbey in very poor spirits, with the knowledge that the tinker and "Brother Marcus" were one and the same, whoever that was, and that it had all been a scheme so that Rhianne could be snatched from us. But why? It did not make sense!

'Let's stop dragging our feet and get back to the woods as quickly as we can and see if we can pick up the trail,' I suggested.

For a few moments I thought Arthur would break down and cry, because that was what I felt like doing, but after swallowing a few times he stood tall, nodded and took charge. We rejoined the men who were outside the abbey with the horses. 'Men,' Arthur said as we gathered around him. 'Men,' he repeated, 'I have made a terrible mistake. I trusted a man, believing he was what he said he was – he even looked angelic - when in my heart I knew unease. I had thought him a very new novice, seeing that he really did not know much about the things of Jesu. Now I am paying the price. It looks as though, because of my error, some evil has befallen us. My sister has been abducted, for what reason I know not. My father is away, and so is my older brother, as you know. It therefore falls to me, as head of the family in their absence, to take command and make sure she is rescued. May God bless our endeavours to bring her safely home.'

'Amen,' they chorused, falling, even at his young age, under the spell of Arthur's natural leadership and charisma – a foretaste of those who would also succumb to his charm and authority in the years to come.

Sending one of the men back to inform Mistress Elise of our plans, we entered the woods.

SEVEN

Winter now being full upon us, the trees - leafless and frightening in their nakedness - added to the fear we were already experiencing. From their lofty vantage point they stared impassively down at us as we made our way through the narrow pathway between them.

Even our ponies felt it as they jerked and baulked as maybe a chunk of wet snow slid off a tree in front of them or one of us sneezed – things that would normally have no effect upon them whatsoever.

Apart from the odd evergreen, the trees stood stark and forbidding, their long, deformed and skeletal arms raised to the sky. As we moved through they began flexing elongated, bony fingers like a wrestler ready to strike, we wondered if they were raising their arms in submission or, possibly, trying to fend off some horror or other. Were *they* scared? Some clutched the grasping hands of a neighbouring tree for comfort. Were they trying to warn us of some, as yet unseen, danger - cautioning us to go back? Whatever it was, as we looked at them we could sense malevolence - so we therefore tried not to look.

The atmosphere around us didn't help - the air low down was still but in the tops of the trees we could hear the moaning of the wind – was it the trees, tormented, warning us, or was it something else? I could feel the creeps starting to sneak up and down my spine. As I have already told you, when things start to go wrong, my imagination goes into overdrive! One fortunate thing was that as the undergrowth was very sparse - it had obviously died down as the frosts ate at it - the going was fairly easy. I noticed, though, that all of us had darting eyes - keeping a look out for anything that might be lurking. Shake Spear was the worst – being so short-sighted he kept on seeing things that were not there, and, I thought, possibly missing things that were. If our plight wasn't so serious, his antics would have been hilariously funny.

However, so far as our tracking was going, the snow had covered any trail and the cold had eradicated any scent. We were therefore at a complete loss as to which way to go or what to do next.

Wandering around aimlessly for a very long time, we finally had to admit we were stumped, as we pulled up our ponies and stared through the shadowy forest to try and find at least one clue.

Arthur let out a huge sigh, 'Whoever has abducted my sister has got to have their lair nearby, possibly in the deeper part of the forest; they must have had a plan and some form of transport to take her so far away. Keep your eyes open for anything unusual. Anything! I wish Merlin were here, he would know what to do.' But Merlin was not here and we hadn't seen him for half a year.

'*There is a castle, high, on the far side of the forest. I found it a long time ago when I was out hunting,*' Cabal whispered into my mind. '*I have never heard anyone talk about it before, so I imagine they do not know of it, although how they do not know of it is a mystery as it looks very old. And it gives me the creeps – my hackles rise every time I get near the place. You will have to try and lead them that way without saying how you know! I am almost sure that that is where she has been taken. There is nowhere else around here. I don't even know of a woodsman's hut or hunter's rest anywhere near here.*'

We had been moving between the trees now for quite some time, with Arthur leading and me at the tail end of the line of men. From the slump of his shoulders and the fact that he had not said anything now for more than an hour, the despondency he must have been feeling started also to bear down heavily on each one of us.

81

Knowing I must help in some way, and trying to think of how to use what Cabal had told me, I dug my heels into my pony, passed the others and drew alongside Arthur. 'I believe we have been walking slightly uphill for some time now,' I spoke quietly. 'So, if we are going upwards, perhaps it would be an idea to try and get to the top so that we have a good view of the countryside around us. We could then spot any buildings or maybe some smoke from a camp fire and try to make a plan.' I looked at the side of his face, which was extremely grim and went on, 'I think we should try as we cannot see anything through these trees.'

Arthur turned and looked at me with very sombre brown eyes. 'I dread to think of what might be happening to Rhianne and I am so ashamed that my father left me in charge and I have failed. But, as I have no clue as to what to do next, Percy, we had better do that and go on up the hill. Lead on.' He spoke, on the verge of tears again, but, like the man he was to become, he gritted his teeth, lifted his chin and commanded the men, 'Turn off here, men. Wite, go with Percy, and we will see just what we *can* see when we reach the top of this hill.' It had by now stopped snowing and a slow thaw had set it. This made the going tricky as we found that, especially on mossy slopes, we could slip and fall.

As we moved further upwards, we suddenly smelled wood smoke. Arthur held up his hand and we stopped. Cabal drew his lips back over his teeth and his ears flattened out, making him look extremely threatening.

'*What is it?*' I asked him.

'*I'm not sure,*' he replied, '*but I have a bad feeling*'.

'I think I can see a light over there,' said Arthur, pointing a little over to our right. 'It keeps disappearing but then ...'

'Yes,' interrupted one of the men, 'I see it too!'

We turned off the path we had been travelling along and came unexpectedly into a large clearing. There was a hut in the centre of it and there was a soft light shining out of the single window. The door was slightly ajar and smoke could be seen to be floating lazily out of the chimney. We all stood silently gazing at the hut and it was only when all of us were completely still that we heard the singing. It was barely discernable but was obviously coming from the small house. It was very sweet and drew us all forward. The ponies stopped and we couldn't cajole them into moving forward so we dismounted and started forward on foot. On reflection, I don't know how I noticed, but I saw Cabal, out of the corner of my eye, and his demeanour was the same as it had been before – he looked frightening! I also stole a glance at Arthur. I could see, like the others and me, how the beauty of the music coming from the hut entranced him. Angelic – that was the only word I could think of; there must be an angel singing in there. None of us, for one moment, thought why such a heavenly sound could be coming out of a broken-down hovel; we were all as spellbound as each other and moved as one toward the delightful singing. As we drew near to the partly open door, Arthur moved forward to look inside. The singing stopped as he pushed open the door.

We all stood alongside Arthur enraptured, gazing at the angel. She had the largest eyes I had ever seen, blue and deep, like the ocean; her skin was diaphanous and her dress shimmered as she moved, like gossamer, as it fell from her shoulders to her feet. We moved forward, as one, to come before this vision.

'Did my heart love till now? Forswear it, sight! For I ne'er saw true beauty till this night.' Shake Spear was the only one to speak – and this merely a whisper!

Cabal, all this time, was making a low growling sound from deep within his throat, tail tucked beneath himself and ears flattened; the ruff on his neck was sticking up and, if we had been aware of it, made him look twice his size. But we were not aware of him! The angel appeared also to take no notice of him and continued to stare at Arthur, beckoning him forward with a languid wave of her elegant hand. She had started singing again and we could see how enchanting she was, with beautiful lips and very even, white teeth. Arthur had just raised his foot to enter the hut when it seemed that all hell broke loose. Cabal, the only one of us that knew something or someone malicious was somewhere in this place, did the only thing that came to mind, which was to lunge forward and bite Arthur on the hand. It wasn't a severe bite, in fact it didn't even break the skin; what it did do, however, was break the spell that had bound us all. We had all been moving as though mesmerised toward a terrible danger. As soon as the spell was broken by Cabal's action, there was a puff of smoke and the whiff of a nasty smell as the "angel" fell to the ground in a pile of black dust. Then, what we actually saw made bile rise up in more than one throat. The hut had completely disappeared and a sudden puff of wind blew away the small pile of dust that had remained of the lovely vision. Our eyes were now coming back to normal from the hypnotic state that had taken hold of us but the hair was beginning to stand up on many a head – well those that had hair! What we had seen was a very large clearing, a bit of a run down hut and what we had heard was a beautiful voice – all seemingly very harmless, that was true, and so we had moved into that clearing toward this vision of loveliness. What we had actually done was move toward the edge of a very high precipice and had all been about to step off! More than one of the men, tough as they were, almost fainted at that realisation and it was as much as we could do to drag ourselves to safety.

'Horrific!' uttered Brosc.

Arthur was the first to recover his voice, as he rubbed the hand that Cabal had nipped. 'Cabal, my faithful hound,' he whispered, having almost lost his voice with fear, 'How can I thank you enough? If you hadn't been here, well I dread to think what might have happened. In fact, can anybody tell

84

me what did happen?' The last sentence was said in a more robust voice as he looked around at all of us.

Many of us continued to remain silent until one or two described what they had seen and then the discussion got quite lively. All the versions were different. It seems that seeing the maiden, if a maiden it had been, had enchanted us all, it was true, but each described her differently – one said she was fair, another said she was dark; then she had blue eyes, no green! We apparently saw the type of lady that attracted us personally.

However, the danger was still not yet past. We heard a scuffling behind us and turned to see the shadows of ... what? They moved fast, whatever they were, and wouldn't let us see just what they were shadows of. We moved away from the edge of the cliff to the comparative safety of our ponies, which were nibbling the grass at the edge of the forest. The shadows continued flitting this way and that, some large, some small. The men were getting twitchy and muttered to one another. Drawing our swords, we moved slowly forward, keeping close together

'What is this place? What are they?'

'They're moving too fast for me to see!'

'It's too dark, I can only see shadows!'

'I can't smell anything, and you can usually smell something!'

Wite went chasing off after one of them.

'Come back!' I yelled at him. I had to call two or three more times for my shout to reach him. He finally stopped and rejoined the group. It was only at that moment, as the moon peeped out from behind the cloud that we experienced another weird phenomenon. We had remounted our ponies and had drawn our swords while we looked around at the things that were flitting about in the trees. We were facing the forest and the moon was at our backs. One of the men tried to strangle a cry as he pointed at the ground. We looked, and the creepiest sight met our eyes. We had first of all looked at Brosc, as he was the one who had called out, and then at what he was pointing at. Because it was so dark, we first of all couldn't make out what was wrong but, as he moved his arm, there was a collective sharp intake of breath when we realised what he was pointing at.

We could see the shadow of his horse and the shadow of his disembodied sword moving about, but not of him! He had no shadow! It took seconds then for all the men to look for their own shadows. Like Brosc, we had none. That, then, was what must be flitting about in the trees. But how! I looked over at Cabal and was relieved to see that he still retained his shadow. Then the moon once more hid behind a cloud.

'How on earth has that happened?' Thatcher called out.

'Magic,' whispered Brosc.

'Is it an illusion?' cried someone else.

'If it is, then we are all seeing it!' exclaimed Arthur. 'Come, Cabal, bite me again,' he cried, holding his hand down towards the hound, but Cabal just whined and crawled toward him with his belly to the ground.

'I don't think biting you is going to work this time. I think this must be an enchanted place,' I said to Arthur, 'and we need to get away from it as quickly as we can.'

'They stole your shadows when you were mesmerised,' whispered Cabal, *and now you're trapped.'*

I was about to ask him who "they" were and how we were trapped, when Arthur gave the command to move out of the clearing and into the trees.

We moved toward them but at their edge found that although the horses moved into the forest, we could not. The two leading men appeared to slide off the back of their mounts and onto the ground. We pulled up and, with swords pointing in front of us, tried to move forward; the same thing happened! Our swords pierced the air in front of us but as soon as our hands reached the first tree there was an invisible barrier.

'It's as though your shadows won't let you catch them! They're taunting you by hiding in the trees!' Cabal said to me.

'Then how on earth are we supposed to move on from here and why haven't they stolen yours?' I asked him.

'I don't know,' he replied, *'but I shall try and find an answer to both of those questions.'*

With that, he went loping off into the forest.

'I fear we are trapped,' groaned Arthur. 'How on earth has this happened?' He slid down from his mount and took a swig from his water bottle. It had started to snow again and the moon, almost full, slipped in and out of the clouds. We were all drawn to our non-existent shadows each time the moon appeared. We were also well aware of those runaways flitting back and forth among the trees, knowing – if they had any understanding at all – that we couldn't reach them. The nearest we got to one of them showed that they were completely black – well shadows would be wouldn't they, except that where the eyes would be – and we saw this particular one blink – we could see right through them and also, when it opened its mouth we could see the forest through the hole. It sent shivers down my spine.

For want of something to do, and to keep warm, Brosc and one of the other men walked the perimeter, exploring every possible exit, only to be frustrated by the invisible wall hemming us in. As they wandered around the places that did not bar them, I noticed that neither of them went anywhere near the precipice.

I recalled that as a very young boy I had been quite adventurous, not seeing much danger in anything that, had I been older and wiser, I might know could harm me in some way or other. The only thing that had scared me a bit was the dark. I remember refusing to go to bed one night as there was a power failure and there had been no electricity for hours. I could hear my mother's voice chiding me as it echoed through my brain, "You'd be scared of your own shadow if you could possibly see it in the dark". I began to wonder if she might have known something about what we were now going through. Were we scared of our own shadows? Well, we were certainly in a bit of a quandary without them!

Shake Spear and Wite started to gather some pieces of wood to try and make a fire. It was terribly cold and getting quite dark, with the moon giving only spasmodic light through the increasing cloud. The snow increased. I thought I could hear very faint laughter coming from various directions in the forest but as it was so soft I believed I might have been imagining it, so put it out of my mind. The men got a small fire going which threw shadows of the horses across the snow, but not of us. I could see the uneasy expressions on their faces as they crouched over the fire.

'It's as though we don't exist,' murmured Thatcher, sounding more like a youth than the brawny man that he was. We were all very twitchy. I am not sure how long we sat around that fire but it was almost out and dawn was just about approaching when Cabal came bounding into our circle. He knocked into a couple of the men and then rushed over to Arthur, who stared, unbelievingly, at him as we all jumped to our feet. In Cabal's mouth, held firmly but gently by his enormous teeth and tongue, was the tiniest man I have ever seen; he was no taller than the length of the bottom of my boot, but perfectly proportioned nonetheless. Also sticking out of his mouth was a very limp piece of material – but, no, it was not a piece of cloth, it was a shadow!

The little man looked a mixture of anger and defiance but also a little scared, if that is possible.

'Put him down, Cabal,' Arthur commanded.

'Cabal lowered himself to the ground, flattening his ears as he did so but, and this was unusual for him, did not obey.

'Cabal,' warned Arthur but Cabal did not move and would not relinquish his hold on his prize.

Shaking his head in disbelief at the hound's disobedience, Arthur ordered one of the men to remove the tiny man.

'Wait,' I cried. Cabal had managed, in a few seconds to acquaint me with the situation.

'Well,' enquired Arthur.

'I think we should first make sure he can't escape if he's released.'

'Well done, Percy. I should have thought of that.'

Turning to the little man, Arthur asked him if he could understand what he was saying and whether he could speak.

'Of course I can,' he spluttered, 'and a lot better, if I wasn't being half drowned by this odious hound's spittle. I have never been so treated in all my five hundred and six years!'

'Five hundred and six years, eh?' Arthur repeated. 'Someone so old and so wise must surely be someone of consequence?' he enquired.

'Of course I am,' he answered. 'I am Ogwin, King of the Faerie!'

I could see Arthur blanch and I believe I turned off colour as well, as we thought of the stories Merlin had told us about this evil king.

'You might be a person of consequence but I wonder whether you are a man of your word; we have heard stories of your evil deeds and so I think it should be us who need to be wise by leaving you in the jaws of my wolfhound.'

'No, do not do that!' he spluttered, his eyes going huge with concern. 'The stories are not true! We have obviously put those stories around to scare children and, of course, to keep people, especially the ones with big feet, away from us. As you can see, we are very small and children are such uncharitable and, dare I say, unholy beings. Why, my Queen and I were shocked when we watched two such abominable little beasts pulling all the legs off a Daddy Long Legs. I don't believe they knew of the pain that they inflicted on that poor creature, nor cared either, by the look on their brutal faces. No, it is us that are afraid of them, rather than them of us. But that is why we allow the stories to circulate so that such as they keep well away from the likes of us.'

'Wait,' said Arthur, believing the little king would never stop speaking, now that he had got into the swing of it. 'What I need to know is, are you a man of your word?'

The little king stretched himself as tall as he could, which was rather difficult in the circumstances, being wedged firmly, and sideways, in Cabby's mouth as he was. 'I have never lied in my life! No man could be king for as long as I, if he lied. Everyone knows that a man gets smaller, not only in others' eyes but also in his own eyes as well, when he lies. Not only that, he shrinks physically as well and as I am by far the tallest in my kingdom it just goes to show that I am also the most honest in it as well! And, as you can see, looking at your size and mine, I cannot afford to have my size reduced, can I?'

'Stop!' said Arthur, holding up his hand. 'How do I know that you are now telling me the truth?' asked Arthur, trying hard not to laugh, although he did, by now, believe Ogwin. Continuing, he went on to say, 'I did not really believe that you existed until now - that is, until I'd seen you in the flesh.

'The king thought for a while and then asked, 'Is there some way I could prove it to you?' He squirmed for a bit and then groaned, 'I wish you would decide something soon, I am getting dreadfully wet in here!'

Arthur gave a very small grin and, holding his right index finger toward the small king's hand, asked him to prove his word by the shaking of hands and on the promise that he would not try to escape if released. He did so and Cabal placed him gently on the floor beside the dying fire. *'So he can at least dry out!'* he said, raising one eyebrow at me.

However, he kept one large paw firmly fastening the captured shadow to the floor.

The little man, once released, shook himself and pulled his garments into place as best he could in the circumstances. He was dressed in what appeared to be a miniature version of the fashion of the day. Greens and browns. I expect that this was so he and his folk could blend in well with the forest. He was very handsome but explained, without any vanity or conceit – more as matter of fact, that all the faerie kingdom was good looking and, contrary to what had always been said of them, did not eat children. 'In fact we do not eat any meats at all!' he declared. 'All animals are our friends. Why, we fly on the backs of birds and butterflies; we travel far with the hare as our mount. Spiders, especially Daddy Long Legs,' he said looking disdainfully at me for some reason or other, 'bring and take our messages through their webs, which hum the most delightful tunes as they carry those missives along. Why should we eat those that serve us so well or be cruel to them at all?

'However, children,' and again he looked at me, making me feel quite uncomfortable, 'as they are so wicked, probably do not taste very good at all.' I tried to think back over my short life to see if I had been cruel to insects or animals. I couldn't recall that I had. Perhaps if this king was five hundred and six years old now, he might still be alive in 1949 and had been watching me. However, as I said, I couldn't remember ever being cruel.

'Whose shadow is that?' demanded Arthur, changing the subject completely, as he could see that the Faerie King was getting quite agitated.

Ogwin, looking down at the shadow wedged under Cabal's paw, appeared at last to be a little embarrassed. 'It's yours, young man,' he replied, looking up at Arthur.

'How did you manage to take it from me and why, and how may I get it back? Come to that, where are all the other

91

shadows and would you please be so kind as to return them to my men?'

'I received a message, in a dream, that some people from the world of men would be coming to my enchanted forest and would take over my charmed clearing and, moreover, would steal it from me. The forest round about is my kingdom and this clearing is where we hold our fayres and festivals. If it is taken from us, The Prophesy says that we shall cease to exist within a hundred years. That cannot happen to us,' he almost cried. 'We have lived here in peace for over two thousand years now and we will not give it up without a fight!' He stamped a very small foot at this. 'We are adept with enchantments, knowing how to fool even the cleverest, and we can destroy. We employ magic we have not used in many a year, you know, if we have to.'

He now stared quite angrily at Arthur. 'We put together an enthralment, which lured you all to the house of the enchanted minstrel. No one can resist her singing, which hypnotises all who hear it. You will recall that it was not really there and you were all supposed to fall over the cliff.' This was said a bit shamefacedly and he showed his discomfort by making tracks in the ground with his foot.

'I believe you have been misled in your dream, or some mischievous pixie has forced his way into your sleep and deceived you, or, and this is more likely, you have got the wrong man – or men!' Arthur sighed. 'We have not come to steal your land; we are searching for my sister who appears to have been abducted. We saw smoke and thought we might have found her. But no, we were fooled and almost lost our lives in the doing - and for nothing. My faithful Cabal has saved my life and the life of my men and, with our shadows being stolen, contrary to what you wanted – which is for us to leave your enchanted circle – you seem to have us here for good now. Right?' Arthur stared down at the little man, raising one eyebrow in enquiry.

92

'You mean to tell me you don't want to stay?   He appeared to be amazed that anyone would want to leave his realm.

'I have no intention of remaining here one minute more than I have to! My sister is abducted and I need to pursue whatever trail is left to me. Even now, I shudder to think that I may be too late. No, Ogwin, King of the Faerie, if I could, I would leave now – this very minute,' Arthur said, choking back a sob as he considered what might, even now, be happening to Rhianne, but he recovered himself swiftly, holding on to his dignity.

The Faerie King gave one of the widest and happiest smiles I have ever seen in my life. He almost did a jig when he grasped that his worst fears were unrealised. 'How happy I am, young sir,' he cried. 'I am very pleased to reunite you with your shadows and then you may proceed.' He took out a tiny whistle, which he put to his lips and blew. Poor Cabal almost shot into the air. Although we could hear nothing, whistles tend to have a painful effect on dogs. The Faerie King took hold of Arthur's lifeless shadow, laid it on the floor and asked Arthur to step onto it. As soon as he stepped onto it, it once again became obedient to his every movement.

While all this was going on we became aware of movement at the edge of the forest. The Faerie King's tiny subjects were moving towards us, carrying our shadows, which they had rolled up like rugs under their arms. Once they had reached the circle, they took a few minutes to find which shadow belonged to which person before rolling them out onto the floor. As we stepped onto them, we spent a short while, before a watery sunrise, gesturing with our arms and legs and making shapes with our shadows – just to make sure, of course! Any stranger coming upon us must have thought us all witless, or taking part in some strange ritual or other.

'Terrific!' Brosc rejoiced as he was reunited with his shadow.

93

There was one slight mix up where Shake Spear and Wite were given each other's shadows. I think this was done deliberately, as one of the little people must have had a distinctly warped sense of humour. As soon as they stepped onto the wrong shadow, they both kept falling over and couldn't stand up. We all chuckled, a sound we had not heard for many a day now, and the faeries joined in, their laughter tinkling around us like silver bells. Ogwin called out in an almost stern voice and a couple of the faeries, tugging at the shadows, eventually joined them to their rightful owners. Order was finally restored.

Ogwin shook hands again with Arthur, warning us at the same time to move away from his enchanted circle as swiftly as possible as, although he had control of a lot of it, it *was* an enchanted circle and sometimes it held surprises even for him and his people, some of which were not pleasant, as we had already discovered.

'You must beware the Mighty Smell,' he warned, but before we could ask him to elaborate, he once again, to Cabal's dismay, blew his minute whistle and he and his tiny entourage skipped off toward the precipice.

Arthur raised his hand to warn them of the danger, when he and the rest of us were surprised and delighted to see a flock of doves swoop down and land directly in front of them. The tiny people leaped in the air, some somersaulting or vaulting, to land gently on the backs of the birds, who flew off into the sunrise with their waving, tinkling burdens on their backs. We stood watching them disappearing until the sun made our eyes water. Taking one last look around, we mounted our ponies and, wondering if the forest would now let us enter, made our way across the clearing. Yes, we got through, all of us letting out our breath at the same time.

EIGHT

Arthur was very worried at the length of time we had been held up in the enchanted clearing and voiced his concern. Many of the men nodded in agreement and a feeling of despondency once again descended upon us.

Shake Spear, however, who had taken up his position at the rear of our team of men, was still confident that everything would work out, commenting, 'Courage and comfort, all shall yet go well.'

We travelled on in silence, each pondering the extremely narrow escape we had just had and it was thus some considerable time before we realised just how hungry we were. However, it was going to be some time before we would stop and eat whatever small provisions we might still have left.

The days at this time of year are very short and it was not long before winter's night started to fall; even though there was now no moon, due to the heavy cloud and endless flurries of snow, it was still easy to travel as the snow illuminated the forest.

We had headed back into the trees and continued travelling upwards, although we had to keep retracing our steps - there were many boggy areas that had not frozen over and thus could not be crossed; at one place there was a sheer drop which almost caused a fatality as the ground nearly crumbled away under Wite, who was leading the string of ponies, and then there was the occasional small cliff that was impossible for the ponies to climb. The boggy areas were the worst, though – they gave us all the shivers - exuding an aura of evil, as though some awful fiend were waiting there just below the surface to drag us down into the mire.

I looked around and could see that it wasn't just me - we all felt it and that fear could be seen as we looked into each other's eyes - eyes that we tried hard to avoid, as fear is highly contagious.

I have never, since those days, ever seen a forest like it - ominous, threatening, menacing! The forest itself was thick and dark, tall and wide and seemed to go on forever. As we got nearer to the castle, there were quite a few very large - clearly old - trees – so wide that two ogres - at least - *must* be hiding behind each one, obviously getting ready to launch themselves at any of us who were careless enough to get too close as we passed. Was it melting snow that was dripping from the branches of those trees, or was it saliva dribbling from the mouths of whoever or whatever was behind them as they prepared to reach over, contemplating the feast that was walking toward them? They got a wide berth.

We came unexpectedly out of the trees, some of which ran directly to the edge of a lake. Darkness had fallen some hours ago but now that we were out in the open the snow reflected an eerie twilight all around us. However, the sight that drew all eyes to it as we rode up the last knoll at the edge of the forest was what was situated on the farthest side of the lake. Set high upon a rock face that slid sheer into the water, there towered an impressive stone castle. Now I wouldn't have thought too much about it as to me all castles were made of stone or rock, but Arthur and the men were overawed by it and stood immobile, with mouths agape, staring up at it.

When I enquired of him much later, Arthur explained to me that the only fortifications he had ever seen were made of wood; either wooden logs or timber frames, with a high walled enclosure made of wooden stakes that surrounded all the buildings. They used the tallest trees that could be found, all fixed together to make the barricade, which was guarded and served by one set of thick wooden gates. If this were the type of fortification that had been made, all the people under the care of the lord of the land thereabouts would enter every night for safety, bringing his family and, usually, all his

96

livestock with him. He had heard of stone castles or those made with some form of masonry but they were mostly only made of stone to a height of around ten to fifteen feet; above that they were wooden.

However, getting back to this particular castle - it was, amazingly, made entirely of stone or rock and was so high that they all thought it could not have been made by human hands - so how had it been made? It gave us all the creeps! There was no light visible from within it, only the reflection of the snow bouncing back from its cold, grey walls. We had this terrible sense of foreboding that something awful was either happening in there at the moment or soon would. It was obvious that something extremely bad had happened in the past, but we did not want to think about that. We all knew we had to go on. I don't believe any of us thought that Rhianne was anywhere other than inside that awful place. Standing for a while, staring up at the edifice before us - huge walls of dark slabs of stone that seemed to vanish into the clouds - we listened for any sound. There was nothing! We couldn't even hear the lapping of the water against the shore, and the stillness was more frightening than any sudden noise could ever have been.

I had learned from Merlin, and from some of the servants that told me stories during the few short months I had been at Sir Ector's home, that magic is really effective where there is water – especially moving water like a fast flowing stream, waterfall or spring. Mind you, I sometimes thought that they only told me these weird stories just to scare me witless. Sometimes it worked because I spent one night searching the corners of my very dark room to see if anything in it, which appeared to be a little darker, actually moved.

Getting back to this lake and from the crawling feelings going up and down my spine again, there was certainly something wicked going on here; even though nothing was moving, you could almost taste the evil.

We could smell decay - rotting trees, rotting undergrowth and worse! Sweat covered my forehead, even in the cold night air, and I could feel the heat from my head rushing through my hair as it stood on end. I couldn't stop my knees from shaking or my teeth from clattering together. The clouds were breaking up and the moon peeped out every now and then. It had started to freeze again and, where the snow had melted and had now frozen, the ponies and we were finding it hard to walk without slipping.

Looking up at the castle, as we drew nearer I wondered what on earth was in there. I didn't want to go in there but, if we were to rescue Rhianne, there was no option.

Because they were now slipping so much, we dismounted from the ponies and led them around the shore.

It was a long walk around the lake, and treacherous. Due to the freezing snow, which clung to the moss at the edge of the lake, it became very dangerous to get too near the water and we nearly lost one of the men who ventured too close. His foot slipped into the icy water and, as another of the men grabbed him and pulled him to safety, I felt, rather than saw, an arm reach out from its icy depths to make a grab at his ankle.

Cabal, however, did see it and rushed at it, lips curled back over his teeth, which were snapping, and he was making the most terrible noise in his throat. The arm with the claw-like grabbing hand disappeared back into the water. Arthur turned round and whispered a shout at Cabal to stop making such a noise; he did not, as yet, want to warn anyone that we were around.

Arthur had not seen what both Cabal and I had, and obviously no one else had seen it either. *'Did you see that, Cab?'* I asked.

'Yes', was his reply, *'It was a water naiad. A very dangerous creature indeed.'*

'A what? I asked.

'Water naiad! It's like a sprite or a leprechaun that lives in water. However, where they are mostly naughty or mischievous, the naiad is spiteful, wicked. It has pointed sharp teeth and will rip the skin off your bones if it ever gets hold of you.'

My blood curdled. 'How frightful! Do you think anyone else saw it?'

'No, I don't believe so. Some people have heard of them and are, therefore, very afraid of them. If they thought any were here, I think we would have trouble getting the men to stay, brave as they are, let alone get them to go any further. They will fight Saxons and the like to the death, but these things are another matter altogether.

'Naiads have sometimes come up on shore and, thinking about it, the conditions are just right for them to do so tonight as it is damp and wet. They cannot allow themselves to dry out, you see, as that kills them, so you rarely see them in summer. You may possibly have seen them when they are dead as they end up looking like the dried, gnarled roots that you find exposed at the base of an old tree. You must have seen them at some time or other and thought that they were just roots. Be careful, though, they are almost as dangerous dead as alive. Obviously they cannot sink their teeth into you anymore, but once they are dead and dried out their carcasses are quite poisonous and, even if the poison doesn't kill you, it can cause a lot of pain and has sometimes disabled the unwary for weeks or even months. I knew a man once who walked about completely mindlessly until ... now how was that? Ah, yes, Merlin mixed some powders for him and he regained his senses. However, he had still forgotten who he was and it was another season before he remembered. Even then he had blanks. Powerful stuff!' He gave me all of this information as we walked around the lake.

I was wondering how I could get my hands on some of this poison as I thought it might come in handy at some time or other. A time like now would be handy, as it seemed that we were in for a bit of a rough ride. But, I thought I had better leave that for another time.

Later, as I was still thinking about them, I asked '*Cab, what do these naiads look like?*'

He sat down quite suddenly, scratching vigorously behind one ear, before continuing. '*Getting some of the poison would probably be a good idea. However, you would need to see Merlin about that because there are ways of collecting it that you would need to observe, so as not to get it on yourself. It only needs a little to send you over the edge. So far as the naiad is concerned, I've only ever seen one whole one – a male, at least I think it was a he! I feel very sorry for her indeed if it was a she!*' he almost sneezed at the thought. '*He was very slimy, dark green in colour and was covered in something like pondweed or seaweed; whether that was his own make-up or whether it was some type of clothing, I have no idea. Anyhow, some of it was short, around his arms and legs and some was long, over his head and down his back. His legs were long and spindly and his feet were like yours, only longer and with long claws; webbed as well. His arms were strong and muscular but his legs were almost useless on land. The things that I noticed most about him were his long clawed fingers and his sharp pointed teeth. Once those two things got into you, you wouldn't stand a chance. His face was free of any growth; it was convex in shape, a bit like a fish, but with holes in it to breath. The holes were quite large, with flaps over them and when they were open, which they were when I saw him, they looked almost identical to the eyes, which were above them, and, of course he had a big mouth with those long sharp teeth. Brosc was extremely lucky there. One second longer and it would have been a different story. In the water, or should I say under the water as they only ever surface to come on land, the naiad is fast, very fast indeed. On land he is slow as he has to pull himself*

100

along by his arms; his legs being fairly useless - he has to drag them along.'

Cabby stopped then and we continued in silence as we walked around the lake toward the castle. The snow, with the moon bouncing off it, brought everything into sharp relief and made it clear as day. I noticed that many of the men kept looking around them and over their shoulders as we got nearer the castle. I, too, looked around to see what it was that was making them uneasy. It felt as though there were many eyes looking at us from somewhere, but we couldn't see from where.

The trees were bare and it would have been easy to see movement if there was anyone in them but there was nothing. The castle loomed high above us, making us feel quite dizzy as we craned our necks to look up at the battlements. When we finally reached the walls, we still had to walk a long way to find somewhere that might let us in. We eventually found a stout door that was studded across with much metalwork where we tried to knock, but our efforts were futile – our hammerings on the door hardly made any sound at all. It felt like we were knocking on a sponge. We would never get in that way.

Eventually, Arthur held up his hand and we all stopped. He turned in the saddle, beckoning us over. When we were all grouped around him he asked, 'Do any of you men have any other idea how we can gain entrance to this place? Brosc? Thatcher?' He looked from one to the next. 'Have any of you been here before?' Shaking our heads, everyone turned to look at the others but no one made any positive response. It eventually became apparent that no one had even known the place existed.

The atmosphere was suddenly charged as we heard groaning. It was very faint but it made us all jump and I don't believe for one moment that I was the only one whose hair rose on the back of his neck.

Wite pointed upwards.

As we looked we could just about make out the shapes of gargoyles, which appeared to have been carved into the walls above the door and around the ramparts. 'I think it was one of them things, up there,' he pointed. We continued to stare upwards but nothing moved and the groaning had stopped. This was getting eerie.

Another of the men snorted and said that that was ridiculous. 'Stone be not something that does move or feel or speak,' he said. 'It must be someone inside.' A couple of the men, looking scared, nodded. However, from where we stood, it still appeared to be deserted in there.

Shake Spear, who had obviously not seen the gargoyles but had been feeling around the stone walls, shamed us all as he declared that 'our doubts are traitors, and make us lose the good we oft might win, by fearing to attempt.'

I looked at Cabal and the hair was standing up on his ruff. '*This is such an evil place, Percy. It* was *one of those things up there that moaned!*' he said to me. '*Don't get too near them, either,*' he warned, '*they breathe unseen fire.*'

'*What do you mean, unseen fire?*' I asked.

'*There is no glow, no spark, no noise,*' he answered. '*If you get too near one, it will burn you up; you will just melt away like wax.*'

'*Cab, if I hadn't seen the hand coming out of the water myself, I would believe you are making up all this nonsense just to scare me!*' I told him. '*However, I shall be very careful but for goodness' sake, if there is anything else I need to know about this place I would appreciate it if you would tell me now. Anyway, how do you know about this unseen fire?*'

Cab sniffed, as if to say I had called him a liar. But being the big-hearted hound that he was he merely looked away from me, stating, '*If you were a little older, I should take offence, but as you are only, how old, ten now?*' I agreed.

'Well, I shall make an exception in this case, due to your extreme youth!' I smiled.

'I told you before that I had come up here when I was out hunting. I had been stalking a rather large and extremely tasty looking hare and had lost track of direction and time when I came out into the clearing here.

'I had been busy trying to keep downwind of the hare - which I have to say now that it still irks me in not catching it, it would have made an exceptionally delicious and filling meal - and I had never seen one as large and the thought of getting my teeth into ...'.

'Cab!'

'Sorry. Where was I? Ah, yes ... when I came face to face with the naiad. We stood, or at least I did, looking at each other for a very short while - me staring - he chewing! I had chased the hare straight into the mouth of that repulsive creature. It was just finishing it off as I got there, almost swallowing it whole. All I could see was one large ear sticking sideways out of its mouth! As it looked at me, smacking its lips together - and very thin lips it had too – well it was lipless really – like a fish, it backed away and slid into the lake. It was then, as I watched it slip under the water and swim away, that I realised how fast it could move.

'It took me a good minute for the hair on top of my head to flatten down. As you can imagine, after this episode I was very careful where I put my feet.

'I walked very slowly toward the castle, just to take a look at it. Like tonight it was eerily quiet and during the day everything stands out quite clearly. There is only a bit of wildlife out here; I should imagine that most animals can feel the evil in this place and have decided to keep a good distance from it. However, as I crept around the walls I noticed the gargoyles. A bird, I am not certain what type of bird it was but it was a fairly large one, was flying toward the battlements and started to alight on one of those heads. No

103

sooner had its claws settled onto the head than it seemed to just melt - it flowed down over the head of the gargoyle and then dripped off its chin. The gargoyle then looked like it sneered, but I didn't know whether I had imagined that or not.'

I grimaced.

'Why are you making that face?' I hadn't seen Arthur come up to me and it made me jump. I also felt a bit guilty when mind-speaking with Cabal. I didn't want to lie to him, so I merely shrugged my shoulders.

'Oh, I don't blame you,' he said to me. 'If I let myself go, I expect I would either laugh or cry myself.

'Come, now, do you have any idea as to how we can get into this place?'

We had come to a part in the wall that had a bit of a bank of grass covered with snow leaning against it. I looked back at the trees and there were quite a few bits of debris, branches and the like, strewn about. As we had walked around the whole of the castle, apart from the west side, which went straight into the water, and had not found anywhere through which we could gain entrance, it looked as though we would have to climb over the battlements. As to how that would be achieved, I had no idea - they were just too high. We had, apart from the quiet groaning when we first got there, still not heard or seen anyone and there were no lights in any of the windows. 'We could try to build a ladder but I think that would take forever. It's just too high and we don't have enough axes to cut down any trees.' We all looked despondent. Somehow, though, we knew we just had to get into that place.

We were tired now, not just physically but mentally and in spirit as well. Arthur suggested we all went back into the forest and made some sort of shelter for ourselves for the rest of the night. We turned and, dragging our feet through exhaustion and despondency, made our way a short distance into the forest - far enough away so as not to be seen from the castle, if anyone was in there, but close enough not to get lost. We found a clearing and, after collecting as much old, dry timber as we could find, managed to make a small, smokeless fire.

Arthur strode up and down, shooing us away as he did not want to be disturbed, first rubbing his hands together in front of him and looking round and about and then holding his hands behind his back, staring at the ground as he walked, a habit he would take with him through life. Everyone that ever met him would soon get to know the "do not disturb" signs of his peculiar walk, and thus keep away. Cabal and I would follow him with our eyes and catch various bits of the thoughts that were flitting through his head. Funny that - although Arthur did not have any of the gifts of the Old Way - he did have some sort of an ability to "show" or "hide" his thoughts and we would only catch portions of them as he strode back and forth. Only those with the gift of the Old Way could communicate effectively with others who also had it.

When I first knew I had this gift I thought I would be able to read everyone's mind. I thought how great it would be when I went home and was able to see when my dad, or, more precisely, my mum was about to give me a thick ear, or when the teacher asked me a question I didn't know but was then able to garner the information from his brain and answer correctly; but it doesn't work like that – it's purely and simply a form of communication between those - and only those - who have the gift. The rest of the time it was just snatches and the odd word - nothing making any sense at all.

We didn't think we would sleep, as, apart from the fact we were so cold and despondent, we were all so very hungry - we had eaten the last of our provisions over six hours ago.

As morning approached, Wite had to shake us awake, so somehow we had managed to get some sleep. Silently he pointed down the track and we saw movement. We immediately set eyes on a very old and very small man walking among the trees collecting firewood. His shortness was caused by the fact that he was bent almost double and had to hobble along, using a stick as a prop – he would probably topple forward all the time without it! He was clothed in filthy, torn rags and had a shock of white hair all over his head and hanging off his chin – in fact he looked as though he had been struck by lightening, the way his hair stood out. Being bent double, the beard dragged along the floor, collecting mud and twigs as he walked, and was almost tripping him up. He had a very long nose with a wart on the end of it, which made it look even longer. He moved our way, muttering as he went, without seeming to be aware that we were there. He was almost on top of us before, suddenly, he stopped, sniffing the air and smelling rather than seeing us, although, when we got a whiff of him, it was a wonder he could smell anything else. He stank!

'Who's there?' he called. 'Come on, I know you are there! Out into the light with you, so that I can see you.' We were already standing in the light and not ten feet from him! 'I'm not afraid of you! Show yourself,' he shouted. He held out his walking stick and was feeling the air in front of him with it as he tried to feel us while he peered out through rheumy, squinting eyes, trying to see who was there.

Arthur walked up to the old man. 'Please, don't be alarmed, old man' he spoke gently. 'We have no intention of hurting you.'

NINE

'Granddad! Granddad!'

Jack turned and looked at his grandsons, slightly bewildered. He shook his head and was soon back in the present, blinking away the past and staring into their faces. 'Why have you stopped telling us the story? You looked miles away just then!' Daniel urged his grandfather to carry on.

'Sorry, boys.' Jack stood up and stretched his arms and back. 'Is that the time? It's very late and I have an early start tomorrow to catch up with all of today's chores. Off to bed now, the two of you, and don't let me hear you chattering away all night. Perhaps you can help me for an hour or so before school, if you are not too tired.'

'Oh, do we have to go to bed now? It's not that late and we have lots of questions,' said Ben. 'How come your dog is called Cabal and the one in your story is called Cabal? Are they the same dog? But they can't be 'cos one is a story and even if it wasn't, you couldn't have a dog that was over a thousand years old! How did you get into the castle? How old did you say Arthur was? Did ...?'

Daniel interrupted, 'Did you see Merlin again? How old were you when you saw him, if you saw him? Did you get back to your father? It's all made up really, isn't it? It's a good story though.'

'Hey, whoa there, you've got my head spinning! There's a lot more to the story but my throat is dry from talking and if you don't go to bed now, not only will I lose my voice completely - for at least a week - but you will be too grumpy for all the jobs I have for you tomorrow and if they don't get done we won't have time to continue the story tomorrow evening anyway. And then I think I should talk about what had really happened to Rhianne.'

The boys looked disappointed that the story had to be put on hold for the night but eventually saw the sense in it. They each polished off a glass of milk, kissed their mother goodnight and, after Daniel gave Cabby a hug, called down their goodnights to their grandfather as they disappeared up the stairs.

Contrary to what Kate expected, they were asleep almost as soon as their heads hit the pillow. 'You are very good with them,' said Kate as she sewed the last of Mrs. Ambrose's curtains. She sighed. It was quiet for some time and then, folding up her work, she went over to her father. Standing behind him and leaning on the back of his chair, she put her arm around his neck and, with her chin on his shoulder, they were both quiet for a little while as they stared into the fire. Finally, 'I didn't want to say anything until the boys had gone to bed, but I've heard that Morgan has been in prison,' she said after a while.

Jack turned quickly in his chair and looked up at her, searching her face.

'He apparently went on a drinking spree that lasted for days, after he found out that I had left him. Mind, it didn't take much for him to find an excuse to have a drink! He spent some time looking for me but, obviously, and thank God, without success.' She spoke very softly. 'Afterwards, when he had run out of drink, he went into an off licence and when the man refused to sell him anything - as he was apparently stoned and falling about all over the place - he went into some sort of mad frenzy, attacked the man, breaking his arm and knocking him unconscious. He stole some drink and took some money out of the till. When he was leaving the shop he fell, knocking over some bottles and drenched himself in beer. The police caught up with him a couple of hours later as, apart from the fact that he stank of booze, he had been recognised by someone outside the shop.' She chewed her lip and looked at her father. 'He will come to

108

get us now, you know! I know he will! He will blame me for all of what happened! That's what he's like. He'll say it's my fault that he got drunk! I think that we will have to go.' She didn't cry – she had got too strong for that now - but she did look extremely worried.

'How do you know all this?'

'Mrs. Ambrose told me. We've become quite good friends, you know. She's well into her 70s but she is like someone at least thirty years younger.

'While I've been making all her curtains and covering her chairs we've talked about lots of things. I told her about Morgan, oh, weeks ago, and she looked out an old newspaper in the library showing the fact that he'd been sent to prison. She said that Morgan was not a very common name and it had rung a bell in her mind. I must admit, dad, that when I read it I felt quite sick. But I know he will come after us. I have often wondered why he hadn't bothered to do so already, knowing what he's like. Now I know that it was due to the fact that he was in prison. I would have thought he'd come here, knowing I didn't really have anywhere else to go, but when he didn't, I began to hope that we were safe, dad. That he had decided it was not worth the effort.'

'And you *are* safe!' he declared. You are not going to leave here. Anyway, where would you go? Let him try to do anything to you or the boys and he'll soon get his come-uppance. Cab and I know a few tricks, don't we boy?' he said as he turned toward the hound.'

Cabal looked up at him with one quizzically raised eyebrow and managed a short wag of his tail, as if to say that he could be counted on.

'Did the newspaper give any indication as to when he would be released?'

'He was given a sentence of six years. That was four years' ago. I suppose he could get time off for good behaviour. I keep hoping that he will not behave himself but

I reckon that, without the drink befuddling his brain, he will be determined to behave himself so that he can get out and "teach me a lesson" as soon as he can.'

'No, I won't let him do that. You must not worry. Look how the boys have come on in the last few years? In another culture they would be old enough to be called men. Ben's growing at a phenomenal rate now and his muscles are challenging mine!'

Kate smiled. Yes, her sons were her pride and joy. Life was worth every sacrifice as long as they were kept safe and happy. 'Dad, you are very good. Just help me believe that we will all be OK.'

'Off to bed now. No!' he held up his hand to stop her from interrupting and, tongue in cheek smiled at her, 'I'm still the boss of this house! Be an obedient daughter now and go to bed. And try to sleep and *not* worry!'

He watched her as she ascended the staircase. Her shoulders were slumped and she seemed to drag her feet as she went up. Jack's heart fell into his boots as he imagined how she was feeling.

At last the house was still. Cabal went outside to do what dogs do before settling down for the night. He always had a good run around the smallholding; sometimes travelling a fair few miles just to make sure that all was well. It was something he had always done! Jack kept an eye on the dying fire and waited for the hound to return. They would then go over the day's events. In the meantime he tidied the room, replenished Cabal's water bowl and, after slicing off the last of the beef, he put down the bone, which still held a fair bit of meat, for his old friend to sharpen his teeth on. Eventually Cabal returned. He eyed the bone but, from the look of satisfaction on his face and his rather large belly, it would be some time before he had a go at it.

'*The boys are becoming young men, old friend,*' observed Cabal. '*Like you said to Kate, if they had been as old as they*

110

are now in the days when you first met Arthur, they would be considered men. Boys died in battle that were not much older than they are! They are quite bright and from some of the questions they started to ask you, it would appear that you might have your work cut out to try and answer them without giving too much away!'

They both sat and considered the situation. Having known each other for such a long time, they were quite content to just sit in each other's company and not even mind speak for, sometimes, hours on end. The only thing was that as they could reach each other's minds they could end up getting very muddled as to what they were thinking of in the first place. At such times, one or the other would put up a mental guard, for sanity's sake. But, this was not such a time and so they just drifted in and out, agreeing and disagreeing, as the case may be.

'Ben almost hit upon the fact that I might be the same dog as the one that served King Arthur.'

'There's no getting away from that, Cab, seeing as you are!' Jack exclaimed. *'When Merlin gave me that blue potion to enable me to travel from place to place, I don't think even he realised its strength – I was only supposed to be gone a week. It was only the fact that you had licked up some as well, so as to accompany me that one time, I eventually realised you, too, could stay with me in any time zone indefinitely - there now being no time limit. It also seems to have had a different effect upon you as well - you just don't seem to age! I've been adding up the years after Griff died. Being brothers, from the same litter, he was about eight when he died - which is quite old for a wolfhound, and you should have met your maker around the same time as him and yet you, well you're still fit and remarkably young looking.'*

Cabal looked extremely pleased at this and couldn't help but preen himself as he tilted up his chin at the compliment. Jack considered his old friend and, although he'd had a light

111

grey coat of hair when he had first seen him, the only difference now was that the grey had turned slightly paler. He had a keenness of ear and eye and a speed to rival any greyhound and his beard still twitched at any sound or smell that might prove to be trouble - or edible!

'Even considering that you have gone backwards and forwards in time with me, and I first met you when I was nine years old, you must now be, let me see, 47 or 48 years old! In fact, in dog years it makes you about 340! If you add the 1500 years since King Arthur's time, I'm afraid that I wouldn't be able to add up the years for a dog. But be assured that that, old friend, is well past your sell by date!' They both found this very amusing and while Jack chuckled quietly, Cabal's only way of showing his amusement was by having what appeared to be a sneezing fit. They eventually quietened down and, when the fire was safely out, Cabal went up and, as was his habit since they had arrived, lay across the boys' doorway while Jack went into what was once the large, walk-in larder-cum-storeroom but was now his bedroom, and lay down to sleep.

Sleep was a fair way off as he considered more the day's events, especially what Kate had told him about Morgan. He had never met this man after that one and only encounter all those years ago, so had therefore never really got to know him and there was always a question mark over someone one has never really got to know. Would he come after her? Was it his intention to punish her? Would his anger have died down; might he give up after all this time, considering it not worthwhile? Is he not afraid of being sent back inside?

These thoughts were jumbling around in his head when a faint, *'Isn't it about time you switched off? You're keeping me awake!'* drifted into his mind. He grinned to himself and bidding his friend *'Goodnight'*, turned over and eventually drifted into and out of a fitful sleep.

TEN

After the previous day's storm there was a lot of clearing up to do around the yard. There were quite a few fallen branches, some of which had pulled down a line of fencing. Jack got the boys piling up some of the broken branches, anything they could manage. 'Nothing is wasted on a farmstead, lads. We will be able to use this wood for kindling when it has dried out sufficiently.' They helped him for an hour and then got ready for school after securing a promise from their grandfather to be ready to continue the story once they got home.

Kate had already set off for work and, shortly before nine o'clock, the boys went off to school. Cabal settled down, all alert, to watch for anything that moved as Jack shifted more of the older bits of equipment that had over the years been shoved to the back of the barn. *'You don't know what you are missing, old friend,'* he said, as he waited for the inevitable rush of mice that had been disturbed. *'There is absolutely nothing like fresh, warm meat!'*

'Cab! I've told you before ...' Jack started, and then stopped. He looked at the hound's innocent face and laughed. 'You really know how to wind me up,' he chuckled. Cabal suddenly moved like lightning and an unfortunate couple of rodents met their maker. Jack looked away and tried not to hear the crunching of small bones. *'I prefer you to a cat, though, Cab! At least you don't play with your food first!'*

By late morning they had almost reached the back of the barn. It suddenly got very still and the light rapidly faded. *'Funny, Cab, it doesn't feel stormy but it has got very dark. Let's go back to the house for some elevensies.'* As Jack turned round, ready to leave, he heard Cabal set up a low growling. Looking over at him and saw that his hackles were rising while his tail balanced this effect by curling right under his belly. The lips over his teeth were drawn right back and in the back of his mind Jack was once again surprised at how frightening he could appear to someone that didn't know him. His fangs were extremely long and could probably crush a man's bones as easily as they had just crushed those of the small mice. These thoughts swept through Jack's mind like lightning. He had been trained well by Sir Ector's men and, moving swiftly to Cabal's side, grabbed the nearest implement, which was a long metal shaft, and was as ready as he could be for whatever might be about to happen. He looked around the barn, which was still gloomy with the fading of daylight, and then started to ask Cabal, in his mind, what was wrong.

'Stop! Close your mind!' was all he got from the hound and both he and Jack shut down their communication with each other and also with whoever or whatever was causing this fearful sensation. He looked in the same direction as Cabal, back into the far corner of the barn – the area that was always the darkest corner in any event. At first he saw nothing and then, very slowly, he could just make out a faint silhouette.

Although Jack had put up a mental guard, he could still think logically whilst keeping those thoughts to himself. He initially considered that the figure might be that of Merlin. However, there were a few things that were wrong with this supposition. First, Merlin always came from some direction or other, either out of a building or from the forest. He made a point of never just materialising, if it could possibly be helped. "It's a great joke to just appear in front of someone," he had once said, "but it then takes so long to explain how or why I had done just that, that once, when I had to spend such a long time trying to explain why I had just done it, I even forgot the reason I had gone there in the first place! No, it's best to arrive in the accepted manner, it saves so much explanation and time - and time, as you know, is precious."

So, although he could appear and disappear at will, he always tried to make it seem he had just arrived from somewhere. Coming back to the present, Jack thought that he certainly never looked like this ghostly wraith. Secondly, Merlin was over six feet tall, slim and elegant and this, whatever it was, was short and - for want of better description - fat. Thirdly, Cabal never reacted to Merlin the way he did toward this apparition. There were probably other reasons that came into Jack's subconscious but the overriding one was the smell. It was worse than the smell he remembered from a few years ago of a field of rotting cabbages after a month of rain or, more awful, that time a decomposing badger had blocked up his drains.

They heard it, at first very low, but then, when it realised it had their attention, it became louder, a wheezing, a cackling. Jack's hair at the back of his neck rose to join that of his dog.

'So, you *can* see me! You have no idea how much pleasure that gives me. You should have been on your guard, you know. You thought you had escaped me but now you can see you are wrong. I am not the sort of person who can be confined for long. Also, time has no barriers for genius! I only needed to find out which time to go to and now I have!' She started to fade and then seemed to rally. 'Ahhh, I have to go back. The enchantment is just not quite strong enough.' Jack could just about hear her now. 'But don't worry - now that I know how, I shall work on it and I shall come back and, when I do, I will have it perfected and then you will be sorry. Merlin can't help you now!' and then she was gone. Jack and Cabal couldn't move. They stared into the corner waiting and searching. After a short while longer, the light returned.

'Pooh, what's that stink?' Daniel stood in the doorway. His voice seemed to galvanize Jack into action. Calling Cabal, he rushed out of the barn, pushing Daniel along in front of him. Once outside he shut the doors and, placing the

115

bar across the front of them, told his grandson that the barn was out of bounds. 'Where's Ben?' he asked.

'He stopped to walk along with Mum. She's finished work early and he's helping her carry the shopping. There wasn't enough for me so I ran on ahead. I thought perhaps you might want some help.'

'What time is it?'

'It's four o'clock. What's the matter granddad? You look ill! Are you alright? Here comes mum. Hey mum, granddad doesn't look very well.'

'Stop fussing now. I'm OK. I've just been working too hard in the barn and didn't realise the time. No, no, Kate. I'm fine,' he responded to his daughter's concern. 'Let's all go inside and get ready for tea.

'However, before I say anything else, I want you all to know that the barn is out of bounds. There has been a chemical leak, which is what you could smell, Daniel, and until I can get the specialists in to clean it up it's too dangerous for any of us to go in there. That's probably why I look pale – I've probably inhaled some of it. I shall lock the barn securely, so there will be no slip-ups for anyone to say they forgot and wandered in by mistake. OK?' He stared at them all, waiting for their response.

Without hesitation, they all agreed.

'Right, you lot go in and get ready while I find a bolt and lock for the barn. Kate, would you mind lighting the fire; I've been in the barn so long it must have gone out by now. Thanks. Cab, come with me!'

Jack and Cabal walked along in silence until they were well out of earshot of the family. They went into the shed, where Jack found a heavy lock and iron bolts for the barn door. Fortunately all the windows in the barn were well over ten feet from the ground and barred, so he was fairly confident that no one could get in that way. No-one physical, that is! He shivered as he thought of what had just happened.

116

As they approached the barn Jack couldn't help but think that it looked so ordinary, and safe. *'What on earth is happening?'* he thought.

'Mab!'

'Mab? What, Mad Mab?' asked Jack. *'That was Mad Mab - that old hag? It didn't look like her. She looked decrepit and so old, like an anaemic prune! And she's got fat! Surely it can't be her? Her magic wasn't that good when we last saw her. And besides, I thought she was well and truly locked up.'*

'Be that as it may, it was her! The smell was her! I got wisps from your thinking – you'd better get your thoughts more under control – and heard you say "badger" and "cabbage" but think, Jack, wasn't it more like a stagnant pond smell? Remember now, how she used to use it to mix up her potions and it was always dripping down her clothes, clothes that she never changed or washed. Come to think of it, I remember someone once saying she never ever washed as she thought that if she did she would wash off some of her power. Consider that! Stagnant pond and unwashed human smell!' Cabal had a sneezing fit as he thought, with distaste, of the fetid fact of Mad Mab. *'What are you going to do?'*

'First, we must not let the boys or Kate know anything about this.'

'The chemical story was clever - well thought up on the spur of the moment. That should keep them out.'

'What I don't understand, Cab, is where did the day go! We were about to go out of the barn for elevensies and it ended up four o'clock! We weren't in there with her for more than about ten minutes - but over four hours have gone by!'

'Yes, that's a hard one! We must have been with Mab a lot longer than we thought. Her spell must have been very strong to keep us bound that long. But not strong enough to do more than that, thank goodness. She didn't seem to be able to step out of her ghostly form into something more

tangible.' He sat on the floor and spent a moment or two scratching behind one ear. Then, jumping up said, '*I'm going hunting and I'll keep an eye out for anything else that might be going on. It's very strange! Nothing has happened for so long, I thought our adventures were only for the telling, not for the doing!*' With that, he loped off into the forest and left Jack pondering the day's events.

'Come on, granddad,' Ben called from the front door. 'Let's eat, or you will be too tired to tell us about Rhianne.' Jack looked across at Daniel who, along with Ben, was eager for the next part of the story. 'OK boys, let me just get washed up and I'll start the story after tea.' He tried to put the day's events behind him as he prepared to launch into the next part of his story, but was only too aware that Mab played quite a large part in it. He wondered if the story, coming to the part that she played in it, had conjured her up. Shaking his head, Jack brought Mab back into his mind's eye of how she used to look and had to mentally agree with himself that she didn't look too bad in those days. Thinking back, she must have been about thirty-five years old when he first saw her and, even then, she was not only interested in potions, spells, incantations but *power*!

Merlin once told him that she had persistently followed him around to see if she could discover the herbs, waters and potions he used. However, he was very wary of her and used to shoo her away whenever he caught sight of her; apart from her annoying presence, he just couldn't stand the smell!

On one occasion she tried to use a particular spell that she'd copied from a travelling magician, which was, now Jack came to think of it, one that could help her disappear; the ridiculous thing, though, was, that as she had decided she could never wash - thinking she might lose her power - even though she could disappear everyone could smell her coming a mile off. Like today! "Humming like a toothless gypsy," was an expression that came to mind – 'One Jack's dad used

118

of a particular pony that had bad breath and a wheeze,' he remembered.

'Granddad! You're miles away again,' Daniel interrupted Jack's thoughts.

'Sorry, boys, I was,' and he started off with the Abduction of Rhianne.

Rhianne had been sitting by the fire in the kitchen when the monk entered from the yard. He asked the child where her mother or her maid was but she had told him that she did not know. Once he realised that the girl was on her own he put his plan into immediate action. Pretending agitation he wrung his hands together, put on a concerned tone of voice and seeming almost to cry said to her, 'Oh my dear child, Arthur has had a terrible accident with a sword while he was training in the yard. Please, you have to come and sit with him while I try and find your mother or the maid. Come, quickly, he does not want to be alone and he is hurt really badly.'

Rhianne, tender hearted and all concern as ever, jumped up and ran ahead of the monk. Once through the door, she turned into the yard but, not seeing anyone there, turned back toward the monk who swiftly covered her mouth and nose with a cloth which contained some substance or other that made her lose consciousness.

The next thing she remembered was coming round on the back of a horse, which was picking its way through the forest. She felt very sick. The monk was sitting behind her and holding her onto the horse with one hand while he held the reins and directed it with the other. He was talking to another man that Rhianne had never seen before and with the realisation of what was happening she could feel the bile rising up in her throat with panic. Even though it was bitterly cold, she felt her body get very hot with fear. 'Where are you taking me?' she stammered.

'Be quiet. Do not speak at all or I shall have to drug you again. I don't want to do that, as I'm not sure what would happen if I have to do it again. I thought you were never going to come round this time.' He spoke quietly but Rhianne felt very scared at his gruff voice. It did not sound at all like the voice of the monk.

'You don't sound like a monk any more. Are you a monk?'

The man shouted a whisper, if that's possible. 'Shut up, I said. No more warnings!'

As the sweat dried on her skin, Rhianne started to shake with the cold as well as with fear. The other man threw a cloak around her and they continued in silence through the forest. It had been almost dark when Rhianne left the warmth of the kitchen and she could have kicked herself at her stupidity: Arthur always had his fencing lessons in the morning. She wished she had remembered that. *'But it's too late now,'* she said to herself as thoughts started to jumble through her brain. *'I wonder where I am. Even if I could escape, I don't know how to get home. I hope they can find me.'* She noticed a piece of material had been torn from the hem of her dress and hoped that that would give any of her rescuers a clue.

They continued deeper into the forest and after many hours of travel she began to lose heart believing they would never find her here. *'I wish my father and Kay had been at home; they would never have let this happen,'* she choked on a sob as she thought of them and was rewarded with a small warning shake.

After what seemed a long journey they came to a break in the trees through which she could see an enormous castle on the far side of a very quiet lake. The horses, conscious of the menacing atmosphere, shied away from the lake and the one upon which she was carried got a dig in its flanks with the man's spurs for its trouble. There was a light showing from

120

one window high in the wall of the castle and they headed toward it.

As they approached, Rhianne became aware of eyes watching their every movement. She couldn't see these eyes but somehow knew they were there. The horses were acting very jumpy and it was as much as the men could do to keep them under control. They eventually reached the area below the lighted window, which was high up beside an enormous wooden door. The other man jumped down from his mount and held the bridles of both horses. The sham monk banged on the door with the hilt of his sword. The door swung inwards immediately and they entered. Just as quickly, the door closed with a loud clang, which disturbed something aloft. It could have been either a bat or a bird, which whirred around their heads, making a terrible squawking noise as it fluttered around, eventually returning to its place high on the castle walls. The monk had to duck quite low as the bird dived and almost fell off his horse.

After they had both dismounted, a very tall man stepped out of the shadows and seemed to glide toward them. He was dressed in clothes the like of which Rhianne had never seen before. He had on a long white tunic that came to his feet. His head was adorned with what looked like a bandage made of the same material, but was extremely elegant. Set into it was a black shiny stone which, when it was seen later in the light, proved to be an almost midnight blue. He had a sash around his waist and a cloak around his shoulders. The cloak also came to the floor. These two items were the same colour as the stone. The sash around his waist held a large, curved sword. The man did not speak but bowed to the monk, placing the fingertips of both hands together in front of him in an almost prayer-like manner, and then turned, expecting them to follow. The monk gripped Rhianne's wrist quite roughly and dragged her along as they followed him into the keep, while the other man walked off somewhere with the

121

two horses. Once inside Rhianne couldn't take her eyes off the strange man. His skin was almost black, as were his eyes, and his face, although thin, was strikingly handsome and would have been expressionless if it wasn't so stern. He held his head very high and did not look at them but pointed at a seat situated underneath the spluttering wall sconce and then glided away.

They sat there for half an hour or more before the door opened. Someone entered, the wind bringing in a chill that was not just caused by the elements. Rhianne looked up and was astonished to see a woman standing in the doorway. She was fairly young and there was a smile on her lips.

Rhianne's heart leapt as she at first thought that there might be some hope but then she looked into the woman's eyes. They were cold and heartless and the child found it very hard to look away from those eyes, which were a mixture of green and dark yellow, *'like a cat'*, she thought. She had long hair, dark brown in colour, and apart from the ends, which were frizzy and wild, the rest was greasy and was plastered, in the main, to her head. She had a small, straight, thin nose with flaring nostrils. Although her mouth, which many a woman would have loved to possess, was full and pink, Rhianne would come to recognise that it had an unfortunate cruel twist to it most of the time. Those that knew her best, and there were not many, would be most afraid when she smiled because that was usually when she was planning to do something really foul. She was of average height and Rhianne thought she must be quite slim but because of the peculiar, and extremely dirty, smock she wore she appeared to be bigger and quite shapeless.

'So, Berryn, my clever, clever man, you have done well,' she commented, patting the man on the shoulder. 'What a pretty young thing she is!'

She turned to Rhianne. 'How old are you, child?' The tone of her voice was even and smooth - like honey - and this confused Rhianne as it contradicted the sharp look in her eyes.

She looked up at the woman but was too frightened to speak. Even if she could, she was so scared that all the spittle had dried up in her mouth and her throat, as a result, was dry - any words would probably not have come out in anything other than a croak. She swallowed a few times to try and moisten her mouth.

The woman laughed at her fear. Then, without warning, she threw a flame of fire at her, which landed at her feet with such an almighty roar and crack of sparks that Rhianne almost passed out. It would be some time before Rhianne realised that the flames and other similar tricks that this woman performed were merely illusion and that she only did these horrid tricks to scare and subdue. However, at this particular time Rhianne did not know any of this. The woman shrieked with laughter and it seemed she would fall over - she was laughing so much. As quickly as it began, it stopped. She jumped in front of Rhianne and, as though speaking to a moron, explained, very slowly and deliberately, the way things worked. 'You can see that I have power. Now, when I speak to you, you answer,' she said, almost caressingly. 'When I say "jump", you jump,' this was a whisper. 'This is very simple, yes?' The woman then circled behind the girl, fingering her hair and letting her hand trail caressingly across her back and down one arm; the touch made Rhianne shiver. Then putting her mouth close to Rhianne's ear, she took a deep breath and shouted at the top of her voice, 'Understand?' at which Rhianne burst into tears and the woman collapsed with laughter.

She eventually got herself under control and yelled, 'Salazar! Salazar! 'Where is that ... oh there you are,' she amended as the turbaned man glided toward her. 'Take the girl to the South-west Tower. Leave her some water and I suppose she can have some food!' she said half-heartedly.

123

'We need to keep her alive, at least …,' and she turned and stared into Rhianne's tear-streaked face. 'At least,' she repeated, 'until we get what we want.'

She burst into peals of laughter as she watched for the obvious expression of horror to appear on the child's face, and could still be heard cackling away as she strode through the door and down a dark corridor to wherever she was going.

'Salazar - a strange name,' she thought in the recesses of her mind as she tried, unsuccessfully, to stop crying. He opened a door, which fortunately led in the opposite direction to that through which the woman had gone - a small relief that did not last long as the corridor, which was very dark and lit only in their immediate vicinity by Salazar's torch, wrapped itself around them as they moved through it, seeming to make grabs at their clothing as they passed along - ghostly hands drawing them into the very depths of despair. She was sure that in some places she saw the darkness move!

Eventually reaching an open archway at the foot of a stone, spiral staircase, the man led the way, holding Rhianne securely by the elbow as they ascended it. Many of the steps had shattered completely and one could easily break a leg or fall back down - a broken neck must surely have happened on some occasion or other.

When they reached the top, the man slotted the torch into a bracket on the wall and, taking a key from a hook beside it, opened a door, which Rhianne observed led into a circular room completely devoid of furniture.

The man walked into the room after he had retrieved the light and Rhianne's breath caught in her throat as she saw more than one dark shadow scuttling away and down various small holes between the wall and the floor. There was only one window, if it could be called that; the sill was no more than two feet from the floor and was wider on the inside than the outside, the outside being only about a hand's breadth wide, thus not wide enough to escape through, and it was

124

about four feet in height. She had never seen anything like it before. The wind whistled through the window making it extremely cold in there. She noticed the man turning to leave and felt panic rise up within her.

'Oh, please!' she wailed. 'Don't leave me on my own!' The man shook his head, shrugged and turned again to leave.

Rhianne grabbed his sleeve and held on for all her might. Her tears were now running uncontrollably down her cheeks and she thought she might faint and probably would have done if the thought of what might start crawling over her had not kept her from doing so. 'Don't take the light away with you. If I cannot see, I shall go mad.'

Salazar looked at her and although his face had been inscrutable in the keep, was it her imagination or did it appear to soften slightly, if only for an instant, at the sight of her tears. He walked over to one of the wall sconces and lit the torch with his own. It took some time to catch as the pitch was old and the wood, like the room, was rather damp. Eventually, when it had spluttered into life, Salazar turned and bowed himself out of the room.

Rhianne heard the key turn in the lock and, biting her knuckles, she backed against the wall to make sure she didn't miss anything that might move. Looking over to the other side of the tower she saw more wall sconces. Running over and taking one down, she determined to crack open the head of any creature stupid enough to get too near her.

Not knowing what time it was - the nights were so long in winter - she stood and waited to see what would happen next. Shortly after Salazar had left, she heard movement on the other side of the door. The key turned and a very old man shuffled in. The little man's head looked remarkably like a burned down tallow candle. The skin on his face sagged in layers as though all the wax of his features had run into folds around it as it had melted and had settled onto his collar and in most places had the same tallow dip colour. He had very little hair, mainly around the lower part of the back and sides of his head, except for one small clump on top in the middle, which could easily have been mistaken for the wick in a candle - it stuck straight up without moving. It's funny, but even when we are very scared, we are fascinated by the ridiculous and Rhianne wondered whether, if it were lit, this wick of hair would in fact burn.

Bringing into the room first a long wooden bench, which, as it turned out, would have to serve as table, seat and bed in turn, he went out again and came back with a large jug of water, a chunk of black bread and some cheese in a rough wooden bowl. After throwing in a very dirty blanket, he sniffed and turned away. He spoke not a word. In fact, no one apart from the woman had said anything since she had been there. Thinking of how isolated she was, she felt the lump in her throat threatening to send the tears down her cheeks again but after swallowing a few times she managed to overcome the urge to do so. The man left and, again, the key turned in the lock with a loud clang that seemed to reverberate around the room.

When her tears had finally ceased, giving her nose a chance to clear, she noticed an extremely unpleasant smell in the room. She couldn't quite place it but it seemed to grow stronger or weaker, depending upon the wind, which continued to blow through the window. She thought it might be the food the old man had brought with him and bent down to sniff at it. It was not the food!

As wretched as she was, she suddenly felt very hungry. She placed the bread and cheese in her lap and, picking up the jug, filled the bowl with some water and drank. Not realising how thirsty she was, as she hadn't drunk anything since she had been at home - a thought that again almost started the tears flowing again - she re-filled it twice more before she had satisfied her thirst. After rinsing her hands in a little more of the water and drying them on her skirts, she bit into the bread

126

and cheese in turn until it was almost finished. Feeling slightly better now, Rhianne pushed all the utensils to the end of the bench and, curling her legs up underneath her, tucked up her skirts, so as to be off the floor away from the creatures, and sat leaning against the wall. It was time to try and consider just what was happening. Fear again swept over her as the room started to darken. She looked up to see that the torch above her was guttering, threatening to go out. Jumping up quickly she rushed over to it with the torch she had taken from the opposite wall and, with a bit of a struggle, the new torch eventually lit. She placed the newly lit torch into its holder and, breathing a sigh of relief, took the burnt one back to her bench to use as a weapon.

The night wore on and at some time Rhianne must have dozed. She awoke with a start, first wondering where on earth she could be and then jumped up with fright and revulsion as two mice, or was it rats, darted away from the scraps they had been consuming from the wooden bowl. She shivered as she thought that they might have been crawling over her. '*No, don't cry*,' she thought. '*Something will happen - I know it will. It has to!*'

She noticed at the window - with relief - that the room was beginning to brighten as morning struggled to assert itself. The wind was whistling around the room and it was still very cold. The ragged blanket had not done much to keep out the chill and it took another hour, during which time Rhianne walked swiftly round the room, trying to keep warm, before a sliver of pale winter sunlight peeped over the rim of the window. She was transfixed, closing her eyes and allowing the sun to caress her face.

'*I have never in my life been so grateful for the sun*,' she thought.

Suddenly, Rhianne heard a rustling and became aware of a presence in the room. She swivelled round, thinking at first that the rats had returned but there, staring at her, was the woman from last night. Rhianne looked at her, and at the same time was aware of everything else that was in the room, *'due,'* she supposed, *'to the shape of it - there are no corners'*. However, the door was still closed and it had not creaked this time so how had the women got in? Had she entered some other way? Rhianne's eyes darted about but she could see no other entrance.

'So, you are not completely dull-witted,' the woman observed, once again using that soft, mesmerizing voice. 'Did I or did I not come in through the door? Did I materialise out of thin air?' she clicked her fingers in the air as she said this. 'Am I really here or am I just an illusion? But I am not going to let you into any of the secrets of my comings and goings. Suffice it to say that you need always be on your guard. Just remember' she pushed her mouth close to Rhianne's face, 'I can see you at any time, even though you can't see me.' Standing up, she walked around the room; then turning she looked at her again with that innocent smile but Rhianne knew better, now, than to think there was any mercy behind it. 'So,' she mused as she made her way slowly around the tower again, stopping to peer out of the small window, 'let us see if you have learned anything since the last time we met.' She suddenly swept around to face the young girl and asked in a very clipped voice, 'How old are you child?'

'Thirteen, mistress,' she replied promptly.

'Thirteen, eh? You have learned something; a bit slow mind but I am sure you will be more obedient, the longer we know each other, eh? Not that I think we will have that much time together before ... but perhaps I shall not mention that just yet!' Again, that smile. 'And "mistress" will do as I am sure you know by now that I will have complete mastery over you – and mystery!' She fell about laughing at the pun she had just delivered. Pulling herself together she continued, 'Don't think you will be able to escape, as there is no escape.

128

Everyone who serves me here knows that fact. None of them can get away from me without my express consent – consent that I never give!'

Her voice rose higher and higher the longer she spoke until Rhianne thought the woman would lose complete control. She started to laugh again, almost hysterically, but managed, finally, to get herself in hand. 'Did you see the gargoyles on the outside of the fortress as you came in?' she gasped in her glee, trying to regain her breath. 'They are the ones that have tried to get away! I always catch them, you know, and I have a very special potion that I make them drink. In fact, it really is quite funny as by the time I have finished with them they actually want to drink it.' She fell about laughing again.

'However,' she said, trying to sober herself up, 'I won't go into detail here. Just to let you know that when they have turned to stone I secure them to the wall. The magic in the potion must be very strong as it keeps them there. I thought that perhaps they would rot away and fall off but, no, they're all still there – every one of them.'

She stood pondering this piece of information for a long minute and then whirled around to face Rhianne. 'If you get too close, little girl, they will melt you with their heat! Their wrath at their impotence is so strong, due to the fact that they must still have their brains - that is, whatever brains they had in the first place - their hate turns into an invisible fire which melts anything that gets too close to them.

'It's quite funny because gargoyles are really supposed to be water spouts but mine are fire spouts'. She thought this an enormously funny joke and did very well in keeping the manic laughter at bay - almost, but Rhianne noticed her lips twitching.

Pulling up her sleeve, the woman looked at a still angry burn just below her elbow, and frowned. 'Yes, I have their measure but they won't do that to me again. Now,' she said turning back again to the girl, 'what a kind person I am to put you in the picture, am I not?'

'Yes, mistress.'

'Better and better. Well, I can't stand here wasting time chatting with you all day. I have my plans to put into action. Did you know …? But no, I don't suppose you do! However, I will tell you! My wellspring has told me that young Arthur will destroy me one day. But there is a proviso and do you know what that is?'

'No, mistress.'

'I have to destroy him first! And I *will*!' With that she gripped Rhianne beneath her ear, pinching it hard. She heard the woman's laughter fading away as she drifted into unconsciousness; the next thing she knew was that she was alone again in the room.

The sun had moved around and on the bench there was a different jug filled with water and some more bread and cheese. '*What did she do? She must have done something to make me fall asleep.*' She knuckled her eyes to clear the sleep from them and looked despondently at everything around her but, this time, refused to let the tears start. '*I must do something,*' she resolved as she nibbled at the cheese.

Realising she had no option but nonetheless feeling very embarrassed by it, Rhianne had to decide which part of the tower room she had to use as a lavatory. They had left her no bucket and so she would have to use the floor.'

Jack became aware that his two grandsons were giggling. 'Why are you laughing, you two?'

Ben looked up at his grandfather and said that it was just the bit about her going to the toilet.

'Well, that is what Rhianne told me when she recounted her story to us all. I wasn't going to leave it out, was I? Besides, I used to read lots of books when I was younger and when I read about people walking for days through the desert or jungle, or wherever, they *never* seemed to go to the toilet. I used to have this vision in my mind of everyone getting fatter and rounder and eventually going off bang – I mean, *everyone* needs to go to the toilet, don't they? So, I believe it needs to be included.'

Both Danny and Ben fell about laughing at their grandfather's explanation and he, too, unable to stop himself, chuckled along with them. 'Let's get back to the story.'

'How degrading,' she thought, *'to be brought to this! I must try to get out of here - and without getting turned to stone - or worse. How did she get into this room? There must be a secret door, or something.'* After pouring some water over her hands and using the hem of her gown to dry them, she looked around the tower and tried knocking at the stones on the wall. Nothing! Solid! They all sounded the same. She stamped on the stone slabs on the floor. Nothing, again! *'How did she do it?'* After trying virtually every stone within reach, she moved over to the window again to see exactly what was outside. It overlooked the lake, which was quite large – what she could see of it at any rate - and was surrounded by a thick forest. The lake was very still, almost like glass, and reflected a little of the sky and the trees of which most, at this time of the year, were bare, although some of them wore garments of snow. *'I wonder if I were to hang something out of the window someone would see it and rescue me,'* she thought. *'Well, it's always worth a try. Nothing ventured ....'* She found the edge of her skirt where there had already been a tear and ripped off another length. There was a rough edge to the window, which she believed would be just enough to keep the material from falling. *'There - I hope someone sees it,'* she thought despondently, believing no-one would, as on the way to the castle they had not passed a living soul, not even seen a woodsman's cottage. She sat down again, biting her lip in her refusal to cry. Just before darkness

fell, her ears twitched as she heard the flapping of wings. She jumped up in time to see a bird pulling at the piece of material she had attached to the windowsill. 'No. Oh, please no,' she cried, jumping up and racing toward the window as it flew away, trailing the material behind it. 'Now, no-one will find me,' she wailed.

A good while passed without a visit from anyone. The light began to fade. Panic again started to rise within her as she realised that no one had come to see her since the little man - presumably it was him who had brought the food – or the woman, had come earlier in the day. There was a little water left in the jug but no food. However, the worst thing was that she had no light and the torches were spent, even if she did have something to light them with. She started banging with her fists on the door. Before long, one hand was scratched and bleeding so she had to give up. She sat back down on the bench, lifting her feet off the floor and pulling her knees up to her chest. It was almost completely dark now and she could feel that she was opening her eyes as wide as she could in the vain hope that she might see anything that moved. Her ears twitched again as she heard something scratching the floor close to her bench. A scream started to form at the base of her lungs when, just before it erupted from her throat, she heard the key turn in the lock. Light blinded her for a second or two but not before she saw a few small, furry bodies scuttling back into the darkness. Salazar stood there with a blazing torch and two new ones to insert into their brackets on the walls. He came into the room and went about this task. He did not look at her at all. As soon as he had finished, he left, turning the key in the lock behind him. The wrinkled man returned a few minutes later, this time he brought in a bucket, which he placed near the spot that Rhianne had used as a toilet. She felt the colour rise up from her throat in embarrassment, to think that Salazar had obviously noticed what she had had to do on the floor and had sent the wrinkled man with the bucket; she was also relieved that she did not now have to use the floor, although she also did not want to use the bucket - someone would have to empty it! *'That woman has a lot to answer for in bringing me into such degradation.'*

Rhianne sat down again on the bench, feeling absolutely wretched. She looked at the bowl of bread and cheese but couldn't bring herself to eat anything. She took the food out of the bowl and poured some of the water from the jug into it. As best she could, after tearing off yet more material from her skirt, she wetted the cloth and washed her hands, face and arms. Once finished, she threw the water into the bucket and wiped the bowl out with her shawl. She drank some water and then sat staring at the door. She daren't close her eyes, even though she knew that exhaustion would eventually send her to sleep, but hoped that she might stay awake until the morning. *'Isn't it funny,'* she thought, *'that we always feel safer in the daylight? I don't know why, because we see much more to be afraid of when it's light. I suppose it's because we imagine more things to be afraid of when it's dark.'*

She must have dozed for a little, as, after a while, she became aware of the bad odour that she had smelled the day before. She wrinkled her nose trying to detect its source. Getting up from the bench she walked around the tower, sniffing now and then and poking different parts of the floor with the toe of her shoe. She heard the odd rustle and felt her eyes darting around the edges of the floor, thinking the rodents were back.

Turning to look for them, as she walked again toward the bench, she almost jumped out of her skin. The woman was sitting on it. She hooted with laughter at the look on Rhianne's face and was holding her sides as her rocking threatened to send her careering off the bench, tears of laughter coursed down her face, leaving dirty trackmarks in

133

their wake. 'Oh, I love it, I love it! I can do just what I want and when I want,' she said, as she tried to catch her breath, 'and there is no-one to stop me. I am so great!

I thought I would let you know that there is a party of men headed through the woods,' she spluttered, between gasps, 'and they obviously think they are going to rescue you!' She swirled around and it was then, as the draught from her movement wafted toward Rhianne that she realised where the awful smell was coming from. It was the woman! She smelled terrible! Rhianne tried not to screw up her nose at the stench.

The woman came close to the girl and peered into her face. 'They will not succeed,' she cooed at her. 'I might even end up with a new collection of gargoyles to put over the archways. I could do with some at that particular spot - it is a trifle bare.' Her eyes were a million miles away as she considered the prospect of her new handiwork. Pulling her mind back to the present, she turned a cold eye on Rhianne and stated, 'Even if they do get into the castle they won't find you. I have given instructions to Salazar to make sure something not very pleasant happens to you if they get too close and he dare not disobey me.' She went off into howls of laughter again as she peered hard into Rhianne's face to watch for the horror that would be written on it.

The light from the torch shone full into the mad woman's face and as she spoke Rhianne was aware of the terrible stench of the woman's breath. She noticed that her teeth were very bad too, some yellow, some brown and some even looked as though they would soon be parting company with their neighbours. The woman continued to speak, 'but I would really like to do the job of disposing of you myself, so I might change my orders.' She fell about laughing again, jigging about the room. Raising her arms high above her head, she swirled around again, almost like a dancer, and then disappeared! She just vanished! Rhianne couldn't believe

134

her eyes. She blinked quite a few times and then rubbed her knuckles over her eyes; her breath caught in her throat while her eyes darted around the room but she just was not there! However, the smell was still there and Rhianne caught just an impression that she was still in the room! Eventually a key turned and the door opened and slammed shut almost immediately. Rhianne thought someone was going to come in but they did not. She did not understand why that had happened. The bad smell slowly evaporated.

The girl sat down to consider what had just happened. First, her heart did a somersault inside her rib cage as she thought that someone was on the way to rescue her. Then she was afraid, not only for them but for herself. Salazar was at least ten times as strong as she was. She wouldn't stand a chance of fighting him off. What was she to do! Are they really coming to rescue her? Was the woman really telling her the truth? Had she imagined or dreamed the whole thing? Was she going completely mad!

Rhianne sat as still as she could – chill allowing - mulling over her problems, keeping an eye on the floor and searching the darkened areas where the floor and wall met, where a rat or maybe some other horrid creature might poke up its head, when suddenly one of the torches spluttered and, as it did so, she noticed that something near the door glinted. Now I reckon that over the last two nights Rhianne had got to know the room she was in pretty well and any deviation from the norm would stand out like a sore thumb.

So, she got down from the bench and, as slowly and cautiously as she could because she knew that anything could happen, moved toward the door. Stopping half way, she returned to the bench and, stretching up, removed one of the torches. She stopped after each step and listened but there was no sound and, more importantly, there was also no awful smell! Stooping down and holding the light in front of her she stared at the spot where she thought she had seen something. Again, that glittering! It looked as though it might be a buckle or a clasp of some description. She bent down to pick it up but although it was only a small thing, she could only lift it but a couple of inches above the ground. It wasn't that it was heavy but it appeared to be snagged onto something quite securely and so, retracing her steps and replacing the torch in its holder, she returned to the door and tried with both hands to lift the buckle. She felt around to find out what was holding onto it and could feel a very filmy type of material attached to it. The material appeared to be caught in the lower edge of the door and was somehow snagged at one corner. Rhianne couldn't see the material, but then it was quite dark, and she thought that once she had removed it from the door she would be able to see it more clearly. However, trying to ease it away was not working so, in desperation, she gave it an almighty tug, almost falling over backwards as she did so, feeling a sharp rip and then it was free. Once released, Rhianne was surprised to find that it was very light in weight; she took it back to her bench and set it down beside the jug to take a closer look at what she had found. There was nothing there! All she could see was the buckle and the bench. But she could feel it.

'What on earth!' She picked it up to make sure she was not going mad and, again, could feel the material. She screwed up her eyes to see more clearly and, this time, as she held it aloft, she realised she couldn't see her fingers. She could see part of her hand and her thumb, but her fingers – the part of her hand that was under the material - were gone. Dropping it in fright, she was relieved to see that her hand was now whole, but in doing so she had knocked into the jug and a small jet of water had leapt over the rim and onto the garment. There were only a few small spots but, where they had fallen, they had turned the garment into a rainbow of

136

colour. Rhianne, now full of curiosity, draped the article of clothing over her arm. Her arm disappeared, apart from the rainbow coloured spots through which her arm showed as a ghostly image. Standing up, she covered herself from her neck to her feet with it and, looking at herself through it from every possible angle, her heart started pumping with the knowledge that she had, literally within her grasp, the means of escape.

The penny dropped as she finally realised how the woman had got into the room without being noticed, 'she's been concealing herself in this cloak of invisibility!' With that knowledge Rhianne knew that she could get out the same way.

'*I have to make a plan,*' she thought, '*as I not only have to escape from this room and the castle but I have to find the people who are searching for me. I can't just wait around and see them turned to stone.*'

But, before she could sit and try to formulate her plan, she was put into the position where she had to act immediately. It might be the only opportunity she would get!

She had heard a step outside the door, which had caused her ears to twitch. Running over toward the wall beside the door, she flattened herself against it, at the same time completely draping herself in the garment. She held her breath as the wrinkled man entered with the inevitable jug of water and bowl of bread and cheese. She felt sure he must see her. He did not at first appear to notice that she was not there but, by the time he did, it was too late. Noticing that the key was still in the door, as the man passed her she gave him an enormous push in the small of his back which sent him sprawling across the room and crashing into the opposite wall - bread, water and pieces of broken jug – and maybe a few mice - flying everywhere.

She observed this only in the blink of an eye as, turning, she was out through the door in a flash and, closing it as swiftly as she could, she turned the key, mentally wishing the old man joy of his supper.

As she fled down the stairs she could hear the tallow man shouting and banging on the door. *'That's the first time I've heard him speak,'* she thought. Knowing she might not have much time if the old man was heard or missed, she made haste to try to reach safety as quickly as she could. However, by the time she got to the foot of the circular stair well she could hardly hear him at all.

At first she thought that she might have to peep out through a crack in the mantle of invisibility, once she had placed it over her head, but found that she could see perfectly clearly through it, that is, when it was light enough to see anything at all. *'It must be invisible in one direction only,'* she thought.

By the time she got to the foot of the stairs, panic started to well up inside her again. It was pitch black at the bottom and, for the last dozen steps or so, she had to use her feet to feel her way, remembering that some steps were broken and some were missing entirely. *'It would be the most stupid thing now to go and break a leg or, worse, my neck!'* she thought. Once she was sure she had reached the bottom of the stairs she tried to remember in which direction she had come when they first took her there but try as she might, she couldn't. Eventually she decided to go to her right as, with illogical thinking, she decided that the opposite to right was wrong. She groped along the wall with her hands, occasionally finding a door but deciding that each door was too warm to be one that led outside; she very gingerly felt each step forward with her toes before moving on.

Carrying on along the corridor she was horrified to see a flickering light getting brighter and then a servant turn the corner and come rushing toward her holding a torch. Almost fainting with fright, she flattened herself against the wall and held her breath, again feeling sure that she was visible, that

138

the servant must see her and thus raise the alarm. Rhianne could feel her heart beating so hard against her ribs that she knew for certain that it must have been clanging throughout the castle and that the servant must obviously be deafened by it as well. The servant, muttering away to himself like a man deranged, did not see or hear her and disappeared around a corner in the opposite direction.

In the brief half-minute that the light had shone in the corridor, Rhianne noticed steps leading down to somewhere, almost opposite to where she was standing. Waiting until it was dark once again and holding her hands out in front of her to find the wall, she moved slowly across the hallway and, again feeling the floor in front of her with her toes, found the top step. There was a very faint glow far down, somewhere at the bottom of the stairway.

It was then a very hard decision. Did this stairway lead to safety? What if that witch was down there. Were her powers such that she was able to see through the garment? Would she turn her into a gargoyle? Would she torture or kill her, as she had threatened to upstairs? How would she do it? Would she torture her for a long time? She tried not to dwell on that one! Telling herself that her situation couldn't be any worse than when she was locked up in the tower like a sheep ready for slaughter, she took a very quiet, albeit shuddering, deep breath and, setting her face like flint, crept down the stairs; stairs that got colder as she descended and seemed to go on forever.

Rhianne was surprised to find it growing gradually lighter as she continued down the stairs. However, she was completely unprepared, and most surprised at what she found when she reached the bottom of that stairway.

She did not know it then, but in this, the deepest part of the castle, down, apparently, even lower than the dungeons and definitely below the level of the lake by the amount of dampness there was upon the walls and the floor, Salazar knelt upon the stone floor before a crystal rock, his heart at breaking point. The light from a single candle danced over the rock, making it shimmer and glisten. However, what drew her eyes was what was encased inside the crystal rock. Entombed therein was the loveliest young woman that Rhianne had ever seen. Salazar kept an attitude almost of prayer as he knelt there, the fingertips of his hands together beneath his chin as he stared at her - a look of complete hopelessness on his face.

Rhianne learned much later that the mad woman had allowed him to keep one candle burning night and day in this seemingly perpetual night before the crystal rock - a concession he would do anything not to lose. He told her much later that he believed that the woman in the crystal rock could see out of it, as her eyes were always open, and whichever way he moved inside this cave-like room they always appeared to be looking at him. He therefore never wanted her to be in darkness.

He stared at her now with eyes of longing, of love, but of despair. Again, later, Rhianne learned that the woman was his wife, Jasmine - a name given her by her parents. When she was born, they named her after a delicate flower that grew in their garden, one of great beauty and wonderful fragrance. Looking at her, as she had looked for almost a year now since the witch had entombed her, Rhianne, along with Salazar, saw a lovely, almost completely oval face, honey bronze in colour, with full, dark red lips. However, the most startling thing about her was her eyes, which, unlike any woman he had ever seen from his part of the world, were pale grey-green. Again he looked at the one crystal tear that was trapped on her lower lashes. He caught his breath as he gazed at her, almost overcome with her beauty and the desperation of their plight. Her dress was of a deep red, matching her lips absolutely and comprised a silk, embroidered bodice and matching pantaloons. She also had red painted nails on fingers and

140

toes. Her feet were bare. Rhianne had never seen anyone with such exotic beauty or, come to that, anyone dressed so sumptuously in her life.

Rhianne learned later that Salazar lived in the hope that one day the woman would relent and release his beloved wife but, whether she did or did not, he couldn't leave her. In the year since all this had happened, he had not seen one sign that the witch would change her mind, but what else was he to do? The mad woman had threatened to add her to her gargoyle collection. There would then be no hope he felt sure. In the meantime, they were both at her mercy. He had to obey or ... but he wouldn't let his mind consider anything further than his obedience – for Jasmine's sake!

Rhianne stood there for what seemed an eternity, taking in everything that was before her and yet not, at that time, understanding any of it. She could feel the misery, in an almost tangible way, that emanated from the man who was kneeling before his wife, although Rhianne did not at that time know that she was his wife. Being the gentle child that she was, she felt a great compassion well up inside her for the man and a great sadness at this scene. She stood very still and tried to quieten the pounding of her heart, feeling that she shouldn't be here intruding upon his grief.

As she was about to turn and creep back up the stairs the man spoke. *'Yes, she is most beautiful, is she not?'*

Rhianne almost jumped out of her skin with fright. She whirled round to look at the man. He had not moved and still had his back to her. He was kneeling on the floor before his beloved and he most positively could not have seen her, facing away from her as he did and, of course, she still wore the mantle.

'I ... ,' Rhianne began, but the man stopped her.

He did not move and he did not open his mouth but again he spoke – she could clearly hear his voice. *'No. Say nothing. You will be heard. Just listen to me.'*

Rhianne's eyes grew wide with wonder and fear as she looked at the man speaking without moving his lips. 'How …?'

Again, he stopped her. *'No, do not speak out loud. Listen to what I have to say. You have a gift, which not many people in this accursed country possess and yet you are not trained in it! Why? Such a waste! You spoke to me in the tower with your mind, although I feel sure that you did not know it. I am speaking to you now with my mind and you hear me. Am I right?'*

She nodded.

'I believe you just agreed with me,' he said, again through his mind. *'I have nearly finished my vigil for today here before my beloved wife. She does not have the gift herself, but I am aware of her misery. She is enduring a living death in this glass tomb due to the malevolence and evil schemes of that mad witch. I have made a vow of silence - that is, I will not speak with my voice, until I have been able to achieve freedom for my lovely Jasmine, so you do not know how much of a relief it is to be able to communicate in this way.'* His expression did not change as he told Rhianne of his feelings. She continued looking at his profile as he communicated with her. *'There is no-one here who is blessed in this way, obviously not the witch, who, although she has this knowledge, is so evil that it is all muddled in her head. No, the only one who can use it effectively in this place is just me - and now you.*

'To continue - a holy man once told me, when I was a child, that those blessed in the Old Way - and mind-speaking is a gift of the Old Way - would secure my good fortune and bring me luck in abundance. When I felt your words in my mind, my heart leapt for joy. It is the first time in a very long time I have had any feelings at all since my beautiful wife was entombed in this dungeon.' Before he got up from his knees, he bowed low, touching his forehead to the ground, saying,

even though he knew she did not hear, '*Until tomorrow, my precious dove*', and then stood and turned to face Rhianne. '*Ah, so you have found the mantle of invisibility. I do not think she has as yet missed it. How did you get it? Ah, yes, I see,*' he said as he read her thoughts. '*Well, she cannot blame me for her carelessness, although she doesn't need an excuse, but I shall help you. I understand there are people in the forest who are looking for you. I will try and help you escape and rejoin them. Yes, you can trust me so do not fear. That wicked woman is considering the best way to torture you and has already said that I am the one to do it, but that I could never do. Even if,* and he turned and look over his shoulder at his wife, *... but we shall not dwell on that. Now, follow me.*' With that he started up the stairs, not bothering to see if Rhianne would follow and not taking another look at his wife.

Rhianne did follow, wondering what on earth was happening. So many weird things had happened since she came into the castle. A mantle of invisibility! She had never known of such a thing. Mind speaking! She had often had a mishmash of words jumbling through her head, which had occasionally given her a headache but she had never before heard of or even considered that there might be such a thing as mind speaking! Mulling these thoughts over in her head now, she wondered whether there was anyone she knew of who could mind speak. '*Perhaps there is no-one else and that's why this is so very strange,*' she thought. '*A mantle of invisibility! Hmm, that is also very strange.*'

Salazar got to the top of the stairs and, reaching back, took hold of Rhianne's hand. She felt reassured by his grasp. His hand was course but dry, not like the sweaty palms of Berryn, who was supposed to be a monk! Monk indeed! No, this man's hand felt kind. She believed she could trust him. Retracing their steps, she suddenly realised they were headed in the same direction as her former prison and Rhianne's heart skipped a beat. Surely he wasn't taking her back! Had she misread him? However, before long they passed the entrance to the tower, hearing, very faintly, the shouting and hammering of the wrinkled man, they turned down another corridor and headed into the unknown. Walking fairly quickly Salazar, who had explored almost the whole castle, made sure she did not stumble. In places where the walls were dripping with water, the floor had turned to a mossy green slime, which made the stone floor very slippery and dangerous. As the hallway narrowed and as the floor sloped gently downwards it got gradually wetter and near a turn in the tunnel-like hallway the floor was covered by about two feet of water. Salazar lifted Rhianne off the floor as though she weighed nothing and carried her for another twenty feet or so until the gradient started to rise again. He placed her down once they reached the dry floor and, walking quite quickly, they finally came to the end of the tunnel. Rhianne's heart fell into her boots. It was a dead end! Where she felt certain there should have been a door there was only rock.

ELEVEN

'Daniel, you look dead on your feet.' Jack looked up at the clock and even he was shocked to see it getting on for 11. 'I'm sorry; I should have realised the time. I suppose I just get carried away.' He got up from his chair and stretched. 'Come along now, get to bed, or you will be next to useless tomorrow.'

'But it's the start of half-term tomorrow, so we don't really have to worry,' grumbled Daniel.

'Oh yes you do! I've got some chores for you both. And, particularly, because I don't get half term holidays, I need my sleep too! Do you think I can keep on talking without losing my voice? Besides, I've got to go into town tomorrow to pick up some machinery parts for the farm and,' he said, looking at Kate, 'if it's OK with your mother, I'll hitch up the cart and we can all make a day of it.'

'Oh, yes,' they chorused. 'Can we mum?'

'Of course you can,' she smiled at them. 'Now, do as your grandfather says and go to bed.'

They gave her a hug and made their way up the stairs. Jack followed them upstairs a few moments later to check on the latches to the upper landing windows. His encounter with Mad Mab had unsettled him somewhat and he felt as though he needed to make sure the house was secure.

'*Not that walls and doors could do much to keep her out if her magic has been strong enough to cross the barriers of time,*' he thought. '*Still, it won't do any harm to check.*' As he got to the top of the stairs he smiled as he heard the boys chatting while they got ready for bed.

'Do you think granddad is a good storyteller? Or do you think it's all real? I don't think they are stories. I reckon he lived in those times and he really did go through the rock doorway into Merlin's cave.'

145

Daniel was just crawling under the covers as he said this, his older brother shaking his head at him while he carried on undressing. 'It's funny,' Daniel went on, 'I sometimes get ideas in my head that these things really did happen, even though granddad never lets on and certainly won't admit to anything.'

'Don't be daft, Danny. How could they have really happened! If they did, well, granddad would be over a thousand years old. I know he looks old now, but not that old.'

'Hey, you two,' growled Jack, pretending to be cross, 'I'm not too old to sort both of you out. Get to sleep now, or we'll *all* feel too old to go on our trip tomorrow.'

The boys laughed and Jack turned to go downstairs. However, he stopped as Ben called him. 'Granddad, what was the name of the old witch who lived in that castle?'

'She never did like her given name; in fact she hated it. She was called Mabel when she was born but anyone who dared call her by it usually ended up being punished. She would go really quiet and sometimes be missing for days as she thought up terrifying ways to get her own back. The potions she was most fond of using gave them a badly upset stomach, which nearly always resulted in them getting a bloated belly and suffering from wind. You've heard of silent but deadly? Well, this wasn't very silent but it was still deadly! For obvious reasons they lost their friends. Or sometimes she used a potion that gave them a rash, which made them look like they had chicken neck skin all over their face or arms. One man, who had the nerve to laugh at her while he called her by her given name, ended up with the biggest nose I have ever seen in my life. It seemed to keep on growing over the space of a month, and not only that but he seemed to be always afflicted with a cold, so not only was it bright red but it had a perpetual drip hanging from the end of it which he ended up having to shake off as he couldn't reach

146

it to wipe it. She nearly always put some potion or other in the drink or food that would have an unpleasant impact on the person who consumed it. She was determined, even then, that no one would laugh at her and made sure that they would be laughed at instead.

There were other unfortunate happenings and as she grew older they became more sophisticated, like turning people into gargoyles and fixing them to her castle walls or worse - that is, if anything could be worse.

Anyhow, she hated being called Mabel, so she shortened it to Mab and as she grew older and became crazier, she was nicknamed "Mad Mab".' Jack had managed to reduce the boys to uncontrollable laughter by this time and then tried, unsuccessfully, to get them to stop. Giving up, he put on as stern a voice as he could and ordered them to go to sleep. Closing the bedroom door, he smiled as he went back downstairs. After intermittent bursts of laughter, eventually all became quiet.

In the meantime, Cabal had come back in and had stretched himself out on the rug before the fire. *'All's quiet out there. No sign of anything, or anybody!'* he said as he put his head down on his front paws and, after inhaling deeply, he let out a great sigh and closed his eyes.

With midnight fast approaching, Jack settled himself in the chair, also closing his eyes. Kate was tidying up her stitching, in readiness for bed. 'I've virtually finished Mrs. Ambrose's curtains. With a bit of peace and quiet tomorrow, I should get them done by the time you come home from town.

Jack's eyes shot open and he turned in his chair, concern written on his face, 'Aren't you going to come with us then? I thought we would have a day out all together.'

'No! I promised Mrs. Ambrose I would have all her window curtains finished and fitted by the middle of next week. I told you she was expecting a big gathering of folks over the weekend and with the storm putting everything back, I have had to do a lot by hand. Sorry, dad, you will have to go without me. Another time, eh?'

'If I had known, I would have put it off for another week or so! I shall leave Cabal here to look after you,' he said, looking at the hound. Cabal appeared to open just one eye and look back at him. 'I don't like you being here on your own. Not with that ex-husband of yours on the loose.' He turned back to the dog. 'You had better make sure you look after her, Cab.'

'Oh, dad,' Kate said as she rested her face next to his, leaning on his shoulder and putting her arms around him, 'I don't think he will come looking for me; not now, not after all this time! In all reality, if anything happened to me they would have to know who had done it and he would get locked up again. I don't think he'll take that chance. I think he will just get on with his life now, and leave me alone. It's not as if the boys are his own children - he won't come running round to see them, so don't worry.' She gave him a final hug and turned to go to bed.

Jack patted her hand and answered, without much enthusiasm, 'I hope you are right, Kate. *Yes, I really hope you are right!'*

TWELVE

Even after their late night, the two boys were up at the crack of dawn, making enough noise for ten. Jack had been up for about half an hour and had already had a good "talk" to Cabal about protecting Kate. It wasn't very often that Jack and he were separated and it felt strange to be leaving him behind but the hound accepted the reasons why. They were due to leave within the hour, so Cabal loped off into the woods to tend to his business and be back in time to see them off.

They loaded lunch baskets onto the cart and hitched up Duke, the horse Jack had bought early in the spring. By the time they were ready, Cabal returned, running across the grass, tongue lolling out of his grinning mouth. He and Jack looked at each other a while, each knowing the thoughts of the other without even having to mind speak. By eight o'clock they were on the road. Jack had told the boys to keep as quiet as they could until the horse had got into its stride. Being first thing in the morning and not having been in harness for a few days, he was a bit skittish. However, within half an hour he was trotting out purposefully along the road.

Ben turned to his grandfather and asked him 'Why do you call your dog Cabal? We are starting to learn Spanish at school and my teacher has told me that "Cabal" means something to do with horses. And then you go and call your horse "Duke" which is usually a name given to a dog. Did you get them in a muddle when you were giving them their names?' The boys both started laughing.

When they had got themselves under control Jack explained, 'I believe I told you a long time ago that I call all of my dogs Cabal. It saves me having to think of a new name every time I get a new dog. I would only end up calling the new one "Cabal" out of old habit in any event! Anyway, King Arthur called his favourite dog "Cabal" as well. If you

149

look at the size of Cabby, you will see that he is one of the largest dogs in the world. In fact, his breed goes back to the days of the kings of old and, when you consider that horses in those days were a lot smaller than the Arab horses we have now, I suppose a wolfhound could easily have been mistaken at some time or other for a small horse.' The boys accepted this and then spent a while in silence, looking around at the countryside but it wasn't long before they got bored with just sitting and staring.

'How long will it take to get to town?'

'Oh, I should imagine we'll be there by about eleven thirty. Why?'

'Would you tell us some more about Rhianne while we are going along?' Ben urged his grandfather.

'Hmm. Where were we then?'

'Rhianne was at the end of the tunnel and there was no way out.' The boys were stumbling over each other's words to let him know where they were up to.

'Ah, yes. Well, to make it all make sense, I think we have to go back to Percy and Arthur first. Where were they?'

'They were talking to the old man with the white hair,' said Daniel. 'He was in the woods with them while they were trying to get into the castle.'

'Right. Well, I shall continue from there.'

THIRTEEN

I had extricated myself from my sleeping blanket and immediately fell over when trying to stand up as one of my legs had gone completely dead. I made an effort to get feeling back into it by stamping my foot but it just felt like I was thumping a swollen sponge on the floor. Eventually feeling came back and, to keep warm, I started stomping briskly up and down and swinging my arms around me to get the circulation going. All the time I was listening to what was going on between the old man and Arthur. The old man appeared to be quite scared and was backing away. However, after listening to Arthur, who was giving him assurances of safety, he stopped moving.

He said he'd been out collecting sticks and moss. He told us he had a small hut not too far away and that we were welcome to go back with him and have some porridge, so long as we left him alone afterwards and promised not to harm him. We had eaten up all the bread and cheese we had brought with us and had given the apples to the ponies. I, for one, had to admit I was feeling a little hollow inside.

I looked at Cabal, who had made a point of going up to the man and having a good sniff all around him. The man hadn't seemed to mind the dog. In fact, he appeared to be perfectly at ease, '*more so with animals than with men*,' I reckoned.

'*He's OK*,' said Cabby. '*I can't detect any evil smell on him. I think we can safely go with him.*'

'What do you think, Percival? Do you think we can trust him?' Arthur had come up to me while I had been listening to Cabal.

'I believe we can, Arthur,' I replied. 'Cabal seems at ease with him and, as you know, dogs have a marvellous sixth sense so far as people are concerned. Yes, I think we should

151

all go and have a warm around his cooking pot. And the porridge sounds inviting!'

We set off, again leading our ponies through the now almost melted snow. It was still very quiet and motionless in the forest. No animals had been seen and no birds sang. It was a forest of fear. An expression I would always use of this place whenever I thought about it.

We travelled on foot, leading the horses, I suppose, for about half an hour and then came to a huge rock. It was about twenty feet high and twenty feet in circumference. It looked like flint and was certainly the colour of it. The most peculiar thing about it, however, was that it had chiselled gouges in it, each gouge bluish in colour and as smooth as silk. Some of them were almost mirror-like. The old man walked around to the other side of the boulder and we found his hut about a dozen paces further away.

He had a peat fire burning and suspended above it was an iron cauldron full of porridge. I was certainly suspicious, looking at this cauldron, as there was much too much porridge for one old man.

'Were you expecting visitors?' I asked him.

'Oh, no!' he responded. 'I always cook a lot of porridge.' He didn't give any explanation as to why, but he did help himself to a large bowlful first. We all relaxed and enjoyed the hot food and, as I did so, I thought that it didn't matter what was happening, I always felt that much better with food in my stomach. I looked around at the others and could see by their faces that it must be true for them too.

'What is the reason for that monolith over there, old man?' Arthur asked between mouthfuls. 'Is it magical?'

The old man appeared not to hear and just carried on eating his porridge, almost as though his life depended on it, and then started breaking sticks into smaller pieces as he added them to the fire. Arthur went up to the old man and made him look up at him. He repeated the question and the old man just pressed his lips together and shook his head. 'Do you know or can't you say?'

He fidgeted, stood up and looked very uncomfortable, shifting about from one foot to the other and twisting his beard in his hands. 'I don't know anything about it,' he whined. 'It wasn't there this morning when I left here. In fact, when we came back, I didn't know if it was really there or whether I had just imagined it. So many weird things are happening just lately that I thought it was another dream.'

Arthur, and most of us come to that, swirled around to look at the grey tower. We walked slowly over to it and around it and one or two of the men very gingerly, touched it. Compared to the ground and the coldness in the air, it was quite warm.

'Do you think it could have fallen out of the sky?' Shake Spear asked.

'Or pushed its way up through the ground?' suggested Thatcher.

I looked over at Cabal to find him backed right away from it with hackles raised and his lips drawn back, showing his teeth.

'Wherever it might have come from, Cabal doesn't like it. Look at him,' said Arthur. We all turned round to look and I don't know about the others but my hair stood on end as well. I had learned to trust that hound, especially when danger or something suspicious drew near. As one man, we all backed away from the stone.

Arthur eventually told us all to mount up, as we were going back to the castle to try once again to get in. He turned to thank the old man for his hospitality but he had disappeared. Arthur asked us if we had seen which way the old man had gone but no one had. He shrugged and we all went to mount our ponies.

'Where's Wite?' asked Brosc. 'I saw him go around to the other side of the rock but I didn't see him come back.'

We all started calling him but he, like the old man, had completely disappeared.

Returning to the rock and, although we were a bit scared, we felt around it to see if there was a chamber or a door or something we hadn't noticed before. We touched it, tapped it and searched with our hands and eyes but to no avail; there was nowhere we could get into it.

'We'll have to go,' said Arthur. 'As much as I would like to find Wite, we have got to try and find Rhianne. He's big enough to take care of himself but she is not; he'll have to follow us … if he can.'

Mounting our ponies, we followed Cabal who loped off ahead of us and retraced our steps to the castle, arriving there about noon.

Up close, the gargoyles looked even more frightening. Where, at night, you could only just make out the fact that they had faces of some description, in the daylight you could see every feature. Most of the faces – in fact there were seventeen gargoyles - were men, three were women and there was even a dog and two cats. All of them, however, looked in agony. *'Keep your distance, my friend,'* warned Cabal, *'and try to alert the others to the danger when you can. Although they are a bit too high to reach, someone might try and climb up!'*

Getting down from our mounts, we led them again around the castle. We finally found a large stone set into the castle wall, almost hiding a doorway, but blocking it up. No-one had noticed it the last time we searched around the perimeter of the castle. 'Isn't this stone similar to the one in the forest?' asked Arthur. 'It's certainly about the same size.' He walked up to it and very carefully touched it. 'Yes, it is warm just like that other one.' Again, Cabal had his hackles raised and his lips drawn back. 'What is it, Cabal?' The dog started to growl; a sound starting low in his lungs and then he would lunge at the stone, barking, and then back off snarling, only to repeat the exercise again and again. We all moved back, away from it. When he thought we were far enough away from it to be safe, Cabal relaxed. Arthur glared at the dog and then back at the stone, with a very worried look on his face. 'Well, there is definitely something strange about these stones,' he said. Cabal is very anxious about them too, not forgetting that Wite has still not re-appeared. Anyway, we can see that that stone is stuck fast into the wall of the castle, so I don't think we could possibly get in there that way.'

Then, as though it had always been there, although none of us had spotted it the night before, we observed a small door, hidden behind the boulder. In fact it was only the top half of the door as the bottom half was stuck fast in the ground. It was almost buried under grass and moss and hidden behind some thick, prickly bramble bushes. The men pulled the bushes out of the way and tried the door. Fortunately it pushed inwards but was only big enough to allow a very small man, maybe a child – 'or one of Merlin's little men,' I thought - through the half-sunken opening. Arthur, without further ado, pushed his way through the hole and we heard him drop a short way down. He stood and, calling up to us, said that he thought he was in a tunnel of some sort. It was very dark.

'Brosc, do you have a flint to make a flame, and a torch?' Arthur stretched and could just reach the top of the mound of earth with his hands. His face was framed by the darkness.

I was a little bit smaller than him and so I found it quite easy to get through the gap but none of the men would be able to make it, as it was too narrow between the hole where the door had been and the rock. We waited until we had the torch lit and Arthur told the men to try and dig their way in. 'In the meantime, we are going to see where this tunnel leads. When we know, we'll send Cabal back to you,' he said. As we listened to Thatcher telling us to take care, Cabal dropped down beside us, the hair on his ruff flattening as he got away from the boulder; with ears flattened and almost crouching on the floor he felt his way along. We heard the sounds the men made as they started to dig away at the entrance to the tunnel, sounds that receded as we moved further and deeper along it. Coming to a part of the wall on one side of the tunnel that was very wet and slimy, I thought that maybe this was the part that went straight into the lake, so I hoped that we wouldn't meet any naiad in here.

'*Me, too,*' Cabal responded to my thought. '*But I should imagine that they would only be in here if there was a breach in the wall somewhere and I cannot think that that has happened as the tunnel would be flooded and we would all be drowned!*'

I felt only slightly reassured at his reasoning.

Arthur trod on a rat and we heard it squeal; it rushed off when he lifted his foot. He then held the torch closer to the floor to see what was there. As he lowered the light we were rewarded, if you can call it that, with the sight of scores of tails disappearing down holes or toward the other end of the tunnel. We had heard weird noises but thought they were just the sort of sounds that rush through tunnels – airwaves, winds and the like.

Making one or two exclamations, and shuddering, Arthur exclaimed, 'I hate rats! Sir Ector also hates rats, but he says that his are more the human kind than these things here.' He shivered, 'I have never seen as many as this; aren't they awful creatures? I can understand now why my father called them that when he said the same thing about some of the men he has met.' He shivered again but then squared his shoulders and we continued.

I looked at Cabal but, even with as many rats as this, he appeared to have lost his appetite.

'*Appetite! Not on your life! In any event it's mice I eat, not rats. I couldn't eat these,*' he said. '*Can't you sense the evil? Even if they didn't choke me, I'm sure I'd throw up.*'

We came to an intersection and stopped. We could hear the rustle and squeak of the rats receding behind us. Thank goodness they didn't come this way!

'I think we should stay together, as there is only one light, so let's go this way first,' and turning to our right we felt our way further along the tunnel. We came, eventually, to a very narrow and slimy set of steps. Bringing the torch down and looking closely, it appeared that no one had set foot on them for a very long time. Holding on to the walls for support as best we could, and that was very difficult as they, too, were very slimy and let off a rancid odour when disturbed, we got to the top of the stairs to find that they led to a small room. We were surprised that the room was not locked. It was empty, apart from a pile of sacks thrown into one corner, and was surprisingly dry. There were two more exits, one of which, a double door, had light showing under it. Cabal went over to the opposite door and sniffed before going to the one with the light under it and sniffed again.

'*I can't smell anyone,*' he said.

Arthur went over to the double door and tried to open it. It didn't move. He put his shoulder to it and pushed. Without warning it gave way and Arthur was propelled through it. Before disappearing completely he grabbed hold of the top edge of the other door and I lunged forward to get hold of his arm. Cabal also grabbed his coat and between us we managed to pull him back into the room. Panting with the effort, but relieved, Cabal and I looked out of the doorway. The snout of a naiad was just disappearing under the water. We had arrived at a room that was probably used by ferrymen to bring their wares to the castle as the doors led out onto the lake which was about three feet below us.

'That was close,' said Arthur, laughing with relief. 'I nearly got a drenching!' He'd obviously not seen the danger that was lurking just below the surface, but Cabal and I had. It would have been far worse than a drenching, we knew.

When I consider those days, I realise now that I had never experienced such fear before, especially those spent at that castle.

'What's that?' he said as he reached toward the edge of the platform. 'Why, I believe it's a piece of Rhianne's skirt. Yes, it is!' he exclaimed as he grabbed at it. 'So, she is here! Well, let's go! We haven't seen any obvious life here so I don't think we'll have too much trouble in rescuing her.' "Tempting the devil" was a phrase that came into my mind. Would it be long before it might be proved right?

'Cabal, faithful friend,' Arthur called the dog to him. 'Take this piece of material back to the men so they will know we have found out that Rhianne is here and then they can try to get to us once they've dug through that gap.'

Cabal waited while Arthur tied the strip of material round his neck and then he retraced his steps along the tunnel. We watched him disappear into the blackness.

Now that the door was open, or should I say now that the door was hanging off its hinges, the light poured in and we were able to see around the room more clearly. We went over to the other door and, surprisingly, it was not locked either. Peering around the corner we could see that the corridor stretched both ways but in each direction it was pitch dark. 'Which way shall we go?' Arthur asked.

'Whichever way we go we shall have to feel our way as it is very dark and we don't want to end up falling down a hole or through another doorway again,' I said. 'We were very lucky that time.'

Arthur turned and looked at me and over the years I was to grow accustomed to that look. 'God will always look after us if we trust in Him,' he responded, and I could see that he had total faith in this belief. However, on the other hand he also put his trust in Merlin and I suppose I just couldn't understand him following the teachings of both Christ and a Druid, although Merlin, too, told me that he believed in the same God. Then, again, I wondered what the monks said to him during his instruction and was amazed that he actually wanted to listen. Not like his schooling, which he hated and tried to get out of if he could.

Perhaps one day I might understand!

In the meantime, my imagination went off into overdrive again as I stared ahead of me. Stretching a long way - or was it a long way? - into the distance was a black vacuum that held innumerable terrors, ready to suck us into its maw and devour us. As we headed towards - what? - and not daring to look behind me at the obvious ghouls and wraiths that were following us, just waiting to be acknowledged to enable them to sink skeletal fingers into our flesh and pull us down into the waiting fiery pit, an agonizing end as the playthings of demonic beings - a shiver crept up my spine, making the hair at my neck bristle outwards and I felt sure my legs wouldn't hold me up as they turned to jelly. I was certainly not going to look behind me even though I desperately wanted to take a peek – just to make sure!

Once our eyes became accustomed to the darkness we found it not too difficult to see as there was a slight glow bouncing off the walls due, most probably, to the dampness. We thought we must have still been travelling along the wall that ran into the lake, as it was extremely wet on the floor and in some places water was trickling down the wall, but only on that one side. We didn't think we were in any main part of the castle because there was nothing in the corridor at all, not even a broom. We came to a flight of stairs at the top of which was another door and we could hear something behind it. However, before we reached it I heard, almost like a scream inside my head, *'Percy, I'm trapped!'* My heart skipped a beat. It was Cabal. *'They've wedged me into a cage of some sort and I can't move – it's so small.'*

Arthur was staring at me. 'What's the matter?' he asked. 'You jumped out of your skin!'

159

'Er, I was wondering what has happened to Cabal. He should have caught up with us long before now. I think we should go back and look for him.'

'Nonsense, he's OK. He'll find us. Never fear. Now, let's go on.' At that he continued up the stairs expecting me to follow. As I didn't move, he stopped and turned, looking none too pleased, and beckoned me on.

What could I do? I wanted to go back and find Cabal. *'Where are you?'* No answer. I tried again. *'Cabal, where are you?'* Nothing! I was frantic with worry but I followed Arthur, as I didn't want us all to be split up and I thought that once we, and the men, were all together again we could try and find my best friend, as that was how I now thought of him.

'Right lads,' said Jack as they turned the horse and cart into a lane leading down to the back of one of the warehouses they needed to go to, 'let's go and sort out what we need and then we'll go eat some lunch.' He led the horse over to the trough and let it have a short drink before hanging the nosebag over his head.

Jack went around the store picking up some machine parts for the tractor and some new hand tools. He checked his list and ordered a couple of new parts for the haymaker. 'I'll also need you to order me some parts for the precision seed drill as well,' he told the merchant. 'I want gallery blocks, singulators and coulters. How long will it take to deliver them?'

After sorting out the various details with the merchant they stretched their legs as they walked about in the small market town. To give Duke time to rest up and have his oats, they make a stop at the pub and, sitting outside in the Indian summer sunshine, Jack had a glass of beer and the boys enjoyed some lemonade while they finished off the basket of food they'd brought with them.

Judging that by now the man at the store would have loaded up the cart and also that the horse had had sufficient rest, they retraced their steps and before long were on the road home, hoping to arrive before the sun went down.

'Come on granddad,' the boys chorused, 'let's get back to the story. What happened to Cabal?'

FOURTEEN

We reached the top of the stairway and listened at the door. All I could hear at first was my own heart hammering away in my ears. When I could get myself under control I heard soft talking. Looking back, I can see that where I thought it was someone whispering, it was in fact people talking in the normal way - if you could ever call anything that was happening at present "normal" - it was just that the door was so thick that it sounded like whispering. We pushed the door as gently as we could to try to see if we could peep in and possibly creep through but, as luck would have it, it had the most awful grinding creak. Before we knew what was happening the door was yanked open, and both Arthur and I tumbled into the room in a heap. We were then face to face with the most awful smelling person I have ever come across in my life.'

'Mad Mab!' Danny and Ben chorused.

'Yes, although I didn't know who she was at the time.' She looked at both of us for a second or two and then burst into roars of laughter, slapping her thighs and almost falling over with the effort of it. I thought she would have apoplexy the way her face went beetroot red. She eventually wiped away the tears as they ran down her cheeks and I could see the dirty tracks that were left behind as they cleaned her otherwise filthy face. While she laughed we scrambled to our feet and she, darting behind us with amazing speed, slammed the door shut, bolting it at the top. I noticed, with a sinking feeling, that it would be hard to reach that bolt without a stool or chair. Eventually she stopped laughing. In the short time we had been in it, we quickly looked around the room for some other escape route and took in most of what was there. It's amazing how much information the brain can accumulate in a short space of time – in this case a very short space of

162

time.   It was a massive room that looked almost like a kitchen. At one end there were lots of things that are part and parcel of wizardry, some in pots or glass jars or in phials balanced over burners, bubbling away. All the colours of the rainbow seemed to be cooking there, some giving off a pretty powerful smell - sulphur and the like – but nothing matched her! The ceiling was very high and, come to think of it, we couldn't really see the end of it, there were so many pots, wooden instruments, cobwebs and other things hanging from it. The room had many similarities to Merlin's cave except where he had a sort of orderly chaos; hers was more like a filthy disorder - and the smell! Directly opposite us was a huge fire over which hung a cauldron. There was a funny looking old man stirring whatever was in it as we came in. However, as we fell into the room he had stopped and was staring at us with a completely blank expression - if an expression can be blank, that is. He had a head like an almost deflated yellow balloon with a sprout sticking out of the top of it.

Eventually the woman spoke. 'It worked.' She clapped her hands like an excited child and bounced from one leg to the other. 'Yes, it worked. Yes, I knew that you would come searching for the girl. She thought she'd got away once, but no, I'm much too clever for her - and you, by the looks of it. Yes, I have finally got what I wanted all along!' She walked round us, cackling with laughter again as she did so. When she came round to the front of us she just stood looking at us for a long minute, with her hands on her hips. She cocked her head to one side and then the other, staring at both of us in the face and then looked us over from head to foot. She finally let out a great sigh and said, almost gently, 'Arthur. You don't know how wonderful it is to see you.' You'd think we had just popped round for tea! Again, she just stared at one and then the other of us. We wondered how she knew who Arthur was because neither of us had the slightest clue who she was. 'Now that I have you, I can at last kill you! Now, how shall I do it? Oh yes. I have to kill you, you know, because, you may or may not know but it has been foretold that otherwise you will kill me and so I have to kill you first! That's sensible, isn't it? The big question is how I should do it. I don't want it to be quick, you know. I have thought so often of how I should do it and I cannot waste all that valuable thinking time on a quick death, but now that the time is here I am at a loss.' She walked around him, weighing him up and umming and aahing. 'I have suffered so many headaches trying to decide on the most appropriate departure route to take you on that special journey from this world to the, er, next. Once again, the anticipation of it is too much; I shall have to think about it some more – a thing I so thoroughly enjoy doing.' I thought she must be deranged but, as I had never met her before and didn't know the first thing about her, was not completely sure, although I thought that most of the signs were there.

'I've got your dog, you know,' she spoke caressingly to Arthur, stroking the side of his face with one dirty finger. 'Why did you tie that piece of Rhianne's dress round his neck? Was it so she could sew it back on again?' She fell about laughing again at her witticism. When she had finally got herself under control she straightened herself up, inhaled deeply and said, almost matter-of-factly, 'I've caged him up and I shall feed him to the little fishes … bit by bit.' Whilst saying this, she looked into an unseen distance, pulling an imaginary dog apart, quite delicately, with her fingers. 'I wonder if I should send you off the same way!' This to Arthur as, smiling sweetly, she strode down to the end of the room, before turning and striding back. Pushing her face into Arthur's, and I did notice how he winced as her awful breath struck him, she asked him, 'Don't you think I am kind?' She smirked when he glowered at her and said, 'But of course I am kind. I was going to add you to my gargoyle collection.

164

But now,' she smiled sweetly, 'I have you at my mercy. So while I think about how I can dispose of you…,' she snapped her fingers and four Cyclops came rushing into the room.

Apart from the fact that each of them had only one eye in the middle of where two eyes should have been, they had the appearance of men but they were so skinny that they were almost skeletal, their skin looking like dried up, sunburned leather sticking to their bones.

I believe both Arthur and I thought we could easily deal with them as they looked too brittle to be strong, but their appearance belied their strength. They divided and ran at us, with one pair on either side of us they each took an arm apiece and sped us off down yet another dark tunnel, our feet not even touching the ground. We tried to struggle and get the better of our captors but they held us with an iron grip us as though both of us were caught in a metal vice. We had no opportunity to escape.

On entering the tunnel the eyes of the Cyclops adapted to the darkness and, to our amazement, switched themselves on like beams of light. Rushing us along at breakneck speed, they eventually reached the end of the corridor and, without ceremony, we were literally thrown into a cell. As we landed in a heap against the far wall our breath was knocked from our bodies and we slid down onto the floor, rubbing the areas of flesh that would eventually come up black and blue. Fortunately we suffered no broken bones.

'Well, Percy,' said a quite winded Arthur, 'what do you think we should do now?' He had got up and started to feel around the cell. I rubbed my arm, where I had fallen awkwardly, and judged where Arthur might be. Between us we spent the next hour feeling round our prison and trying to see if there might be some way out. It was built with huge blocks of stone and, banging on them, it confirmed that there would be no way out that way. The door was solid wood with no grille or window in it.

The cell was pitch black.

Before long, with the cold gradually creeping into our bones, we sat down and held on to each other for warmth. Speculating on what might happen to us and wondering who this wretched woman was, we started to drift off to sleep, or were we suffering from hypothermia?

'Percy, help me! They are going to throw me into the lake in this cage! I won't even be able to try to swim away and the naiad will get me!' Cabal was calling me and the agony in his words woke me up as nothing else could have and made me begin to sweat with fear for him. I felt such a lump forming in my throat as I thought of him either drowning or being eaten by those awful water sprites. What on earth could I do?

As I pulled my tunic away from my neck, so as to help me breathe more easily, my fingers came up against the cord that held the dragon dust. I jumped to my feet. We couldn't help Cabal locked away here and we wouldn't be able to help him if we were transported back to Merlin's cave – it was so far away, but we could certainly help him more if we were free, than locked up. Merlin would know what to do.

'Percy, my friend, help m...'.

I had a terrible fear as his thoughts were severed from my mind believing that it may, even now, be too late; that he might be struggling under the water, fighting for breath or against the naiad. I tried to mind speak with him but there was no response. I tried also not to let my mind imagine the worst. Well, if we couldn't help him here, I reckoned Merlin would be able to do something about it, that is, if Merlin was in his cave. We hadn't seen him for so long, I was beginning to wonder if he really existed at all. Still, I was hoping that he did, particularly for Cabal's sake; also if we didn't get away from that smelly excuse for a woman, Arthur at the very least would end up dead, so I called him over to me.

He was struggling to wake himself up but began feeling his way toward the sound of my voice. Once I felt his touch,

166

I put my arm around his shoulders, took a pinch of the dust and threw it above us. It was still hard to come to terms with exactly what I was throwing over us, but even in the darkness of the cell I could see the dust glittering as it settled onto and around us.

Then we were both blinking our eyes and shaking our heads due to the brightness of the light, as we materialised in Merlin's cave. One of the first things I saw, when I could focus properly, was Wite sitting cross-legged against the wall eating an apple. Surprised at seeing him and forgetting the urgency that had necessitated our escape, I asked Merlin, 'How did he get here?'

'Through the standing stone! I needed him to do something for me,' he replied matter-of-factly and then, staring at me beneath one haughtily raised eyebrow, demanded, 'More to the point, young man, what are you two doing here? I gather you used the dust? I hope you realise how precious that stuff is! I have just about run out, you know!'

My mind suddenly came back to the urgency of the situation and, almost tripping over my own tongue in a hurry to get everything out, I tugged on Merlin's arm, stumbling over the words, 'Merlin, we got into an old - well, not so old really, witch's castle but she caught us. She locked us in a cell while she said she had to think of a way to kill Arthur. She's got Rhianne there somewhere as well because we found a bit of her dress! Also, we must hurry and save Cabal. He's been captured by that mad woman who's going to throw him into the lake and the naiad'll eat him. There's no time to waste! How far is it to the lake from here and …'.

'Whoa, shhhhh. What on earth are you going on about? You are making no sense at all! Cabal! Arthur! Rhianne! You'd better start at the beginning, lad, as I have no idea what you are talking about. And, Cabal can look after himself.'

'No! He can't! He's caged up and can't get out!'

Although Arthur was obviously shaken up and bewildered by his sudden transportation from dark cell to brightly lit cave, once he saw Merlin, he put two and two together, accepting that Merlin's magic had been the power behind everything that had happened, and quickly interjected, 'What are you talking about Percy? Cabal went off to get the men to help us find Rhianne. He's probably somewhere in the castle with them now, because we haven't seen him since. You aren't ill, are you?' Arthur was suddenly all concern. I had completely forgotten that Arthur knew nothing about mind speaking. Also, he had either forgotten what the witch had said about feeding Cabal "to the fishes" or he was suffering from amnesia. Had he bumped his head against the cell wall? I couldn't think about that right now – the urgency of Cabal's plight was the major concern here. We could feel Arthur's bumps later.

Merlin stopped what he was doing and, concentrating more on what I was saying, started to realise the seriousness of the situation. He told us both to sit down and speak to him one at a time, starting with me. I explained that we did not have much time, because Cabal was about to be thrown into the lake inside a cage, that is, if he wasn't already in there. I tried not to look at Arthur but I could feel his eyes boring into the back of my head as I spoke, waiting for an opportunity to interrupt. I saw Merlin hold up his hand more than once to silence Arthur, who was certainly not happy to wait. I did not need to tell Merlin how I knew what had happened to Cabal as Merlin also could use the Old Way of communicating but I realised that I would need my wits about me when Arthur started asking questions. I was panting, when I had finished, as though I had run a marathon.

Merlin, deep in thought, started to stroke his chin as he considered the problem. Arthur, meanwhile, was almost jumping up and down in an effort to let Merlin know that I must be in some state of shock as none of what I had said had

actually happened. He knew that the mad witch had said she
had him caged up, but that was probably not true at all. There
was no proof she had him. She was probably just making it
up to scare them.

'It's Mabel!' he stated.

'Who?' we chorused.

'Mad Mab! I wondered when she would show herself
again. It's been nearly twelve years since she did her last
dastardly act.'

Merlin then took us both by surprise as he strode off down
a tunnel, beckoning us to follow. He took us into a room that
held an enormous array of bottles and jars perched on every
available ledge or table. He rummaged around at the back of
a shelf, wiping cobwebs away without a thought; realising
what he was after was not there. I began to feel very
frustrated that he couldn't find what he was looking for – if he
had tried to tidy everything up, perhaps he would be a bit
better at finding things! Didn't he realise the seriousness of
the situation! He looked over at me with one raised eyebrow
and I felt myself blushing. I really would have to keep my
thoughts under control, especially where he was concerned.

Tutting, as he searched, he poked around the
paraphernalia on the table until he came to a peculiar small
green jar with a cork stopper. Humming another of his
tuneless tunes (it could have been the same one all the time
for all I knew) he prised open the bottle, using what must
have been a very tough thumbnail, sniffed the contents,
choked a little and then nodded. 'Yes,' was all he said, in a
slightly coarse whisper, as he strode back into the main
chamber of the cave, beckoning us to follow - as if we needed
to be told! Again that look from him (and blush from me)!

Before long he started to hum again. As I listened to him,
in the back of my mind I wondered just how he could ever
have been a famous bard. I understood that they usually sang
their stories – and all had the most melodious singing voices.

Listening to him, much later, I had to admit that there was a resonance to Merlin's voice that was mesmerizing - he was also an expert harpist – I had seen his famous harp hanging up in the cave – and that instead of singing he spoke the words with that, peculiar to himself, hypnotising voice as he plucked at the harp strings. Also, the harp itself appeared to be singing, so magical were its notes. Yes, when Merlin performed before an audience, no one moved - they were awestruck. However, getting back to the story.

Sitting us both down in front of the huge Glass he explained to us what he was about to do. Arthur, at a loss as to what this was all about, was told by Merlin to just trust him - there was no time for explanation at the moment. 'We have to try and concentrate on the Glass. We've got to get inside that castle. I need you to tell me something you saw in the castle that we could make appear in the Glass. Once you both agree, and try to find it in the Glass, it will be easy. Then, I want you to shake this bottle,' he lifted it up in front of us, 'using your finger as a stopper, and then lick off the small amount that will stick to your fingers. It is important that we all lick our fingers at the same time, if we are to arrive at the same place together. I will show you.' He shook the bottle, holding it between his finger and thumb, the open end being against his forefinger. He showed us the thick green blob that stuck to it. He then handed the bottle to Arthur who did the same, and then to me. Again, it was another obnoxiously smelly potion. 'I will count "one, two, three" and then we all lick our fingers together. Understand?' We nodded. 'Good. Now think of something in the castle that you can both remember.'

We sat for a while, staring at the Glass and suggested a couple of things each, which the other couldn't remember. Neither of us wanted to mention the woman; the last thing we needed was to come face to face with her again, especially after Merlin had told us who he suspected she was. Suddenly

Arthur suggested the cauldron that the wrinkled old man had been stirring.

'Yes,' I said, 'I remember that!' Hoping that the witch was not in the kitchen, we all looked into the Glass until very gradually the cauldron appeared, then the fire and the hearth, along with that part of the room, which, at the moment, was empty of anyone. Once Merlin saw the room reflected through the Glass, he turned to us to check whether we, too, were sure of what we saw.

When he was satisfied, he whispered, 'Fine, now both of you concentrate on the Glass and get ready to lick your fingers. Ready?' We nodded. 'One, two, three.' We all licked our fingers. Wow, what an amazing experience! It felt like we were all flying through the sky on top of a rocket. Everything was shooting past us at a terrific speed. It lasted, what, about ten seconds and then we were all in, what did Merlin call her? - Mad Mab's kitchen.

I looked at Merlin and Arthur but all I could see was a vague impression of them, like vaporous outlines – like Cabal when he attacked those two boys on the farm, I recalled. I spoke to them, but it was as though, as I mouthed the words, I was a million miles away, and hardly any sound came out - a bit like the feeling I got when I once had to have gas to have a tooth out. I saw Merlin and Arthur nod in slow motion and then, as if by silent, mutual agreement, we all turned and started to walk towards the doorway that would lead to the lake.

I felt relieved when I heard Cabal again, but he, too, seemed a long way off. It was an enormous relief to know that he was still alive. He was calling my name and I could see that Merlin also heard him. But not Arthur! We spoke to him in our minds to try and encourage him that we were on our way but as he just continued to call, it was obvious that he could not at this time hear us. Perhaps in our present state he was not conscious of us.

Before we had taken half a dozen steps or so, a door opened behind us and we all turned, again in unison, and, it seemed, in slow motion, to see who had come in. Of course, it had to be the witch - and it was - together with the old man. Arthur and I were petrified. We tried to find somewhere to hide but we couldn't move and as we gaped at the pair of them, the woman started to spin around, looking this way and that, bending down to search under the table. 'Who is there?' she screamed, eyes swivelling in her head as she surveyed the room. 'I know you're here. Come out!' She carried on searching the room while the little old man stood there, not knowing what was going on and looking terrified, the little bit of hair at the base of his skull standing out sideways and the bit on top standing up straight - a most ridiculous sight! She sniffed, as if she could find us by trying to smell us. In the back of my mind I wondered how she could smell anything other than her own rotten stench – surely that must overcome any other scents in her vicinity. But they do say (and who, by the way, are these "they" people and where do "they" get their information from?) – hmm, yes "they" do say that smelly people get used to their own horrid odour and eventually aren't aware of it any more! The worse for the rest of us, eh? So maybe, the witch could smell other things, over and above herself!

Merlin, Arthur and I, ignoring her, turned, as one, and continued out of the room, leaving Mab searching for us high and low.

We passed a room in which hung the four Cyclops, each one of them drooping limply from hooks on the wall like old coats, or, more, like rag dolls. Merlin, and thus we, went into the room and checked them over. I saw him nod a couple of times as if agreeing with someone and then we came floating back out of the room.

We carried on down the corridor until we came to a door, bolted at the top. 'That's it,' I thought. 'Now we're stuck!'

Merlin, however, disappeared straight through the door without opening it, so we followed. It was a weird sensation going through something solid but at the time it seemed completely natural. I thought there might have been a bit of a strain to get into and then maybe a pull or drag to get out, but, there was no feeling of a door or any other obstruction being there at all.

We re-appeared on the other side of the door and were surprised – well, I was if no-one else was - to find ourselves facing a small jetty that ran out into the lake. At the end of the jetty was a cage in which crouched poor Cabal.

Now, I think I have mentioned that there were various gifts that those who were blessed with the Old Way could have. Although Merlin, Arthur and I seemed to move as one, in whatever state it was that we were in, Cabal couldn't see us, so it soon became obvious that this was not one of the gifts he had, not at that particular time at any rate. I tried to mind speak to him but, although I could grasp some of the thoughts going through his head, he couldn't hear me and as he couldn't see any of us there was no way we could give him any reassurance.

He looked so pathetic, squashed up in that cage; it was obvious that the enclosure was much too small for him as he was scrunched up in the most uncomfortable manner within it.

I saw a boat, with very high sides, moored up and two men who were about to cast off; they had finished loading up what was on the jetty and had only the cage left to take. They were a long way off and, as I have already said, we seemed like we were moving in slow motion, so it appeared that we just weren't going to reach the boat in time to save my friend. My stomach did a somersault as I thought of the terrible end that awaited Cabal and, looking back, due to the fact that everything was going so slowly, the somersault seemed to last minutes instead of seconds.

I thought I might be sick - no I couldn't do that - I'd choke if it went on for too long, as everything at the moment seemed to be taking forever!

However, even with all these disheartening thoughts coursing through my mind, Merlin continued on his way, and, oh no, started humming again! What on earth could make the man hum at a time like this? Had he no idea of the importance and urgency of the situation? Was he not too scared that Cabal might be thrown into the lake? Had he no feelings at all?

It was then that I saw the most amazing thing I have ever seen in my life. As Merlin hummed, there was a brightening of the sky, a glow, which started on the far side of the forest and rose, filling the sky with a riot of colour, which was eventually reflected in the lake. I thought perhaps that morning was coming or a full moon was rising. Then, with my mouth dropping open in amazement, I saw the most incredibly stunning creature rising up into the sky. It was huge! I thought it must have been at least the size of Buckingham Palace. It wasn't, of course, but it just seemed like it at the time. If one were to have to describe its main colour, it would have to be brilliant red but then when it moved, sinuously, undulating, the colours changed through all the different shades of purple, deep blue, gold and green that glowed iridescent and seemed to blend and change as it winged its way into the sky.

We all stopped, oblivious to anything else, to marvel at it as it flew, obviously thoroughly enjoying the experience of flight. It flew straight up into the air, lighting the whole sky with its brilliance, and then appeared to dance as it swooped to and fro, swirling and dipping, waltzing on air!

I sensed, rather than heard, Merlin continue humming his tuneless tune and, as it got louder, could feel myself getting very irritated with him. He would spoil this astonishing experience - why was he making such an almighty racket?

174

Then, to my amazement, I heard the creature start humming along with him. Even though I had often wondered why Merlin insisted on trying to sing, when it was obviously not his forte, I now had an understanding of it. It *was* music; it was also *beautiful* music and, how can I describe it other than to say it was, otherworldly. There was definitely something exciting about it – magical!

Anyway, getting back to this wonderful sight, I was aware, out of the corner of my eye, of the two men almost falling over each other as they jumped out of the boat and bolted straight along the jetty as though all the demons in hell were after them, past us – without seeing us of course (although they did look vaguely familiar to me) - and on into the castle. Looking back, they were quite comical in their haste. I wonder what that old witch did to them for disobeying her commands! But I wasn't concerned for them in the slightest.

We stood there for I really do not know how long watching the amazing spectacle being danced and played out before us and then, finally, the music stopped.

The creature let out a roar of triumph straight up into the atmosphere, just like the victor in a battle, and as it did so a flame erupted from its throat, shooting upwards and lighting up the night sky for probably miles around with the beauty of its brilliance.

Then it turned and looked directly at us - huge eyes, pale yellow irises with greenish-black elongated pupils like a cat - for a good few seconds before moving - so I realised that it, at least, could see us. Then, it circled twice more and, sweeping down in a graceful arc, using giant claws, very gently picked up the cage that held Cabal, flew up over the treetops and disappeared, the colourful luminosity gradually fading as it went.

I felt as though I had been holding my breath for hours and then, as I let it out, realised that we had turned and were moving off, alongside the castle walls. Once we were safely away from the water's edge, Merlin pulled us all together, threw some dust in the air and we were instantly back in his cave.

'Well,' he murmured thoughtfully, 'that was very interesting. Yes, and very gratifying.'

'Was that all he thought of that amazing experience,' I thought. *'Oops!'*

He turned and raised an eyebrow at me! Then smiled.

He took us both along to yet another side room in the cave, made us sit down and gave us a refreshing drink of lemonade.

The next thing we knew, we were waking up on some fur skins on the floor of the cave. Merlin was nowhere to be seen but there was a note telling us that everything had worked out just as he planned and that we were to wait for him here until he came back.

I looked at Arthur and asked him 'Well, did he think we would just go off on a jaunt without knowing what had happened? But, what did you make of the creature in the sky?'

Although Arthur had an amazing sense of fun, when things were serious he couldn't even think of smiling let alone being merry. This was one of those occasions. He looked at me with those solemn eyes of his, shook his head as if to clear it so as to concentrate on what I was saying and then replied, 'What creature?'

'The dragon – the one Merlin sang with last night!' I responded.

'Merlin sang with? What are you going on about? Merlin can't sing,' he said. 'Everyone knows that! I really think you must be unwell. I keep forgetting you are only ten. You have been acting very peculiarly of late and, once again, I don't know what you are talking about. In fact you seem to be talking a mighty lot of rubbish lately. I shall have to get

176

Merlin to give you a physic.' At that, he sat down on the fur rug and said that, as he was still tired, he would rest a little longer and suggested, if I wanted to get better, to do the same. With that, he turned over and settled back to sleep.

I lay down again on my back and, staring at the ceiling, wondered if I could possibly be unwell. I felt fine and, after feeling my head – which had no bumps on it, although a few bruises I had gained in Mab's castle - thought I must be OK. But then I had been having some very strong dreams lately – or were they dreams! Perhaps I would discuss it with Merlin when he came back. He might have a cure for it. On the other hand, he might need to have a look at Arthur, who may have had a bump on the head in the mad witch's cell.

FIFTEEN

I could feel myself drifting back into that peculiar trance-like state somewhere between being half-awake and half-asleep. I don't know how long I lay like that but I was suddenly jolted awake by being pounced upon by a chronically happy animal. I looked up to find two large paws on my shoulders, pinning me to the floor, and one slobbering tongue licking my face. I had just started to sit up after he had bounded off, running - in an almost sideways position - around the room a couple of times, when he came tearing back to knock me over again. I couldn't help laughing as Cabal started sneezing with joy.

Arthur sat up and grinned at the scene before him, laughing every time I started to get up and Cabal knocked me back down again.

Cabal caught sight of Arthur and went through the whole rigmarole again with him; it was then my time to laugh at him. Chaos reigned for a crazy few minutes. Finally, order was restored when Merlin came striding back into the room. He had a sack thrown over one shoulder and carried a glass jar under his arm, which appeared to be full of roots.

'Well, this is a fine thing, eh lads?' he chuckled as he stood in the middle of the cave. 'Glad to have him back?'

'Oh yes,' both Arthur and I chorused. 'How did you find him? Where was he?' I asked him.

'Later,' he replied. 'I have to store these bits and pieces before I forget. I don't want them to end up useless.'

'What have you got there?' asked Arthur.

'I've got the dismantled cage that Cabal was locked in; perhaps you would like to re-assemble it for me. I have some dragon droppings in this sack, which must be stored at once, and I have some naiad root in the glass jar. I need to get the root secured in a dry place, so that I can grind it up. I think

178

I've found a good use for it - and soon,' he grinned wickedly. His voice faded away as he strode off down one of the tunnels. 'I won't be long,' he looked over his shoulder and called to us. 'Give the hound some food and water. He's mighty hungry.'

Cabal was sitting in the middle of the cave and wagging his tail as though he was frightened it might stop working.

'Come on Cab, let's get some food into you.' We poured him some water, which he lapped up, still wagging his tail. Arthur threw him a huge beef shinbone that still had plenty of meat hanging from it and Cabal fell upon it with a will; the tail stopped wagging - eating was a much more serious occupation.

While Cabal was eating, Arthur, now wide-awake, decided to explore the cave and wandered off.

After a short while Merlin returned looking exceptionally pleased with himself.

'Tell us where you found Cabal, Merlin? And what was that that we did? It felt like sleepwalking! And what on earth was that stuff you gave us to drink? I can't recall another thing until just before you came in.'

Merlin walked over to the huge hanging Glass and called me over to join him. 'The drink was nothing special - just something to help you sleep after your frightful experience. But, the sleep walking is something known in the trade as "ghosting"! It's sort of being there, but not being there, if you know what I mean! I shall teach you all about that another time, but first of all, I think we ought to see what we can do about Rhianne. I understand, from extraordinary sources, that she has tried to escape but, unfortunately, is trapped again. I could see her, and a rather astonishing looking man, at the end of a dark tunnel. A large stone was blocking their exit. Now, I have tried to get into that tunnel but Mad Mab has put a spell at that entrance and, unfortunately, I cannot yet deduce what type of magic she's used and it might take me some time to discover what she has done.

'However, I was able to track the dragon's flight, primarily through listening for Cabal and when I eventually got to them, not only was there a wonderful great pile of droppings which was quite ripe – the dragon must have, er "dropped it" before she flew to save the hound – and just right for collection but there was also a large amount of naiad roots for me to gather as well. I had almost run out of the root and this lot will keep me going for quite a long while. A most fortuitous turn of events.' As he winked at me with another wicked grin, I thought how great it was to be his friend. I was to learn that when he was with people he did not know or, more particularly, did not trust, his face was inscrutable and he appeared very unfriendly and unapproachable. But now, with me, it was alive with emotion and glee. I could almost imagine what he was thinking of getting up to next as I caught the odd word that rushed through his mind.

Arthur re-entered the main chamber of the cave and grinned with pleasure at Merlin.

'Ah, Arthur, come over here,' Merlin beckoned him over toward the Glass. 'There is much to do. I want you to remember the place where you entered the castle; the place where the men were when you and Percy dropped down into the tunnel.' Arthur stood before the Glass remembering.

'You have to rejoin the men and, when you do, I want you to take them to the top of the Tor which you will see as you look due eastwards. It's quite a way and will possibly take you about two hours by horseback or more to get there. From the crest of the Tor you will look down onto the plain and find, in the distance, a circle of standing stones. You do not need to go down to the circle but make camp on the western side of the stones where you will find a rough stone dwelling, rather dilapidated but it will shelter you from the elements. You are to wait for me there. I may be a day or two in arriving, but, as I said, wait for me. The men will need to be rested and ready for what will most probably happen when we are all together again. I shall be sending Percy elsewhere but we all need to play our part if Rhianne is to be rescued. I have organised Wite to meet you there; he will be bringing some pack ponies with him so there will be plenty of food and drink for all of you.'

I had wondered where Wite had gone.

Merlin stood Arthur in front of the Glass and as soon as the castle came into view - the men could be seen sitting despondently beside the entrance, which had not grown any bigger - Merlin threw some dust over Arthur and the next thing that could be seen in the Glass was Arthur striding toward the men. The men jumped up as they saw Arthur and that was the last I saw of him until we met up at the Tor. As Merlin turned toward me the picture faded.

SIXTEEN

'OK Percy, Arthur will do his part and now you have to do yours. Come over here.' I had been standing a few paces away from Arthur, watching what had been going on, and now Merlin took me over to his workbench.

'I am going to give you some naiad root in a small glass container. Now you must remember that this is very dangerous stuff and if you get any on yourself something terrible could happen to you – or worse.' I found it hard to imagine something worse than "terrible" happening to me. 'So listen very carefully to what I want you to do with it,' Merlin continued. He spent the next half an hour giving me instructions and was very patient, as I had to ask him to repeat himself more than once. When I apologised, he just smiled and said it was best I made sure I got it right, as one slip up could cause havoc at best and at worst - well he said that he didn't want to even think about that.

Before long I was standing in front of the Glass. Merlin was sending me back into the castle but this time there was no green blob to lick to make me invisible and I would be going back alone! No, this time, if Mab were around, she would definitely see me. I could feel my stomach start to gurgle a tune and my knees, not to be outdone, joined in by beating time with it. I knew I looked green with fear. Merlin looked across at me and scowled.

'Come, come, Percy, you know you can use the dust if you are really desperate but you need to know that if you do use it this time you will only end up back here and will miss out on a most breathtaking adventure! And,' he said nonchalantly, 'I thought Rhianne had a small place in your heart - best there than a small place in the ground eh? Or stuck high up on a wall!' He knew how to hit hard when necessary.

I felt the uncontrollable blush rising up my neck again anyway and tried hard not to look over at Cabal. Merlin very kindly pretended not to notice.

'So, concentrate now on Mab's kitchen.' He stood behind me with his hands on my shoulders as we stood before the Glass.

Before long the kitchen came into view. There was no one there but that wasn't to say she wouldn't walk in at any moment. Before I had a chance to think any more, Merlin had sprinkled some dust over me and I was once again transported through those castle's walls and stood before that bubbling cauldron. I remembered the door that we had all disappeared through when we were trying to save Cabal and decided that I had to find another exit that would hopefully lead to Rhianne. I didn't want to go down to the lake again, so knew not to use that particular door, and I didn't want to go back through the tunnel that Arthur and I had entered, or should I say had fallen, through. I looked over at the corridor that led to the cell in which Arthur and I had been imprisoned, albeit briefly, by the Cyclops and tried to stop the shivers creeping up my spine.

I tiptoed across the kitchen, away from the cauldron after which I reached the first door that I had not been through. I put my ear to it, listening for any sign of life. Nothing! I was just about to creep along to the next door - which was the only other door I had not been through, when I heard footsteps approaching toward the kitchen from the other side of it. I quickly went back to the door near the fire and, opening it, disappeared through it, thinking to make my escape. Horror of horrors, it was a larder or some sort of store cupboard! What would I do now? It was too late to come out and try one of the other doors. If they needed anything from it, they would find me without any trouble at all and all will have been in vain. There was nowhere to hide inside it and no way out other than the way through which I had come. I stood as still as I could, hardly daring to breathe, believing that whoever was outside must be able to hear my heartbeat, going like the clappers as it was inside my own head. As I listened, with my ear pressed tight up against the wooden door, I could only hear one person moving about. No words were spoken.

As my eyes gradually became accustomed to the darkness and the bright spots and stars eventually started to settle down, I found a very small crack between the door and the frame. I believed that if I bent down a bit more I would be able to see into the room. All well and good but, as I bent down, my backside, which wasn't very big at my age but at this time was obviously colossal, dislodged an earthenware pot that had been sitting on a low shelf and sent it crashing to the floor, sounding, in that confined space, like the almighty explosion of a bomb going off. I held my hands to my ears, grimacing at my misfortune and waiting for the inevitable.

Was I surprised when the door handle was grabbed and the door crashed back on its hinges, as it was yanked open? No, I expected it.

Mab, who chose just that moment to walk into the kitchen to join the old man, grinned wickedly at me; I was still crouched down inside the cupboard with my hands over my ears and my eyes squinting up, surrounded by broken pottery. 'So, little man, I have you back. And where is your other little friend?'

I opened my eyes wide and goggled up at her as I started to stand up again. The tallow man had been shuffling across the room with a bundle of wood for the fire when I had made my big mistake and he had discovered me. Mab turned around and, taking the wood from him, told him to tie me up to the chair, 'and don't worry about tying him too tight either,' she ordered him. He did as he was told and I wondered, in the back of my mind, just how I was supposed to throw any dust over me to get away, with both of my hands

184

tied together behind the back of the chair. '*Thanks a bunch, Merlin,*' I thought.

'What's that? What did you say? Eh? Come on now, I heard you say "Merlin". Is he involved in this? But then, I would expect him to be – him and his infernal plans and his great love for Arthur,' she almost spat out Arthur's name. She strode up to me, still holding the bundle of wood, which she had taken from the old man so as to enable him to tie me up, in the crook of her arm. I had forgotten that she could thought-read even though not really too well and so I hastily put up my guard. Cabby had tried to show me how to do this and Merlin had had a bit more success, but I was still not really that good at it - I kept forgetting and lowering my defences. I stared up at her, trying to look innocent and puzzled at the same time but probably looking more guilty and scared than anything else. I thought for a moment she was going to whack me with the bundle of wood but, after staring at me for a long half-minute, she turned and threw it into the scuttle beside the fire.

'Come, Minion, we shall need the strongest potion we have to get this, this …'. She turned back to me and demanded my name.

Gasping for breath, mainly through my terror but also because she smelled so bad that I was finding it hard to breathe anyway, 'Percival,' I whispered.

She thought it hilarious that I was so frightened and started cackling with laughter. 'Fine, my brave little man' she spluttered sarcastically after a while. Turning towards the old man she said, 'Come with me and let us get my friend Percival here, my most powerful "truth" potion and then afterwards we shall have ourselves a new gargoyle for the castle wall.' She carried on cackling as she disappeared through a doorway, which seemed to lead down a very dark tunnel. 'Perhaps we'll put him directly over the castle entrance. Never had one so young or so pretty before, be quite a change …'. Her voice trailed off as she disappeared down the passageway, the old man shuffling along after her.

I was now in a fix. I tugged at my arms but my hands were securely tied behind the chair by the rope and my feet didn't touch the floor as each ankle was tied to a chair leg. I felt trapped and very vulnerable, tied the way I was. I didn't know what she meant by a new gargoyle but had a squirmy feeling in the pit of my stomach that it might have something to do with me becoming like one of those stone heads on the castle walls. I carried on struggling with my bonds but all I succeeded in doing was making the knots tighter and my wrists very sore, something that brought more mirth to the mad witch when she noticed them. What on earth was I going to do?

Before too long she came bustling back into the room, arms loaded with scrolls and other odds and ends. The tallow man came shuffling back after her with his arms full of bowls and phials filled with different coloured liquids. Smashing everything as she did so and creating quite a few small explosions and mini-smoke fires, Mab swept everything off the table with the back of her arm and placed the scrolls onto it.

After looking through two or three, she sighed with satisfaction as she found the one she wanted. Holding it up to the light to read it through, then keeping it open on the table by placing on each of the four corners any heavy object that came to hand, one being, I noticed, a bronze dagger, another a brass owl, she started, slowly, to gather together the ingredients for her concoction. However, before she'd opened up the scroll I noticed that the table looked more like a butcher's block than anything else as there were more than a few slivers of wood chopped out of it. A horrible shiver went up my spine.

'Right, Minion, light the burner and then I want you to help me mix these ingredients in the dish as I call them out.'

She swirled around and grabbed him by his tallow wick - as I had started calling that bit of hair that stuck up in the middle of his head - and pulling his face very close to hers she growled a whisper, 'and don't get anything wrong or you will be joining this little man - and your brother,' she cackled, 'on the castle walls!'

She started speaking again, this time to me as she stood behind the table and checked the scroll. 'There were some men sitting outside the castle walls. They weren't doing much but another of their number turned up with some ponies and they rode off. Well, you can imagine I don't want anyone else coming here to disrupt my peace ...'.

'Peace! Hmm, I wonder if she knows the meaning of the word,' I thought.

'... so I have sent my Cyclops off to deal with them.'

'Oh, no!' I shivered.

'More pretty trophies for my walls,' she chuckled.

So, I was right to be afraid. It looked very much as though Arthur and the men were being rounded up and they and I were going to be turned into gargoyles. How on earth could I get away and at least try to warn them? I was by now shivering uncontrollably with fear as I thought about what might possibly happen to them - or me. Forcing myself to come back to the present where nothing, as yet, had happened, I turned my eyes as far as they would go to see what she was doing and listened to what the witch was saying to the tallow man.

'Two drops of the green liquid, one white wafer.' She cuffed the old man around the ear, shouting, 'Don't break the wafer, you stupid oaf; it has to dissolve whole. A spoonful of the grey powder.' She stirred these together and I could hear a popping noise. 'Now, gently, one drop at a time until I tell you to stop, mix the red venom into the ground toenails of the giant until it forms a stiff paste.' How revolting - I wanted to throw up! She turned and stared at the old man, as he gingerly lifted the stone jar. 'Don't you dare drop any on *me*! If you do I shall throw the lot over you and you'll burn to a crisp,' she screamed at him. How did she expect him not to spill any with her awful threats hanging over him and that awful odour wafting into his face? The old man was quaking with fear but as carefully as he could, even though he was shaking like a leaf, he started to drip the red, steaming, drops one by one into the bubbling mess that was already cooking in the dish. She was eventually satisfied that she had the right consistency and told the old man to stop. He replaced the stopper in the jar and, by the sweat standing out on his brow and top lip, I could see how relieved he was to put that particular jar down.

But - what was it going to do to me?

'Now, little man, I have to wait until the mixture has cooled and so, while it is doing so, you can either tell me everything you know, voluntarily, or I shall have to make you drink this wonderful concoction, and then you will tell me everything I want to know, but it will have a terrible effect on you as well. I have to warn you that I have only used it twice before and the individuals who drank it were never the same again.

'I remember one man,' warming to her story she started spluttering out drops of spittle as she laughed. 'He was an extremely clever and popular man from the village; everyone looked up to him and asked advice from him and he seemed, well, so wise. But he wasn't very wise to try and stand up to me now, was he? So, once he had drunk my mixture, he believed, after the initial effects of the potion had worn off, that he was a cockerel. He strutted about cockadoodledooing and pecking at his dinner for a twelve-month before he came to his senses and, then, when he did, was so ashamed of himself that he packed up and left. We've never seen him since!' She acted out the scene and howled with laughter, slapping her thighs and almost falling off her stool, as she recounted the story of the poor man. Her mood changing just as rapidly, she swirled around and shouted at me, 'So, do you want to become a chicken, or are you going to tell me everything I want to know?'

I had had a couple of minutes to think and in that couple of minutes I had come to the conclusion that, even if I did co-operate with her, she wouldn't keep her word to me. She would definitely do something bad either way - probably forcing the potion down my neck. I therefore decided to try and outwit her by spinning some sort of tale and at the same time try as hard as I could to put Merlin's plan into action, although at the present time I did not know how that would happen before it was too late for me. I could feel my heart in my boots as everything looked like it was going terribly wrong. I had already put up my mind barrier and hoped that Mab couldn't read anything that was currently going through my head that would confirm I was lying or let her know just how sick I was feeling.

Mab was staring at me, waiting expectantly for my answer. 'I will try,' was all I said.

She looked surprised and a bit disappointed as I think she wanted to use her concoction but said, 'Well, there must be a bit of sense in that silly head of yours. But,' and she pressed her foul-smelling face close to mine almost felling me with her breath, 'if I get one little hint that you are lying to me, the potion goes down your throat. Minion, here, will hold your nose and pull your head back and I shall take great delight in pouring it into your pretty little mouth! I haven't done this for a long time now and I *do* find it great fun.' Off she went again, howling with laughter.

It took almost three attempts before she could eventually pull herself together, take a few deep breaths, and demand, 'Now that you've proved he is involved, tell me, where is Merlin? Which cave is he using at the moment? Does he have any new potions? Does he know you are here? Does he know where "here" is? More importantly, where is Arthur?' Her face darkened suddenly. 'To think I had him in my grasp and he got away!' She stamped her foot in frustration. 'You do not know how angry I was when I found that you had both escaped, but Minion here knows, don't you?' she spun around and leapt at the man who held up his hands to ward of another attack.

'So,' she turned slowly back to me and demanded, 'what do you know, eh? Eh? Whoa, whoa, Mab, he cannot answer all these questions at once,' she chided herself, laughing and almost going over the edge again. 'So, little man, first question first. Where's Merlin?'

'The last time I saw him he was in his cave.'

She goggled at me for a second or two and then, spluttering, said 'I know he's in a cave, you dolt. He's always in a cave! But which one? Eh? Is it the one at Tintagel, the one at Cadbury? Glastonbury? Come on, come on, which one?' She stamped her foot again in fury, just like a spoilt child.

She was obviously a manic-depressive, the way her moods swung so rapidly! I had got to the point where I knew I had to answer her very swiftly, just to try to keep her on the sane side of her mood swings.

'I don't know the name of the place but I know that my dad had taken me to the place that is a good few miles past Cadbury.'

'Ahh,' she sighed, 'now I know. Well, we will have to see what we can do to trap him there'. She had a very self-satisfied look on her face as she skipped around the room, wafting her stench around.

I would have tried to speak to Merlin, to warn him, through my mind but had found in the past that if I was too far away it didn't work. Probably similar to trying to physically talk to someone who was too far away: even shouting wouldn't help. The main reason, though, was the

190

fact that if I tried to do so, Mab would latch onto it in a jiffy. That just would not do. This thought ran through my mind in a flash as I followed Mab around the room with my eyes. Merlin, I decided, would have to look after himself and I was sure he was capable of doing just that. More to the point, though, was whether he was in a position to help me! I had an awful and growing suspicion that I was soon to need help or some sort of an escape route but reckoned that I was going to be on my own on this one. I replied with half-truths to the rest of her grilling, after I realised that I had more than likely dropped Merlin in it, but she appeared to be satisfied with my answers.

She finally turned and, stroking her chin, stared at me, as a malicious grin spread slowly over her face and I felt my heart sink once again into my boots. 'It seems such a pity to waste my brew,' she purred, 'and I think I have all the information I need'. Her face went hard but, even so, she looked very excited at what she was about to do. 'Hold his nose, Minion, while I pour it down his throat.'

SEVENTEEN

'Well, boys,' said Jack, 'let's stop for a while and stretch our legs; give poor old Duke a rest. Some of this stuff in the cart makes it quite a heavy load for him to pull, especially as we have been going uphill for the past few miles.' They pulled over to the side of the road where Jack loosed the bit and checked some of the clasps to make sure nothing was rubbing the horse and further secured the cart and equipment. Duke started to crop the grass while the boys climbed up onto a style and looked into the field. Once satisfied, he joined the boys and pointed out one or two places that could be seen from this high vantage point.

'Come on, granddad. What happened to you then? Did you drink the potion?' Danny and Ben's questions were once again tumbling over one another.

'I think I had better get back to Rhianne first.'

'Oh, no! Can't you just tell us if you drank it? Just to put us out of our misery!

'Sorry, lads, that would spoil the story!' He sat down on the grassy bank and leaned back against a tree, looking very pleased with himself as he saw the effect he was having on the boys. Danny told him that it wasn't fair that he wouldn't tell them if he drank the potion or not. Jack just grinned at them and continued.

'Rhianne and Salazar had come to the end of the tunnel but, where there should have been a door, there was a huge rock blocking the exit. Salazar walked up to the rock and stared at it for a few moments. Rhianne, who had thought that freedom was so close, collapsed onto the floor. She was too upset even to cry. It was then that they heard sounds coming down the tunnel. They both turned to peer back down through the darkness. First they saw a gradual lightening, as someone approached with a torch. They then got a whiff of a fairly unpleasant odour as a breeze wafted it toward them. Rhianne started to shake. Then finally they saw Mab and the old jailer man on the far side of the tunnel at the edge of the water. Mab shading her eyes with her hand from the glare of the torch peered down the passageway and spying Rhianne started chuckling.

'So, my pretty young thing; thought you'd get away did you? Well, how wrong can you be?' She looked down at the expanse of water between her and the girl and considered the best way to get across. Obviously she couldn't get wet - she might wash off years of power! She looked around and eventually her eyes stopped as they alighted on the old man.

As Rhianne desperately tried to think of what to do next, she watched as Mab tried to get the tallow man to pick her up and carry her across. You will appreciate it when I remind you that she didn't wash. Well because of the overwhelming odour, the poor man was almost fainting when the woman tried to climb onto his back. As this water was about two feet deep at its deepest point, it soon became obvious that she would have to get a little wet and even this would have been too much of a wash for her. Apart from anything else, her skirts draped themselves around the poor man's face and, as he couldn't see to stop himself, they both tumbled onto the floor. It would have been quite comical, under different circumstances, to watch this little old man trying to pick up a much bigger woman, especially one who would, due to her close proximity, make him pass out before he'd gone more than a few steps. However, thinking that capture was seconds away, at that time, Rhianne was petrified.

She let out her breath in relief when, after a while, it was seen that they were not going to be able to cross the expanse of water in the tunnel; it was obvious the little man was just not capable of carrying Mad Mab. She slapped the poor man a good few times on top of his head with the flat of her hands after his knees had buckled under the strain and then gave up, striding angrily back along the passageway.

'I'll be back! You can't get away!' She turned to Minion. 'Stay here while I go and get my travel potion.' She strode off down the tunnel, taking the torch with her and leaving the old man's side of the tunnel in darkness. Why she hadn't sent the old man across to get her, Rhianne would never know.

Once she had gone, Rhianne turned round to speak to Salazar. Her heart leapt inside her. He was gone! 'Salazar,' she whispered, not wanting the old man to hear her, and forgetting to mind speak, 'where are you?' No answer. She suddenly remembered that she could mind speak and called him again that way. There was still no answer and she wondered if she had imagined the ability or, if she had not, whether she had somehow lost it. *'Have you hidden yourself in the mantle of invisibility?'* she queried. Still no answer. She decided that if she held both arms out as far as possible, so as to touch the sides of the walls, and walked toward the end of the tunnel, she would, eventually, be able to touch him. She walked from the edge of the water, right up to the rock but he was not there. The old man watched this odd behaviour and must have thought she had gone out of her mind. Similarly, Rhianne's thoughts were following the same pattern, *'I must be going mad,'* she said to herself on a sob. Leaning back against the rock, she was surprised to find it exuded warmth; however, of Salazar and the mantle there was no sign.

EIGHTEEN

Back at the cave, Merlin was just finishing reading up on an exceptional incantation for authority, as he wanted to make sure he had complete control over the situation that had to arise when he eventually came face to face with that mad old hag - Mab. He was just rolling up the scroll, humming with satisfaction as he did so, when a bright flash of light from the direction of the Glass, heralded the arrival of a guest. Hurrying across the room he came face to face with Salazar. A wide grin spread slowly across his face as he greeted the extraordinary looking man. Salazar looked at Merlin and in the same split second they both realised that they were of the same source, but different order, of druids. They bowed to one another and Merlin greeted him in the correct but completely mysterious language, incomprehensible to anyone else, of the High Druid Order. Salazar responded to him in the same way but spoke only through his mind, after explaining that he had taken a vow of silence.

Once the formalities had been fulfilled Merlin set refreshments before the man and, although he was bursting with curiosity and questions, kept his peace, observing the correct procedure until the man, once refreshed, eventually looked up at him, ready to proceed.

Over the next hour Salazar told Merlin about his life in Britain and how he had finally come to the here and now.

'My father came to Britain with the Romans about forty years ago, just before they were recalled to Rome. He was slave to a man called Justus Fluvius. Justus Fluvius was not a very healthy man, suffering much from bad circulation due, in part, to the damp weather in this accursed land. However, my father, being a druid of the highest order and with a considerable knowledge of herbs, potions and the like, was able to alleviate a lot of the pain from which the Roman

suffered and, thus, the man found he couldn't do without him. As is the way of things when you spend so much time with someone – even in a slave/master relationship - you either become friends or you become enemies. Well, they became firm friends and Justus Fluvius, to show his favour and to make sure that my father was content, gave his consent for him to marry a young woman that he had fallen in love with who was also a slave. Then I was born. I grew up in the same household as my father and spent some of the happiest days of my life there. My mother was a very loving soul and that, together with a father who spent every available hour with me that he could, made me a very contented child indeed. I can remember my mother very well, even though she died during my seventh year. After that, my father taught me, when he found I was receptive, the secrets of the knowledge of the Old Way. I grew proficient and, together with my father, we succeeded so well, being able to heal sick people, give prophecies and the like, that we, due to the great gifts and favours we received, were able, eventually, to purchase our freedom. However, as I said, my father and Justus Fluvius were by now great friends, and were growing somewhat old and comfortable together so, although we were free, he elected to stay in his household. Justus Fluvius had said to my father that he had already made arrangements for him to be freed once he had died, but that it was better he show initiative and prudence by purchasing his own freedom before that time.

'The Roman must have known, for, as is with the way of all flesh, he died shortly thereafter and, not long after that, so did my father - unusual that, in a druid, as they tend to live on for years, as you know. I believe that they had enjoyed one another's company so much in this life that my father just wanted to go to be with his best friend in the next – besides, there was no one left who could play chess as well as he! This said with a wry smile.

196

'I stayed on at the villa for a short while but eventually decided that I had to follow the way that was calling me. However, before I left I fell in love with and married the most wonderful person I have ever met – Jasmine. I was able to purchase her freedom as I had, by then, become very wealthy indeed.'

Thinking about his wife, his shoulders slumped; he fell silent and his face became extremely sad. Merlin did not interrupt his reverie but waited silently until the man was ready to continue. Recalling himself to the present, the man eventually did so.

'We lived within the fortress of Portchester for some few years but then, as I said, I continued to practise my arts and, as I did so, felt the call to continue my travels north. In fact, the call became so strong that I knew I had no choice - it was ordained for me to do so. Some way into our journey, we came upon a castle, deep in the forest, beside a lake. It was an evil place, as we would soon discover.. The most peculiar thing was that I did not read any of the signs of the sickness within it. With hindsight, I believe it must have been enchanted and that enchantment had befuddled my brain. Also, the rain had been falling constantly for days and we were both soaked through, chilled to the bone and exhausted when we arrived there; too tired, I am afraid, to have been aware of the malevolence in the surrounding atmosphere.

'My father had often reminisced on the beauty of Africa: the warmth, not only of the land but also of the people, the vibrant colours and the food. I believe I must have been dreaming about what my father had told me of his homeland and was yearning for some warmth and beauty - I was certainly not aware of the aura of evil surrounding that place. However, I digress - I was talking about that accursed forest and castle. We hammered on the castle gates and were eventually escorted into the keep, where we met the witch. At that time, of course, I did not know she was a witch.

197

'She smelled awful but seemed friendly enough, even though somewhere in the recesses of my numbed brain, I felt that something was not quite right. I have thought long and hard about this and the only conclusion I can come to is that we must have been drawn there under some sort of spell.

'We were taken to a room on an upper floor where a big fire burned in the hearth and a peculiar little man brought us some refreshment. Jasmine and I were grateful for the respite from the cold and rain and were only too pleased to remove our wet garments and warm ourselves before those roaring flames. We put on dry clothes while we draped the sodden ones over benches before the fire to dry.

'After eating a few mouthfuls of the food and drinking a little wine, we fell into bed and slept the sleep of exhaustion, or, more likely, it might have been something else!

'The next morning, as we dressed in our now dried travelling clothes, we thought to thank our benefactor before continuing our journey. We came out of our room and, walked to the head of the stairs where we were greeted by the woman. She bade us good morning and escorted us into her kitchen, where she set before us a mountain of food to choose from, so that we could break our fast. We thanked her not only for the food but also for her hospitality and she smiled back at us, but only with her mouth not, as I noticed now that I was more alert, with her eyes. I felt a little uncomfortable but tried to set it aside as I ate some porridge and drank a little beer. It was, I thought, just my unfamiliarity with the people of this strange land, who tended to be very suspicious of strangers and who, unfortunately - because of the cold I believed – wash only when it is warm enough to do so or when they deem it extremely necessary! This woman looked as though she never reached either of those conclusions!

'When we had had a few mouthfuls we arose from the table to take our leave but the woman said that it would be considerate of me if I gave her something in return for her *kindness. I was more than a little confused, as I had always thought that strangers, especially travellers in distress, should be helped if one had the means to do so, and, looking at the pile of food still sitting on the table, this household certainly had the means.*

'I asked her what I could possibly do for her and, even now, I shiver at her reply.

'"I need to be able to exterminate someone. I do not wish to say who it is or why; suffice it to say it has to be done. I have a small crystal that has told me you would be coming this way and that you have supremacy of power in the Old Way. I have a little knowledge of the Old Way but my understanding, I have to admit, is limited. I am still learning, you see! You know and will thus tell me the enchantment I need to be able to do this, er, deed."

'I can remember that I looked at her in horror. Jasmine, who was holding my hand at the time, gripped mine so hard that her nails almost broke the skin in the palm of my hand - I could feel her fear. 'I do not understand what you mean,' I replied.

'I couldn't believe it when she turned toward me with a face that was so suffused with anger and with lips that, because they curled back over her teeth, made her looked almost feral. Stamping her foot she screamed at me, "Don't lie! You understand me completely! You will do as I say or it will be the worse for you. I might not have your great powers but I do have supremacy in one particular area that seems to have gone out of fashion at the moment and if you do not do as I say I shall have no choice but to implement it. I must warn you, though, that I have not yet perfected its reversal, so it could be that if I have to use it, it will stay forever that way. Now, tell me!"

'I can remember that I was so disgusted at what she had suggested that, clamping my lips together and shaking my head, I grasped Jasmine's hand firmly as I turned to leave.

However, as her eyes held mine, I found it an extreme effort of will to pull my gaze away. I eventually did, but before I could take more than a couple of steps, she spoke.

'She had been staring at me for a long half-minute and then said, very calmly for her, "Stop!" I turned and looked at her. "You will live to regret your decision, my friend, but you will eventually give me the spell. You think you do, but you have absolutely no choice in the matter," she snapped.

'The next few minutes are still utter confusion in my mind. It seemed as though the room filled with smoke, swirls, flashing lights of mainly dark green, blood red and grey, miniature explosions and unintelligible incantations, the like of which I had never before come across in my learning. It was as though hell had come to visit and complete chaos reigned. My father, you, of course, will understand, had taught me only that which was for the common good. Looking back, I now realise why I had had such trouble in understanding what had gone on - I had been taught the things of healing, goodness, light; this was all sickness, evil and darkness. Even though I was strong and intelligent, at that particular time I was absolutely petrified and impotent.

'Before long the mists cleared and a quietness descended - a stillness I had never experienced before or since. My head spun and I felt numb both mentally and physically, and weak, as though I had been drained. Everything seemed the same as it had before; however, the woman was staring at me with such a quizzical look on her face, as she twirled a tassel on her belt backwards and forwards over her fingers, that I went cold, knowing that something was very wrong.

'I suddenly realised why she was looking at me in that fashion as I spun round to find that Jasmine had completely disappeared. I searched the room with my eyes, looking into every corner until I had to accept that she was not there. I could feel the bile rising in my throat. Swallowing, I called her name, gently at first and then by shouting at the top of my

200

lungs. No response - not from Jasmine at any rate - but the woman started mimicking me, which added to my frustration and fear. For the first time in my life I felt that I could kill someone, as I looked at this witch. I could feel my hands clenching and unclenching as I imagined myself attacking her. I moved forward, almost against my will, to grab that filthy throat but that was not my way and so I stopped.

'She suddenly burst into peals of laughter, slapping her thigh with the palm of her hand and almost falling over in her mirth.

'"So, you can kill, then, can you? Excellent! It won't be so hard to give me the details I have requested from you now, will it?" she wheezed as she tried to catch her breath. "No, don't even think of attacking me or you will never see your lovely wife again," she gasped as she held onto her sides, not even trying to stop herself from cackling.

'As I stood there she eventually stopped laughing and, finally getting herself under control, just stared at me for a very long time, then asked me if I wanted to see what had happened to my wife.

'I could not trust myself to speak and even if I tried I don't think words would have got past the tightness in my throat. She beckoned me to follow her, warning me that should I try to do anything to her, Jasmine would be lost forever.

'After grabbing a torch which she lit from the kitchen fire, I followed her out of the room and she led me along a passageway and down the many steps toward the dungeons. I could feel fear crawling up my spine as the corridor through which we travelled became bitterly cold and very wet, the water dripping onto us from the ceiling in quite a few places.

'I couldn't wait to get to Jasmine as I felt sure I could rescue her somehow; equally, I thought that if she had somehow locked Jasmine away in this cold and damp place, she would surely catch the ague and die. Our people, even though we may have been born here, do not have the physical make-up to guard against the chills and dampness in this brutally cold and wet land.

'The darkness in these passageways gave way grudgingly, shadows seeming to become tangible as they parted to let us through, crawled around us and then closed ranks, creeping along closely behind us as we made our way along, curious as to the outcome of the drama unfolding before them.

'The witch walked to the end of the hallway and we went through yet another doorway. After walking for a further minute or so, we turned down a flight of steps to a rock-lined dungeon.

'There, in the centre of the dungeon was a standing stone made out of crystal and entombed within it was my poor wife, Jasmine. I froze as I looked at her and then, as though someone had passed a lightning current through me, I hurled myself at the glass, pulling the scimitar out of my belt as I did so and tried to hack through it to free her. I can remember watching the sparks fly off the crystal as my sword struck.

'The witch howled with laughter at my efforts, which, as you will probably have guessed, were futile.

'I turned in anger to face the witch and took a couple of steps towards her. Stepping back - and she did look a little worried - she held up her hand at my approach and, although I could have cut her down there and then, something stopped me from doing so. I stood there, scimitar raised, but knowing I couldn't make that final move.

'"Very sensible," she said, slowly letting out her breath. I believe she was really not sure at all that I would not strike her down. "Now let me just put you in the picture. As I have already told you, if you attack me, she will be lost forever. If you attack the crystal you will not be able to break it – it is unbreakable - but you will cause your wife severe pain – the noise caused by your hitting the stone will reverberate for hours – very painful. Now, go on, take a look at her. Go on, go on," she shouted then as she pointed toward my wife.

'I walked back to the rock and noticed a crystal tear suspended from her lower lashes. That tear had not been there before! I felt sick at the thought that I had caused her pain.

'"Yes, she is alive and will remain so, just as long as you do what I require." There was no compassion in her face or her voice as she turned to leave the room.

'In the recesses of my mind I realised that I would need to have all my wits about me to prevail over this mad woman. Who was to say, that once I had given her what she demanded, she would not dispose of both of us? Speaking to her with as much civility as I could manage, past, I have to admit, an enormous lump in my throat, I called to her, "Madam". She turned and waited for me to continue, merely raising one eyebrow. "Please do not leave her here in the dark; she has always feared the darkness." I waited to see what she would do but she just shrugged and turned away. I called to her again and she turned and stood still, staring at me. I eventually realised what it was that she wanted from me. "If you let her have light I will instruct you in the incantation you want."

'The smile that came from the mad woman was almost angelic. Almost! "Well, if you had been more amenable in the first instance, we should not be in the position in which we now find ourselves or, should I say, your wife would not be in the position she now finds herself. But, that cannot be helped. What is, is – and," her face hardened, "until you finish the job, she will stay where she is! I shall instruct Minion to bring a candle here every day. The candle will be one of the largest I have and will last for twenty-four hours. However, I want complete obedience from you or that concession will cease. Understand?" I nodded. "Excellent! Now that we understand each other I believe we shall get along famously."

'She was at least true to her word in that one respect. I made a point to check that the candle was placed there every day; I also went along to spend time with Jasmine whenever I could. I do not know whether she could see me but I suppose it was for my benefit as much as hers that I went along and, of course, I had to check daily that the candle was there; if I had had my way, I believe I would have checked hourly - just to make sure it was still alight. However, I knew that no sudden breeze would blow it out – it was as still as the grave down there.

'But now, what will happen? The witch will stop sending Minion down with a new candle and, even now, my poor wife could be in darkness. She might lose her mind!'

Merlin tut tutted and said that between them they should be able to do something about that but in the meantime asked Salazar to continue his story so that he had all the facts to hand.

'As I said, I had promised to teach the witch the death enchantment. I told her that as this was such a powerful spell, it needed to be absolutely correct and, what with the collecting of the right herbs – some of which needed to be fresh and only grew at certain times in the year or during the night; some only at the new moon - and the making of the potion as well as the accurate incantation, it would probably take the best part of a twelvemonth to perfect. I can remember her smiling at this and saying that that was an acceptable timeframe.

'Mind you, she was not at all pleased when the next thing I did was write down that I had decided to take a vow of silence, such vow not being retracted until my wife gained her freedom. As you can imagine, the witch was furious and, after shouting and screaming - spitting and frothing all the while - it took all her self-control, such as that is, to accept the inevitable. She came, finally, to the conclusion that the spells and ingredients would be best written down, as then she wouldn't forget anything and, if she did, she could always go back and check on it. "And," she added, in a very self-satisfied way, "if anything should happen to you in the meantime, I will have a record!"

'That, thinking about it, was just about a year ago. I had to be very careful in her training as, although I did not think I could possibly bring myself to give her the correct spell for what she wanted to do, it had to be near enough for her not to be suspicious. In the meantime, I was trying to find a way to free Jasmine. So far, I have had no success whatsoever.

'About seven days ago, one of the mad woman's servants, a man called Berryn, arrived at the castle with a young girl.'

'Rhianne!' said Merlin.

'Yes, Rhianne. The witch wasn't too pleased at the time, for she had instructed him to bring Arthur. She felt that the time had come for me to give her the final instructions to enable her to dispose of him. However, she wasn't too displeased with Berryn, as her thinking was that if she had Arthur's sister, the family, and even Arthur, would come looking to free her. Then she would be able to get her hands on him. In fact, she wondered why she had not thought to abduct her or someone else in the family before now. "It's all coming together," she laughed, as she clapped her hands and danced up and down.

'She then had Rhianne locked up in the tower. Somehow Rhianne managed to get her hands on the witch's mantle of invisibility and escape. That's when we met – well, met on our own, so to speak. She has the ability to mind speak and with a little bit of encouragement we were able to communicate. She had found her way down to the dungeon where my wife is imprisoned and from there I tried to help her escape.

'That has now all gone terribly wrong, as while I fell through the doorway of the standing stone and arrived here, she is still in the castle. I would have tried to return through the standing stone, but even if I could have found it, it was obviously only meant to be used one way so I couldn't go *back. It was confusing to know where I was – I seemed to be drifting in space. Once I was outside the standing stone and knew it was impossible for me to get back, I did what any druid would do at a time like this and that was to mind-speak the incantation of finding - that was when I entered through your Glass doorway. I am so sorry to have to bring all these troubles to you. When I passed through that rocky portal I had the mantle of invisibility over my arm, so Rhianne doesn't even have the opportunity to hide from that evil woman.*

'That is, therefore, where my story ends. I have now left two women at the mercy of a witch who obviously does not know the first meaning of the word.' Salazar's face looked the picture of despair.

Merlin, who had been striding up and down for the last part of the story, stroked his chin, staring at the African as he considered what Salazar had told him. 'We live in interesting times, brother. The single standing stones are doorways, of course, but are also, unfortunately – well in Britain anyway, as you have found out - only one way and there is a reason for that which I shall explain another time. But, to get back to the present, all is not lost! It is all part of the plan which, even now, is being put into action.'

'Goodness me,' exclaimed Jack. 'Is that the time! We'd better get going if we want to be home before its dark.' He took a swig of water from his flask as they all jumped up from the bank, and, untying Duke, they clambered back up onto the cart and started for home.

NINETEEN

'What did Merlin mean, granddad, when he said that it was all part of the plan?' asked Ben as they settled down for the last leg of the journey home. 'We know that you went back to Mad Mab's castle but you got caught. Did that spoil the plan?'

'No, it didn't spoil the plan, but *I* now needed to get away. So, where were we? Ah, yes …

'All I could see was this phial of bubbling liquid. As it drew my eyes towards it, the rest of the room seemed to have disappeared. My knees would have started knocking together if they hadn't been so far apart, being tied separately to the two front chair legs, as they were. I considered what might happen when I was force-fed that vile potion and felt that I might throw up before I'd even swallowed it.

The old man had pulled back my head which, of course, made my mouth start to open but, before she started to pour it down my throat - and, do you know, I could feel the heat from the glass bottle against my lower lip - I said the first thing that came to mind. Even now, as I think about it, it's amazing that it worked. I reckon someone somewhere was looking after me!'

'What did you say?' prompted Danny.

'Well, as I said, the witch was just about to pour the liquid down my throat and all our eyes had swivelled round to look at it - glass phial, still bubbling with that deep red brew and steaming away as though it was still being held over the flame - when I asked her if, before she did so, I could have a last meal. A bit like the condemned man before his execution, I thought. And I did feel like that condemned man!

She looked at me and laughed, saying that I had more guts than she would have thought possible for someone in my

207

unenviable position, and was crazy if I thought it would help me.

Her laugh made my blood run cold, even though I was fairly close to the fire and could feel the heat from its flames.

Nevertheless, she scooped a bowlful of the stew out of the cauldron and set it on the table in front of me. I asked her if she would release my hands so that I could hold the bowl and, after pointing out that I could hardly escape as my legs were tied securely to the chair, she nodded toward the old man to untie them. I held the bowl to my mouth but, as the broth was so hot, I started to blow on it to cool it off. While I waited, I asked her why she was doing what she did and, again, was rather surprised that she told me – but then I have heard that when some people, especially mad ones, have put a plan together, they are so vain that they need to tell someone so that at least one person knows just how brilliant they are!

'It's quite simple really,' she said. 'Merlin and I were fairly close at one point. Well, as close as someone could ever be to that standoffish, self-opinionated, self-important old … – he's a cold fish, you know! Doesn't have any feelings for anyone except himself. I tried to get close to him, but he just didn't want to know.'

'I wonder why!' I thought, trying not to wrinkle my nose as I did so and, more importantly, trying to keep that particular thought to myself.

'And me being such a good catch - intelligent, powerful and not bad looking either.' She tossed back her hair, which didn't really move – the greasy bits stuck, as it were, to her head! I tried hard not to grimace, as she was not at all attractive, although I expect she probably was when she was a lot younger – and cleaner! I reckon it had been a long time since she had come into contact with a mirror, or soap come to that. I believed she must have something wrong with her sinuses as well! She continued. 'By going after Arthur – yes he is my prime target – I shall also capture Merlin as well - so

208

you might consider him a bonus - two birds with one stone, eh!'

My mind went off at a tangent as I wondered if she was the person who started that saying, considering that a merlin was a bird and Arthur well, he was really the son of Uther Pendragon – "Uther Chief Dragon", and a dragon flew!

However, getting back to point in question, 'Why do you want to capture them?' I asked.

She peered at me as though I were completely bereft of any brain. 'I don't just want to *capture* them,' she stated and then raising her voice as though I were deaf, 'I want to *destroy* them! Deprive them of life! Make them cease to exist! Cut them short in the prime of their lives! Do you need any other explanation?'

She stared into the fire with a very excited but thoughtful look on her face and was talking more to herself than to me as she continued. 'Merlin I shall probably be able to secure for a while, maybe a long while! I don't want to finish him off just yet as he may come in useful. Perhaps I can make him tell me some of his more complicated spells. Hmm. But Arthur, well he has to be annihilated.' I shivered; I couldn't help it. She laughed. 'Yes, my little friend, well might you shudder. With Arthur, you see, it's either him or me. As you can imagine, so far as I am concerned I'd rather be the one to stay alive. Yes, the prophecies tell it. I've checked and double-checked and it always comes out the same - so it must be true. You know the truth when it stares you in the face and in these cases it didn't just stare me in the face, it didn't blink either.' I did know she totally believed this but, nevertheless, at the back of my mind I wondered how often she did tell the truth or even have any idea of it.

Another saying popped into my mind, 'You shall know the truth and the truth shall set you free.' That was one of the verses from the Bible that Arthur was often repeating. Funny, as at that moment I realised that her "truth" and Arthur's

209

"truth" were two totally different concepts; I felt an ease and a security that really went against my present circumstances. I did not know where it came from – maybe someone, somewhere was speaking into my mind even though I could not hear a thing - but I knew that everything would work out. I could feel myself relaxing.

Suddenly she stopped talking as she sat by the fire watching me and then, almost absentmindedly, taking another bowl from the shelf, she filled it up with some stew for herself. She, too, blew on it a few times and then took a sip. 'Make yourself ready, boy! It won't be long now! Your freedom will last as long as this stew! As soon as I have drunk it, you are going to go through the experience of a lifetime' - this said with a devilish grin on her face. I had continued blowing on my stew without drinking any as it was still much too hot but I watched her through my eyelashes over the rim of the bowl as after a few more seconds she took another sip, and then another. My eyes narrowed as I watched her for what seemed an extraordinarily long time, when all of a sudden she seemed to go stiff, as though an electric current had passed through her; she clutched at her throat as she fell forward onto her knees. She looked over at me in horror and hate, her eyes bulging out of her head like organ stops, as I put down my bowl and just sat staring expressionlessly at her.

After twitching a couple of times she fell onto the floor, shaking all over. She pointed at me with a trembling finger and opened her mouth to say something but all that came out was, 'Ag ag ag'. Nonsense, all she could say was nonsense - gibberish. She clapped a very unsteady hand over her mouth as she carried on staring at me for a few more seconds, hate and fear filling her eyes.

She continued holding a shaking hand over her mouth until she thought she might be safe. Taking her hand away, she tried a few more words - more rubbish; to stop herself from saying any more nonsense she pressed an ever weakening hand over her mouth again and then, finally, with eyes rolling up into her head and her body twitching quite violently, she conveniently passed out.

Still watching her but without wasting any time I had been untying the rope around my ankles and, jumping up as quickly as I could, was ready to try and outrun the old man but, as it turned out, he was only too willing to help me. He had been untying the rope around my other ankle as I made haste to release myself.

After deciding on our best route of escape he was happy to tell me a bit of his story. His brother, he told me, had been rude to Mad Mab by laughing at her and she had therefore tricked him into drinking the same potion that she had been going to force-feed to me. As a gargoyle, he had adorned the castle walls now for over ten years.

The old man had about given up hope of getting his own back on the witch, let alone getting his brother freed or escaping. He looked down at her lying on the floor with her mouth gaping open and the spittle hanging out of it in long slimy threads.

Still without any expression on his face, 'What a nauseating sight,' he whispered, 'and what an obnoxious person she is. Shall we throw her into the lake?' He said this with no emotion in his voice whatsoever. 'Do you think those carnivorous fish, or whatever they are, will turn their noses up at her? I reckon they would.'

'No,' I said. 'We haven't got time for that and I don't want to be responsible for anyone's death. Even hers!' In the back of my mind I wondered if I would live to regret that decision. However, now was not the time to consider anything other than getting away.

Merlin had told me that the naiad root, which I had managed to slip into the cauldron before my disastrous "escape" into the cupboard, would have an immediate effect on the witch, and it had - almost. But, he did not know how long it would last, as he did not know how powerful Mab was or had become. He had told me to get away as quickly as I could and try to find Rhianne. I was only too pleased to do this as I had worried about her so much since the day that she was abducted. The old man warned me not to tarry but to follow him quickly, as he knew where Rhianne was.

As I followed Minion along the corridor leading away from the kitchen, he told me that the witch was quite insane. Not only had she disposed of more people than he could count by turning them into stone-like gargoyles and fastening them to the castle walls, she had also done the same to her cat and to some other animals as well. He said that she had loved the cat, if you could use the word "love" in her case and was extremely annoyed with herself after she had changed it into stone because the cat had been very useful in assisting her in carrying out certain spells. She had a room full of scrolls and over the last year or so, now that the cat was not around, she had tried out some of the magic on him but he had turned out to be not at all receptive and so she had given up - thank goodness. Now she tried most of her experiments out on herself; sometimes it had worked and she had become quite powerful; sometimes it had gone wrong.

As they rushed along the corridors of the castle, he recalled one of those instances where she'd ended up seeing everything double for a least a week and kept walking into doorframes or missing the chair altogether because she had "sat" on the one that wasn't there and had fallen on the floor because of it. He hated it when things went wrong because she would always take it out on him, mainly by boxing his ears; however, at this particular time she kept missing as she was aiming at the "him" that wasn't there more often than not - seeing double that is.

By the time he finished recounting his life at the castle - and I think he had spoken more in those few minutes than he had in the last few years, as he was quite out of breath when he stopped - we had reached the foot of a flight of decomposing spiral stairs. The old man said his name was not Minion - as the witch had insisted on calling him - but Hive, due to the fact that he used to keep the beehives for the lord he had worked for, and he informed me that his brother was called Mead, as he used to make the drink of the same name from the honey he obtained from the hives and that his sister, whom he hoped to rejoin one day, was called Honey - for obvious reasons.

Getting back to the present, he told me to watch my step or I might fall, as many of the stone steps leading to the tower were crumbling.

We eventually, almost out of breath, got to the top of the staircase without mishap and, after Hive had taken down the key, opened the door to a circular room. It made a loud creak as it was pushed back and I stepped out of the way only just in time to save myself from being knocked out by a large earthenware jug aimed at my head. It did scrape along Hive's shoulder and he cried out, but more out of shock than from pain.

'Percy,' gasped Rhianne and, when she was over her surprise, rushed into my arms, holding me very tightly and exclaiming, 'Oh, I am so glad to see you! But what on earth are you doing here? You haven't been caught as well have you?' This said almost in despair.

Well, I must admit I didn't know where to put myself; even at that tender age, to be hugged by someone that I felt more than a passing interest in made me feel quite peculiar. However, if ducking earthenware jugs was a way to be hugged by someone as lovely as her, well, bring in the potters! She let me go and, looking suspiciously at Hive, grabbed my hand and said that together we could overcome the little man, as we had to escape as quickly as possible. 'Where is the witch? Quick, let's run! Let's get away before

213

she finds out. Grab that little man and lock him in the tower.'
The words were tumbling out of her.

'Rhianne,' I tried to quieten her. 'I've drugged Mab but I
don't know how long it will have an effect on her. Hive,
here, is quite OK. He will, I am sure, show us how to escape.
We must be quiet and not panic. Lead on, Hive.' As I gave
him this instruction, I felt that some of the training I had
received along with Arthur, including that of authority, had
rubbed off onto me – I felt just a little embarrassed at giving
orders to someone who was obviously a lot older than me and
also a little taller as well. Nevertheless, he seemed to be
ready to accept them.

We got to the bottom of the stairs and followed Hive
along the same route that Rhianne and Salazar had taken the
last time she had tried to escape. 'There's no way out that
way,' Rhianne said, beginning to panic. 'He's trying to trick
us. That's where the woman caught me the last time,
bringing me back and locking me up again in that awful
tower.'

Hive said that they had taken a wrong turn, as there was a
short flight of steps, which led up to an opening where the
woodsmen brought in the fuel for the fire. We'd gone too far
before, ending up in the flooded part of the castle. We found
the steps, as he had said, hidden behind an extremely old-
looking, shredded tapestry depicting what appeared to be a
white dragon. Making our way to the top of the steps, we
stumbled upwards over quite a few pieces of loose twigs and
branches and unlatched the door, which, surprisingly, opened
quite easily. We stepped out into the cold night air, stopping
only then to get our bearings.

Hive, however, was not one to waste time. 'Make haste,'
he said, 'Let's get away from the lake and find your friends'.
As we stepped out from the comparative safety of the
doorway, he started away from the lake and towards the trees,
pulling Rhianne along behind him. It was very cold and the

wind, which was howling as it bounced off the now very choppy waters of the lake, was trying to grab at us and pull us back with its icy fingers. A mixture of snow and icy rain flew almost horizontally into our faces, attacking us like miniature whips. I grabbed hold of Rhianne's other hand as I felt that we might stand a chance if we held on to each other. Hive said something but his words were whipped away by the wind. My eyes were streaming with tears as the cold wind blew into my face making it very hard to see. Holding on to Rhianne for dear life, we eventually got around the corner of the castle and flattened ourselves against the wall. The wind here, although still quite strong, was at least not trying to blow us into the lake.

Hugging the castle walls, we made our way around to an area near the front gate where we had initially found the sunken door into the castle. From there, Merlin had given me directions to travel to the Tor, where we were to meet up with Arthur and the men.

Morning was rapidly approaching and, as we were able to tread more securely, we picked up some speed. We passed in front of the main gates and Hive stopped. He looked up at the gargoyle that was once his brother Mead. Rhianne and I both stared up at them and experienced an assortment of emotions, ranging through pain, hatred and longing, which emanated from the stone-like heads.

'I'll not rest until I can free you, my brother; I must see if there is anyone who can help,' said Hive as tears, not just from the wind, coursed down his cheeks.

'*What a sad situation,*' I thought. '*I wonder if Merlin can do anything about this.*'

'Yes,' said Rhianne. I almost jumped out of my skin. I didn't do or say anything there and then, as I didn't know if she was answering Hive or responding to me. Was it possible that Rhianne might be susceptible to the gifts of the Old Way?

We had reached the path where we were to turn and travel eastwards toward the Tor, when my blood turned to ice in my veins. We heard a terrible, low growling sound right behind us and spinning around were confronted with the drawn back lips and dribbling fangs of a naiad. Rhianne screamed and Hive's normally yellow colour drained from his face, leaving him almost bloodlessly white. For a few seconds we were rooted to the spot but before anything else could happen, I recalled what Cabal had said about them being very slow on land, I grabbed both their hands and we turned around and ran – straight into the arms of the mad witch. Our propulsion caused her to make a bit of a turn, facing away from the naiad and thus obscuring her view of the present danger.

'So, my pretties,' she said as she spun round, catching and holding both Rhianne and I by the wrist, 'you thought you would succeed in overpowering me and get away, eh? Ag, ag!' she twitched involuntarily. Turning slowly, she moved us along and we were forced back to the castle doors from where there would be no escape. She stared at Hive with eyes that were demonic - the whites had turned to red and glowed as she looked him over from head to foot – was that because she was evil or was it the result of the naiad root poison. 'You, I will deal with later,' she spat, almost convulsing once again. The poor man just stood there, head bowed and quaking in his boots. 'I think that now might be the time for you to join your brother; it would even things up nicely – a good match - you are very alike!' she spluttered. I think she must have had quite a strong constitution because, though the poison kept trying to take her over the edge, she managed, somehow, to keep it under control.

Making sure that we were securely held in her grasp, she turned us toward the castle door. However, in all the confusion of running into Mab, we had spun completely around and she now had her back to the naiad. Rhianne, gripping her lower lip with her teeth, looked over at me and

216

confirmed my previous suspicion as she spoke into my mind, saying '*Get ready to run!*'

After getting over my surprise I replied, '*Eh? What do you mean?*' But, at the same moment that I was mind speaking the last couple of words, the witch let out an agonizing yell, and whatever had caused her to do so culminated in her letting go of both our wrists as she spun around to face in the other direction. Without more ado I grabbed Rhianne and, with Hive trailing, we ran at what seemed like breakneck speed eastward, through the forest, toward the Tor, until our lungs were almost bursting with the effort. We eventually stopped, legs like rubber and breath, coming in rasps - steaming through our mouths. Hive caught up with us, in a sorrier state, as he had certainly not been used to moving at any pace quicker than a shuffle over the last few years.

He collapsed onto the fallen log upon which Rhianne was also resting, his breath more like a saw slicing through an old log that had rusty nails in it than a man breathing hard. I was leaning over with my hands on my knees, trying to get my breath back and stop my heart from thumping. Being young, both Rhianne and I were soon back to normal and were able to speak again. We waited a bit longer until Hive was also able to talk.

'What happened there?' I asked.

'The naiad got hold of Mab,' Hive replied. 'I expect she's dead by now. I've never known anyone get away from them before, so I reckon she's gone. It's a wonder she didn't know it was there! I expect that potion you gave her was quite mind-numbing.' He said all of this very matter-of-factly, showing neither joy nor sorrow. I wondered if the witch had succeeded in removing all emotional feelings from this poor man.

'Well, I don't know whether she will or won't manage to get away from that creature,' I said, 'but I do know that we have to get to the Tor, north-east from here, to meet up with Arthur. Are you with us, Hive? Now that you have got away, we can meet up with Merlin at some time and I am sure he will know if anything can be done about your brother. If that witch could have done something, she hasn't or wouldn't, and, if she is dead, well there is no way she could do anything now anyway, so let's get a move on.'

We had now recovered our breath and, between us, Hive and I took turns in enlightening Rhianne on the niceties of the naiad. She made the observation that she was glad it had got the witch and not them.

By now the morning was well advanced and we made swift progress through the forest. It was extremely cold and, as we did not have very warm clothing, we moved quite quickly, just to keep warm. In any event, we wanted to be there long before dark as we were concerned that if it was a moonless or even starless night we might end up travelling in a circle and ending up where we started – perish the thought! Besides, if we had to stop overnight in these conditions we would not survive! The shoes that Rhianne had been wearing when she was abducted were house shoes made of linen and wool sewn onto soft, thin leather soles. By the time mid-day had approached she was limping - the shoes had now become sodden and were hanging in shreds – it was only then that we noticed one of her heels had blistered and was bleeding. She certainly couldn't travel any further on foot.

There was nothing now that we could do except stop and rest. Rhianne obviously needed to clean her feet and rest them but for the life of me I couldn't think of what we could do to get to the Tor by this evening; it was obvious that neither Hive nor I were strong enough to carry her. I looked around to see if there might be anything that we could use to make some covering for her feet but, being winter, there was not even a leaf to be found. At the moment the sun was shining and the wind had dropped but there were still intermittent, gentle flakes of snow drifting in from the north showing that the bad weather had not yet left us; so it was certain that if we didn't move soon we might all freeze to death. We searched around and even though there was a lot of wood we had nothing with which to light a fire. No, we had to move on as soon as possible.

'I'm so sorry, Percy,' Rhianne choked on a sob. 'I seem to have caused such a lot of bother. I'll strip off some of my skirt and perhaps we can wrap it around my feet.' So saying, she started tearing strips of cloth.

It wasn't such a bad idea, but it wouldn't be long before the damp would soak through and her feet would be drenched and chilled to the bone again. But, as it was the only idea we had come up with, we set to, and wrapped her feet as best we could. I felt the small pouch hanging from the cord around my neck and considered sprinkling us all with the dust but in the back of my mind I knew what I might miss and so, mentally apologising to Rhianne, I decided against it. Besides, Merlin had made it abundantly clear that it was important we met up with him in accordance with his instructions, so he therefore probably wasn't in his cave.

Rhianne looked at me and nodded; I shivered! '*Send Hive off to do something or other*,' she spoke directly into my mind. I think I must have looked witless as I stared at her with my mouth hanging open like a moron – definitely not the right thing to do when you are trying to impress a female! Pulling myself together I turned toward Hive and asked him if he knew where we were. He shook his head.

'Would you mind just going up to the top of that knoll and looking around to see if you can spot anything? We need to find the Tor that is supposed to be near here. Can you whistle?' He nodded. 'Good, so can I. If you get lost, whistle!'

When he had gone, Rhianne looked at me with those disconcerting, blue eyes. 'I thought as much,' she smiled – a

219

bit lopsidedly. 'You can speak in your mind as well, can't you? You just apologised to me for something, I know not what!'

Oops, I was glad she hadn't read my mind then! Instead, I answered, 'Yes, and Merlin thought you might have the gift, but didn't quite know it yet.'

'Does he mind speak then?'

'Yes. As far as I know there is only him, me and Cabal.'

Rhianne started as I mentioned the hound. 'Cabal! What, a dog can speak?'

I smiled at her. 'Oh, yes! There are no obstructions in understanding him in thought. He obviously cannot speak through his voice, he just doesn't have, as he puts it, "the equipment". So, as I was saying, there is only Merlin, me, Cabal and now you.'

'And Salazar,' she said.

'Salazar?' I looked down at her as she spoke this strange name.

'Yes. He was at the castle working for the witch.' I ground my teeth at this and Rhianne looked up at me. 'No, you've got it all wrong, Percy. Salazar is just as much a victim as everyone else that Mab gets hold of. His wife had been captured by her and Salazar has had to obey her, or else …'. Rhianne recounted the awful story of what had happened to Salazar and the entombment of Jasmine, his wife. Her voice trailed off as she finished binding her feet.

Hive returned, quite excited – well for him, at any rate, excitement was no more than speaking a bit quicker. His face, however, showed no emotion whatsoever. He had seen the Tor from his vantage point. It would only take about half an hour of determined walking to get there. We both looked at Rhianne who showed us, by the set of her jaw, that she was up for it. I had been thinking, while we were resting that, as I had been exercising quite regularly with Arthur and had gained muscle and strength that I had not possessed before, I could possibly help carry her – for a short while anyway. Although she was older than me, we were of a height, so it might not be too difficult.

'Would you mind if I gave you a piggy back?' I asked her.

She looked really confused and, after a short while, exclaimed, 'But I have never ever given you a pig!'

It took a while for the penny to drop but then I burst out laughing as I thought of what I had said and how she had misinterpreted it. Both she and Hive looked at me as though I had finally lost my mind and the more I looked at them, particularly the thought that they considered me mad, the more I couldn't stop laughing, tears streaming down my face, the laughter probably a mixture of what I had just said combined with the fact that we had escaped the mad woman and relief that as we were nearly at the Tor we would finally be safe. Anyway, eventually, I did stop falling about. Explaining what I meant by it, they caught on and then, adding the deed, I found it very easy to carry her for the next ten minutes. Hive took over for a while, but could only manage about five minutes before he was puffing through a face that had turned an unflattering crimson - the poor man certainly sported a diverse range of colours on that face of his! We stopped then and rested while we all caught our breath.

TWENTY

We had reached the edge of the forest and could see the Tor in front of us. It would be a long climb up but at least we were on the last leg of our journey. I wondered what would happen when we finally got there. Were the men, especially Arthur, there? Had the Cyclops captured them? Had they escaped? One relief I had was that Rhianne was now safe. Another was that Mab was more than likely dead. Hopefully, now, we were safe and perhaps could just all go home.

Although we were now walking on grass, which was a lot softer than the stones and brambles in the forest, it was still wet and very cold but Rhianne was determined to give both Hive and I a rest from carrying her.

We started up the hill, both of us with one of Rhianne's arms around our shoulders so that she did not have to place her full weight onto the ground, and after about five minutes came to some flat terrain. Straightening up and peering up the hill we saw some of the men. I reached into my pouch and, finding my penny whistle, blew the highest note I could find.

Within seconds the men were tearing down the hill, Arthur in the lead with the widest grin on his face that I have ever seen, considering that in strange company he was usually a very serious person.

He threw his arms around Rhianne and, after checking that she really was alright, clapped me on the back and started to escort us up the hill. He organised the carrying of Rhianne by one of the men – a job that Shake Spear made sure was his, an easy job for him, as he was so big.

When we reached the top we were given refreshment and shelter. The men had built a rough structure beside the stone ruins, which kept them safe from both wind and rain, and Thatcher was busy waterproofing the roof.

Tanner gave Rhianne some hot broth to drink and while she drank he removed the rags from her feet; after bathing and soothing them with some ointment he wrapped them in a dry, warmed sheepskin.

Arthur joined me as I sat by the fire, warming myself. He gave me a jug of broth and a chunk of bread. 'Now, Percy, I owe you more than you could possibly know in finding Rhianne but, for the present, tell me everything that happened.' As I recounted the story his eyes never left my face. He looked grim as I told him about Hive and his brother Mead and turned to speak a few words of commiseration to the man; then looked harsh as I told him about Merlin and what the witch had in store for him.

He looked very angry as I told him how that mad woman had sealed Jasmine in the glass tomb but was completely surprised when I told him about what she had said about Arthur himself. I had been in two minds as to whether I should tell him or not but then the thought, "fore-warned is fore-armed" jumped into my brain, so decided he should know.

'Why? What could she possibly want to kill *me* for? I'm just a nobody – a younger son of a minor lord! I am absolutely no threat to her at all!' He stalked off, walking up and down, alternately rubbing his hands in front of him and then grasping them behind his back, ruminating. I knew I could say nothing to him about who he really was; Merlin had forbidden it. In fact I just remembered in time to put a guard on my thoughts - it would never do for Rhianne to guess that this supposed brother of hers was not all she had thought him to be.

After a while he came back and sat beside me. We stared into the flames of the fire and it was some time before either one of us spoke again. Rhianne was exhausted and had gone to sleep, covered over with a large, warm fleece and some blankets; probably the first time she had felt able to do so for a good many days and definitely the first time she had been warm.

I looked at Arthur who, after staring into the fire for long minutes, returned my gaze. He smiled that rare and enchanting smile of his as he threw one arm around my shoulders and thanked me again for all I had done in the release of his sister. 'We have known each other for such a very short while and yet you have proved one of the truest friends I have ever known. I know not where you come from and care even less, but if anyone had been sent a guardian angel ...' he choked on the rest of the sentence, being completely overcome by emotion.

'Arthur, please, you are making me feel very embarrassed,' I cut in on him, feeling the flush creeping up my face.

Taking control of himself once again, he opened his eyes wide in amazement, as he did not understand my reluctance to receive praise from him. I was later to learn that men in those days went out of their way to do daring deeds solely to be praised for them and have songs written and sung about them. It goes without saying that he couldn't understand my discomfiture.

I went on to ask Arthur what had happened since he had re-joined the men. He said that, having met up with them some time in mid-afternoon, and, after Wite had brought the provisions, they had mounted up and entered the forest in accordance with Merlin's instructions.

'We had moved away from the lake and the castle and were making our way along a path between the trees when it all went very quiet. Well, it was quiet to begin with but now it was eerily quiet, apart from the slurp of the ponies' hooves in the mud. When we had started out it was still bitterly cold but the wind died down and a chilly and persistent drizzle had started to fall, melting most of the snow. It dripped off the trees and seemed to find every available gap in our clothes, running down our hair, down our necks and between our shoulders. Soon we were all pretty wet and very miserable.

'Anyway, the ponies knew something was up first, and started snorting and rolling their eyes and it was as much as we could do to keep them going the right way and stay in the saddle at the same time – they were very jittery. We finally had to draw in the reins and stop. Our mounts appeared to have more sense than us at that time, as they bunched together for comfort and protection. None of us spoke! We were all very uneasy, not to say a little scared! You know how superstitious some of the men are! So we formed a circle with our backs to each other, drew our swords and waited to see what would happen or if anything would, or whether we could continue on our way. It was getting dark anyway but now the darkness seemed to draw in on us. We had thought that we might get to the Tor in the daylight. Now, it seemed impossible.

'Then all hell seemed to have been let loose. We saw the lights! They rushed out at us from all directions and after a short while, as they got closer, they almost blinded us. I was the only one who had seen them before but the men were petrified, thinking they were the very devil. I had to steady them.

'"Get ready men!" I whispered in as calm a voice as I could muster and just loud enough for them all to hear. The ponies were extremely nervous but they kept close together.'

'Shake Spear stood high in his saddle and, with spear raised high, yelled, "And God befriend us, as our cause is just". Then they were upon us.

'It took some time for all of us to realise who our adversaries were but one of them turned as it got near to me so as to attack the man on my left, and my suspicions were confirmed when I recognised one of the Cyclops as its beam shone past me. I remembered how strong they were and held on to the reins of my pony for dear life. "Aim for the lights, men," I yelled when I saw the horrified looks on their faces. They are not ghosts or spirits. You can defeat them!"

'One of the men had been pulled off his mount and was being dragged away at great speed by one of those creatures. However, because of the mud, its feet were getting clogged up and Wite managed to save him as he raced after them, slicing the air with his sword and bringing the hilt down onto the Cyclops's head. The creature fell to the ground like a rag doll, dropping his captive, who immediately swung up behind Wite. They then returned to help the others. I noticed the Cyclops' light went out as he fell.

'Shake Spear was screaming like a banshee as he whooped and whistled, getting his mount to run this way and that while he shook his spear and, true to his word, didn't strike anyone. He frightened the life out of me, though, who knew he wouldn't hit anyone, so I don't know what the two human prisoners we had just captured thought of him. I only know that they took fright and, in their haste to run away, almost knocked one another senseless when they turned their horses into each other and fell off.

'"Wisely and slow; they stumble who run fast," declared Shake Spear as he saw them scrabbling about in the mud.

'We only fought for about five minutes but it felt like more. After the third Cyclops was injured, the last one ran over to it, grabbed it by its arm and they sped off, back toward the castle. Tailor was slightly injured when he was dragged off his pony and has a broken arm as a result but, apart from that, we all survived.

'Shake Spear has become most popular with all of the men, as he has been making up and singing songs about their derring-do. They are all now very pleased he came along. I know he can't see very well, but he'll go far, that one! He can certainly tell a tale or two.'

We carried on walking about the camp as Arthur updated me on events and I wondered if this Shake Spear might have been the original bard or, if not, one of his ancestors. As things stood, though, I couldn't ask, as I wasn't supposed to know anything about anything, let alone the future.

Arthur, who had once again become serious, continued, 'However, as I said, there were at least two men who appeared to be directing those awful beings and we managed to capture them after they fell off their horses. We have tied them up and the men are taking it in turns to guard them, though they don't need much care as one of them has a broken leg, so he couldn't get very far if he did try to escape. The other one has had a knock on the head and has been unconscious for most of the time, but we are taking no chances as he could be faking it.'

Nothing much more had happened on the way and they had just sat about here for the last two days waiting for Merlin to arrive. Arthur said that he was really surprised when he saw Rhianne and me making our way up the hill. 'How did you manage to free her?' he asked. I continued my story, telling him about how I had duped the witch into drinking the stew. His eyebrows shot up at that. 'She'll come after you now with a vengeance,' he stated. 'Merlin said that she never lets anyone off the hook if they have bested her at any time,' he added. 'You will have to get Merlin to make an enchantment for you to keep you safe from her.' I ended by telling him that I thought she was possibly dead, eaten by the naiad. Arthur shook his head, 'Don't you believe it! It would choke on her, I reckon. I bet it spat her out and has been vomiting ever since.'

We continued staring into the fire for a while and then Arthur, taking charge again, organised sentry duty and most of us settled down for the night. I suppose I worried a bit about Mab coming after me but, like all healthy ten-year-olds, especially after all I had been through, exhaustion and the warmth of the fire soon sent me to sleep.

TWENTY-ONE

We awoke to a misty morning. As I looked around at the vapour swirling about, I thought I was beside the sea, especially as the Tor, floating above it, resembled an island. Although the fire had not gone out during the night, it was extremely chilly at the beginning of another winter's day. The ponies were snorting and the steam from their nostrils made them look a little like miniature dragons. Wite went over to them, untied them and took them to the spring that rose up behind the ruin, where they had their fill before they started cropping the grass close to the edge of the water. He left them tied, but with a long rein and came back to join us as we worked to stoke up the fire.

Some of us stared in awe as we stood high on the Tor and looked down at the plain towards the standing stones; they seemed to move, beckoning, as the mist swirled around them. At times they looked like giants staring into the distance, waiting for I knew not what. Arthur saw me staring at them and suggested we go and have a look.

'Some of us looked around at these stones when we arrived. They're very impressive. I have no idea how they got here or whether they were already here in the first place,' he said. 'One or two of the men wouldn't come and look. They remembered Wite disappearing after looking at one similar to them when we met the old man and ate his porridge and they were not going to take the chance of something happening to them, even though Wite has since re-appeared none the worse for his adventure - and with some provisions for us.'

Leaving the top of the Tor, we strolled down towards the plain and then walked all the way around the outside of the stones – they were huge. It was very quiet there, quite eerie. Not wandering off on my own, I kept close to Arthur for, as he had already been in there and had come out again, I thought it safer to stay with him. We stopped first just outside the outer circle of stones and stood looking up. They were impressive. They must have been at least three times the size of a fully grown man and each must have weighed more than all of the men here could carry or pull. So, how did they get there? Some of the stones formed arches, being balanced on two or more other standing stones; some had fallen down. I continued following Arthur around the outside until we had gone full circle; we then ventured inside where we found another smaller, although more obscure, circle and at its centre was what can only be described as a table or altar. I felt my flesh creep as I considered what that altar might have been or even was still used for. As these thoughts went through my mind my mother's voice echoed through it, telling me off about my over-active imagination. I turned and looked at Arthur who was studying me. He was now twelve years old, as he had passed another birthday since we had first met and the boy had almost disappeared. Yes, it was true; boys became men at a very early age in those bygone days. 'Well, friend, what do you think this place is?' he asked.

'I have no idea, but I don't like it one bit!' I answered.

'Merlin said we had to wait for him here and that he would join us within a couple of days, so we had better do as he says and then see what happens. We were supposed to be meeting to try and free my sister but that has now been achieved, thanks to you. Perhaps, when he arrives, we can all just go home. Let's return to the others.'

We took one last look around - as the mist was clearing we stood and watched a misty sun start to make ghostly patterns through the different arches - before we started back to the others.

Rhianne was trying on some leather ankle boots that Tanner had sewn for her during the night. She looked up as we entered the camp and smiled a rather crooked smile as she beckoned us over to her. Sitting down beside her, she turned serious, stating, 'We must try to save Jasmine. That witch will not let her have any light now that Salazar has gone missing and I have escaped. The poor woman will end up thinking that we have all left her and she might die – or go mad – that is, if she *can* still reason and if she is not already dead!' Rhianne held her face in her hands in despair at the thought of Jasmine in the crystal tomb, terrified and alone.

Just then Hive came up and in his usual voice, devoid of any expression, as was his wont, continued, '… and so, as I was the only one who ever went down there - apart from Salazar, that is - I expect the candle will by now well and truly have gone out and she will be in complete darkness.'

'We have to wait for Merlin,' said Arthur. 'We cannot do anything until he comes. You said yourself, Percy, that you only escaped by the skin of your teeth. I don't for one moment think that the witch is dead. She's probably had a setback or two over the last couple of days, but she is much more crafty than to die at the hands – or should I say fangs – of a naiad! I should imagine that she's probably got it hanging from the battlements as one of her new gargoyles by now.' He stomped up and down, hands behind his back, with a very grim expression on his face, an expression, I could see, that was mirrored in every face around.

'I can see that I am arriving at just about the right time!' called Merlin, as he strode through the mist and up the side of the hill, with the wolfhound trotting at his heels. Being so engrossed in all the problems that were attacking us from every side, we hadn't even been aware of his approach. Merlin moved so quickly up the last part of the incline that I noticed even Cabal was finding it hard to keep up with him without breaking into a run.

'Merlin,' we chorused as both Arthur and I rushed to meet him. 'Just in time is an understatement,' I groaned as we met up with him. We ran alongside him as we all returned to the campsite, Merlin making introductions as we eyed the strange looking man accompanying him. Rhianne, ever practical, handed Merlin and Salazar a drink of beer to refresh themselves as they settled down beside her.

Merlin leaned back against the stone wall of the ruin. 'Tell me what has happened,' he asked as he sipped at his drink. Seconds later he held up his hand, stopping the cacophony of noise as at least three people were trying to talk at once. 'Rhianne - you first.'

We each recounted our stories, looking from Merlin to Salazar and back again, especially when we got to the part about Jasmine. Rhianne looked up at Salazar with such pity in her expression that it was as much as she could do to stop herself from bursting into tears. Salazar, on the other hand, kept his noble face inscrutable.

Cabal had run around sniffing and checking out everything and everyone and I was taken off guard as he growled at the two prisoners. I had not really taken much notice of them as there were too many other matters to be considered and quite a bit of catching up to be done. However, when Cabal sat down on his haunches and curled his lip at them I decided to go over and investigate. Imagine my surprise when I looked at two men that I believed I knew as boys – Alf and Bryn! The one with a face of an angel scowled up at me as I stared down at him. He obviously did not know me but looked exactly like an older version of the same bully that had attacked me at the farm and who had, in turn, been attacked by the spectral dog. Was it one of his ancestors? I then felt drawn to look down at the other captive. I almost jumped as I looked at the same bright red hair and hateful expression of an unconscious Alf! '*No*,' I thought; '*it can't be!*' I then looked down at Cabal who looked up at me with one quizzically raised eyebrow. He didn't speak to me about it; well, not then at any rate but it was obvious to me that Bryn and Alf, or their ancestors at least, were still the nasty pieces of work I had known them to be in the 20th Century, where I came from. Some time later Cabal commented on the likeness of these two to the devil and his brother that I had come across at the farm. I wondered if they were, in that later millennium, looking for me, or had they given up or been scared off by Cabal. It was a sobering thought. After a while, I walked back over to the group surrounding Merlin.

Merlin sat us all down and said that he would take each one of us at a time for a walk and tell us what he wanted us to do. There was not much time but it had to be done. He knew what we were like and that if he told us all together we would get muddled, possibly doing someone else's work and then it would all go wrong. Over the next couple of hours he took us in turn, up to the edge of the Tor, gave us our instructions and then brought us back. First Arthur, then Rhianne, me and then Hive. Salazar he had instructed on the way here. He took all the men as a group and I could see them nodding as they listened to their instructions. Then he got us all together.

'You must *not* discuss this amongst yourselves,' he ordered. 'We have until the full moon rises tonight to put our plan into action. Rest now, it will be a very anxious time ahead and we will need to be as alert as we can. The witch is not dead - I would know if she were and she will come here! Oh yes, she will come. It is ordained!' He fell silent for a long moment and then turned, 'Cabal, come with me.' He and the wolfhound walked off into the distance.

And it *was* an anxious time. Not much was said during that afternoon, as we were all too worried about saying something we had been told not to and creating the chaos that Merlin said would make it all go wrong. The men were very busy checking and cleaning their weapons. However, one thing I can remember very clearly was that Salazar spoke into my mind. I became aware, as we all sat around the fire, that he was seeing if anyone else in our group could mind speak and that as he was going round the circle, questioning each mind he came to, he was getting close to me. I was in two minds as to whether I should put up my guard but considered that if he was accepted by Merlin, then who was I to challenge him! He eventually got to me. *'Can you hear me, Percival.'*

'Yes,' I replied. *'And so can Rhianne, I believe.'*

'Ah, yes, she can,' he responded. *'Anyone else?'*

'Not anyone here at the moment,' I answered, *'but Merlin and Cabal are able to, but you probably already know that.'*

'Yes,' he said. *'It might come in useful when we meet up on the plain later on. However, because I know the witch can also mind speak, albeit not very well, we had best take care.'* I agreed and we then closed our minds to each other.

TWENTY-TWO

Jack pulled into the yard near the barn and stared at the house. He had wondered, some distance away as he drove along the lane, why there was no smoke coming out of the chimney. He whistled for Cabal but there was no response. Trying hard to push down a rising feeling of panic he jumped down from the cart and headed toward the house.

Looking grim, he ordered the boys to stay where they were. 'Take the horse over to the trough and start unhitching him. I just want to check the house.'

He walked over and let himself into the cottage - a great, rambling, stone-built place constructed some time late in the Seventeenth Century. He had looked into the time of its construction when he first moved in with his bride - a long time ago now - and because of the "witches' rests" on the roof, could be fairly certain that it was built around that time.

Kicking the door shut behind him, he descended, in one bound, the two steps that led into the main room and strode over to the fire.

For the most part out of habit, but in the beginning because of self-preservation, his eyes scanned the whole of the large room in seconds just to make sure nothing was out of place. Was it his imagination or did the shadows - and were they shadows - scuttle away upon silent feet to conceal themselves in the corners of the room or slide down under a chair or skirting board, ready to make a grab at any unsuspecting ankle?

No, everything was as it should be - nothing appeared to have been disturbed, although that did not mean that it had not!

The large, old, hardwood table - bought at auction many years ago and which had possibly been the kitchen table from one of the old stately houses that had fallen into disrepair -

234

dominated the centre of the room. It covered a floor made of hard wooden boards, which was softened by a large, colourful ragweave mat spread out in front of the sizeable fireplace. An ancient oak dresser covered almost the whole wall facing the fireplace.

A set of open stairs ran up the side of the wall opposite the cottage entrance, which led to the two large rooms above.

Enough of the room: what took pride of place was set over the mantelpiece. Fixed to that wall hung an impressive shield; tall and rectangular in shape, it was made primarily of leather which had clearly darkened over the years. It was obviously loved and cared for as the sheen upon it showed that it was regularly cleaned and oiled. The motif upon it, however, was very hard to discern - over the years it had dimmed and darkened - in fact one would really have needed to be informed of what it was in order to be able to fathom its outline but, once identified, the heart leapt within the breast - yes - a red dragon! Starting to rear up on its hind legs and with wings just beginning to unfurl - arms raised showing talons extended and a huge mouth with lips curled back from rows of countless pointed teeth - the creature stood ready for, what? Flight? Fight? One could never be sure. It was outlined very faintly in gold, or maybe it was bronze, on an ebony background.

The light from the brass paraffin lamps - the only items he allowed on the mantelshelf - would play across the surface of the shield and, Jack thought wistfully, almost make it come to life. He would catch his breath as he watched the flickering lamps dance across the now dulled yellow eyes and fan-shaped ears. On the odd evening he would just sit and stare at it - sometimes with a look of such melancholy on his face that anyone coming across him would think that his heart must surely be broken.

But, coming back to the present, nothing looked out of place and Jack heaved a sigh of relief.

The boys had nervously, and therefore quietly, started undoing the trappings on the horse, keeping one eye on the house to see what was happening and straining their ears to hear if anything was untoward. Their grandfather's visual search of the room took mere seconds but, because they were a little scared, the boys felt it was a lot longer.

He finally came back out of the house. 'Well, your mother's not here. Reckon she must still be at Mrs. Ambrose's house, fitting the curtains.'

'Would Cabby have gone with her?' Ben asked.

'I would think so. I left him here to take care of her so he's probably gone along as well.'

The three of them got to work unbuckling the horse and getting him settled with a bag of feed. They unloaded the goods Jack had purchased into the biggest shed and then went and washed up, ready for tea. Jack cleaned out the grate, re-stacked the fire with tinder and lit it. Afterwards, he got the boys helping him by preparing their tea while he got washed.

He went into his room and, stripping off the shirt he had worn all day, tossed it into the corner whilst opening the cupboard to get out a fresh one. His heart almost stopped in his chest. Inside the cupboard lay Cabal, bundled up with his four legs bound together by a stout rope and a ligature around his neck. His eyes bulged, staring but unseeing, out of his face and his tongue was hanging out of his mouth. 'Dead!' whispered Jack as his gorge rose and tears welled up in his eyes. He reached up to the shelf below the window, where his hooking knife was always kept, quickly reached down and cut the cord round Cabal's neck, at the same time shouting for the boys to bring water. He started massaging the hound's neck, noticing with an uncomfortable dread that Cabal's body felt cold. Jack's eyes were brimming with tears as he held the hound to his chest and rocked backwards and forwards.

'Granddad, what's happening?' said Danny, white faced, as he rushed into the room. Ben was just behind with a pitcher of water. Jack took the water and, soaking his old shirt, started wiping the area round Cabal's neck, gently dabbing at his neck with the cold, wet cloth. He trickled some water into his mouth and prayed to whoever might be listening to do something; well prayed was an understatement – he was literally screaming inside his head. Silently, very silently, a voice inside his mind whispered, *'Alive.'*

'Quick, boys, open the windows. Wedge open the door. Help me get him into the kitchen. I thought he was dead but I think he's still alive.' They gently, but struggling nevertheless because of the size of the hound, managed to get him into the kitchen. Jack bent down and put his ear to the hound's nose. He felt a very faint breath of air. 'Come on my old friend, fight, start breathing. What would I do without you?' he croaked past the lump in his throat.

A shuddering intake of breath!

'He's alive.' Ben jumped up and danced around the room. Danny 'Phewed' and they all looked relieved.

As Cabal started to breathe more easily, even though each breath was rasping and rattling in his throat, his eyes began to return to nearly normal and he almost focused on the three anxious faces before him. Jack gave him some water but, after the hound started choking on it, he reduced the amount to a trickle at a time. 'Oh Cab, what a scare you have given us. What on earth has happened here?'

'Morgan,' Cabal spoke into Jack's mind.

Jack went white. He noticed that Daniel had also gone pale. 'Are you OK Danny?' he asked.

'I had a feeling that my stepfather might have been here,' he replied. 'It's just as though I felt the name "Morgan" come into my head. I hope he hasn't done something horrible to mum!'

'Oh no, Kate! I had forgotten all about her! Cab, stay!' Jack ordered the hound – not that he could yet move! 'You two boys stay here and look after him. Keep giving him a little water and bathe his neck. I am just going to look around to see if I can find anything outside.' With that, after rushing upstairs and back down again, he went out into the yard. The boys looked at each other and then went to the door to see what their grandfather was up to. He was gone quite a long time and when he came back he looked really worried, although when he noticed the boys looking at him he tried to remove the worried look from his face.

'What's up?' asked Danny.

'Everything looks normal apart from the large barn. Where there was the chemical leak, something has burned through the wooden wall and there is now a hole. Don't go anywhere near there,' he ordered the two boys.

He looked over and could see Cabal trying to stand, although very unsteadily. 'Go upstairs, boys, and get your walking boots on and your coats. We are going down into the village to see if anyone has seen any strangers.'

While they were gone he talked with Cabal. As Cabal could talk with his mind and didn't have to talk with his vocal chords there was no strain as he conversed with Jack.

'Morgan came in a car. We heard it pull up and Kate went to the door to see who it was, just as he was about to knock. She was so shocked, she couldn't move. He grabbed her and bundled her into the car.

'I went for his leg but it was as though I suddenly had no strength in me whatsoever. He kicked me in the throat and while I was struggling to get my breath he slipped a noose over my head and then the lights went out.

'He is a very big man, old friend. I can't help you any more as I don't know what happened after that. I am sorry I let you down.'

Jack went over and put his arm around the dog, stroking his head.

'No, don't blame yourself, my friend, you did not let me down. I'm sure the witch is involved here somehow, because

238

there is evidence she has returned and has been able to burn her way out of the barn. Now, you need to get your strength back. Do you think you will be alright if I leave you? I am going to take the boys down to the village to see if anyone knows anything. I'll be back later.'

The boys came back down the stairs as Jack shrugged himself into an old coat. They turned towards the village and Cabal, probably out of habit more than any other reason, dragged himself slowly and painfully up the stairs to lie across the boys' bedroom doorway. In any event, from there he could see and hear anything that might go on in or outside the house.

While they were walking down to the village they hardly spoke as each had their own particular thoughts as to what had happened and what might happen next. However, Jack thought it best to voice his suspicions about Kate.

Ben finally asked, 'Do you think, then, that it was my stepfather, granddad?'

Knowing this was not a time to prevaricate or cushion his suspicions, 'I am afraid that I do, Ben,' he replied. 'I can't think of anyone else that would want to harm your mother, or my dog, come to that. But, I have never actually met Morgan, apart from that one time, and even then we did not speak, and I only know what you and your mother have told me. From that, he seems a very bad man but it's only now that I can see how evil he is. The wicked thing he did to Cabal shows just how much. I only hope that …um, yes, well …' and he would not let his mind or his speech venture further. Suffice it to say they all looked pretty grim.

As they entered the village, they noticed Mrs. Ambrose sweeping the path from her front door to the gate. They went up and asked her if she had seen Kate. 'She came by about three o'clock and hung the rest of my curtains and they do look very nice. Why, whatever is the matter Mr. Percival? You look quite upset.'

'What time did she leave, Mrs. Ambrose?'

'She was only here about an hour and then left. She said she wanted to get your tea ready.

Mrs Ambrose looked at their worried faces and asked, 'Has she not been home?'

'No, Mrs. Ambrose.' Jack hesitated but then decided to be plain with the old lady. 'I believe her ex-husband has abducted her. She did come home but I think he must have found out where she lives and then ... oh, why was I not there when he came! I am always there! Only today I had to get some spares and some new farm equipment.' Jack, quite distraught, took time to pull himself together. 'No, it's not good thinking that way now, is it? What we have to do is think about what we should do next to try and find her. Mrs. Ambrose,' Jack said, 'he tried to kill my dog. He put a noose around his neck and left him for dead. I believe that it's only because it happened fairly recently that we were able to remove the cord in time.'

At the old woman's enquiry, Jack said that Cabal appeared to be recovering quite swiftly.

Mrs. Ambrose opened the gate and told them all to come inside. Jack started to protest, saying that there wasn't enough time to stop, that they had to keep going. 'Unless you have a plan, Jack,' she said, and Jack wondered at the familiarity of the change from the formal "Mr Percival" to "Jack", 'you will not be able to do anything and will just end up going round and round in circles and that will never do. Come in, now. Sit down and we will think of what can be done. I'll put the kettle on, so come into the kitchen while I make some tea. I must admit that I do love tea. A wonderful invention,' she confided to them as she put the kettle on, got the tea caddy down and started to warm the pot.

They had by then all sat down in Mrs. Ambrose's very comfortable kitchen. While the kettle was boiling she suggested Jack telephone the police, more to give him something to do than anything else, as he was obviously very ill at ease. Unfortunately, because the village was very small there wasn't a police station in it, but there was a policeman who lived at the edge of the village and, with luck, he might be in. She looked up the number and gave it to Jack who rang him. He was in and said that he would come along to Mrs. Ambrose's house, enquiring in the few shops and the pub on the way. He said he would be about half an hour. 'Enough time for us to start making some plans?' enquired Danny.

Mrs. Ambrose had a cupboard that seemed to be full of medicines and pills. She was rummaging through to find a salve that she said was very good for bruises and sores. 'I'll pop up to your house with you when you leave here, and put some of this on your dog's neck. I've also got some medicine that will take away the soreness in his throat.'

'That's very kind of you Mrs. Ambrose,' said Jack.

They drank their tea and before long there was a knock. The policeman entered through the front door. He had a nodding acquaintance with Jack but knew the boys quite well, as he did most of the children who attended the village school. 'I'm sorry but no-one saw a stranger; well, not to describe anyway,' he told them, 'but someone in the pub did see a Hillman Minx car going nor-east out of the village. He only noticed because he'd had one of those cars himself, what some 35 years or so ago, and didn't believe there were any still about. It was cream coloured and there was a number plate that started "HTW" but he didn't get the rest of the number. I've passed the information through to the station and they said they'd get onto it. I'll need some information from you, though.'

They sat for the next twenty minutes, describing Morgan, or at least what he had looked like four years ago. The boys, surprisingly, as they were so young at the time, could remember a lot of detail. 'He is about five feet ten with dark brown, curly hair and dark brown eyes. He has a bit of a beer

241

belly,' this from Ben, 'and he always shaved twice a day because he had a thick beard otherwise. Mum said that most people thought he was good looking; although when he got into a temper, he didn't look good at all; in fact he looked very bad.'

'One funny thing, though,' said Danny. 'He doesn't have the end joint on his right index finger. He said he lost it in an accident but he never told us how.' Jack shot a quick look at Daniel as he volunteered this information, noticing as he did so that Mrs. Ambrose also turned quickly to look at the boy.

'That's very interesting and important,' said the policeman. 'I'll pass that on to the station so they will have a bit more to go on.'

They then described Kate so that the police could be on the lookout for two people travelling together with those descriptions.

'You'd better go home now so that we know where you are if we need to get hold of you quickly.'

None of them wanted to go home, but they could see the sense in it. If Morgan had taken Kate in the car, well they weren't going to catch up with it on foot, were they!

Mrs. Ambrose, who had never ventured up the hill to Jack's home, got her Mackintosh out of the closet and said she would come along with them to treat the dog.

They entered the cottage when it was almost fully dark. Cabal tore down the stairs and went straight to Mrs. Ambrose, nuzzling her and wagging his tail. Jack started to light the lamps on the mantelshelf and stoke up the fire, while Mrs. Ambrose set out her unguents on the table.

'Cabby,' Jack scolded him, 'that's being a bit familiar, isn't it! Sorry, Mrs. Ambrose, he's not usually like that, it must be the after-effects of his close call.'

'It's OK, Jack. I'm used to it with animals. I get on well with nearly all of them you know. Now, Cabal, isn't it?' she leaned down to stroke the dog. 'Stand still and let me take a look at your neck.' She carefully moved the hair on his neck to one side and could see the welt that had sprung up because of the cord. She tutted a bit and then gently spread the ointment onto his skin. All the while he was licking her hand! Jack, shaking his head, couldn't believe it. Next, she measured some medicine into his drinking bowl, added a little water and then told him to drink it all up, which he did, all the while wagging his tail furiously.

'I don't know what's got into that dog,' Jack said, staring at Cabal, worrying that maybe lack of oxygen to his brain had made him a little deranged. 'Also, I don't know how to thank you,' he said as Mrs. Ambrose screwed the cap back onto the bottle. 'Please share our supper and then I shall take you home.'

'Now, I'm fine, Jack. I've had my tea and there's no need for you to be walking me home. I shall just trot along now and pop back in the morning to see how the invalid is doing. It's only two minutes down the lane anyway.' And, without more ado, she was up and gone.

It was still some time before the boys could be persuaded to go to bed but, after promising to wake them up should anything happen, they finally went upstairs and, following their very long day travelling and the shock of their mother's abduction, fell, like all youngsters do, into the sleep of exhaustion.

Jack flopped down into his rocker, stroking Cabal's head, and they started to finally catch up on the day's events. Jack told the hound about the car and the direction in which it was last seen heading and told him about the missing part of Morgan's index finger.

'*Mordred!*' Cabal exclaimed when he realised the implications of who it must be – Mad Mab's sadistic and evil oft-times partner in wickedness. '*Do you think he has been able to time travel? It certainly looks like it! Mind, he's changed a lot if it is Morgan. I didn't recognise him at all.*'

243

Jack considered this possibility.

Cabal then gave him a description of what Morgan looked like. Jack was surprised, because as far as Cabby was concerned, he appeared to be a little different to what the boys had described him as looking like. He had a completely shaven head - so, gone was the dark, curly hair. He had an overload of muscles and, after Jack enquired, apparently no beer belly.

'Looks like he has been working out while he's been inside,' said Cabal. *'What I can't understand, though, is why I didn't recognise him. Now I come to think of it, the smell of him was the same but he looked so different; he used to be so skinny and wimpish and now, what with all the muscles and his face filling out ...'.*

'Yes, he must have been doing that in prison,' interrupted Jack. *'You're not the only one to get it wrong, though; I should have recognised who he was when he got Kate to marry him. But, like you, I didn't recognise him - at that time he was tall, but mainly fat instead of muscled whereas in Arthur's day, like you say, he was skinny and wimpish. Mab must have put a powerful spell on him to change his appearance so much. I wonder how he couldn't manage to get out of prison in all that time, if it is him! I bet he was mad at being locked up like that!*

Jack considered this for a while and then, shrugging his shoulders, decided, *'Well, whatever, I am only going to give the police a few hours to do something tonight and then I shall start my own investigations.*

'I shall ask Mrs. Ambrose if she will have the boys - that is, if I can persuade them to stay, and then we'll go hunting. Talking of Mrs. Ambrose, you were a bit familiar with her tonight! What was all that about?'

'Mrs. Ambrose? Oh, nothing!' Cabby, all innocent, was very amused and even though his vocal chords couldn't physically allow him to laugh, the look on his face was as

near to amusement as you could get. *'Mrs. Ambrose, indeed!'* he said on a sneeze and then decided to settle down to tease Jack for a while.

'Cabby, come on now, what is so funny?' Jack was getting annoyed.

'You think she's Mrs. Ambrose? Well, she's not Mrs. Ambrose.'

'Not Mrs. Ambrose! Then who, for goodness' sake, is she?'

'She's - or should I say he - is Merlin!'

Jack jumped up out of his chair, knocking it over and smashing his mug in the process as it dropped onto the floor. *'Whaaat!'* and then recalling that he needed to keep quiet or he would wake the boys, continued silently. *'But Merlin has never been able to time travel!'*

Jack looked at the hound and, remembering Mad Mab, things that had been niggling inside his head started to slot into place.

'Do you think he has managed to do it? No, silly question!' he admonished himself. *'If Mrs. Ambrose is Merlin, then the answer would obviously have to be "yes". And if Mab has somehow got hold of the spell, or whatever, she will be - no,* has been - *trying her hardest to do the same. Merlin will need to know. Come on … oh no, we can't leave the boys on their own. Cab, can you look after them?'*

Cabal looked a mixture of ashamed and affronted, knowing that Jack must think him completely incompetent, especially as he'd allowed Morgan to get Kate.

'Sorry, old friend, I don't mean to make you feel bad, but I am a bit worried about you, especially with the damage to your neck.' Jack reached out toward his friend and checked the wound on his neck only to find it completely healed. *'Yes, you are right - it must be Merlin! Stay here and keep an eye on the boys and I will be back within the hour.'* He grabbed his coat from the hook and was gone in a trice.

245

Cabby went upstairs and lay down, completely alert, outside the boys' doorway. No one was going to surprise him this time.

The memory of Jack's young family's arrival, all those years back, flooded into his mind and he didn't know whether it was the shock he had just sustained with regard to Cabal, Kate or Morgan or even the fact that Merlin appeared to have travelled through time to the 20th Century, but as he remembered them he recalled his daughter's distress when she had arrived on his doorstep with her two young sons - his grandsons - Ben and Daniel. Once she had finally made up her mind to leave her cruel husband - the boys' stepfather, who was obviously both a bully and a coward – she decided she was just too tired to do anything other than go home to her father.

From that first day when they had turned up at his home until now, four years had passed. *'Four years! Can you believe it?'* he thought.

Jack, having been taught well by Merlin, could recall the distant past as though it was only yesterday. *'Though sometimes I can't remember much about yesterday!'* he had often joked.

As the years had gone by they had settled into life at their grandfathers. Kate became more independent and the boys grew in strength and confidence.

TWENTY-THREE

Mrs. Ambrose, or should it be said, Merlin, was sitting on the wall outside the house swinging her - or his – legs when Jack arrived, some five minutes later.

'I thought you might get here a bit quicker than this, Percy!' he said. 'I knew that husband of hers would have a try at getting at her, but I didn't think he'd outfox me. Just shows how wrong each of us can be – even me! Besides, I thought it would be Mab that would make the move, not anyone else – especially that retard!' he stated.

Jack couldn't help but stare at her - or should he say "him" - goggle-eyed. It had been years since they had met and, although he had seen him masquerading in many disguises, he was still astonished at the transformation. "A man of many guises" people had often said of him. 'I can't believe it's you! You really *do* look like an old woman.'

'Well, of course I do. That was the whole idea!' But its all illusion – you only see what I want you to see! I am still exactly the same,' he harrumphed. 'It's pretty weird, though,' he said thoughtfully, 'because it's you and not I that's been blessed with a natural ability to travel through time *and* needing very little help from me. That is part of the reason I summoned you in the first place. You're unique! However, I have to admit that I had tried for years to travel across time and it was only by mere chance that I came across the right potion to combine with the correct spell. I had managed to hop backwards and forwards on several occasions, but the longest I ever stayed anywhere in a different time zone was about thirty seconds. I'd hardly had the time to wipe the surprised look off my face before I was whisked back again to where I started! Wham! In fact it was just after the time you and Arthur appeared in my cave, when we went off to rescue, or should I say Moon Song managed to rescue, Cabal from a watery grave, when I found the plant growing next to the dragon's droppings.'

'Moon Song?' Jack queried. 'Who is Moon Song?'

'Moon Song! You know Moon Song! Oh,' he appeared flabbergasted, 'you are dense sometimes Percy! The dragon!'

'Ahh, yes,' Jack thought, a slow smile spreading over his face, 'so that is the name of the dragon.' Even now as he thought of her, a shiver went up his spine. She was the most amazingly beautiful creature he had ever laid eyes on, then or since, and Moon Song was a very appropriate name for her because like that first night she rose as the moon over the treetops and sang, along with Merlin, the most haunting of melodies.

Jack was suddenly brought back to the present as Merlin jabbed a gnarled old finger into his shoulder. He was again surprised because when Merlin *was* Merlin he had the most beautifully shaped hands he had ever seen. "A musician's hands", his mother would have said, which he supposed he was, in a way, as he could play the harp more like a musician than a magician, even though he didn't sing the songs but spoke them. But, then again, he had the most melodious speaking voice Jack had ever heard, then or since.

'You are wandering, young man, and are not listening to a word I have been saying. I don't believe you are aware of the seriousness of the situation!'

'Sorry, Merlin.' Jack had to laugh inwardly at being called "young man" again by Merlin. 'However, I can assure you that I am completely aware of the seriousness of the situation. Anyway, I can't stay long; I have to get back to the cottage. The boys are alone. Well, Cabal is with them but I said I wouldn't be long. We're going to have to start looking for Kate tomorrow. I've never got to know this Morgan fellow - well not as Morgan anyway - but from the description we have of him we now know that he is not who we thought he was.'

248

Jack waited for Merlin to make the appropriate response but he might as well grow wings and fly as Merlin just waited patiently for him to continue.

'And I don't like anything I've heard about him.' Merlin still stood waiting. 'Oh, OK - it seems that his right index finger is missing and, if that is so, it looks like Mordred has also been able to time travel and, not only that, but he has also been able to stay here, albeit locked up in prison, and usually a time traveller's time in another time zone is limited. *And* trust his mother to give him *her* name - what conceit!' He stopped, thinking of the time he had met Mordred's mother, the extremely ambitious sorceress, Morgan le Fey and then, forcing himself back to the present, continued, 'Also, it looks like Mab's been able to time travel.' Now Merlin's satanic eyebrows did shoot up in surprise at that one - and it took a lot for that to happen so far as he was concerned as he was usually one step, if not one leap, ahead of whatever was going on.

'She appeared to me in the barn about a week ago and there are signs that she's burned her way out of it. By the way, she said something quite peculiar. Something like "Merlin won't be able to help you this time". So, can you help us?'

'Can I help you? Can I help you?' Merlin spluttered looking and sounding affronted. 'Well, of all the dumb questions I have ever heard in my life! Why do you think I am here? Nothing happens by chance, you know!'

He scratched his chin and thought for a moment. 'I reckon she's stolen one of my scrolls.' His lips twitched as a funny thought entered his head. 'I bet she's taken one of the old ones. Ha, yes! I reckon she's taken a rough draft thinking it a completed scroll and she either thinks she can stay here or she thinks I won't be able to get here because I'll not remember the spell without the scroll.' Merlin creased up laughing, or should I say cackling – looking and sounding like a really old hag as he tried to get the laughter under control.

'Did you know, Percy,' he croaked as he finally stopped laughing, 'that we druids never commit anything to paper? No, I didn't think you knew that. Well, when the Romans came here they slaughtered all the British druids because they were terrified of their power over the people and their mysticism and, therefore, all that wealth of knowledge was destroyed overnight. Well, we do now write quite a few bits and pieces down but - and you should feel very honoured that I am telling you this - we never actually complete it! If she has stolen anything of mine, it will be useless to her. Anything that cannot be committed to memory is not worth remembering, my boy. My spells are my own – nobody else's.'

'How is it that you survived the slaughter? Jack enquired.

I thought I had already told you! I was on a flying visit to China to see the dragons hatch. Did I not say? Well, I was and that was when it happened. So I was the only one left. When I returned, my cats told me. As you can imagine, I was horrified. That's why no-one ever knows which cave I may be in at any one time! *And* that's why I have so many caves – and cats!'

He stood looking way off into the distant past until, shaking himself out of his reverie, turned his eyes once more upon Jack. 'Anyway, getting back to these scrolls, I believe Mab thinks she has the whole spell.'

'He really does put his all into a spell,' Jack thought.

'Of course I do, young man!' Jack remembered he could mind speak, as Merlin answered his thought.

'Well, we'll see,' he continued. 'The only thing that really worries me is that I shall have to now try and find out how she might have got hold of *my* scrolls! She's either been able to get into one of my caves - which means that I shall have to update my security spells or, and this is even more worrying, she's been able to get to one of my little men. Hmm, if that's the case, she must have something over him! No, I can't believe even then they would ever consider being duplicitous. All my men are completely honourable; I have always been a good judge of character. Still,' he said, shaking off his thoughts, 'I can't worry about that right at this moment because we need to find Kate. Go home, get some rest and come back tomorrow morning. I shall be working through the night to discover where she is and I shall find her, Percy, never fear. I shall certainly find her!'

He turned to go back into the cottage but stopped, thinking of something that had jumped into his mind. 'You remember the prophesy, my boy? Arthur, when he died, would be taken across the sea to Avalon? And he was!' I nodded and he continued.

'All the signs are right that Britain is coming to that stage in its existence where the prophesy looks like it might be reaching its climax! It is in desperate need of Arthur's return - High King of all the Britons. So, just you keep looking at the signs, my boy; keep looking! He will return when Britain is in dire need and you will know him, even if he doesn't have the same name!'

He stepped across the threshold of his cottage and, glancing back over his shoulder, lifted a gnarled old hand in farewell.

Jack started to turn away to return to his own home but stopped and looked back. As he waved to the old woman standing in the doorway, he suggested, 'Merlin, I think we should call each other with the names by which the boys know us. It could be a little awkward trying to explain your sudden appearance, especially with what you look like at the moment and also, so far, the boys believe that the stories I tell them are just that - stories. At least I think they do! So, from now on I shall call you Mrs. Ambrose and I think you should call me Jack.'

'Sensible, my boy, sensible. I am glad you've learned something from me,' he responded, as usual taking all the credit. 'Anyway, I have a plan. It will be no good until tomorrow, so go home and get a good night's sleep. Return here in the morning, with the boys, and we'll start putting the plan into action.'

Merlin was walking back through the front door when he stopped and turned back to Jack. 'I'm glad Daniel told us that bit about Morgan's index finger? Yes, we certainly know who that is, don't we?'

He turned and went in through the front door calling out, 'Good night, Per … Good night Jack.'

Nothing untoward had happened while Jack had been away. Cabal trotted down the stairs as Jack entered the kitchen. While Jack made a mug of tea he told Cabby about Mrs. Ambrose, forgetting, of course, that Cabal already knew who she really was. *'You remember we were talking about Mordred, when we were told of the man with part of his index finger missing, Cab? Well, it looks as though we were right. Mordred, or Morgan as we now know him, was sent here by Mab. I wonder how she did that because he's obviously been here for many years! She must have been messing around with time travel for a long time. And, she left him to rot in prison for a good few years as well. I bet he was furious about that! Possibly, whatever happened went a bit wrong, having to spend all those years in prison as he did. I wonder if her powers are as strong as they used to be,'* he mused. *'Well, Merlin is up to speed on that aspect so we'll just have to see what happens tomorrow. I don't suppose for one moment that the police will be able to locate the car. I think that might be a blind, to have us running around in circles. I think that what's happening now is something that should belong to the times of legend and myth, so I don't think any policeman is going to believe half of what we could tell him. They'd probably think they'd be doing us a favour by locking*

252

us up! No, I think we're on our own with this one. Daniel was the one who set us onto the right track when he said about the missing finger. Hey, I think that's enough for now Cab. Let's get some sleep. We have a colossal task ahead of us and we're going to need all our strength.'

As they settled down to sleep Jack recounted the little he knew about Mordred. He was, or had been in the time that he had known him, about ten years' older than Arthur and was the son of a sorceress called Morgan le Fey. Both mother and son were evil and had always kept to themselves, learning as much as they could of the Old Way but not listening to the wisdom of the seers - those elders who advise with regard to a knowledge of revealed things – but instead have both gone back through to its evil side down the iniquitous route to that place of chaos - the place of madness! Therefore, rather than using their powers for the good of all, they hoarded up power only for themselves. Mab, another evil sorceress, spent time with the iniquitous duo. Mordred and Mab became very close – well as close as anyone with no heart can get – whilst pursuing their evil schemes, each one trying to outdo the other in thinking up the most heinous spells and enchantments. And all that notwithstanding the smell! It was quite probable that Mordred had no sense of smell – he couldn't really, being as close to Mab as he often was!

'Go to sleep, Jack!'

TWENTY-FOUR

The next morning, almost before cock crow, everyone seemed to arrive in the kitchen at the same time. Although they had somehow all managed to get some sleep, they were more than eager to get started to find Kate. Jack knew he had to keep silent on the fact that Morgan and his old foe Mordred were one and the same. He wondered what effect that would have on the boys if they ever found out. Would they believe it?

In no time at all they were all, Cabal included, heading down towards Mrs. Ambrose's cottage. She was in a flurry of business, packing this, stirring that, reading something else.

'Come in, come in all of you,' she said as they knocked on her door. 'I haven't heard anything from the police, but then I expect they will have come to you?' she queried. As they shook their heads, she turned back to what she was doing. 'I have packed a few things that we'll need for our journey and have hired a car.' She turned to Jack. 'You can drive, can't you?' she asked. Smiling as he said that he could, she breathed a sigh of relief. 'Good, because I pretended I was you when I phoned for it. Jack could believe this, as Merlin was an excellent mimic. 'Boys, please take all of these things out onto the porch and wait for me there. Let me know when the car arrives. I want to speak to your grandfather.' The boys lifted the packages and baskets out onto the path and sat down to await the arrival of the car.

When they were alone, Mrs. Ambrose, speaking in a very quiet voice, told Jack that she knew where Morgan was taking Kate. 'She has tried very hard to cover her tracks but I found, and with some difficulty I can tell you, that Mab has arranged for him to take her to the place of standing stones, where we once had that confrontation with her – you know - the time after she'd abducted Rhianne. No, do *not* interrupt me,' he held up his hand as Jack went to speak, 'There isn't time to go into all the details. Now, and I hope this won't alarm you too much, she has been harnessing evil forces, one of which has advised that her powers would be unbeatable if she could revisit the stones and present an offering. I believe Kate is that offering! Now, control yourself, Jack! We shall save her, it won't happen!'

'How do you know?' Jack asked, white to the gills.

'As I said, it's a long story and I have my sources! And,' he exclaimed, changing the subject, 'if I am not mistaken, here comes our transport. This should be good; I haven't travelled on anything so fast since I went on that trip with Moon Song over to China. Hrrmph, yes, well, let's go. I'm not at all sure how we are going to overcome the problems facing us, but I reckon we might try and do something similar to the last time. We shall see. Well, come along, make haste – let's go!'

They climbed into the car – an estate, thank goodness - Jack in the driving seat with Mrs. Ambrose sitting next to him. The boys sat in the back and Cabal stretched out in the rear with all the packages. The clock on the dashboard said 10.55am as they set off through the village.

They stopped at the end house to speak to the policeman but he could give them no news. They, in their turn, told him no more than that they were going to some places where they thought she might be. 'We'll call you if we need assistance,' said Mrs. Ambrose.

'Granddad,' Ben interrupted Jack's reverie. 'Where *are* we going?'

'Not quite sure yet, lad. I'm just following a hunch.'

'Well, if we are going to be travelling for a little while, will you finish the story you were telling us on the way home from the town? It's not that I don't care about mum, but it's more like, well it will take our minds off things for a while.'

Mrs. Ambrose raised a quizzical eyebrow at Jack and then added her urging to that of young Ben. 'Oh I love a story,' she purred. 'Do let me persuade you to continue. I'm sure I can catch up with anything I may already have missed. You don't have to start from the beginning for my sake.'

Jack frowned at her but she had turned away with an amused smile on her face.

'OK boys,' he said. 'But I don't want *any* interruptions. It's hard enough worrying about your mother, let alone telling a story and driving at the same time without having to answer questions as well.' He gave another quick glance at Mrs. Ambrose who stared straight ahead, the picture of innocence.

'So - the afternoon disappeared and, as evening fell, Merlin got us all to go down into the circle of stones on the plain. He had previously told us what our positions were, so each of us searched around and took up our places. Merlin stood very still in the centre of the circle of standing stones. Arthur and I stood between the two stones that supported one of the lintels within the inner circle. It was very quiet. Even if there were any night creatures making a noise, that noise did not penetrate the circle of stones.

Cabal wouldn't come inside the circle. He stood just outside, the hair all over his body standing straight out – making himself look as big as he could - a warning signal which was, unfortunately, counter-balanced by his tail, which was tucked right under his body, showing his fear. He held his head low with ears splayed out like shelves either side of his head and his lips were curled back over his fangs. If he had to come in to rescue us he wouldn't want to but he would; however, for the present he was a silent sentinel on guard just outside.

Merlin raised his staff high above his head. Suddenly light radiated from the eyes in the silver falcon's head atop the staff like a shaft of light from the sun, lighting up each standing stone as he looked at it. He himself appeared to have been raised about a hand's breadth above the ground and was staring straight ahead. In this position, he started very slowly, as though wedged onto an invisible, slow motion potter's wheel, to move in an anti-clockwise direction. He told us afterwards that, as he looked down the pathway of each shaft of light, he saw histories and prophesies the like of which he had never seen before. At some he stared in wonder. At others he appeared to be searching - sometimes finding, sometimes not. Many times a look of sheer horror could be detected. All these reactions could be seen, but only in his eyes – they were the only parts of him that moved or showed any emotion. Only one ray found nothing but blackness – to that road he was barred!

The light from the tip of the staff was suddenly extinguished, leaving us all in pitch darkness. We had already been told not to move but now we dared not move until we could see.

Gradually our eyes became accustomed to the dimness, which eased as the moon started to rise. We saw Merlin sitting on a small, fallen stone, at the edge of the circle. We started toward him and as we got close he looked up at us with a dazed expression and then, recalling who we were, held up his hand, palm upward, to stop us. He looked exhausted and old. We stood, waiting for him to speak, staring at this man as the rising moon gave his face and falcon's head cap a silvery-grey unreality.

'I have seen down the pathways of time!' he whispered in a very croaky voice. We had to strain forward to catch his words. Pointing at Arthur he stated, 'You have a hard part to play in this life, young Arthur. But play it you will, and men will revere your name down those pathways of time.' Then he shook his head to bring himself back to the present.

'Come,' he said, jumping to his feet, 'there is much to be done.'

Without further ado he was up and striding back toward the campsite and, as we had stood so still before, we were now almost running to keep up with him. Of course, Cabal

257

had no difficulty and always enjoyed a run, particularly as it was going away from those hated stones.

I had understood some of what Merlin had thought but it was extremely jumbled and I guessed I might have a chance to ask him later.

We had asked him earlier if, now that Rhianne was rescued, whether we could just go home. There were a couple of arguments against this – one of them being that Jasmine still had to be rescued. However, the main one was that Merlin knew that this confrontation between his and Mab's powers was pre-ordained and thus could not be set aside – there would be a high price to pay if he did not make a stand! Mab would automatically win and her victory would produce dire consequences for all concerned.

Merlin now rummaged around in the sack he had brought with him and eventually brought out two objects that looked slightly familiar to me. He held them up to the moon and slowly, very slowly, they started to illuminate. The Cyclops' eyes! Merlin turned and grinned at me. 'I don't know how she did this or where she got them from, but, when I was travelling around, along one of my favourite pathways, I came to the forest outside the castle, where that old witch lived with these peculiar specimens. I had seen them when we went to rescue Cabal. Two of these horrid beings were laying dead just inside the forest and it looked as though a battle had taken place there, although there were no other bodies or weapons about. I went over to them and pulled these eyes from their sockets and pocketed them to examine another time. Purely by chance – or was it? - sometime later when I was working on a new enchantment, they were lying on a workbench in my sky study tower when they started to glow. The moon was just peeking over the rim of the windowsill and had alighted on the eyes of the Cyclops. After a while, because I was studying a sky chart at the time, I wondered why my candle was illuminating it so brightly that night. Turning around I saw these eyes glowing. Amazing! So, I left them there in the moon's glow where they appeared to have consumed all of its light. When I put them back in my sack they went out but when I brought them out into the open again they lit up.' He was ecstatic at his find. All I could think about was that they looked just like a couple of 200-watt light bulbs, but I tried to look impressed. 'I have a great use for these illuminations,' he stated. 'Now, you lads get prepared; in another hour we shall return to the plain. Salazar and I have a lot to sort out.'

I never did find out what he and Salazar discussed but I shall never forget what happened that night. I had heard that it was amazing to watch two sorcerers at battle. One never knew what would happen next. However, as I had never seen one of these events before I really did not know what to expect. Suffice it to say, we were all extremely nervous as we did not know what would take place should the unthinkable happen. Selfishly - what would become of us all if Merlin lost!' Jack took a quick sideways glance at Mrs. Ambrose but she appeared to be taking no offence.

'Well, Arthur and I checked and oiled our short swords, making sure they came easily out of their sheaths and counted a dozen arrows at least in each of our quivers.

The men, obviously, had their equipment always at the ready. Rhianne would not hear of being left behind with one of the men to guard her but insisted on coming with us. She said that it was all or nothing, even though none of us had any idea of what was going to happen.

The sun had almost sunk behind the hills to the west and was shedding an eerie light over everything, casting huge shadows where the stones stood; anything could have been lurking behind them in the darkness!

'It's time,' said Merlin. 'Come, let's go down to the plain.' He and Salazar started to descend. I can still remember how I felt. I looked at Cabal, whose hair was again standing on end. The men all looked grim. My knees were playing a tune against each other and Rhianne looked extremely pale but, as she took hold of my hand, I forced myself to be brave. Arthur was walking along rubbing his hands together, but then it was fairly cold, while Hive, well he always looked expressionless anyway, just looked a lighter shade of pale.

We all followed Merlin onto the plain.'

Mrs. Ambrose suddenly interrupted, pointing as they came over the rise and there, in the distance, majestic upon the plain, stood the stones, tall and grey. There was not much sun now; it had been almost obliterated by a mist that had started forming some half an hour ago, and thus the light from a watery sun cast eerie shadows through those gigantic structures.

Ben asked, 'Granddad, is that the same place that you have been telling us about in your stories?'

Jack had to think quickly but a quick nod from Mrs. Ambrose suggested, into his mind, that at such a time as this nothing but the truth would suffice. 'Yes, Ben, it is.'

'Then how do you think that Morgan knows about it, if you think that that's where he's taken mum?'

'That's a hard one, eh?' Mrs. Ambrose spoke into Jack's mind.

'I don't know, lad,' he responded, 'but I can see another car parked over there at the foot of the hill. Let's go and investigate.'

They pulled up behind the car. It was cream and it was a Hillman Minx, "HTW" being the first part of the number plate. 'Looks like they *are* here,' said Daniel, 'but I can't see them anywhere.'

'Let's go up to see if they are anywhere in the stone circle,' Mrs. Ambrose was already striding up the hill as she spoke.

They all followed, Cabal running on ahead. He stopped abruptly, only halfway down the incline and waited for the others to catch up with him.

'What's up with him?' she asked, forgetting his fear of the stones. Darkness had rapidly started to close in on them and, although it was still too early in the year for it, chilliness seeped up through the ground, through their shoes, making them all start to shiver. 'Keep together,' Mrs. Ambrose ordered them, as she delved into her large shoulder bag.

Bringing out a powerful torch, she led the way over toward the standing stones. Shining the beam of the torch this way and that, they made their way around the whole of the outside before venturing inside.

Cabal kept his distance outside the stones but, keeping pace with them, padded back and forth well away from the circle.

After they stepped inside the outer circle, Mrs. Ambrose ordered the children, 'Stay here and do not move,' putting great emphasis on. *'no matter what happens'*.

They looked scared and Mrs. Ambrose, not to mince her words, told them that their lives and that of their mother might depend on them staying just where they were and doing just as they are told. If Morgan got hold of one or both of them, he would have a further bargaining power, which might mean that they lost their mother forever.

Feeling very bad about having to put the situation to them quite so baldly, she made them promise, which they did, and then she turned and, with Jack alongside her, strode toward the centre of the stone circle.

They were gone for some time before returning to the boys where, looking over their heads, they could see Cabal staring at them just outside the circle.

'Well, boys,' Jack whispered, 'everything is quiet and there is no sign of anyone else here at the present, but Mrs. Ambrose has said there is evidence that someone has been

261

here and it looks like they'll be returning. We'll just have to be patient and wait.'

'What for?' asked Ben. 'How do you know it will be them that will be coming back? Will they definitely be coming back? What is going to happen? Will mum be OK?'

He was getting agitated, so Jack placed an arm around his young shoulder in a firm grip, trying to calm him down.

'We are almost sure it will be Morgan and your mother that comes back. I am certain that he has an evil plan and this is a lure to get us all here. However, I do not know what that plan is but I do know that we shall all do our utmost to free your mother and send this Morgan creature packing for good. Now try to keep your wits about you. Worry keeps trying to get the better of you, I know, but it never helps so try your hardest to keep it under control. You must know that I am worried sick as well, but if I dwell on it, well I can't think straight and the battle is half lost before we start. We all love your mum. Just remember that. Love is the strongest weapon we have.' Jack turned as Mrs. Ambrose called him over. 'Stay here,' he told the boys and walked over to join her.

And then the mist swirled around them in earnest.

TWENTY-FIVE

Ben grabbed Daniel by the elbow and pulled him close, so that, with one of the huge stone structures at their backs, they could feel a little more secure. Daniel could just see Cabal's head if he turned and looked over his left shoulder; the dog was shaking and looked very scared. Daniel knew that dogs were more susceptible to changes in the atmosphere than humans, so Cabal's fear was not helping him feel any easier.

As the mist swirled around their feet, the cold grew more intense and it wasn't long before both boys' teeth started clattering together - was it cold? – more than likely it was fear! The mist came and went, thinning one minute and then becoming dense the next, coiling and uncoiling – a serpent ready to strike? – had they listened to too many of their grandfather's tales? They caught glimpses of him as he stood in front of one of the stones and Mrs. Ambrose, who must have been standing on one of the stones because she looked a lot taller; must also have brought a long coat with her because she certainly looked warmer than they felt. Before very much longer, in the eerie quietness that always accompanies the mist or fog, they noticed that Mrs. Ambrose was using her torch, which was piercing the fog as she searched with it. It was an extremely strong beam.

Just as suddenly as the mist rolled in, it hastened away – scampering off to its hidey-hole as though sucked away by some huge, invisible extractor fan, or was it by the indrawn breath of a giant?

The scene before the two boys became like something out of a science fiction film. The stones began to pulsate with a life of their own. No, they didn't move – well not just then anyway - but they appeared alive nonetheless. The dullness had gone from stone or slate grey, gradually turning to vibrant colour and light, which surged and danced along and through them like an untamed electrical force; it sang and buzzed and fizzed and zinged as it chased backwards and forwards over and through the boulders. Mrs. Ambrose was now nowhere to be seen but they were relieved to see their grandfather's profile and he, like them, had his back to one of the stones and was hanging onto it for dear life. Perhaps Mrs. Ambrose was hidden from their view, clutching a stone in like manner.

Then they noticed, in the middle of the circle on an altar-shaped stone, stood a man the like of which the boys had never seen in their lives. But without the shadow of a doubt they both knew who he was – Merlin. They had listened to too many of their grandfather's tales to not recognise him when he appeared. They looked at each other, eyes goggling, for confirmation that they were not hallucinating. Daniel pinched himself, just to make sure. Turning back to the scene in front of them they saw him raise his staff high above his head. Like the story most recently told by their grandfather, it was as though it had come to life.

Suddenly light radiated from the staff's silver falcon's head like rays of light from the sun and with the occasional flash from the ruby eyes. Merlin appeared to have been lifted about a hand's breadth above the ground and was staring straight ahead. Again, like the story, he started to move very slowly - 'as though wedged onto a slow motion potter's wheel' Ben whispered – 'in an anti-clockwise direction'.

Merlin stood stock still, except for his eyes – they were the only parts of him that seemed not to be made of stone. The electrical current gained momentum as it continued to dance and sing, moving around the circle from stone to stone, illuminating the area as it went. The boys noticed shadows and flashes as it zipped along. More than once they thought they could see groups of wraith-like people standing around watching all that was going on. They appeared and disappeared, only to appear again somewhere else within the stone circle.

Ben rubbed his eyes, thinking they were playing tricks on him but Daniel, pointing out the ghostlike shapes, confirmed that he wasn't imagining it.

Then suddenly the light from the tip of the staff was extinguished and the colours and sounds from the stones faded away, leaving them all in an eerie, silent half light. After that, the electrical force continued intermittently to play through the stones, lighting up places here and there but even this eventually weakened.

'It's happening for real,' whispered Daniel. 'Just like in one of granddad's stories.' The boys had already been told not to move but now *dared* not move. Gradually their eyes became accustomed to the dimness; then the moon started to rise in earnest.

When they could see clearly again, they noticed that Merlin had stepped down from the altar stone and was placing various bits and pieces into the folds of his robe. His lips were moving as he did this but no sound came out of his mouth. Before long, he stopped and beckoned Jack over to him. They conferred for some three or four minutes, Jack nodding, sometimes speaking and pointing at a couple of things that they couldn't see, after which he returned to his place. Neither of them appeared to acknowledge Mrs. Ambrose, wherever she might be.

Merlin did a circuit just inside the inner circle of stones, his staff held aloft, sprinkling something around the altar. As the moon caught the indentations on his falcon's head cap and staff, it sent bolts of light around the circle, bouncing from stone to stone and reflecting back and forth across the expanse in between.

Gradually the electrical dance through the stones became still but it still gave off a charge now and then. The colours, however, remained in the stones, which dimly lit up the area all around. Suddenly, Merlin stopped. He turned and faced toward the east raising his arms as he did so. His robe fell full from his wrists, making him look even larger than life; his falcon's head cap and staff held high.

Everyone held their breath.

She was smelled before she was seen! But she must have been very sure of herself because there was no suggestion of fear or failure in her bearing as she stepped out from behind one of the larger stones, even though she was slightly taken aback at the sight of Merlin. She stared at him for a full minute before she spoke.

'Myrddin, my old friend,' she gushed; finally, 'I really did not think you would come.'

'Not so old, Mab, and definitely not a friend,' he retorted, 'and, as you can see, I am not an illusion!'

'Now, now, Myrddin, there is no need to be quite so snappy. Think of the wonderful times we have shared over the years,' she responded. 'However, be that as it may, I am rather surprised to see you here; I thought I had wrapped you up in that cave for at least a couple of millennia! How on earth did you manage to get out?'

Merlin did not deign to respond. He had found out years ago that one of the things that really annoyed Mab, apart from being called Mabel that is, was being ignored. She almost steamed with irritation.

Then, realising she was not going to get a reply, she just shrugged and walked closer to the centre of the stones, noticing, only just in time, that there was a phosphorescent mark etched into the ground encircling the altar.

'Ha, very clever, but not clever enough!' she sneered. 'Did you think I wouldn't see it? But it is quite ineffective; it won't damage me and it won't stop the inevitable.' She lifted her arms and leapt over the magical line, landing, for all her excess weight, quite lightly in the centre of the altar, throwing some powder over the line as she flew. 'So, now – what was to keep me out, will now stop you from coming in.' As she landed, she noticed Jack standing against a stone. 'I see you,

Percy. You thought you had got away with outwitting me, didn't you? Well, mine will be the vengeance! Wait until you see what I have in store for your soon to be not so lovely daughter!' She stepped down from the altar stone, still staring at Jack as she uttered her threats.

Jack had been warned by Merlin not to react to her threats and so, although he was obviously very concerned, merely moved his weight from one foot to the other whilst clenching and unclenching his fists. Remembering things in the past, he thought how he had always trusted Merlin; he would have to continue to do so now.

Putting that awful grimacing smile back onto her face - which they wished she hadn't, her teeth being in the bad (and, Jack noticed, in some places now missing) state that they had become - apart from the foulness of her breath - she turned back to Merlin. 'We have only a very small time to wait and then you will see what you will be unable to do anything about.' She chuckled and swirled around in her glee. It was as much as Merlin could do not to choke on the terrible smell that wafted toward him.

Mab searched the sky, counting on her fingers as she did so, and then, when she believed the time was right, clapped her hands and held out her arms in what looked almost to be a loving, welcoming gesture.

It was another breath-holding moment. No one moved. There was a slight fizzing of electricity over one or two of the stones but even that was not what she was waiting for. Finally, when they all believed that nothing would happen, they saw a similar electrical current moving over the altar stone. It appeared to be outlining something, or someone, and then going out. It did this a few more times but, gaining momentum, carried on swishing around until it finally completed its purpose. They all stared! On top of the altar stone, looking as peaceful as death, lay Kate with her arms crossed over her chest.

Merlin went to move forward, remembering just in time that he now could not cross the barrier that the mad witch had placed around the altar. She screeched with laughter as she saw his dilemma, dancing up and down on the spot like a maniac and swirling around like a dervish, clutching her sides as she rocked backwards and forwards. 'Myrddin,' she was eventually able to gasp, 'when will you give in and admit that I am now more than a match for you?' She wiped the laughter tears from her eyes with the hem of her skirt, leaving dirt tracks down her cheeks. It was as much as Merlin could do not to sneer at her excuse for womanhood.

Jack had his hands behind his back and had to force himself to unclench them before his nails cut into the skin. His beautiful daughter certainly looked dead. He glanced over at his grandsons and their faces were washed white with fear. He couldn't move. He still had his part to play in what looked now like a futile contest.

'Ah, but Mab,' Merlin responded calmly, 'what would you do if you did not have me to perform in front of. No other audience could ever appreciate you as much as I!'

She considered this for a moment, preening and puffing out her chest in self-importance, with her face showing pleasure at his words. Then changing her looks back to the uncompromising sneer that was more normal to her, she snorted, 'Don't think you can sweet-talk me into giving up my plan. I have been waiting for this moment for,' she searched for a word and not being able to think of one that fit, merely uttered, 'ever! I can now get back at all my enemies, you included, you old fraud. No, I don't need you to witness or appreciate my supernatural powers. When I see what I can do, that is satisfaction enough for me - for now!'

She stopped talking and walked toward the altar, looking down at the still form of Kate. 'She looks so like her mother, Myrddin, ' she murmured. 'Only a few slight differences,' she amended as she ran her filthy fingers down the side of

Kate's face and through her hair. Turning slowly, she looked slyly over at Jack as she made these observations.

He was trying, unsuccessfully, not to look angry. Of course, this caused the mad woman's mouth to twitch with amusement.

'OK, Mab, what do you want?'

'Want?' she placed the tips of her fingers together, pressing her forefingers against her lips. As she looked over the top of her grimy hands at Merlin, she became very grave in both word and demeanour, so that it was obvious to all, just how serious the situation was.

Taking a deep breath she stated that which had been her driving ambition for as long as she had been able to plot and plan. 'What I want you cannot provide! So - what I really want is to be renowned as the most famous and celebrated sorceress of all time - feared - and thus claim as my right the adulation and servitude of the whole world. That is my aim - that is what I want and that is what I am going to get! Can you provide that Myrddin? If you, can,' she purred, 'fall down on your face and grovel before me now, and even then the girl might be spared.' She waited and seeing that he had no intention of doing so, curled her lip at him and turned away.

She moved around the altar table, contemplating the woman lying there, then, turning back to him, stated, 'But, what I want, before all that, is this: Arthur slain – he has to be you know, as everyone knows the prophesy – him or me! I know that he is in Avalon - "sleeping", but that's not good enough for me: I have to see him dead. Next, you, Myrddin, stripped of your powers – what would you be without them? – Nothing! A nobody! You would be ridiculed throughout the entire world, for all time – past, present *and* future. Then – Rhianne's beauty destroyed – you wouldn't let me have her for Mordred – Kate had to do - so I want to make sure no-one else wants her; Percy imprisoned forever so that I do not have to put up with his annoying presence any more – the pest. Also, as you know, I have a score to settle with him! Hmm,' she turned and looked over at him. 'Perhaps I could imprison him in the eternal dungeon, where he would see Rhianne on the vision wall – see her beauty age, become marred through my spells, turned to ugliness – yes, I am sure I can make her quite repulsive; she would be mocked by all.' The witch started cackling at her ideas. 'Kate, I'll leave her as she is, kept in a state of lifelessness – the useless offspring of a "great love" – great love indeed! That only leaves those two boys over there – orphans, yes that is what I want for them.' She stopped - breathing heavily at her exertions; then stood looking at them all, one by one, completely satisfied. Once she had regained her breath, 'There are other things,' she added, 'but this is what I want, Myrddin. Otherwise Kate dies. So, you asked, "What do you want". That is what I want. But can you provide it, Myrddin? Can you deliver?'

Hope sprung up in Jack's breast as he listened to the mad woman's dialogue; it meant that Kate was not dead, as he had feared, although he was sure that what Mab wanted was something they would not be willing to provide.

Merlin stood for a short while contemplating all that Mab had said. 'What, Mab, is the difference between Kate being in a continual state of lifelessness and being dead? And how can Percy be imprisoned but at the same time leave orphans?'

'There you go again; always splitting hairs.' She stamped her foot in anger. Twisting around to face him she answered, 'At least with one option you have hope!'

'True.'

Mab stared at him as the minutes went by without him moving, let alone saying anything else. Before too long the witch started to get quite twitchy. She had time, but not a lot, to go through the enchanting required to sacrifice the woman that was at present in a deep sleep - one from which she had to be roused in order for the offering to be accepted. She did not intend for Kate to live. Oh no! She needed for her to die but she was just playing with Merlin and all those present. However, she believed she could compose herself for as long as it took for Merlin to amuse her with some offer or other – something quite unacceptable, of course. They stood there for almost half an hour.

She couldn't take any more - also there wasn't much time left. 'Well, what are you going to do? Do you accede to all my wishes? Do you want the girl to die?'

Merlin looked down at Mab with such a sad look that victory danced in Mab's breast. Her eyes shone as she continued to search his face. Then, surprising her, he changed the subject completely.

'Mab, have you journeyed down the avenues of time? I have, and I know what each one of them has in store for mankind; more, I know what each of them has in store for me – and you! However, there is one that I cannot gain access to. I will consider sharing all the mysteries of my druidic learning with you if you can penetrate that avenue and share it with me.' He stopped speaking and stared straight at her; even time seemed to hold its breath. 'That is my answer to you.'

Mab stared at him, eyes bulging. To learn the druidic mysteries from Merlin was something indeed. His knowledge went back to time immemorial. His teachers had been from the highest druidic training, not only in this land but others; not only in this time but also throughout the ages; yes – he had travelled far. He knew of and understood the uses for potions, herbs, spells and incantations that had never even been dreamed of by others – *'especially me,'* she thought. *'I can get what I want from him and then, because I will know as much as he, I will dispose of him – at the right time of course. But, to be able to know a mystery that is barred from him - that must surely be the turning point in my life! And, if he thinks I will tell him what the secret avenue says, he must think I am mad!'* These thoughts went rapidly through her mind and took mere seconds to collate and file somewhere in her brain. Merlin did not even need to read her mind as what she thought was written large on her face!

'Where are these avenues of time to be found then, Myrddin? If it is something that is going to take too long I cannot agree. I need to get this sorted out now, tonight, as the timing and seasons are, for this moment, my strength.'

'Mab, look around you. There before you are the arches of time. Not only do they give you the hours of the day but they also give you the months of the year and the years of the century, millennia - and more. Don't let it end for you there, though. They also give you time throughout the ages. Go one way and you will see what has been – you can learn from that. Go the other way and you can see what is to come – you can use that knowledge. But, see, over there, that large, dark stone set by itself? That is the stone of darkness. It revealed nothing to me – I was barred. Tonight, though, is the night where Mars lies directly behind the full moon, giving the moon a red glow, which in turn gives a power so infrequent that only the most knowledgeable know of it.

'The stones know it - it can be seen in their lightning dance and song they have been performing throughout this night. Tonight, even the dark stone will have to give up its - secrets! However, it has refused to give up its secrets to me.'

Mab's mouth was almost salivating at the thought of gaining all this knowledge and power for herself. Merlin was using all his wisdom to make sure that his timing was completely right.

'What a terrible effect greed has on people,' he thought. Looking at Mab's countenance he could see just how ugly it made her.

'After tonight, Mab, Mars moves away and the same conjunction will not occur again in many generations, so all of us here will be long gone and the stone's secrets - well, they may be lost forever. Perhaps you may gain access,' he cajoled her, 'where I have been refused. Perhaps you, too, are not to succeed.'

'Perhaps! There is no "perhaps" about it. This time – and I have studied - I shall succeed where you have failed! Show me what you did and I shall know then what to do.'

'Ah, there is one very minor problem,' Merlin said apologetically.

'A catch!' Her voice rose to a squeal. 'I knew there would be a catch.'

'No, no, not a catch. It's just that you will need to stand upon the altar stone.'

Mab swirled around to look at the stone table upon which Kate lay. She turned her head and looked back at Merlin. A slow smile spread over her face as she raised her hand and clicked her fingers. The boys jumped out of their skin, as a man seemed to walk right out of an adjoining stone pillar. 'Morgan,' whispered Ben, as he flung a protective arm around his younger brother's shoulder. Daniel looked around the pillar and saw the effect Morgan's appearance had had on Cabal, whose head was so low it was almost to the ground and his teeth were bared in readiness for attack.

'Ah, Mordred, beloved, come here,' beckoned Mab. 'I want you to hold on to this lovely woman for me while I perform a little rite here on the altar stone. Jump over that obvious circle of phosphorescence,' she curled her lip in disdain as she glanced at Merlin. 'The woman - and I think you know her don't you?' she chuckled, - 'take her down from the alter table and I want both you and her to sit below it. Do not leave the circle.'

Mordred, although obviously very strong as could be seen by his muscular frame, had more than a little difficulty in dragging Kate from the stone as, being unconscious, she was a dead weight. His face was suffused with blood at his exertions. However, as could be seen by Merlin's eyes, he obviously had taken delight in making Mordred's job more difficult than it should have been as he made Kate, by the use of a seldom used thought incantation, a lot heavier than she actually was.

Mab sprinkled a little of some powder or other over the shining circle, allowing Merlin to enter. Once again, he climbed up onto the altar stone and raised his staff. Again the scene was played out as he was raised, slightly above the ground, and saw visions through the avenues of time. Mab caught sight of some of the visions but was obviously not in a direct enough line to see them clearly.

Then, once again the light from the staff went out and he got down from the altar.

'Fine, Myrddin. I need to know the spell.'

'There is no spell, Mab. You only need the light.'

'Give me your staff, then.'

'My staff works only for me, Mab. However, I have a light that you can use.' With that he delved into one of the folds of his robe and brought out one of the Cyclops' eyes. As it came into the open it started to glow. She knew at once where he had got it as she turned and sneered at him. 'Keep it raised above your head, Mab, and look down its rays as it bounces off the stones.' Merlin's voice had become quite croaky and he seemed drained of all energy. At Mab's insistence, he left the circle and she once again sprinkled something across the ground to stop him gaining access.

As had Merlin not so long ago, so now Mab stared down the avenues of time. Like him, she had a look of wonder on her face but never once a look of horror as she viewed the wickedness played out in some of the scenes before her. She obviously took great delight in their performance – in days past and those still to come. Eventually she came to the dark stone. Merlin looked up at the moon. *'Not quite time yet!'*

'Myrddin, you've tricked me! I cannot penetrate the stone,' Mab called.

'It's not quite time yet, Mab. Mars and the Moon are not yet quite lined up. A few minutes, seconds maybe. But you may as well use your most powerful spells. Perhaps that is where I failed.'

Mab started her incantations. She stared at the stone and had eyes only for what would be found in that mass of minerals. She was determined to know its secrets and hoped, as she learned them, that she would become the most powerful enchantress of all time. As she spoke, the stones once more increased their intensity in electrical cracking and buzzing and the mists, again, started to rise. The stones appeared to be swaying to and fro in a mesmerizing dance. Jack could feel the hair standing up on the back of his neck as Merlin started to hum one of his tunes. He shouted to the boys to turn toward the stone, not to look and to hold on for dear life. They didn't need to be told twice. Cabal shot between their legs and the stone, not caring that he was almost squashed by them, and quaked with fear. However much he feared the stones, he did not want to be left behind or left out of whatever was or might soon be happening.

Suddenly Mab stopped - staring in horror at the dark stone – her face drained of all colour, making the dirt stand out in sharp contrast. 'I can see the face of a man in an agony of great suffering,' she screamed. 'I cannot bear to look at the purity of his face - it is burning my eyes in their sockets! He wears a crown of thorns,' she moaned as she wrapped her arms around her own body in paroxysms of pain and fear. 'Just looking at him is blinding me, aah but I cannot look away!' She screamed a scream that enveloped the whole of the night air, making the boys hold their hands tightly over their ears. And then, 'I should not have looked where I was not bidden,' this almost a whisper.

Many things then happened at once. Mab passed out. When he saw this, Mordred, dropping Kate, leapt over the circle toward the boys. He held a knife and it was obvious

275

what his intentions were as he lunged toward them. Mordred had just reached Daniel, arm descending in a stabbing motion, when a large, red, reptilian tail wrapped itself around him. Like the time Jack had been saved by the ghostly dog in the forest, this creature was also very indistinct in outline – 'Like clear, rippling jelly that I could almost see right through', thought Jack. 'In fact, I don't think many of us here can see it,' he supposed. Mordred was so shocked that the knife fell from his grasp. Jack, who had been halfway across the ground towards the boys, stopped as the scene playing out before him mesmerised him. He watched the thrashing tail bounce Mordred against the ground in quite a fury and then throw him high into the air and out onto the plain. Mordred, together with Mab, who had fainted and who had fallen from the altar stone, suddenly started to twitch as electrical forces played over their bodies. Out of the blue, unbidden but welcomed by the evil duo, a white dragon swiftly plucked the pair from where they had fallen and, placing them gently on his back, flew away. The air around the departing threesome rippled and shimmered and Merlin, staff raised and light blazing toward them, watched as they gradually disappeared. They were being transported from this time to another. 'God help the people into which time and space they would eventually arrive,' he thought.

'*And God help their noses,*' Cabal responded.

Merlin was not worried about doing any more against Mab; he was content with the knowledge that it was going to take a long time for her to regain her power. As she and her evil companion departed the spell that had held Kate in her comatose state weakened and was finally broken: she began to revive.

Merlin continued holding his staff aloft as he started to hum his tuneless tune and all gathered there were amazed, if not a little alarmed, to see the stones start twitching, moving closer together, swirling and clattering, buzzing and sparking

– and, Ben wondered, did he see an eye open and close in that high stone? The group observed this strange and fascinating phenomenon and, unable to move, merely stood and waited. The buzzing and clattering stopped as Merlin lowered his arms. All was deathly still and everyone stood with baited breath to see what would happen next.

No one dared move, nothing stirred! It was like a tableau. The stones still had their colourful luminosity, which drifted slowly back and forth throughout their length, gradually picking up speed but apart from that, nothing moved. We waited.

A sudden, mighty rushing wind – a roaring of the elements. We held onto our coats as they were whipped around us. Thunder clapped and lightening cracked as, with an enormous clattering, the stones finally rattled and clamped together and then another deathly hush pervaded the night. Slowly, from within one of the lintels, a huge eye did blink! Inanimate stones were transforming into a living organism! The mist faded away, as a red dragon shook itself and rose up from the ground where the stones had once been; curling its tail and wrapping itself around Merlin, Jack, Kate, Cabal and the boys, lifting them up off the ground and placing them on its back before taking flight across the countryside. The beauty of this wonderful beast again enthralled Jack. As it and Merlin joined together in song he lay back within the folds of its scales and luxuriated in all of its loveliness. The dragon flew high; soared and then dived, flying through trees and over lakes, capturing the light from the moon which rippled along the whole of its iridescent length, dancing along its colours as it progressed - a truly beautiful sight and an absolutely awesome experience. Daniel and Ben were dumbstruck and could only stare at this amazing creature. Following the colourful light which danced along its length, they were enchanted by the beauty but, again, were also disturbed to see that their shadows did not quite match their actions – the shapes looked like different people – spectral people who appeared also to be watching them. 'No,' they thought, 'it's just our imagination - an enchanted dream.'

They were completely unaware of time, although everything that happened, happened during that one night. Merlin ministered to Kate, while he sang, gradually bringing her back to full health. After a half-hour or so the music stopped, Moon Song descended and they all got down. Neither of the boys had been able to speak. Was this all a dream? The dragon shook itself and then curled up again, this time to rest. Daniel noticed that a few reptilian scales had worked loose from the dragon's skin, if skin it was, so he picked them up and put them in his pocket.

Merlin, gathering them together, led them around the side of the hill until they came to a rock upon which he tapped twice with his staff. The rock swung open and they all entered, the rock doorway closing silently behind them. They descended a flight of rock-hewn steps into an inner chamber like that described in some of Jack's tales. Merlin told them all to sit down while he checked some charts and organised some refreshment. The refreshments arrived, delivered by a very little man who was dressed all in green. He carried a tray upon which were wooden cups filled with – lemonade? Whatever it was, it was delicious and most welcome. Kate had finally regained complete consciousness and couldn't stop hugging her sons – for once they did not mind. She was laughing and crying all at the same time, especially as she had believed she would never see them again. She sipped at her drink as she looked from one to the other, a huge smile on her face. They, in turn, grinned back - so glad to have their mother with them, safe, once more.

Jack, who had been stopped from drinking his lemonade, by a quick look and shake of his head from Merlin, went over to his family and joined in the embracing. 'Dad, I don't know how I will ever be able to thank you,' she said, on a yawn.

'Ooh, sorry, I feel quite sleepy. I shouldn't though, should I? I would have thought that as I've been "asleep" all that time I wouldn't need to close my eyes for days.' But she couldn't stop yawning. 'I suppose it's weakness.' As she was speaking, she turned to look at her sons who, also, were now both fast asleep. 'Fear must have made it a very exhausting experience,' she yawned again. Leaning back against the wall, she, too, succumbed to the effects of the lemonade.

'Now, Percy, come here.' Merlin crooked his finger at Jack. He went over to him and stood beside him in front of the great Glass. Jack felt as though it had been a million years ago since he had stood there and yet at the same time it felt like it was just yesterday. 'Look,' Merlin pointed. 'What do you see?'

Jack's heart missed a beat. He must have been hoping to see her – his beautiful wife, Rhianne. There, seated beside and trailing her hand through a clear stream, she sat, a little older but still very beautiful. Gently, Merlin said, 'I know you have had no choice, Percy, my boy, as she was unable to stay in your century for long or you in hers; Arthur, too, is still alive - sleeping - in yet another, different time than this! What, pray, have you told your family about her?'

With a catch in his voice, he merely replied, 'I just say that I have lost my wife.'

'To get back to the now, if you want, she can join you for a short while.'

If I want! Is that some kind of understatement!' Jack thought; without looking up at Merlin, and being unable to speak, he just nodded.

Merlin, mouthing something completely unintelligible to Jack, clapped his hands and there she was, standing in front of him.

Merlin coughed and disappeared along one of the corridors to his chambers. 'My powers on this occasion are very restricted. You have but half an hour so make the most of it - don't waste it,' he called over his shoulder.

Rhianne smiled at Jack and held out her arms to him. He rushed over to her and embraced her, almost crushing her in his joy at seeing her after all this time. Cabal, too, joined in, licking her hand and sneezing his delight before moving off and giving them time to be on their own. Eventually Jack let go and held her at arms' length, looking at her hair, her face and then kissing her hands and lips. 'Oh, how I've missed you! You are still as beautiful as ever,' he whispered into her hair as he once again, this time more gently, held her close.

'And I have missed you, so much,' she responded, a tear trembling on the end of her lashes. 'One day, my love, we will be together for all eternity. This I know.'

He nodded again, unable to speak. As she leaned against his shoulder she turned and became aware of Kate and the boys asleep across the room.

'Oh,' she exclaimed quietly on a quick intake of breath, 'are these our family all grown up?'

'Ah, yes.' He took her hand and led her across the room where she stood looking down at Kate and the boys.

By now the tears were streaming down her face as she looked at them. She knelt on the floor beside the boys and touched their faces.

Looking at each one in turn, she commented, 'Kate looks like me, I think, but a little darker.' She looked back at Jack, 'and our grandsons are very handsome, like you. What are their names?' she looked up at him and smiled through her tears – a rainbow through the rain. 'Oh, how I wish things could have been different but it was not meant to be. I'm glad you raised them in a time that is more peaceful than mine - it is more peaceful, isn't it? Although I expect every age has its horrors.

I do miss my daughter, though. And I miss you more than anything. It's almost like a real pain in my heart when I want

280

you near and you aren't there. You would think it would get easier as time goes by, but there are days when it's almost unbearable.' She caught her breath on a sob and then, recalling the short time they had together, dried her tears and determined to smile and hold on to every last minute they had left.

Jack and Rhianne spent the rest of their short time catching up on each other's news. They sat together during the whole of this time with their arms around each other, Rhianne making the most of looking at him, her daughter and grandsons in turn, while Jack's eyes never left her face.

How time is relative to the activities at hand! All too soon the half hour had vanished, gone in time like a flicker of light. Merlin, looking serious and sad at one and the same time, returned and told them to bid one another goodbye adding that there would probably be other times when they could meet.

Rhianne, almost stumbling in her grief, walked over to her daughter. 'Farewell Kate, my heart'. Her words caught in her throat as she laid her hand upon her only child's head. She turned and lightly did the same to her two grandsons before turning back to Jack. They held one another tightly for as long as they could and then, with Jack and Merlin standing well back, the wizard threw some dust over Rhianne, and she was gone.

They saw her sit down again by the stream and then the picture in the Glass faded. Jack felt elated and devastated, full and empty, at one and the same time. 'Goodbye for now, my darling, lovely wife.' Merlin decided to leave him alone for a few minutes.

He returned some ten minutes later and, all businesslike, advised Jack that the time had come to return to the plain. Moon Song will take us back and then, after that, you will have to use your powers of story-telling to its greatest effect to say how Kate's rescue came about.

Jack, once he had pulled himself together, wanted to know what had happened to Mab and Mordred. 'Oh, you don't need to be worried about them! The white dragon has taken them back to the dark ages, I expect, where it will take them a very long time to recover. Mab's mind has been affected by what she saw in the forbidden stone. The revealed things are for man; the hidden things are for God! Mab should have known that! Mordred, well he is just a lump of brawn - there has never been much brain there, you know – he thinks he knows the arts of sorcery but he is completely useless without his mother's and Mab's powers. You will all be absolutely safe from her and him for many a moon now. Apart from anything else, I need to return. Arthur still needs me, you know! My life's work is to serve him. So, have no fear, I'll keep an eye – if not a nose,' and he thought this was very funny, 'on the mad woman. Come, come, there is no time to be lost.' Between them, they carried the sleeping Kate and boys up out of the cave and down to where the dragon lay dozing. Cabal trotted beside them. Dawn was not too far away as the dragon took off, flying this time straight to its lair – the place of standing stones. Jack, once again, luxuriated in the flight; it might be the last time he saw this beautiful creature. She landed and curled herself up as she settled back onto the land. After Merlin and Jack had removed Kate and his grandsons from within the folds of the dragon's back, she settled herself down to her normal position. Merlin stepped up beside the altar stone, raised his staff and a blaze of light shone from it in every direction, dazzling and blinding anyone who dared look.

Just as the first few tentative rays of the sun peeked over the horizon to check and see if it was worth getting up, Merlin spoke the spell of restoring and watched as Moon Song settled back into her resting place. A few sparks of electricity danced along her body, backwards and forwards from her head to her tail before she finally drifted off once again into her long, long sleep; she would be enjoyed, for the foreseeable future at any event, only by those tourists or day-trippers who thought that she was merely a circle of gigantic, pre-historic standing stones. It would be only the very observant that would be able to see the odd streak of red running through the greyness of those boulders, or maybe detect a sleepy eye taking a lazy look around before closing again to rest for another hundred years or so - or until she is drawn back again by the mesmerising song of Merlin.

Dawn eventually broke and the sun, seeing that all was now well, shone confidently straight through a stone archway onto the altar in the middle, dancing and bouncing its rays back onto the group of people who were now leaning against some of the outer standing stones.

She gradually shone brighter and warmer, dispelling the mist. Daniel awoke first, looked around and seeing his mother rushed into her arms. 'Mum, you're safe!' Ben, too, hurried toward her and they all danced around together. 'What happened, Mum?'

'It's a long story, Danny, and I think I shall need a bit of a rest before I even begin to tell you what happened. However, we are all safe. Thanks, I know, to your grandfather.'

'And Mrs. Ambrose,' said Jack as he strode over to them. Mrs. Ambrose came bustling across to them, all businesslike as usual.

'What's happened?' said Ben. 'It was pitch dark a few minutes ago and now it's morning and mum's here, and I'm confused. Where's Morgan? More to the point, where's Merlin?'

'Whoa there, young man,' said Mrs. Ambrose. 'As you can see, your mother is back with you safe and sound and Morgan will not be bothering you any more - well not for a very long time at any rate. He has been, er, arrested again and this time will spend a very long time, hmm, locked up – top security,' Mrs. Ambrose spoke on a cough. 'And you must have been dreaming about one of your grandfather's stories – Merlin, indeed!'

Ben looked a bit bewildered but said nothing else. Daniel just stared at his grandfather but decided he would save his questions for later. He had thought he had been dreaming, too, *'but, it's funny if both Ben and I have had the same dream,'* he mused.

Walking down the hill all together, they tumbled into the estate car and started off for the nearest café to get some well-earned breakfast.

Jack looked back to the top of the Tor just once and then across at the giant structures - how innocent those "standing stones" appeared, resting where they had dwelt since, *'I don't know when,'* he thought.

Cabby wagged his tail, as he looked up at him, only too pleased to be away from them.

Mrs. Ambrose and Jack were fairly worn out by the night's events. Unfortunately, Daniel and Ben were as lively as ever. Kate said she would take a turn at driving so that Jack could have a rest on one of the back seats. With both grandsons either side of him it was not long before they badgered him into completing the story. 'Seeing as how we've been to the top of the same place, granddad,' urged Ben.

'Yes, while it's all still fresh in your mind,' agreed Daniel.

'Oh, OK.'

TWENTY-SIX

We finally reached the top of the Tor and walked down to the plain where Merlin held up his hand for us all to stop. He called Salazar over to him, pointing to the large stone directly opposite. Salazar strode over to the stone and disappeared behind it. Summoning the men, Merlin told them to place themselves around the outside of the stones, at about an equal distance from one another. They walked off to do his bidding.

'Arthur, Percy, come here,' he beckoned us. 'You, too, Rhianne.' We all stood before him. 'I have given you your instructions, but before anything else happens, I want you to know that should anything untoward occur, that is - should anything happen to me - you are to take your instructions from Salazar.

'No!' exclaimed Arthur. 'Nothing is going to happen to you, is it?'

'I don't suppose so for one minute,' he replied. 'Have faith and stop arguing with me - we don't have the time. These instructions are just in case we are split up and you will then need to follow someone else's instructions. Salazar knows what to do.'

'But he can't speak,' said Arthur.

'He will make his instructions clear, even if he can't speak,' Merlin replied. 'Rhianne.' She looked up at him. 'Call me old fashioned, but I don't want you anywhere near this central stone. If that witch gets hold of you, it will cause no end of a problem and we already have all our work cut out to put one plan into action, without adding complications. Now, go over and stay with Cabal - he needs someone with him as he won't even enter the outer circle - for some reason or other known only to him he's petrified of these stones.'

'But ...' she started to reply.

'No! No buts! Just do as I say; there is not much time.'
He looked up at the rising moon. 'It will be hundreds of
years before this happens again. Hurry now. To your places.'
We all took up our positions, as he had instructed us; Arthur
and I standing with our backs against a stone on the outer
circle waited to see what would happen next.

Merlin held up his arms, looking like a huge bat as the
folds of his gown fell from his wrists to the ground. There
was a humming, which emanated through the ground and up
through our feet, making us all shake. I turned around and
looked at Rhianne, who was as white as a sheet. She was
crouched down with her arms around Cabal's neck. He had
his lips curled back over his teeth.

The vibrations running all through the area gradually
increased as the giant stones started to rattle and shake and
take on a luminescence and colour that changed as movement
rippled through them. Merlin stood motionless, arms still
raised, as the mists swirled in from the east. I looked at
Arthur who was staring straight ahead. Suddenly all eyes
were drawn upwards as something - what was it? - flew low
overhead. We carried on searching the sky with our eyes and
then, again, it flew above us, eventually settling beside one of
the fallen stones just beyond the outer circle, disturbing the
mists about as it landed.

'A dragon,' I whispered. 'A white dragon!' It was not a
beautiful dragon like Moon Song, but showed hard, lifeless
eyes that stared out of an almost lion-like head and with
crimson smoke coming in short puffs from its nostrils –
smoke that would soon turn to fire, I thought. Where Moon
Song's scales rippled with luminescence and colour, this
other dragon's skin looked sickly, similar to the underbelly of
a dead fish.

'Ah, Mab - I thought you would make a grand entrance,'
said Merlin as he watched her alight from behind the dragon's
head, followed closely by Mordred.

As she stepped down and started to cross the ground toward the altar stone, a light breeze, which had been slowly stirring the mist on the ground, gradually carried a whiff of her odour across to us. Yes, she had definitely arrived!

'You've brought your lackey with you, I see!'

Mordred looked daggers at Merlin and would have done something, had the witch not held up her hand to stop him. 'Not now, Mordred, my love, we will be satisfied when we have had our way, do not fear,' she was sickly sweet as she spoke to him. He sulked. Merlin smiled – inwardly.

'But now, Myrddin, my old adversary, how are you keeping? Unwell, I hope.'

'Sorry to disappoint you, Mab, but I am very well. I was wondering to what I owed the, er, dubious pleasure of seeing you.'

'Always the gentleman, eh?'

'Ah but of course, and I believe we should always get the pleasantries over with as soon as possible so that we can get down to what it is you really want. Time and tide and all that, you know, Mab. If you have looked at the position of the moon, as I know you have, you of all people will know that we do not have time for idle chit chat.'

'Patience, patience!' ('That's a laugh, coming from her,' I thought.) 'But, now that you have mentioned it, I suppose we should get down to the nitty gritty.' She lifted a hand and clicked her fingers. Mordred, still with a sullen look on his face, came forward with a scroll and some containers. He scowled over at Merlin because his smirk gave the impression of confirming that Mordred was acting as the servant he had been accused of being. He was not well pleased and his face reddened in anger.

Merlin turned away and looked at Mab as she spread the scroll out onto the altar stone, securing the corners with the heavier containers. She moved her hands over the scroll, muttering an incantation as she did so. Merlin still looked on, unmoved. There were a few zips of electrical energy but they did not come to anything. Mab looked slightly annoyed and then tried again. Same result. She stamped her foot in fury and then remembered she had an audience. Squaring her shoulders she put on as nonchalant a front as possible, as though this was what she was expecting all along and, opening one of the containers, tried a new approach. She sprinkled some powder over the scroll, weaving a spell as she did so. Again, the same, result – a few buzzes and then – nothing.

Merlin wanted to laugh but knew that if he did so Mab would go completely out of control and then nothing would be achieved. So, with difficulty, he kept his features deadpan. All the problems Mab had been causing had to be sorted out tonight. Such a cosmic opportunity of these particular planets being in this particular alignment wouldn't happen again for many generations.

Keeping a completely non-committal expression, Merlin could not, however, resist one jab, asking Mab, 'Do you need a hand?'

She swirled around, glaring at him. 'Are you being funny, Myrddin, because, if you are, I shall throw a lightning bolt at one of your men, or even at one of those children over there - you'd spend eternity trying to find the pieces to fit back together again in order to give them a decent burial.' She pointed at Arthur, or was it at me?

'Now, now, Mab. As if! My respect for you, you know, knows no bounds!'

She stared at him again, confusion writ large on her face. Deciding after a short while that he might not be mocking - and then saying to herself that she didn't care anyway - she shrugged her shoulders and turned back to her somewhat ineffective spell-making.

'Do you think you could tell me what it is you are trying to do? It could be that we could come to some agreement without the exhausting need to go through all this enchanting. You look really busy at the moment and I haven't even started. I would hate you to break out into a sweat!'

'Good grief,' I thought, *'so would I!'* Cabal, in the distance, sneezed, while I heard Merlin's silent chuckle as each of them heard my thoughts.

'If we are to make a spectacular display between us, surely it would be only fair to know why we are doing it. Don't you think it a bit one-sided for you to be huffing and puffing over there, while I stand here completely bemused by it all? If I knew what it was that you wanted, we might come to some agreement, eh? It can't be Rhianne, as we have her back,' he turned and pointed, 'as you can see!'

'Oh, I can't think while you keep prattling on, and, no, it's not her, and you won't come to any agreement in any event! I know you won't. I wish you would just shut up! I'm sure it's all your silly chitter chatter that's making me go wrong. Just keep quiet! And, as I said, we won't come to any agreement because I want what you don't want and that is Arthur dead! What is it that you want?'

'Ah, yes! I can see there is a problem. Still, now that I know what it is, I can start my counter-measure. As you know, Mab, I initially wanted Rhianne back but now that that is no longer necessary I have a small question: how did you get away from the naiad?'

Taken off guard, Mab's face turned bright red with – what was it, embarrassment or anger? She took a few steps towards Merlin and he noticed, as she did so, that there was a slight limp to her walk. 'Bit your leg, did it?' he tutted, shaking his head in sympathy and seemingly full of concern. She stopped, thought better of it and, deciding to completely ignore him, turned and limped back to her scroll. 'Is it still alive?'

We could see by the stiff set of her shoulders that she was fighting to keep herself under control but refusing to be angered, and changing the subject, she said. 'I have been looking into the dark crystal, Myrddin. I have seen things that would turn your hair white – that is, if you have any hair under that ridiculous skullcap of yours. I was looking, particularly, for anything to do with our friend Salazar and that lovely wife of his. This is what I saw: Britain is going through a time of testing in these days. Kings are fighting over the High Kingship of the land, each one wanting this powerful position for himself, without even looking to see if they have the brains, let alone the brawn, to achieve such prosperity.'

Merlin noticed that these attributes must, to Mab, be the pre-requisites of a successful ruler - nothing about wisdom, peace for the land or a love for the people had even entered her thought process.

'They have been so short sighted with their in-fighting – depleting their might in the process - that they have allowed the Scots to invade from the west, the Picts from the north and the Saxon from the east.

'I have been consolidating *my* allies, evil though you may think them, from the south. Britain is in a stranglehold, my old friend! And, do you know? I reckon that even without my help they will all destroy themselves and I could then just walk into the job and take control – however, it wouldn't be any good if there was no-one left to rule, eh? And half the fun is subduing the populace!

'But,' then her look turned sour, 'as it is, there is always good fighting the bad and so the dark crystal gave me a further word of warning. It showed me, and it was well after I had entombed the woman in the crystal rock – and that must definitely have been forward planning on my part – that she had a power peculiar to herself. So, I know it must be the woman that I hold that you have come for.'

She looked around for Salazar but he was still hidden. 'You already know the prophecy of old which cautioned me that I needed to kill Arthur or he would destroy me. Well, if anyone were in my place they would say that it is only natural that I should seek his death. So, for the woman, we might come to some arrangement, eh?'

We all held our breath. What power, we were wondering, did Jasmine possess?

Merlin stood, waiting for Mab to speak. He had the patience of a saint. However, he had already told me that Mab hated silences. One way to make her lose her cool – and thus make mistakes - was to not take the bait. She stood looking at Merlin with her eyebrows raised. Eventually, she did lose her temper and it took all her self-control to try and contain herself before she could continue where she had left off, but she was not well pleased.

Without any prompting from Merlin and almost dancing in her attempt not to stamp her foot she went on, 'Her power lies in a special ability to see in advance, but only up to one whole day. No further than that - just one day! If I were to release her, her loyalties, as told me by the dark crystal, although primarily to her husband would ultimately be to Arthur, as both she and Salazar would pledge their loyalties to him as High King of Britain. Should he become High King, he will bring peace to this land.' She remained quiet for a long minute. 'He will not become High King! I shall not release her but I shall use her; I shall kill Arthur - no, he will not become High King of Britain as you so hope - and I shall rule this land.' Her voice rose to a crescendo as she declared these last few words and it seemed that the entire universe was holding its breath, making the air so thin it was very hard to breathe. Nothing moved - it was one of those times where you will look back and always remember where everyone was – but even so, everyone was ready, like coiled springs waiting to be released.

Mab broke the spell of the moment as she turned back to Mordred, whose smile, like hers, did not reach his eyes. 'Let us proceed, my love,' she said to him.

We all, very slowly, let out our breath.

Before they could move, Merlin spoke. 'Mab,' have you seen down the Avenues of Time?'

She turned and looked at him, surprise written on her face at his change of tack. For a few heartbeats there was stillness, then, 'I have seen all that I have needed to see in the dark crystal,' she replied.

'Ah, but that only told you "ifs",' he responded. 'The Avenues of Time will tell you what definitely will be. However, I must warn you that there is one avenue that is excluded - well, it is to me at any rate - as I was not given permission to look down it.'

This, he knew, would whet her appetite, as Mab had such an inflated opinion of herself and her magic that she believed nothing could be barred to her. 'Where are these avenues?' she demanded.

'You are standing among them,' he told her.

'Where?'

'Look around - the standing stones! You must have wondered what they were here for?' he queried.

She looked around at the stones, watching as the colours undulated through them accompanied by the occasional electric charge, and her countenance lit up as understanding gradually dawned.

'But what do you want in exchange? I know you, Myrddin, you are after something.'

'You said, yourself that Jasmine had a peculiar gift. If that is the entire gift she has, then she cannot be much trouble to you, or much of a loss come to that. You know yourself that you can see into the future and, if you can see what the Avenues will divulge, what need do you have of her? Just being awkward, Mab?'

Mab leaned against the altar stone and considered this for some few moments. Again, her arrogant self-importance rose to the fore and she decided that she really did not need the woman. '*In fact, she has been taxing my powers by keeping her there,*' she thought. However, she did not believe that that was what Merlin really wanted.

'What is it you really want, Myrddin? The woman cannot mean that much to you, you who has the gift of prophesy!'

Merlin smiled – inwardly. 'You know me too well, Mab. What I need to know is what the forbidden avenue will tell me. But, I expect you will keep that secret to yourself too, will you not? However, that is a chance I have to take.'

Mab stood and considered this for a while but it was all too much for her - she must know! 'OK, you can have her, but not the knowledge of the forbidden stone – that I will keep to myself. I will give you the spell of binding that has been keeping her there.' She handed over an extremely small scrap of parchment with almost unintelligible markings upon it. Merlin looked at it, noticing that some of it was missing, and nodded, pocketing the parchment within the folds of his robe. He did, however, pick up from Mab's mind the thought that he would not live long enough to use it and free Jasmine.

Merlin then proceeded to tell her how to look down the Avenues of Time. 'It is so important to use the light I have given you and to line it up with the moon and Mars. You have to catch the rays from the moon and bounce them off the light that you hold in your hand onto the standing stones. You will know it is ready to look down that avenue when the moon turns red.'

She looked wary, trying to discover any trap, but, after staring into the limited amount of the future that she already had access to, she decided there was no catch and, to be on the safe side, she encircled the altar stone with a potion of exclusion to anyone trying to enter.

Merlin smiled. Innocence was written all over his face.

As Mab began her contemplation of that which the stones would reveal, the mists, which had evaporated during their interchange, again rolled in. Mordred, who had been banished to await his mistress just outside her enchanted circle, edged backwards until he stood firmly against one of the tall stones. Mab, as Merlin had instructed, held the light aloft and as the reflected shafts were lined up, stared down each Avenues, finally coming at last to the Dark Avenue. She started to repeat an extremely evil-sounding incantation – making us all feel quite sick as we watched a thick sulphurous, not only in colour but in smell, vapour emanate from her mouth and nostrils, and then she stopped. All was still for a full minute as Mab stared ahead.

As the picture cleared, her eyes started to bulge and a low scream began to rise from within the depths of her being, gaining volume as it climbed up her throat and then erupted from her mouth. Merlin read what was in her head and, as he closed his eyes, could see within his own mind what she saw. However, where the vision burned deep into her being causing harm, Merlin only saw it in a second-brain fashion that would cause him no danger.

There was, he saw, a huge precipice at the end of a long, almost imperceptible downward sloping pathway and many people were moving towards it. All along the edge of the precipice there was fast, loud, passionate music playing as the vision played out in his mind. Mab could see herself caught up in the middle of the crowds. At first she was fascinated by all the things that were going on and enjoyed watching what all the people were doing – especially the evil ones. She drifted along quite happily for a while but eventually became aware that there were so many people all moving along in one direction and that she was caught up in it and could not escape. Try as she might, she could not break out of this river of people who were moving slowly down the slope towards the edge. Eventually she could see into the maw of the

294

precipice, although no one else was aware that it was there - until it was too late. She saw kings, some of whom she had glimpsed in one or other of the Avenues: a few were fighting other kings, there were lords carousing, some were drunk, engulfed in their own pleasures and pursuits, warriors slipped towards the edge as they fought tooth and nail against other enemy warriors, while the common man suffered and the land around them perished; she saw invaders, marauders, strange peoples: pillaging, laughing, crying, dancing as they edged towards the, as yet unseen, pit.

Mab was caught up in the crush of these people and the river of bodies, growing ever thicker, made it impossible to get away – she, too, was being pushed toward the blazing pit. She tried to warn everyone around her, so that they might turn around and take her to safety – she wasn't concerned at all about them, only for herself - but the noise was so great that she couldn't be heard, or they chose not to hear her, let alone take any notice. As she looked over the edge of the precipice she could see the dragon – no, two dragons, one white and one red. Hope suddenly flared in her as she saw the white dragon, but was soon extinguished, as she realised he couldn't see her in the crush of people, let alone hear her in the cacophony of noise.

The white dragon was slashing its tail to and fro as it fought the red dragon but its aim was to take hold of as many people as it could and drag them down screaming to perish in the flaming pit.

All the time it was fighting, the red dragon had its work cut out to overcome the great onslaught as it, too, was plucking people from the flames also with its tail, but this time was setting them down safely on the far side – there were not that many saved! Those that were put down safely on the other side were sobbing as they, from the safety of the other side, were struck dumb at the sight of so much suffering and so many lost souls. Even if the white dragon was

295

unsuccessful in capturing people and pulling them into the pit, the crush of people heading towards it was so great that there was no way out, other than by falling or being pushed over the edge, even as they tried, ineffectively, to claw their way back through the horde.

Mab, caught in a stream from which she was unable to extricate herself, was carried swiftly over the edge of the abyss. Too late, together with many others, with her scream penetrating the air, she saw her life flash before her eyes and the horror that greedily awaited her for all eternity, as she tumbled over the edge. The vision faded from Merlin's mind.

Brought back to the present, he heard a blood-curdling scream pierce the air as Mab cried out for help. Mordred rushed toward her but was thrown high into space as, forgetting, he hit the exclusion line. No one looked to see where he landed as our eyes were fixed upon the witch, whose hair was standing on end as it steamed - that is, the hair that wasn't plastered to her head stood on end while the greasy bit steamed. Her eyes were bulging out of their sockets and the veins in her neck stood out as she clenched her teeth together. Her arms were waving about like dislocated windmills.

The air again started to vibrate as the stones rocked to and fro, colour and electricity fizzing through them, increasing at an alarming rate.

'Come, quickly, all of you. Salazar, change of plan - quick, hurry.' Even Cabal, overcoming his fear for a short while, moved into the circle, as Rhianne, running alongside him, held on for dear life to the ruff of his neck. Merlin wrapped his cloak around us all, enveloping us not only in the garment but also with his protection. We stared again at Mab who, with eyes rolling around inside their sockets, continued to scream, albeit in an ever decreasing volume, in terror, calling out for someone we had never heard of; even Merlin had not heard this name before.

'Hellion, Hellion, to me, to me,' she called.

We were completely amazed as a huge white face - a dragon with the face of a lion - appeared as it descended from the sky toward Mab. As it swooped down toward the ground it gently - oh so gently - plucked her from the altar stone. It twisted its neck and placed her tenderly upon its back beside, we noticed, an unconscious Mordred. Then the white dragon took flight.

Merlin started to hum. *'Here we go again!'* I thought, although I was not prepared for what happened next. The standing stones started clattering together, buzzing and fizzing as they did so, jumping up and joining together as they came to life.

I could feel my eyes standing out of my head as I watched what should have been inanimate stones link together becoming vibrant in colour and full of energy and life - I was drinking in the splendour, once again, of the most beautiful of dragons - Moon Song!

We were all held in a powerful grip, being gathered up in her embrace and gently laid in the folds of her back between two gloriously shimmering wings. She did not feel at all like I imagined - her scales were dry, silky and smooth, delicate and yet strong, beautiful in their iridescence. Pointing her head toward the skies, she took off after the white dragon. Merlin carried on humming and Moon Song joined in.

Before long we could see the smoke trail of the white dragon – Hellion – in front of us. We had to get to Jasmine before the witch had a chance to get to her and, judging by the speed of the white dragon, we would have our work cut out for us.

The witch had obviously spotted us, as her dragon started to spurt out more and more red smoke until we were completely engulfed in it, not being able to see anything, so thick was the mist. Moon Song wouldn't be outdone, however - she soared into the cool, clear air in the upper atmosphere, which, unbeknown to Mad Mab, gave us a good vantage point. In this clearer air we were able to travel at a faster speed and it was therefore a complete surprise to Mab when, coming from a slightly different direction, we landed almost head on with her outside the castle gates.

The two dragons shook themselves, fluffing out their wings and puffing smoke - making their bodies look sleek and powerful. Along with Mab and Mordred, we slid to the ground and made for the castle door. Mab was ahead of us but not fast enough to close the door before we could get in. We saw a flash as the light from the moon bounced off the dagger that Mab had pulled from her belt as she dashed across the castle grounds.

Cabal had already caught up with them and, as Mordred turned to strike Arthur down with his spear, Cabal pounced, knocking the villain to the ground and biting off the end of his finger in the process. This awful bit of flesh and bone almost choked the poor hound and, while he was trying to cough it up, Mordred made his getaway; bleeding and screaming in pain at his lost member, he tore off into the darkness.

Salazar rushed through the door with Rhianne close behind. They, too, had seen what Mab was intending and, as they knew where Jasmine was imprisoned, they ran like the wind to try to save her. I watched as they ran across the courtyard and disappeared into the keep, while Arthur and I followed. However, when we eventually arrived in the keep, everyone had vanished. We could hear running footsteps but they echoed so much that they could have been coming from any direction.

We stood still, heads spinning this way and that to try to discern the right way to proceed.

Cabal, however, once he had disgorged the offending finger, came rushing in and, his nose being what it is, he found the scent immediately and darted off down one of the passageways. We followed, but we needn't have bothered. It was, once we eventually got into the castle, all over in a moment.

Merlin met us, coming from the direction of the dungeons, as we followed Cabal down the corridor. He walked toward us with Rhianne holding onto his arm and with Salazar and Jasmine following. That couple were holding hands and just staring at one another, smiling. Salazar eventually started talking to his wife and it was amazing, after being with the quiet man for so long, to hear a voice that sounded as rich and powerful as the man himself. Jasmine was a delight to behold. She was as beautiful and graceful as Rhianne had described her.

'Where's Mab?' asked Arthur. 'Don't you think we ought to get out of here before she comes back?'

Merlin raised himself to his full height and looked affronted. 'Do you think she is more powerful than I?'

Arthur looked abashed. 'Sorry, Merlin. Not thinking straight! Brain's been overworked. But I did see dragons, didn't I?'

'Moon Song!' Merlin exclaimed. 'Oh no – those dragons have forever been at odds with one another,' and then he dashed out through the door; after a heartbeat we followed, hurrying through the main gate. The sight that met our eyes was breathtaking and very frightening. How we hadn't heard their commotion was a mystery, as the dragons were and had been fighting tooth and claw – and fire. There were many rips and tears along the wings and flanks of both of them, together with more than a few scorch marks. Moon Song was tiring, but so was the white dragon – Hellion. As we all gathered in front of the main gates leading out of the castle, we watched as they circled each other, looking for an advantage, smoke steaming out of their nostrils as their chests heaved with the effort. It was looking very much as though the white one would win after he suddenly found an advantage and fastened his teeth into Moon Song's throat. She was now bleeding profusely and, as could be seen by the droop of her head, weakening rapidly. Letting go of her throat, the white dragon fastened his enormous teeth onto one of her wings and started to thrash her around like a whippet with a mouse. We all had to duck a few times as she was whipped over our heads.

At sight of this, Salazar raised his arms and spoke some of what I now knew was not quite so much mumbo jumbo. Jasmine stood beside him and declared that all would be well. Arthur knelt down, bowed his head and prayed to his God, while Merlin surprised me by kneeling down and joining him.

The battle between the two dragons seemed endless. The noise they made deafened us and it made me feel sick to see them biting into one another, tearing off chunks of flesh and spitting scales. The flames being snorted out of their nostrils more than once scorched our clothes and we were lucky not to get our flesh burned as well.

As they pounded the earth with their feet it felt as though an earthquake was occurring and it was as much as we could do to stay upright. It was one of the scariest experiences of my life. I reckon the upbringing in my own century was not as rough as those of the times of Arthur, but when I looked at the others, their faces gave the impression that what was happening was perfectly normal.

The white dragon's eyes had turned red and angry as it tore into Moon Song and there was and would be no mercy from him; you could see it in those eyes and by its demeanour. When both dragons raised themselves to their full height on their hind legs, the white one towered many hands higher than the other and, bringing its arms down with all its strength it looked like it was knocking the sense out of her head and the breath out of her body. We felt ill; it seemed as though the end was near. I know I was in tears and not ashamed at that time to shed them.

But, and we cannot quite remember when it happened, the red dragon started to get the upper hand. The fight went on for some considerable time longer and then quite suddenly it was all over. The white dragon's fire suddenly turned to steam and he turned tail and fled, haltingly at first, it must be admitted, as he was sorely damaged. Moon Song hung her head as she gasped for breath but then she raised it and trumpeted a dart of flame into the air – her declaration of victory. We all applauded and danced with joy. Both Merlin and Salazar went over to the creature and, after putting their hands upon her and muttering something or other, she regained her breath and her wounds started rapidly to heal.

Arthur stood and gazed at the magnificent beast and, seemingly in a trance, declared, 'I shall have the red dragon as my standard'. His voice was soft, as I believe he was deeply touched by what he had seen. The young man had prophesied, although not knowing his future, or even who he really was, he did not realise that he had done so. 'Yes, when I become a knight,' he amended, slightly embarrassed by his declaration, 'I shall use the red dragon as my banner!'

'So, Merlin,' I asked, 'What's happened to Mab?'

'Come and see.'

We all, except Jasmine and Salazar, followed him down one corridor after another and through the dungeons until we came finally to the deepest and darkest one of all. At the bottom of the steps Merlin held his torch high. This, then, was where poor Jasmine had been entombed for the past year. How awful! But there, now in front of us was Mab - staring at us with a look of absolute horror and hate on her face – completely surrounded in crystal.

'Goodbye, you old witch,' said Merlin. 'Until we meet again - which I hope will not be until hell freezes over!' We all turned and left, leaving the mad witch in total darkness, where she belonged.

'How did that happen?' asked Arthur.

'I had the cloak of invisibility rolled up in my tunic,' Merlin grinned. 'I just wrapped it around myself and ran behind her as she headed toward Jasmine, not that she would have seen me if I had not had it, engrossed as she was in her desire to kill her.

When she got to the dungeon, she said the spell of releasing to free Jasmine from the crystal rock so that she could destroy her. I knew I had to be there because she had given me the spell at the altar stone but part of it was missing. I had to time Jasmine's release to the second.

Well, as soon as the crystal was open Mab pulled Jasmine out and, when the old witch had raised her hand to do the dirty deed, I shoved her into the crystal and said the spell of reversing. As it turned out, on hearing it, the spell she had put on her was a very simple one, but so old that most of us druids have either forgotten it or don't use it any more. I reckon she must have come across it in the archives. Then the rock closed around her and she was trapped. Not before time, I say, eh? She will need to raise her arms to achieve the spell of releasing – but she's stuck – big, big problem!'

He looked at us all to receive our acclamation of his genius. We, of course, obliged.

'And where is Mordred?' I asked.

'Oh, he's a coward. He's run home to lick his wounds. But, even though we need not worry about him for a while, keep him in mind and keep vigilant - he'll be back.

Rhianne, holding onto Merlin's arm once again asked, 'Why didn't you come and rescue me when I was in the tower? I was so alone and so scared.'

Merlin stopped and got them all to sit down. 'I'm sorry Rhianne, but it had to be the way it was. Anyway, how do you think all things have worked out the way they have if I had not been exceptionally busy and, believe it or not, taking care of you all? Who do you think it was who made all that porridge?' he turned and asked Arthur, 'not an easy task!'

302

Our mouths dropped open.

'Who do you think it was who created all those avenues through the standing stones; an even harder task? And who do you think was keeping an eye on this accursed castle? *And* who do you think arranged for that piece of your dress to be plucked from the castle window, Rhianne? It's not easy being a hawk, let alone flying without the aid of a dragon!'

We all looked ashamed but suitably impressed as well. We apologised to Merlin for not trusting him enough.

Hive, very hesitantly, spoke up at that moment. 'I know I haven't the right to ask, but is it possible to free my brother from his life of hell on the battlements?'

Merlin turned then and looked at the man with great compassion. 'My friend, you have every right to ask for something that is good. Let us go and see.'

We all trooped back outside, where Moon Song was resting. She opened one eye and studied us as we turned to look up at the faces adorning the fascia of the castle walls. Going back to her rest, Moon Song left us to look more closely at the gargoyles. We noticed that each face had its mouth open and tongue hanging out – well, they were supposed to be spouts, weren't they!

Merlin, together with Salazar, raised their arms and again used their powers of incantation. There was an almighty crack of lightning and rumble of thunder. Rain started gushing down, but only over the castle walls, and, as it did so, began to loosen the mortar around each head. Very soon the faces changed from stone to flesh and, one by one, the heads disappeared back through the walls and into the castle.

We then all walked back inside the gate and Hive gave a shout of joy as he rushed to embrace his brother, Mead. I had never seen his face show any emotion and I must admit I had thought him a very peculiar looking man indeed but, seeing his brother freed, there was such a transformation that, if I did not know him I don't believe I would have recognised him -

303

he actually shone. It was weird seeing the two of them together; they were so alike – two peas in a pod, even down to the "candle wick" on top of each head. They were as effusive in their gratitude as in their emotions and I believe Hive again spoke more in those five minutes than he had spoken in the last ten years. It was very emotional seeing the brothers walking about arm in arm. There were many others wandering around (including a dog and a couple of cats, looking bewildered) so Hive gathered them up and told them all that had happened.

Again, one by one, they came over to Merlin and couldn't thank him enough. They also didn't burn anyone any more.

When we asked him why they had melted everyone when they had been stuck on the castle walls, Merlin explained that the heat of their anger and frustration at being turned into gargoyles had made them burn; their uncontrollable anger being directed at anyone or anything that came near. That - plus a particularly nasty spell that Mab had placed on each one of them. Now that they had regained their liberty from the castle walls, Merlin told them that they were each free to return to their homes. The atmosphere around the castle became lighter until it seemed almost festive. *'It even smells better!'* sneezed Cabal.

'Let's go home too,' said Arthur who, like the rest of us, was wilting with exhaustion.

Moon Song, now refreshed, once again took to the skies and just before dawn we alighted after the red dragon landed upon the plain near the Tor. Shaking herself and making sure she was completely comfortable she rested her head upon her front paws, tucked in her wings and with a couple of deep breaths closed her eyes. After some buzzing and crackling the place of standing stones once again took upon itself the shape it had held for many thousands of years!

Merlin gathered us all up, waking the men, who had fallen asleep – I wonder how that had happened! We ascended the hill and made our way back to the ponies. I did notice that the men kept giving Jasmine a funny look; I expect they wondered where she had come from. We sat around the fire while the men broke camp, saddling the ponies after taking some refreshment that Merlin was dispensing to each of us - except me, that is.

Without exception, all of us couldn't wait to return to the Caer and all the comforts that came with it.

Later that day, Lady Elise was overjoyed when we entered the compound. She wept and laughed at one and the same time as she held her daughter close. She couldn't stop thanking Arthur and me for what we had done and finally shook Merlin's hand, nodding her thanks to him, suddenly unable to speak.

'Lady,' Merlin responded later, 'I know I have asked you and your husband for many things in the past, of which you and he are the only ones I could ever trust with my secrets, and I have no right to impose on you once more but, again, I would be obliged if you will assist me!'

'Please go on, Merlin.'

'Would you extend your hospitality to Salazar and Jasmine? They are freemen – man and wife. He is my brother - a druid of the highest order and she has a special gifting. I can assure you that they would be as much of a blessing to you as you would be to them.'

'Of course,' she smiled at him. 'You should know that you do not even need to ask. I should be ashamed to deny you anything after all that you have done for me.'

Merlin thanked her and then apologised, saying that he needed to take his leave at once.

Things soon started to settle back to normal. Arthur and I, once again, took up our combat training in the mornings; we were certainly improving, especially as we now knew how much it would benefit us and those we needed to protect, or what might possibly happen if we were out of practise.

Arthur spent much time at the blacksmiths having an armband made of bronze and red gold, which he wore on his upper arm. It was, not surprisingly, made in the design of a dragon. He also had a shield made primarily of wood and hide and upon which was stained, with red dye, another dragon. I don't know how he could remember anything about any dragons, not after the draught of forgetting that Merlin had supplied everybody with, but somehow he did.

In the afternoons Arthur did his school work and I sometimes sat in with him when the monk - and from then on we made sure we knew exactly who he was - came to teach him the things of Christ - mostly only on rainy days, for me, though. I still don't know whether it was because I wanted to hear about Him as well, or whether I just wanted to vet the monk!

However, best of all, Cabal and I took up our games in the forest. How I loved that hound.

Merlin came striding into the house one blustery spring evening and announced that Sir Kay would soon be returning as he had completed his stint with the king and it was now someone else's turn to do that particular duty. He walked straight over to the side table and poured himself a long draught of beer. 'Ahh, that's much better. I have been walking through these woods for much of the day without stopping for any refreshment.' He turned and looked at me, beckoning me outside. 'Percy, come walk with me in the yard.'

I got up, looked over my shoulder at Arthur and shrugged. *'No Cabal, you stay with Arthur.'* Cabal halted at Merlin's command and stayed in the doorway, watching us as we moved away. I could tell he was most put out not to be included and could almost see him strain to try and catch the words. Following Merlin outside, I walked over to the large barn, where the blacksmith shoed the horses, and stood looking down at him as he sat leaning against the horse

306

trough. He warned me to put up my mental guard, as he did not want anyone to know what we were talking about, not even Cabal. 'I am tired, Percy, after our last encounter with that repulsive witch – she has really drained me. However, what I have come to say is that you, my boy, have to return to the 20th Century. As I told you, I do not want to be disturbed by all those heavy boots stomping about all over my hill while they search for you – and that they have started to do! I need a long rest to recover my powers.

'So, I will call you again, one day - when you are a little older,' he brightened. 'We still have to kill that giant you know, but he will keep. In the meantime, I have called the dragon and on the first mist of her breath you will be carried back to your father. I shall stay on here for a little longer, in any event at least until Sir Kay returns, and then I must away to rest and take you home. Learn much for me for when you return. I will need to gather much information from you one day.'

At the mention of the dragon, the memory of her came flooding back and I recalled the shocking battle she'd had with the white dragon. 'Merlin,' I asked, 'why did you kneel with Arthur and pray instead of standing with Salazar when Moon Song was in such danger?'

He looked down at me as we walked along, sighed, thought for a while and then said, 'Magic, as often as not, is just a trick and I am so good at it that for me it is merely great fun. It's all an illusion, really! However, there are times, young Percy, when you come up against such extreme evil that only extreme good can combat it. That was one of those times.' He then hurried forward, beckoning me to follow. I was left to ponder what he meant.

We returned to the main hall, where Arthur had been busy organising our supper and spent an enchanted evening listening to Merlin as he recounted, harp in hand, many tales of witches, dragons and the battles he had witnessed against the Picts, Scots and Saxons - and, of course, Mad Mab and Mordred.

Cabal lay stretched out against the hearth, soaking up its warmth as he dozed in front of the fire, although I could feel on that first night that he was still miffed at not being included in my conversation with Merlin. Merlin continued to entertain us each evening, but Cabal wasn't interested in hearing Merlin's stories - he'd heard them all before!

TWENTY–SEVEN

During late spring the days grew longer and the woodpile grew higher as less of it was required in the fireplace – a very small blaze soon heated the whole room.

Another evening, I looked at the hound with a feeling of great tenderness and sorrow. I had, on one of our forays through the forest, had to tell Cabal that as soon as the autumn mists arrived, I would be gone, for a while at any rate. He wanted to know where I was going and when I would be back but I was unable to tell him so that he would be able to understand. However, I did promise that I would one day return. Putting up my mental guard so that he wouldn't know what I was thinking at that time, I did wonder whether he would still be around, dogs having fairly short lives compared to humans, as you know, and wolfhounds having the shortest lifespan of any in the canine world. But, we shouldn't think like that, so in the meantime I took pains to enjoy a peaceful summer.

I took great pleasure in my adventures with Cabal in the forests, where he continued to teach me to stalk prey and not become preyed upon in the process. With Arthur I had a great time learning how to use the sword and bow and arrow and wondered how I was going to explain my new muscles to my father when I returned to my own time - still, I'd cross that bridge when I came to it.

I wasn't too keen on learning how to be a courtier, though, as it seemed a bit soft, but it had to be endured as everyone else had to do it. I'd tried to shy away from it but the ear-bashing I had received from absolutely everyone made it not worthwhile escaping. They really couldn't understand my embarrassment at soft-soaping everyone (as I thought that that was what it all amounted to). But I treasured the times that Rhianne was in our company. She had changed a lot from the time I had first seen her; I expect anyone would after what had happened to her over the last few months. I was going to miss her too - a lot. Thinking of her I would sneak a glimpse at Cabal, who *always* seemed to be watching me at that time.

Five or six months after our adventures with the mad witch, Sir Ector and Sir Kay returned. They rode into the compound on a beautiful day in June and Arthur and I, who had been sparring for most of the morning and were quite exhausted, were lounging on the stone step, taking a well-earned rest and eating our luncheon.

Sir Ector and Sir Kay rode straight through the gate and up to us. Sir Kay had grown a lot in the last six months and, sporting his new, obviously unused, suit of chain mail - yes, he was making a very grand impression - he looked down his nose at us and in an extremely haughty fashion, declared, 'Well, father, it looks as though we have only just returned in time. These two layabouts look like they definitely need something to do to keep them out of mischief.'

Arthur and I looked at one another for a good few seconds and then burst into such uncontrollable laughter that both Sir Kay and Sir Ector thought we had either taken leave of our senses or had caught more than a touch of the sun.'

As autumn approached, I looked ahead with a sense of expectation and trepidation. I wanted to go home and see my mum and dad but I had grown very fond of the people that I was now spending my time with.

My last day was with Cabal and was one of extreme sadness at our imminent separation. I must not have been concentrating while we were walking through the forest. The mists had started to rise, reminding me that I would soon be going away. Tripping over an unseen root, I tumbled and fell quite badly down a sharp incline and into a ditch, cutting myself in various places. What a way to go!

TWENTY-EIGHT

I awoke with the sun shining on my very sore face. I looked around for Merlin or Arthur or even Cabal but all I could see were the tops of trees and a farmstead, which sat just the other side of them. I groaned as I moved, touching my swollen eye and very sore nose.

As I peered over the tops of the trees I saw, with a leap in my chest, my father, along with a dozen or so other people, searching – yes, searching for me. My heart somersaulted with joy as I thought of my father worrying and desperately trying to find me. I fumbled in my pocket and brought out my whistle. Putting it to my swollen and tender lips and at the same time making ready my handkerchief, I blew with all my might. Everyone stood still. I rose up, on very unsteady legs, fluttering my handkerchief as I did so.

My dad saw me first and ran up the hillside. I collapsed into his arms but by then I didn't care. I could let go - now that I was safe - and that was all that mattered.

Many days later he told me that I had been very ill – delirious – I had had a fever and had been muttering about Merlin, Arthur and the like. I can remember asking him how old I was and seeing him look quite concerned, believing I was still rambling in my mind. He could see that I was restless and wouldn't be happy until he told me, so, after telling me that I was nine, I relaxed and so did he.

It took me several more days to get well enough to leave my sick bed. My mother had come home after helping her sister with the new baby and she and dad took turns looking after me, making me feel very special. Once I was out of bed, my dad asked me what had happened. Not wanting to make matters worse than they already were I told a bit of a white lie and said I couldn't remember anything after entering the woods.

311

Mum and dad looked at one another, after which dad said it would probably come back to me later on. I then asked *him* what had happened.

'It really was a most peculiar day, Jack,' he said. 'I was busy for a couple of hours with heating and cooling metals and bending them to see how far they would go before they cracked, when those two young lads, white as sheets, came haring into the enclosure looking like all the bats from hell were after them. Alf, the younger boy, had teeth marks on his upper arm and ear which looked like it came from a large animal – a wolf or something – and both of them were gibbering like idiots.'

'Which they are,' I said to myself.

'They kept muttering something about having some fun with you when it all went wrong and something – whatever it was – attacked all of you.'

'I can't recall any of that!' I responded, which was not quite lying because I knew that the something – whatever it was – had not attacked me but had attacked them, it had actually been my saviour. So, it looked like they had got away with what they had done to me – well, in this life anyway!

'We then rushed out to look for you and, well, you know the rest.'

TWENTY-NINE

The car pulled up before Mrs. Ambrose's door. Jack helped her into the house with her belongings and the boys could see them conferring for a short while before he returned to the car. They had no idea as to what Mrs. Ambrose and their grandfather had been talking about.

'Merlin,' Jack asked, 'how is it that Mab fell for the same trick twice? I can understand her wanting to know the answer to the forbidden stone once, but felt sure she wouldn't fall for it a second time!'

'Ah well, lad, I am afraid that I couldn't possibly say. She is either not up to scratch,' he chuckled at the pun, as Mab, not having washed for a long time now, spent quite a considerable amount of time doing just that – scratching, 'Or maybe her pride made her think that this time she could overcome! Evil, though, can never overcome good – and that's a fact!

'However, to get back to us, I have done a little spell-making, Percy. No, don't look at me like that! Sometimes the "hocus pocus" works!' he chuckled. 'I have arranged that the cottage now belongs to Kate and the boys. I shall make everything ready for them while I am still here and they can move in tomorrow. They will think it's their house and that they bought it from me, and so will all the villagers. I'll also sort things out with the policeman. So far as everyone is concerned, I have moved away. Everyone will forget about me after a while, well at least I believe I won't seem important to them anymore, not now at any rate. However, I shall see you again, Percy, now that I know how to hop to and fro. So, goodbye for now.'

Merlin, in the guise of Mrs. Ambrose, ushered Jack away from the door toward the car and took his leave of them all. Jack was too tired to object. He knew without a doubt that he would see Merlin again. When he got back into the car, Kate shifted gear and they went on up the hill to his cottage.

'You and the boys should stay the night, Kate. It's late and I think perhaps we should spend a little time together before you go home. And it's now safe to go home!' She just nodded. All of them were very tired.

The boys crawled out of the car and dragged themselves into the kitchen. Drinking some milk before they went off to bed, Ben looked at his grandfather and grumbled, 'I thought you were supposed to be telling us the story of the Glaston Giant! It's taking you a long time to get round to it!'

'Don't be so rude, Ben,' his mother scolded him.

'It's alright, Kate. I don't think he means to be rude; we're all a bit tired, to say the least, after this evening's turn of events.' Turning to Ben, he said that as soon as they had all got their breath back he would tell them what happened when he met the Giant.'

'But I thought that was what you had started to tell us this time,' he replied.

'Oh, no, Ben! That's another story!'

In a very short while both boys had gone up to bed. Kate sat for a while and had a cup of tea with her father and then she, too, said her goodnights and disappeared upstairs. Cabal returned from his evening run and, using his wet nose to push up Jack's elbow for a bit of attention, settled down beside him.

'Let's not even think about it tonight, old friend. I'm desperate for my bed,' he said to the hound.

'Me, too.'

Upstairs, the two boys, weary - not only from the day's exploits but also from the drink that Mrs. Ambrose's had given them earlier - were taking off their clothes before crawling into bed. 'It's funny Mordred has a bit missing from his finger, just like Morgan!' observed Ben as he let out his third or fourth yawn. Just before he dropped off to sleep, he

314

asked his brother a question. 'Do you think all that dragon stuff is just a story playing on our minds because granddad keeps on talking about them? It couldn't be real, could it?'

In the semi-darkness Daniel was secretly placing the iridescent scales he had found near the Tor into a matchbox.

'It wasn't a figment of our imagination,' Danny whispered dreamily to his brother, who was by now fast asleep. 'It was real!'

NOTES

I hereby acknowledge that my character, Shake Spear, is guilty of appropriating for himself several one-liners from a possible distant relative's future plays. Or maybe it could have been the other way round ...

Whichever way round it may have been, I should like, in any event, to acknowledge and thank William Shakespeare for his works and inspiration.

The following - an extract from the next adventure, which is at present under construction - brings Jack back again, through the mists of some 1500 years where Merlin, tricked by the mad witch, waits for Jack to unlock the spell of binding and set him free. Once again, Jack, Arthur and Cabal are drawn into an adventure where good and evil take their stand.

The Glaston Giant – a tale of Merlin

I don't know how I got there that day, but I found myself sitting on the cliff overlooking Tintagel Island. It was one of those beautiful golden autumn days – still and warm - and as I looked down I could see the sun winking back at me from a crystal sea and the island itself gleamed as though it were an emerald jewel actually floating upon it. As I said, I had been there before, when we used to go on our special days out, but I had never seen it look as beautiful as it did that day. In fact, I couldn't have kept away from it if I tried – I was drawn, like a moth to a flame.

It took me a while to make my way down the cliff face, as it is very dangerous, being steep and crumbly. As soon as my foot stepped onto the beach the day suddenly grew darker. I knew it was not far past noon, as I had only recently eaten some of the food that my mum had packed for me and, like you two,' he said to his grandsons, 'I reckon I could tell the time by my stomach!

I finally crossed the narrow bay that led to the island. The sun, although high in the sky, was almost obscured by a slowly rising mist, looking like a hazy floating orb. It was eerily quiet. I couldn't hear the seabirds any more and the sea didn't break on the shore but made noises similar to the hissing noise you hear when you put a seashell up to your ear – far away - mind it could have been the hissing noise you get from snakes, or would that be serpents? Also, I began to be disorientated and couldn't tell from which direction it was coming. When it first started to get dark I thought I'd better hurry back across the causeway, as I wasn't sure how far the sea would come up - but halfway across I got completely lost.

It got very chilly and I could feel panic starting to clutch around my head like a vice. If I went in the wrong direction I could end up being blocked in when the sea rose - I could remember that some of the sides of the rockface on the mainland side were sheer - and then I might drown. It now started getting even darker and I almost jumped out of my skin when I saw this ghostly shape unexpectedly rise up in front of and over me. It looked like a huge monster with arms raised to grab me. I froze – it appeared to be drawing me towards it. I held my breath –I was literally too frightened to breathe. The mist swirled around my legs looking and feeling like slithering serpents ready to strike or perhaps wrap themselves around me to strangle me and I think that scared me more than the dark shape. I could feel the moisture from the mist starting to drip off my hair and my clothes were really clammy and cold where they clung to my body.

Starting to shiver and shake, I realized I had to get away from the monster and try to find my way out of the bay or I might never be seen again. After a few seconds, when I realised that nothing was moving except the mist as it swirled around, thickening and thinning, it allowed me to see that the dark shape was, in fact, a huge rock on the island. I took a step forward and could see the mouth of a cave and, as I strained my eyes to peer ahead, could see that the mist inside rose no more than knee high. I stood there for what seemed an eternity, but which could only have been a half-minute.

Making a life changing decision, I slowly edged my way around the inside of the cave, my eyes gradually becoming

318

accustomed to the dimness all around, and could see that, inside, the walls were not as black as they had at first appeared: there was a dark green luminosity to the inside of the cave which bounced around and gave back some light.

The dripping continued inside the cave and echoed around it like water falling into a deep well. I was getting dizzy and starting to panic again. My heart was banging inside my rib-cage and I could feel the blood rushing through my ears. I put my hands over them and told myself to stop it. It was very hard to keep myself from panicking as, on looking behind me, out into the open the mist had grown so thick it looked like a curtain and, also, I believed that the tide, which now sounded a lot louder, had started to rise.

I had never been over to the island on my own before and was beginning to regret that I had done so. What if the sea filled the whole of the cave! The sides were fairly smooth and there didn't appear to be a foothold anywhere so how could I get above the waterline if it did rise? I didn't know what to do. I couldn't go outside again, at least not until the mist cleared in case I walked straight into the sea and, then, that would be the end of me!

In the grip of this mist I felt myself becoming colder and colder and eventually started to drift into some sort of dream world. I could hear the condensation dripping from the roof of the cave and echo around inside it but it seemed like a million miles away. I shook my head to try and clear it and thought I had better start moving, more, at that moment, to keep my circulation going than in the hope of finding a miraculous way out, so I continued to explore the cave as best I could in the dimness, in the hope of escape. Groping around in the semi-darkness, I eventually found a small ledge about shoulder height and decided to climb up. I huddled as far back on the ledge as I could and, with my back leaning against the wall, gripped my knees to my chest, hugging them with my arms so as to try to keep as warm as possible.

I don't know how long I sat like that but I believe the mist and the hissing of the sea (if it was the sea) made my mind drift again and I fell into some sort of slumber, even chilled to the bone as I was – or could it have been a trance? I still, even after all these years, cannot decide which.

'Ah, there you are, Percy,' said a very melodious voice and I awoke with a start. I could still see the inside of the cave and the mist but it appeared to be on the other side. It was as if I had fallen backwards through the rock wall and was looking back into the cave through a distorted glass window. I was very disorientated and, as it was still quite dark, I felt myself drifting away again.

'No, no, no! No time for that now,' said the voice, all businesslike. 'You've found the doorway. Come, quick, let us get out before it closes. I didn't think it would take you this long to find me! Still, you've finally made it, so let's go!'

I turned around and saw the strangest sight ever. A very tall man stood there. Very, very elegant. From his head to his feet he was dressed as no one I had ever seen before in my life.

He wore a midnight blue, almost black cap, which was very close to his head – a bit like a swimming cap, I thought. It covered his hair - that is, if he had any hair. Looking back, I never saw him without that cap, so I never found out if he had hair or not. However, if he did have hair it would have been very dark due to the fact that his eyebrows were black - eyebrows that almost always had a quizzical look to them. Stitched - I believe it was stitched - onto the cap was a silver plate fashioned into the shape of a falcon's head whose eyes were made of the most magnificent rubies that glowed and flashed as he moved. He wore a long robe, also in midnight blue. I would have thought that it would have impeded his walking but it appeared not to hinder him in the slightest. He always walked with very long strides and I can remember that

320

at that time - and when I think of it even when I was fully-grown - I always had to run to keep up with him.

He held a staff in his hand, which was about six-and-a-half feet long. He used it for many things. He could use it as a weapon.

I once saw him point it at a man who was running toward him to hack at him with an axe. Now I, personally, would have turned and run like the clappers – in fact, looking back again, I believe I did. The man, who was huge and wild, looked completely mad. He was dressed in a bear-skin, which probably made him look even bigger, tied around with a thick leather belt, and half his face was smeared in blue woad. He was screeching and howling like a banshee as he ran at us but, as I said, as soon as the staff was raised at him, the man dropped dead in his tracks!

Now that was something, I can tell you!

I have also seen him use it to hit a fish on the head in a stream for his supper. It had many uses, and one day I shall tell you more as to what they were, but mainly it was used for walking.

The staff was made of what appeared to be wood, but it was almost black in colour and had very intricate designs, like hieroglyphics, carved into it. He must have known what they all meant but every time I asked him he always said something like, 'Not now, Percy, I shall tell you when we have more time.'

I don't think he ever found the time to tell me, now I come to think of it. The staff was extremely tough, as at one time a knight tried to knock it away with his sword and the sword was the thing that broke! It was also topped with a silver falcon's head, complete with rubies; it was obviously much smaller but it matched his cap.

He was strikingly handsome, with piercing black eyes and, I believe, could have been any age. Over the time of knowing him, at different times he could look anything between 35 to 135 years old. At this time, however, he looked fairly young – late 30s, I would say.

I was very bewildered and thought I was dreaming. 'How did I get here?'

'How did you get here? How did you get here? Percy, you are having fun with me, are you not? No! No, I cannot believe you are unaware of what is going on. Like me, you have slept a long time, much too long. But you must know something?' he queried. 'I hope it is not too late! Anyway, to the present, come, quickly, take my hand. We have little time. If we don't get out now, we will both be trapped in this crystal prison, perhaps forever.'

At that, he took my hand and, pulling me with him, we stepped forward – well, we fought forward: it was like being suctioned through rather than stepping through - out of the glass rock, out of the cave, out of the darkness and mist and, as I was very soon to discover, out of the 20th Century.

'That was very close. I can still feel the pull. I shall tell you another time how I came to be trapped in there. But now, we must hurry.'

He started to walk, with his very long strides, from the mouth of the cave. Holding on to my elbow, he almost dragged me along. 'Wait, wait!' I yelled. 'Where are you taking me? What is going on? Who are you?' I thought I was being abducted.

He stopped and peered at me with those piercing black eyes of his; eyes that could change from black to golden brown – like a hawk - as they reflected his temperament.

'Percy, Percy, my dear boy, you couldn't forget me could you? Don't you remember me?'

I looked up at him and there was a vague stirring in my memory but I just could not grasp it. I hate those times when a remembrance enters your head and then, before you can grab hold of it, it rushes right out, down one of the corridors inside your brain. I've spent ages in the past trying to

322

backtrack through my mind to find what had just jumped in and then out of it; opening doors inside my head and still not finding what I was looking for – extremely frustrating! Anyhow - to continue: I carried on staring at him, mouth probably hanging open like a moron and so, on reflection, he must have thought me a complete half wit.

'Its Myrddin! Myrddin! He looked at me expectantly, nodding as if I knew who he was and would respond, and then, quizzically, 'Surely you must remember. We spent a whole year together. No? Do you not remember Cabal? Or Sir Ector? You must remember Arthur! Do you not remember your quest? You must remember that! How I sent you off? How you went? You must remember, as you've come back the same way. You must remember that I needed you to learn more and grow more before we go after the giant!'

That was it! I was now getting very nervous indeed, thinking I had met someone from the local lunatic asylum. My mum had repeatedly warned me about these men and had told me to always give them a wide berth; I had never experienced anyone as crazy as this man before in my life, let alone one dressed in such a fashion. Although he hadn't attempted to harm me I must admit that I was ready to run – and I was a pretty fast sprinter in those days.

'I do not remember any quest or know how I came here, so how could I remember how I was sent, if you say I was sent? And my name is Jack! You've got me in a muddle with someone who must look like me – this, er Percy!' I felt completely bemused by everything and not a little scared. It was peculiar as well, as my family name is Percival and my friends at school called me "Percy". I was trying very hard not to cry and, being the youngest in the family, I had always used tears as my best form of defence – and whinging - but I could see that that wasn't going to do me any favours here. Also now I thought about it, I had better stop using the

323

waterworks, well, I mean, I was going to be twelve quite soon!

'Jack, Percy, its all one to me! Keep quiet, you are making much too much noise and keep still, Percy, I do not want the enemy to see you or hear you and I suppose I had better try and refresh your memory before we go much further.' He sat on the sand and leaned back against the outside of the cave and, drawing a dragon in the sand with his staff, said 'You came here on the dragon's breath!' He started nodded at me, again raising his eyebrows in expectation of my agreeing with him.

The hair on the back of my neck stood out at this and I felt as if a million spiders were running up and down my spine making me shiver. I had heard this dragon stuff talked about in the village but I thought it was just a story to keep children safe indoors when the mist started rolling in off the moors. I had heard how people had wandered for days on the moors and been attacked and killed by wild animals - or was it the dragon? But this man - Myrddin? - spoke as though the dragon existed. And it wasn't just as though he believed it but as he spoke I started to believe it too, even though I didn't want to!

'I sent you out on the dragon's breath, into the future, to find out how our battles would progress. What the Picts and Scots were up to. Where the Saxons and Angles would encamp. How many were there in their respective armies? Who were their leaders? Who were loyal and who would prove false. Would they fulfil their quests? How did Arthur fare?' Did you find this out for me?

He suddenly stopped speaking and turned to me. 'What year did I send you to?' He stared at me again with those penetrating black eyes. I felt myself being drawn into them and I don't believe, for one minute, that I could have lied to him to save my own life! 'Come, lad, tell me, what year is it now?'

324

'1951. I was born in 1939. I don't believe in dragons. I don't know anything about any battles. I was a mere babe during the war.'

'1951! 1951! Well, my spell seems to have been a wee bit more powerful than I intended. 1951 indeed!' He rubbed his chin and drew his brows together as he strode up and down, mulling this over. Eventually, 'No wonder I was so weak that that witch managed to entomb me in that cave! Tell me what you do know about the battle! Was Arthur in it? You do remember Arthur? You know, Arthur, Chief Dragon, or Pendragon as he is known, son of Uther?'

'Do you mean King Arthur?' I laughed, yes I actually laughed. ' But he's only a legend. He's not real. He never was! I've read about him - lots. Everyone says he's only a myth. And, it wasn't a battle, it was a war, World War II. Everyone knows that.'

'Well, not everyone knows that because I don't know that! He spoke in a very sarcastic way to me. 'But a king, yes, that I do know! The greatest king! Well, you do have some intelligence, though I was beginning to doubt it. Yes, Percy, I do mean King Arthur and he is no myth; he is real. What else do you know? Apart from a world war, that is. No war could cover the whole world – there aren't enough swords for that.' The man turned to me. 'What have you got to tell me, Percy? Lots, eh? You've been gone so long.'

'So, you don't know everything, then, do you?' I was getting a bit too cheeky now. 'The war *was* over the whole world ... and don't keep calling me Percy? My name is Jack! And I do not know who you are! I have never heard of Myrddin. I don't know what is going on. I don't know where I am. I don't know how I got here. I don't know who you are ... I want to go home'. I was, by now, almost in tears.

'Hush. I don't know this and I don't know that. You do go on! I sent you off to find out so much for me and now you come back with all these "I don't know this or I don't know that". And keep your voice down. We cannot warn them,' he said. 'Not now that I have had to wait this long. Well, we have a few hours before morning. So I suppose I had better answer some of your questions. Start then', he ordered.

I sat staring at him. This strange man stood there waiting to answer questions that I didn't even know I wanted to ask. I was completely mystified and in the back of my mind felt sure I was dreaming. Like all dreams, they take their course, so I just kept looking at him (and pinching myself, just in case I was asleep. I wasn't) and waiting for the next thing to happen or, alternatively, waiting to wake up!

'Oh, well, if you won't start, I will. Perhaps then, *you* might get started. Don't keep looking at me as though you have lost all your wits, lad, and please shut your mouth. Try to concentrate on what I am saying instead of looking like a complete dolt. Hmmm, its possible you did lose your mind whilst travelling on the dragon's breath! It has been known. Well, that is I chance I had to take. Let me see if I can answer your questions.

'I call you Percy, because that is your given name. You came to me, as I said, on the dragon's breath, as someone with the gift of the Old Way. There are only a few of us left - more's the pity. I gave you the name Percy, an honourable name, as you must have some royal or druid blood in you somewhere, like me, otherwise you would not know as much as you do - or did, at any rate,' he mused. If it has been slightly changed to that of Jack …'.

'Slightly!' I thought, *'It's nothing like it!'*

'Well, maybe it's not,' he appeared to respond to my thought! How did he know what I was thinking?

'Even, so, 'he responded, 'well, so be it! Things change, things move on! Ah, yes, if I remember correctly, my name was changed slightly, too - Merlin, yes that's what they called me in later years, Merlin!. The Romans called me Merlinus Ambrosius! Sounds grand, doesn't it? Merlin's my name!'

326

He could see that the blood had drained from my face and that my eyes now stood out of their sockets – the proverbial organ stops.

Yes! Now I understood!

His eyes lit up as he exclaimed, 'By the Sword, you know! I can see it written on your face! So, tell me, what did you find out in these fifteen hundred years?' He sat down, placed his elbows on his knees, the tips of his fingers together and, staring over the tops of them, waited for my answer.

At the mention of the name of Merlin it all came flooding back – Arthur, Cabal, Mad Mab and (blushing) Rhianne. I looked up at Merlin and saw him smile. He did not smile often. His work and his quest were too serious for that. But when he smiled, the sun shone and the angels sang, and I would have followed him to the ends of the earth. Some say I was hypnotised or mesmerised! No, that was not it. It was his quest and, after I had met Arthur, it became my quest, too! It was contagious! He knew many things, exciting things. At times I believed he knew everything that was going on in the whole world. But he took me under his wing. He taught me many things about the Old Way – a way he said that came from the beginning of time. A way that people had lost as they grew more "sophisticated". A good way. A way that led to adventure. As some of those adventures rushed into my mind a flight of moths started dancing in my stomach. Yes, from whichever year I had last met him, I realised how much I had missed him. The yearning for all that Merlin did and was grew back in my heart and my ambition again was to follow him once more into the adventures, which, I believed, only he could create.'